THE NURSE'S PREGNANCY WISH

CAROL MARINELLI

HEALED BY THEIR DOLPHIN ISLAND BABY

MARION LENNOX

KT-377-247

MILLS & BOON

First published in Great Britain 2023
by Mills & Boon, an imprint of HarperCollins*Publishers* Ltd,
1 London Bridge Street, London, SE1 9GF

www.harpercollins.co.uk

HarperCollins*Publishers*
1st Floor, Watermarque Building,
Ringsend Road, Dublin 4, Ireland

The Nurse's Pregnancy Wish © 2023 Carol Marinelli

Healed by Their Dolphin Island Baby © 2023 Marion Lennox

ISBN: 978-0-263-30593-7

01/23

MIX
Paper | Supporting
responsible forestry
FSC™ C007454

This book is produced from independently certified FSC™ paper
to ensure responsible forest management.
For more information visit: www.harpercollins.co.uk/green.

Printed and Bound in Spain using 100% Renewable Electricity
at CPI Black Print, Barcelona

THE NURSE'S PREGNANCY WISH

CAROL MARINELLI

MILLS & BOON

CHAPTER ONE

PARAMEDIC ALISTAIR LLOYD knew exactly what everybody called him.

He even answered to the name at times.

For the most part it didn't bother him.

Now and then it irked.

It was cold, wet and raining in London—slushy sleet that seeped down the back of a person's neck and meant entering the very warm Accident and Emergency department caused his ears to sting just a little.

Alistair was working with Brendan today, and Brendan was extremely good-natured and very good at his job—though not quite as pedantic as Alistair.

That was the reason for his nickname: Perfect Peter.

Alistair never strayed from protocol.

Frankly, if it had been his call, Alistair would have alerted the Accident and Emergency department of London's Primary Hospital prior to the arrival of this patient. Brendan, who had been treating while Alistair was driving, had chosen not to.

'What now?'

Libby Bennett's friend Dianne, who was working in Resus, looked up from the leg she was holding as a doctor applied traction. They both saw a patient arriving on a spinal board with his head strapped down.

'I'll go,' Libby said, and then frowned. 'Who's that Brendan's working with?'

She only asked because she'd thought Brendan was rostered on with Rory.

'Perfect Peter.' Dianne rolled her eyes and got back to the leg she was holding. 'Good luck…'

Libby, who had only been working at The Primary for three weeks, was far too new to know what Dianne's roll of the eyes and rather sardonic 'good luck' meant; she was just worried about her fridge! It was being dropped off at three—the only time the driver could do it. Rory had offered to move it up the two flights of stairs to her apartment, and had roped in the older, rather portly Brendan into helping him—and now Rory wasn't here.

Still, it wasn't the patient's problem, so she made her way over and smiled down at the young man who lay on the spinal board. 'Hello, I'm Libby.'

'Marcus…'

Her new patient was a young gentleman with a clearly fractured wrist, though he was smiling and possibly appearing a little too happy, given his predicament.

'Marcus is a twenty-seven-year-old male,' Brendan said, 'who fell from the first-floor window of his flat.'

'It was an accident,' Marcus elaborated. 'We were just messing about…trying to get the best control.'

'Gaming,' Brendan further explained. 'Marcus was standing on the bed and he says he fell backwards through the closed window behind it.'

'Gaming?' Libby blinked.

It wasn't particularly relevant, but Libby wanted to engage the patient in conversation while she assessed him and decided where best he should be placed. She'd also heard the 'he says he fell' in Brendan's handover, which raised flags as to whether the patient might have jumped or been pushed.

'I never knew it could be so dangerous!'

'Obvious right wrist fracture,' Brendan continued, 'but apart from that—'

'I'm fine,' Marcus said. 'Can I get this thing off my neck?'

Marcus had been strapped to a spinal board and had on a cervical collar.

'Not just yet,' Libby said.

All precautions had been taken, Brendan told her, with a slight edge to his voice. And Libby listened as he explained the scene he had found on his arrival, and the distance the patient had fallen, and the fact that Marcus had been sitting up when they had arrived.

It really did sound like an accident that had happened while Marcus and his friend had wrestled for the gaming control, although Brendan informed her that the police had also been on scene, and they were currently speaking with the friend and would soon be coming in to interview Marcus.

There were certain standard operating procedures in place for falls, and this patient was borderline. While his fall had been broken by some bushes, the distance he had fallen was close to the cut-off that meant his injuries could be more serious than were obviously apparent. She was just coming to a decision when she glanced up at the other paramedic—the one who should have been Rory but wasn't, and whom she thought Dianne had said was called Peter—and he silently mouthed two words: *Long fall.*

He did it so that neither Brendan nor the patient could see, letting Libby know that he was also concerned by the distance the patient had fallen. He had been on scene too, after all, and it was good to have all the information.

'Straight through,' Libby said, gesturing to Resus, but her patient started when he saw the red sign and realised where he was headed.

'Why am I being taken in there?'

'It's just a precaution because of how far you've fallen,' Libby explained. 'Don't be alarmed by all the equipment—it's just until we know that you're stable.'

'I've only hurt my wrist, though.'

'Even so,' Libby said as they wheeled him in, 'it's better to be cautious and get you properly seen to.'

Still Marcus objected. 'I told them I could walk…'

'Well, it's best you don't,' Libby said as she moved the stretcher alongside the flat Resus bed and tried to reassure him. 'Marcus, it's best we take all precautions. Let me worry about all that. Believe me, I'm very good at it.' She made him smile as they set up to move him. 'I'm a professional worrier, in fact…'

She wasn't lying. Libby, even though she tried her best not to, worried about almost everything!

Because, if she didn't worry enough, things tended to fall apart.

The fridge being a case in point!

Not that she was thinking about that now…

Dianne came in to assist with the move, as did a couple of others, but, glancing up, she saw Peter checking that the brakes had been secured on both beds and refusing to be rushed.

'Come on, Alistair,' Dianne chided, and Libby frowned. Hadn't Dianne just told Libby that his name was Peter?

Whatever his name was, he nodded, seemingly more in affirmation to himself that all was well than for Dianne's benefit, and then returned to the head of the stretcher. It was then that she discovered his eyes were the darkest brown.

A deep, chocolate-brown, with spiky black lashes and gorgeously arched brows. He was drenched—no doubt frozen—yet somehow Libby couldn't help but notice he still managed to look incredible. His black hair was wet from the rain, his skin pale, and he was clean-shaven. She also noted that he stood a head above everyone else, both in stature and presence.

Though their eyes met for less than a second, it was enough that Libby felt her cheeks redden.

She could blame it on many things—sliding the patient over, the heat in Resus, or the fact that she'd been racing around all morning—only it wasn't just that.

She was suddenly aware that she must look an utter fright. She'd been in full PPE for most of the morning, so her blonde curls were dark with sweat. As well as that, her hair tie had snapped on her arrival at work, so her curls were now being held back with a crepe bandage.

The heat on her cheeks would not fade, and it was actually a relief that it was Brendan who was the treating paramedic and giving the handover, as she was about to turn into one burning blush.

'What do we have?' Huba, the emergency doctor, came in as Libby set about doing her patient's observations.

'A fractured wrist,' Dianne responded a touch tartly, glancing over to Libby.

It was clear that Dianne thought she had overreacted.

In the end, there wasn't actually a chance to have a word with Brendan about her fridge, because he was being summoned by his very good-looking partner. So Libby put all thoughts of fridges and stairs completely out of her head as she called X-Ray and then dealt with Marcus, who was concerned about his friend.

'I've told the police it was an accident,' he fretted. 'Why are they questioning him?'

'Marcus, I don't know what the police are doing.' Libby was honest but firm. 'For now, let's focus on you.'

'But I'm fine. I could walk if you'd let me.'

'Libby, go and have your break,' Dianne cut in, clearly a bit miffed, because she was in charge of Resus today, and didn't think the patient needed to be in there—though she'd had to accept the decision, and since there was a bed free for him she didn't challenge it.

It was quiet for a Thursday morning.

Well, no one was allowed to say the Q-word, or comment on the fact that it was unusually Q for a Thursday, because the second they did the Bat Phone would buzz, the doors would fly open and everyone in the waiting room would simultaneously collapse—or something similar.

So for now Libby took her morning coffee break and headed to the kitchen beside the staffroom. She retrieved her cheese and biscuits from the fridge and then put her hand up to compare the height of the staffroom fridge to what she thought was the size of the gap in the wall of kitchen units at her new and exceedingly tiny studio flat.

Oh, God, even if she did somehow get it up the stairs, Libby wasn't at all sure that the fridge she was having delivered was going to fit.

'Libby!'

Brendan made her jump, and she stopped mentally measuring the fridge and watched as he speed-filled his mug with coffee—paramedics never got long between jobs.

'You're going to need to find someone else to help me with the fridge,' he said. 'I'll be there as soon as we're finished, but Rory's off sick. I've got...'

He gestured to the dark hunk behind him, who was helping himself to some biscuits. A lot of biscuits! He had three in his hand and was munching his way through them as Brendan tried to rope his colleague in to assist Libby with her fridge.

'I didn't catch your name,' Libby ventured, but instead of enlightening her he helped himself to more biscuits as Brendan explained her predicament.

'Rory agreed to move Libby's new fridge with me,' Brendan said. 'The driver's dropping it off at three and she's got no one to help her…'

'I didn't know that I was just paying for delivery,' Libby explained.

She realised that without even trying she was blinking and batting her eyelashes—her green eyes, which on a normal day cheerfully greeted everyone, were flirting of their own accord!

'But it turns out I have to arrange people to lift it. I thought the price was good value for money.'

'She paid him up-front.' Brendan laughed as he told his colleague. 'How long have you lived in London now?'

'Three weeks,' Libby said.

'It shows,' Brendan said, then turned to his partner, who Libby hadn't heard speak out loud yet. 'The thing is, now Rory's off sick and I need someone to help me lift it.'

But the man shook his head. 'I've got a physical assessment tomorrow,' he said, while dipping a biscuit in his coffee. 'I'm not hauling a fridge.'

He didn't so much as look at Libby, just denied his assistance in a deep, sexy voice, and Brendan gave Libby a helpless shrug of his shoulders, as if to show what he was up against.

'I'll find someone,' Libby said, blinking her eyelashes with disappointment now.

She didn't really know many people in London. And,

given it was pouring with rain, who would want to drag a fridge up two flights of stairs?

A fridge that might not even fit when it got there.

'I'll ask around,' Libby attempted in an upbeat tone, and smiled at Brendan. 'What time do you think you'll get to mine?'

'All depends what time we get our last job. It could be quite late,' Brendan warned. 'Make sure you get someone to help me, Libby…'

'Of course.' She nodded and watched as the hungry paramedic, whose name she still didn't know, took another handful of biscuits and completely ignored both her vivid green eyes and her plight.

'We need to get going,' he told Brendan as the radio on his shoulder summoned them.

'We haven't cleared yet.'

'I have,' he said, and walked off.

'God…' Brendan sighed, screwing the lid on his mug and following his partner out. 'No rest for the wicked!'

Libby smothered a giggle as Brendan huffed off.

Whatever his name was, it was no wonder they called him Perfect Peter, Libby thought as she ate her cheese and crackers and drank a huge mug of tea.

He really was *perfect*.

Not just tall, dark and handsome, but all brooding and silent—and self-centred enough that he wouldn't help with her fridge.

Libby tended to go for that type, but she was determined—*determined*—only to date nice, safe and sensible guys from now on.

The kind of caring and thoughtful guy who was strong enough to manage a fridge. One who would gallantly put his stupid physical assessment in jeopardy for her…

And who didn't mind about her ovaries.

With a weary sigh she leant back on the chair.

Libby was, despite her bright smile and friendly nature, not having the best day. She had *finally* been contacted by her home GP regarding a gynae appointment, having been referred *ages* ago. Seriously, ages ago. In the weeks prior to the appointment she'd have to undergo blood tests, and a detailed ultrasound, but she should be able to fit the investigations in as she was going to be home in Norfolk for her mother's sixtieth birthday at around the same time.

Libby needed to text her response, and confirm the appointment time for the tests, only she hadn't yet done so.

The trouble was that she wasn't sure if she wanted to know why her periods had dropped to every two or three months—or the reason for a few other issues she'd been dealing with.

She was oddly tempted to call and tell them she'd moved, just so the investigations and appointments would be cancelled. But then she would have to start the process of finding a new GP in London, and go through all the waiting again to find out she might have fertility issues, as her GP back home had suggested.

She'd been upset by the possibility, and felt she had nowhere to turn.

That was partly due to the fact that her boyfriend at the time had been hurtful, rather than helpful, and although Libby had got rid of him quick-smart, now she felt even more alone. Her close friend Olivia hadn't been as helpful as Libby had hoped either—although in fairness she'd been pregnant herself at the time, and busy with concerns of her own. And Libby didn't want to confide in her mother, who made Libby's low-grade anxiety look like a walk in the park.

It was something she didn't want to face, but Libby knew she had to get answers.

It was just so very hard facing it alone.

Draining her cup, she put it in the sink.

'Rinse it,' Paula the ward domestic warned. 'You wouldn't leave your own cups like that—'

'Sorry,' Libby said. 'Actually, I do leave my own cups like that at home!' She smiled at Paula as she washed and dried her mug. 'I keep meaning to get a routine, but I leave cups everywhere. Still, that's no excuse,' she said, and put away her mug.

She headed back out towards the department and bumped into Ricky, one of the porters.

'Ricky!' She beamed. 'I have a fridge being delivered this afternoon. One of the paramedics has offered to help, but not till the evening…'

'No chance,' Ricky said.

In the end, her 'long fall' patient was possibly the most willing in the department.

'I'd do it Libby,' he said, 'if I wasn't stuck here.'

Marcus had had his X-rays, been interviewed by the police, and his cervical collar had been taken off. Now he was waiting for the orthopods to review his wrist.

'That's very kind of you.' Libby smiled. 'It's a shame about the broken wrist…'

'I could ask my friend. He should be in soon, now that the police finally believe it was an accident.'

'There's no need for that,' Libby said, and her smile hid her sudden concern, because the formerly ruddy Marcus had gone a little pale. 'How are you doing?'

'I feel a bit sick, to be honest.'

'Okay,' Libby said, running another set of obs. 'Have you got any pain—aside from in your wrist?'

'Not really. Maybe a bit in my shoulder.'

'That's new, is it?'

His blood pressure was low and his heart rate was starting to creep up. Summoning Huba in, to reassess him, Libby lay her patient down.

'Let's increase the fluids,' Huba said, instantly concerned at his sudden decline. 'Any pain in your stomach, Marcus?' she asked as she examined his abdomen.

'Not really.'

'Okay.' Huba looked over to Libby. 'Can you page the on-call surgeon, and also the path lab, and see how the cross-match is coming along.'

'What's wrong?' Marcus asked.

'I just want to be sure that you're not bleeding internally,' Huba explained. 'Sometimes shoulder tip pain can be a sign of bleeding into the abdomen, and you're looking very pale.'

He was looking so pale, in fact, that by the time Dianne had come back from her break the surgeons were diagnosing a ruptured spleen and Marcus was being prepared for an urgent dash to Theatre.

'Good call,' Dianne said a short while later, once Marcus was in Theatre. 'I'd have had him in a cubicle.'

'I might have too,' Libby admitted, as together they wiped down the Resus bed, preparing it for its next guest. 'Perfect Peter was quite insistent that he was to be treated as a long fall.'

'Well, he was right,' Dianne said.

'Why do you call him Perfect Peter? What's his actual name?'

'Alistair.' Dianne laughed. 'We just call him that…'

'Behind his back?' Libby sighed, completely understanding his nickname—he was seriously gorgeous after all. 'I looked a right fool.'

'Sorry about that.' Dianne smiled again, then got back

to discussing their patient. 'Thank goodness Marcus was able to give a full statement to the police before he went to Theatre, or his friend really would be in trouble.'

'Gosh…' Libby said, placing a fresh sheet down and a roll of paper. 'All that from gaming!'

Marcus's parents arrived then, and Libby showed them into Interview Room One, where Huba came and spoke with them. She had a lovely, calming nature, Libby thought as Huba explained what had happened.

'Josh said he was sitting up and talking after the accident.'

'He was,' Huba said, nodding, 'and he was holding his own all the while he was here. However, given the distance he fell, we were keeping a close eye on him…'

It wasn't such a quiet day after all, although Marcus was safely out of Theatre by the time Libby's shift ended. She popped up to the unit at the end of the shift to check on him, and was warmed to see his mystery friend sitting with his family in the small waiting room.

'How is he doing?' she asked.

'He's asleep,' his mother said. 'The surgeon said it all went well.'

'I'm so pleased.'

Josh spoke then. 'I'm going to buy him his own control as a get-well gift—no more fighting over it…'

They all laughed.

Libby was indeed pleased that it was a good outcome, and she smiled as she made her weary way to the underground to travel the two stops to her home. Her mind kept drifting to the handsome paramedic who had so clearly insisted that all precautions be taken on scene, and had done what he could to ensure that the gravity of the situation had been quietly stated.

In truth, she would have sent the patient to Resus anyway, until the doctor had carefully assessed him, but his actions had helped articulate the standard procedures, which had made it easier for Libby to stand her ground with Dianne.

Still, all daydreams about a certain gorgeous paramedic faded as she walked through the rain to her small block of flats and down the side entrance.

There to greet her was the biggest fridge ever—right by the stairs up to her apartment. It was thankfully shielded somewhat from the elements, but only because it was half blocking the driveway to the little parking bay behind the flats.

Her fellow residents were having to manoeuvre around it, and they were bemoaning the fact.

Oh, God. Why hadn't she measured it? How had she failed to secure help?

It was just the story of her impulsive life—the very reason that Libby was stuck at five p.m. on a grey winter's night in London, feeling homesick and wondering if she'd made the right move.

Her moving to London hadn't actually been that impulsive. She'd always wanted to work in a major city hospital and well... London!

But the very sociable Libby missed her many friends—especially the ones from the tiny amateur theatre group she'd belonged to. Of course when she had five minutes to breathe and take stock she'd look to join one here. She also missed the team at her old A&E department, who had been friendlier than the ones at The Primary. Her old colleagues had known that despite her fun, flirty nature there was a serious head on her shoulders. An anxious head too. And they had known she took her work very seriously, but could still manage to smile and laugh.

Not like the London lot.

Or was it just that there were so many of them?

Three weeks in and there were still so many new faces to get used to each and every shift. Names to remember. Nuances to learn.

Garth, the consultant, was decisive.

Huba was a little hesitant.

May, the Nurse Unit Manager, was all smiles and friendly comments, but as sharp as a whip...

Even the London way of speaking was taking a little getting used to.

And then after her shift she would return to her tiny little flat, and though she had never minded her own company, it felt very different being alone in London.

Three weeks in, and pretending to love it so as not to upset her mother was starting to take its toll. She missed her parents, even if they were a little overbearing.

And now she had her failing ovaries to face.

Or not.

She could just put it off, she thought again. Could cancel the appointments and start all over again.

It was a tempting thought.

'Don't be stupid, Libby,' she scolded herself out loud. 'It's time to sort things out.'

She was twenty-eight. Well, twenty-eight and a half. Actually, closer to twenty-nine...

If she put this off, she might well be thirty by the time—

Thirty! Yikes!

Hauling her mind back to the present, Libby attempted to be positive. Brendan was a paramedic and very used to difficult extrications—although it was generally getting patients *down* stairs rather than *up* them.

Why hadn't she thought this through?

Why hadn't she worried adequately?

Libby had acquired the skill from her mother, who worried about everything.

From early morning right through to sleepless night, Helen Bennett worried.

Often with good reason.

Libby's father was a firefighter. All too well Libby could remember creeping down the stairs and seeing her mother's pale face as she anxiously watched the television screen or paced the kitchen.

Sometimes Libby would join her.

Nearly all the time her father would come home unscathed, but there had been more than a few hospital visits to see his colleagues and friends. And, very sadly, she also had the memory of her father getting ready to attend the funeral of a colleague.

Still, Helen Bennett's worrying wasn't just for her husband. It was channelled towards her daughter too.

Growing up, it had been a litany of warnings.

Don't get in a car with someone who's had a drink.

Of course not.

Don't walk home at night alone.

Libby's heels were usually so high she avoided walking as much as she could!

Don't take the night bus.

As a teenager, right up until she was eighteen, her father had always picked her up. She'd left home at eighteen, but even ten years on it would seem Helen would rather her daughter lived at home and was escorted there by two guards after a late shift. Now that she was in London every incident on the news had her mother texting, convinced that Libby must somehow be involved.

Everything in Libby and her father's lives was said and done so as not to upset her mother. Or, rather, everything was secretly done or said so as not to upset her.

Libby was determined not to be like her mother—especially as she had the adventurous spirit of her father. So when her latest relationship had gone south, Libby had decided that so, too, might she.

London.

Only, in this instance she hadn't been cautious enough.

Her innate impulsiveness had won, and now she was living in a flat without a bedroom. As it turned out, the video she'd watched had been of a one-bedroom flat in the same complex, rather than the studio flat she had eventually signed up for. It was her own fault she hadn't read the fine print.

Now, nearly all her stuff remained in storage, as it would have filled the shoebox flat ten times over. Libby had commenced work two days after moving in, and now she had to start looking for somewhere else.

As well as that, her great friend Olivia, who had planned to come and see her, had put off the visit because with hubby and baby there was nowhere for them to stay. Well, even if she'd had a one-bedroom place it would have proved a dreadful squeeze. But Libby wasn't thinking about that now. Even if she hadn't seen as much of Olivia since she'd married, it had been nice knowing she was near…

Her phone bleeped and she pulled it out, hoping it was Brendan to say that he and Rory were on their way.

But instead it was a reminder, asking her to confirm her appointment for an ultrasound.

'What the hell?' A guy in a delivery van who had struggle to manoeuvre around the fridge wound down his window and shouted at her.

'Sorry!' Libby called back.

'Stupid cow!' he yelled, and angrily reversed out.

It was then that all her positivity faded.

His horrible words played on repeat inside her head and

it was just the final straw. Libby sat down on the steps, unable to face the fridge, put her head in her hands and for the first time since she'd arrived in London gave in and cried.

Why had she moved here?

It felt like the unfriendliest place in the world.

There was no one she knew to bump into at the shops, as had *always* been the case back home—a dash for bread had often ended up with an hour or so spent in a café, catching up with an old friend, a new friend, a friend of a friend...

Back home she'd have had an army to help her with her fridge...

When she'd moved in to her old flat it had been pizza and wine and fun...

Hearing the roar of a motorcycle, Libby kept her head down, guessing that its rider would no doubt shout at her too.

And, anyway, it felt good to cry.

It felt good, for a moment, to stop being the new one, the happy one, the funny one, the stupid cow—or whatever these people who didn't know her chose to describe her as.

No, she wasn't crying about the fridge. It was about not having any friends in London, and those wretched tests that were looming, and the struggle of being a worrier by nature while also a little wild at heart...

She was mid-sob, and had given up on finding a tissue, when she heard that very nice, very deep voice.

'Is Brendan here?'

She saw black boots, and as her eyes drifted up they clocked an awful lot of black leather.

'Peter!' She stared up at the handsome paramedic and could have kissed him for showing up to help her. But then she realised she'd got his name wrong. 'I mean, Alistair...'

He just stared back at her. On second thoughts, she could

happily have kissed him for no reason other than that he was gorgeous! Instead, she sat back on the steps and looked up as he peeled off his black leather gloves and spoke.

'My colleagues call me Perfect Peter behind my back— or to my face to annoy me. It would seem the nursing staff at The Primary do too.'

'No…!' Libby attempted, and then realised there was no getting away from the fact. 'Gosh, I'm so embarrassed.'

'Good,' he said, as if pleased by her mortification.

'It *is* good, actually…' Libby agreed, and watched him frown.

'Why?'

She couldn't bring herself to admit that she'd been pondering on the way home how she was going to have a little fantasy about a hot paramedic called Peter. A hot paramedic called Alistair would be much easier!

'Alistair's a nice name.' Libby settled for that. 'Are you here to help with my fridge?'

'I believe so—unless you've managed to rustle somebody else up?'

'No.'

Gosh, he was seriously good-looking. She had noticed, of course—clearly everybody had, because he wasn't called Perfect Peter for nothing—but now he was dressed in leather and riding a motorbike that would cause her mother to lose her mind if Libby were ever to get on the back of it. So there was a rebellious edge to him too.

'Are we waiting on the steps in the rain?' Alistair asked. 'Or are we going up?'

'We'll go up,' Libby said, delighted by the turn of events and seriously hoping that Brendan would be delayed.

Without thinking, she held out her hand, as a friend might, to be hauled up.

He didn't take it.

And nor should he, of course. They weren't friends or anything.

She wouldn't have held out her hand to the horrible delivery driver had she been here when he'd dropped off the fridge.

It was odd, though, because it felt as if he'd denied her assistance because her gesture had been flirtatious, although he was probably just annoyed at having to lug her fridge. Especially as he had his physical assessment tomorrow.

He'd pass. Libby was rather sure of that from looking at him!

But they wouldn't be waiting in Libby's little flat, because as they started to go in a car squeezed up the drive and Brendan waved.

'Here he is,' Alistair said, as Brendan got out of the car and huffed his way towards them. Then he added rather drily. 'My lifting companion.'

'Is it an important assessment tomorrow?' Libby asked.

'Very.'

'Look, I don't want you getting injured. I'm sure that Brendan and I, between us—'

He cut her off with a look. Not a macho chauvinist look, just a blunt look that told her what she already knew: there was not a chance in hell of her and Brendan moving it.

'Thanks so much for this,' she said, both to him and to Brendan. 'I really do appreciate it…'

'Which one's yours?' Alistair asked, looking up at the flats.

'Two hundred and one,' Libby said.

'Second floor?'

'Yes.'

He proceeded to go up the first flight of steps, to see

what they were up against, and then drew a finger picture of the layout for Brendan.

'Can't we just get on with it?' called Brendan.

'You don't learn safety by accident,' Alistair called back, quoting an old saying, and Libby wanted to giggle as Brendan muttered and rolled his eyes.

Alistair certainly planned his lifts!

Brendan was to go first, while Alistair got the heavy end. Libby stood by as they lifted, feeling useless. All she could do was grab the electrical cord when it slipped and trailed on the ground.

'Leave that, please,' Alistair said.

'It might cause an accident,' she pointed out.

'Leave it,' he said through gritted teeth as he took the full weight of the fridge.

'I'm just trying to help…'

'If you want to help, then go up and open the doors,' Alistair replied.

Libby climbed the stairs to her flat and propped open all the doors, then quickly threw a few cups in the sink and kicked a bra behind the sofa-bed. Glancing across the room, she looked at the gap in her doll's-house-sized kitchen units and lost all hope that the fridge was going to fit there.

She could hear them coming up the stairs—Brendan's heavy breathing and Alistair's clear instructions. She hovered at the door, rather like a family member might linger in the corridor when there was a sick relative in Resus.

'Right,' Alistair said, and then, 'The flat's just to the left…'

She stepped back from the doorway, and it was Brendan who gave instructions now. 'Down in three, two, one—now.'

Brendan was red-faced and sweaty. God, she hoped he didn't have a heart attack or something dreadful.

After a brief respite, they rocked the heavy fridge the remaining short distance into her flat.

'Where's the kitchen?' Alistair asked.

'Just here is fine,' Libby said, and Brendan gratefully straightened up then arched his back. 'Completely fine! I can slide it from here. You guys have done more than enough. I mean, honestly, I can manage from here…'

Brendan seemed relieved, but Alistair looked at her suspiciously. 'I'll push it through.'

'No need,' Libby said, and found that she was blushing as if she herself had been heaving the fridge up the stairs.

'You haven't measured it, have you?' Alistair accused. 'That's why earlier today, at work, you were standing with your hand on top of your head in the kitchen…'

She should be flattered that he'd noticed, let alone recalled what she'd been doing, but instead she was embarrassed as he brushed past her into her tiny, tiny kitchen as Brendan leaned against the wall and got his breath back.

'It will fit,' Alistair said, reluctantly hissing between clenched teeth.

'I don't think so…' Libby gulped.

'So you let us drag it up here, thinking it wouldn't fit?'

'I need a fridge,' Libby said, shrugging. 'It might have had to live in here for a little while.'

She saw his eyes take in the studio flat and the sofa-bed she had not folded back this morning.

She was burning red as he pushed and rocked the fridge over to the units, then left it standing in the middle of the kitchen.

'It doesn't fit, does it?' Libby checked.

'It will, but you have to let it stand for three hours,' he said.

'Oh, no.' Brendan shook his head. 'It's been upright since it's been dropped off, so it should be fine.'

'It wasn't very upright on the stairs,' Alistair said, turning those heavenly chocolate eyes to Libby. 'Keep it unplugged for three hours or you risk damaging the compressor.'

'Sure…'

'*Then* you can slide it in.'

'I shall. Look, thank you, guys. I'd offer you a cuppa, but I don't have any milk…' She glanced at her new fridge as if in explanation. 'Or a beer. But…'

'Have you got any glasses?' Brendan asked.

Actually, she didn't.

All her glasses were in storage, with the rest of her stuff. She'd been planning to buy a few cheap ones to see her through on her next day off.

Libby did have four mugs—all of which were now sitting in the sink. She rushed over to wash them, before handing a clean one filled with cold water to Brendan.

'Alistair?'

'No, thank you.'

'I've got chocolate biscuits,' she said, but they both declined. Clearly they were more than ready to go home.

'Seriously,' Alistair said as he left, 'wait three hours.'

'I shall. Look, thank you. It really was kind. Thank you, Brendan. And Alistair, I hope your physical goes well tomorrow.'

He simply nodded, and then was gone.

She breathed a sigh of relief as she closed the door behind them. No one that sexy had ever been in her little doll's house studio flat before.

Actually, no one that sexy had been so close to her bed before!

She looked at her fridge with delight, and gave it a little pat. She thought about Alistair's sternly delivered wise words about waiting three hours. But surely she should check that it worked? Just briefly…?

Impulsiveness won out and Libby plugged it in.

Light.

Yay!

Forgetting all Alistair's warnings, she pushed the fridge back and was delighted to find that it fitted.

Just.

Certainly she wouldn't be able to put a broom or a mop by the side of it—or anything, really. But she had a fridge, and she could now have real meals. In fact, she would go shopping right away…

Picking up her bag, and still in her coat, she opened the door to find—

'Alistair!'

'I dropped a glove…'

'Oh.' She cast her eyes around the bedroom/lounge and realised it must be in the kitchen. 'I'll go and have a look.' She gave him a lovely smile. 'Wait there.'

But he did not wait there…

It might have been disconcerting to have a man ignore her request to wait at the door, but they both knew exactly why he brushed past her and in two long strides reached her kitchen.

'Good God!' he said, when he saw how quickly she'd dismissed his instructions.

He yanked the fridge out, turned it off, and gave her a long and tedious lecture about oil and compressors…or something like that…

Yet he made 'tedious' sexy! She could have gazed into those velvet eyes for ever, whatever the subject matter.

'Have you no patience?' he demanded finally.

'None,' Libby admitted happily.

Absolutely none. Because though she had known him

for just a few minutes, and had only met him for the first time earlier that day, she was suddenly frantic for his kiss.

'I often tend to regret my impulsive decisions…'

Libby's voice trailed off as she realised she was warning herself that chasing after a kiss from this gorgeous man was foolhardy at best.

After all, she barely knew his name.

'Regret?' he asked, with that lovely full mouth, and she saw his jaw was a touch darker than it had been this morning.

'When I don't think things through.'

He opened his mouth, as if to say something, and then he chose not to. Bizarrely, she wondered if he might be thinking about kissing too.

Libby didn't usually have such random kissing thoughts.

Clearly nor did he usually have the kind of thoughts he seemed to be having, because he suddenly seemed a bit shocked. He looked away and took a step to the side and swiped his glove from the floor.

'Come on,' he said, and took her arm.

'Where are we going?'

'For a drink and dinner. We're going to wait out those three hours together. Have you got your keys?'

'Yes, I was about to go to the shops.'

They headed down the steps and Libby took out her phone.

'Where should we go? There's a pub near the Tube station that looks like it does decent food…'

'Okay.'

'I'll meet you there.'

'I can give you a ride.'

'Oh, no. I'm not getting on your bike.' She shook her head.

It wasn't her mother's dire warnings that held her back.

A stint on Orthopaedics and her time working in Emergency had put Libby off motorbikes for good. However, she did really, really want a drink and dinner.

'I'll meet you there.'

'Why? I've got a spare helmet.'

'I have a very strict rule,' Libby said, smiling. 'I don't go on motorbikes. Or anything with two wheels, come to think of it…'

She thought it was probably still cold and wet outside, and since it was too far to walk and not look like a drowned rat, she said, 'I'll get a cab.'

'Sure,' he replied. 'No cheating, though.'

'Cheating?'

'Dashing back in…' He glanced to her flat.

'I don't cheat,' Libby said, thinking he really seemed to know her far too well.

Because she'd have loved to dash back in, tidy up a little—herself, rather than the flat—and not look quite so bedraggled for her evening with the sexiest, most perfect paramedic.

'Look, I'm calling for a cab now.'

Annoyingly, he waited till her car arrived, and ten minutes later they were outside what appeared from the outside to be a very nice pub. Only, on entering it, they discovered it turned out to be one of those family ones, full of boisterous children and frazzled parents.

'It's noisy,' Libby said, a bit taken back by all the people. 'Should we have booked?'

But it would seem there was space for them after all.

They were led to a high table with bar stools, where they disrobed and de-leathered. Libby perched on her stool and tried to look at the menu rather than at his lovely forearms.

He wore a grey jumper, and he had gorgeous black

hair on his arms and a jut of black chest hair at the base of his neck.

And he'd caught her looking.

She flushed and fought for something to say. 'I'm getting this,' Libby said. 'I mean it.' She would have no arguments. 'I was going to get you some wine or whatever, for moving my fridge, so this makes it easier.'

'Fine.'

Not even a smidge of protest!

He decided to have steak with pepper sauce, potato wedges, no salad and water, while Libby was tempted by the scampi, because she hadn't had it in for ever. But she didn't want to smell of fish. Not that they were going to be kissing, but she couldn't help considering these things, because she considered everything—and hadn't they shared a charged moment back in her flat, when he had confronted her about the fridge? Could kissing be on the cards after all?

She was being ridiculous.

Libby decided she would also have steak, but with salad. And, because she wasn't going home on a motorbike and she was exhausted from worrying about her fridge, a glass of wine.

She returned from the bar with their drinks and two tokens. 'We get a free trip to the dessert station!'

'Cheers,' Alistair said, and they chinked glasses. 'Here's to your fridge.'

'It's been awful not having one.'

'It really wasn't worth crying over.'

'It might have been when my neighbours found out it was *my* fridge blocking the drive.'

'True... How long have you worked at The Primary?' he asked.

'Three weeks.' Libby sighed. 'And I still feel like it's my first day. I worked in Norfolk before, in a tiny hospital

compared to The Primary. I can't believe how busy it is…
how much of an area it covers.'

'And it's getting bigger…' he agreed.

Their meal arrived and Libby was glad she hadn't ordered the scampi, as the steak looked delicious.

'I'm starving,' Alistair said. 'So how come you moved
from Norfolk?'

'I just…' Libby thought for a moment. 'I was very happy
there, but I wanted to know what it was like to work in a
big trauma centre, and I really wanted a couple of years in
London. So…'

'You like Emergency?'

'Reluctantly.' Libby nodded.

'Reluctantly?' He frowned.

'Well, it's very…' How best to say it? 'I adore it, but I
can't stand it at the same time…'

He frowned again.

'I worry about everything.'

'Except fridge compressors,' he pointed out, and Libby
laughed.

'As I said, when I don't worry enough—or when I worry
about the wrong things—I tend to regret it…' She looked
right at him. 'I got caught, didn't I.'

'You did.'

Only, she wasn't regretting it now!

And, from the way he held her eyes for easily seventeen
seconds, neither was he.

Eighteen seconds.

Nineteen…

She dragged her eyes from his beckoning gaze and tried
to get back to the question and best explain how the daily
witnessing of the fragility of life affected her.

'Take our friend today, who had the gaming control-
ler accident.'

'The long fall?' he checked.

'Yes. It's put me off standing on a bed for life…'

'Do you regularly stand on the bed?'

'Yes.' Libby nodded and he smiled, but then she asked a more serious question. 'Does it trouble you? I mean, you must see far worse than I do.'

After all, he would see the patients who didn't even make it to the hospital, and he would see seriously injured people outside of the relatively controlled and resourced environment of A&E.

'Most of the time it's a lot like social work,' he said.

'Not all of the time?'

'No…' He was clearly thinking about her question as to whether the sights he saw troubled him. 'I guess it makes me appreciate life—and it's perhaps taught me not to take unnecessary risks…'

'Yet you ride a motorbike?'

'Well, I was once thinking of being a rapid responder,' Alistair said.

And thankfully he was looking down, slicing the last of his steak, so missed her little shudder.

Libby actually grimaced as she made a mental note never to fall for someone who zipped around on a motorbike for a living.

He looked up. 'What do you think of London?'

'I'm sure I'll love it,' Libby said, 'when I get a chance to see it. My first round of days off was spent arguing with my estate agent.'

'About…?'

'I thought I was getting a one-bedroom flat. I signed the lease without viewing it…'

He stared, but thankfully didn't tell her how stupid that had been.

'How long's the lease?' he asked.

'Three months,' Libby said.

'Well, at least you got that part right.'

'All my things are in storage—as I soon as I saw the place I knew there was no way they'd fit. I do actually have glasses and a fridge of my own…even a bed…' She let out a glum sigh. 'I've had to put a hold on the delivery and just buy a sofa-bed and a few cups and a kettle and such while I work out what to do…'

'And a fridge?'

Libby nodded. 'I'll probably sell it to whoever leases the flat after me. Although…' She rolled her eyes heavenwards.

'Go on.'

'As much as the agent may have exaggerated the size of my dwelling, the price is on a par with the area and I *really* like it… I'm trying to decide if I can survive in a shoebox just to be close to the underground, the parks…' She smiled. 'It's a lot greener than I dared hope. Do you live close by?'

'A few miles,' he said. 'Regent's Canal—just a short walk away. Do you miss home?'

'There hasn't been time, and I'm in touch a lot.'

'How old are you?'

'Twenty-eight,' Libby said. 'Well, twenty-eight and a half…'

He smiled.

He was just so easy to talk to…

They clicked—or at least it felt like that to Libby as she told him about her friend Olivia and her husband and baby.

'I was telling her about this gorgeous bar, how incredible it sounded, and she said that when she came to visit she really wanted to try it. And do you know what happened?'

'Yes,' Alistair said.

'You don't.'

'I do,' he said, mopping up the last smear of pepper sauce with his steak. 'She asked if you'd babysit.'

Libby's mouth fell open. 'How did you know?'

'Because I work with a lot of parents of young children and they're always on the scrounge for babysitters.'

'Do they ask you?' she smiled.

'No, because when I congratulate them on their happy news I make a point of telling them upfront that I won't be babysitting.' He topped up his water. 'Not even if I'm a godparent.'

'Oh.' Libby looked across the table to him. 'And are you a godparent?'

'Twice. Each year I take them to see a pantomime and the Christmas lights…'

'Pantomime!' Libby was delighted, and told him about the tiny little amateur theatre group she had been so heavily involved in. 'I have to find one here. I mean, there are loads, but…' She sighed. 'I'll be a very small fish.'

'Were you a big fish at home?' Alistair asked.

'I played the narrator in *Joseph*,' she told him proudly. 'Admittedly, it was a very small production…' She waved at him to go on. 'Your godchildren?'

'Well, I also try to do a daytrip in the Easter school holidays, and one in the summer—even if it's just a visit to the ambulance station…'

'They must love it.'

'Oh, yes. So their parents know better than to jeopardise that by asking me to give up a Saturday night so they can go to a wine bar.'

'I tend to get caught on the hop.'

'Well, be careful,' he warned, 'or you'll have your friend, husband and baby all crammed into your flat and you looking after the baby while they go to the bar…'

He must have seen her pressed lips.

'Do *not* get a bigger place,' he warned.

He was the first person to make her feel better about having the tiniest flat in the world.

'If they want to come and see you then they can book a hotel—or tell them you'll catch them the next time you're home.'

'I like your way of thinking.'

'And find the name of a good babysitting service should they actually come and see you.'

'They'll never come!' Libby laughed, and then her laughter faded because she knew it was kind of true…

Not so much the babysitting part—she loved babies—but she did feel a little adrift from her friends who had settled down…

Alistair made being single sound like an attribute—something to relish. Gosh, he made saying no to friends with children sound possible…doable. He was just so… in tune with his own priorities. He did not sway to please, and she liked that.

Really, really liked that.

'So, you have a physical assessment tomorrow?' said Libby. 'Is that a work thing?'

Alistair nodded.

In fact he was near the end of a long application process to get into the Hazardous Area Response Team, and was eventually aiming to work for the Paramedic Tactical Response Unit.

In truth, he rather doubted he would get accepted into HART. Not because of the physical assessment or the studying or anything like that. It was the team player part.

He was very independent, and although he liked being in a team at times, he liked taking charge and working alone too. The HART application process was thorough, and there was no showing only your best side to advantage.

All sides were being scrutinised.

So he wasn't letting anyone in on his plans. Well, a couple of colleagues knew, like Brendan and Lina, but aside from that he was trying to keep it under wraps. He didn't want to discuss it now, with Libby, so he left his response at a nod and moved on.

'Do you want dessert?' he asked.

'Always.' Libby smiled and pushed a token towards him. It was then that their fingers brushed—or rather, their fingers met.

It felt electric.

But also more than electric. Because when you come into contact with electricity, the natural response was to pull back.

Neither of them did, so Libby amended her thought inside her head. It felt *magnetic*, because now his fingers were toying with the tips of hers.

And he didn't let go. In fact, he turned her hand over and commented on the smooth pale skin.

'For someone who must use alcohol rub a thousand times a day, you have very soft hands.'

'Because I use hand cream a thousand and one times a day,' Libby said, smiling. 'Well, that's possibly an exaggeration...'

She examined his very neat nails and rather lovely long fingers and thought how nice they felt, lingering in her own.

'Yours are soft too.' She looked up to his smile and met his eyes. 'Do you use hand cream?'

'Much to Brendan's mirth, I do.' He nodded.

For the first time in memory, Libby found she actually didn't want dessert. Instead, she wanted to sit playing with his fingers and marvelling at the feel of his skin against hers.

'I'm so pleased you dropped your glove and had to come back.'

'I didn't drop it,' Alistair said, and she looked up from their joined fingers to chocolate-brown eyes that knew how to flirt. 'At least, not by accident.'

'Oh!'

She loved it that he didn't hide it—that he didn't pretend this night was an accident. She loved it that he had, in fact, engineered it. Thinking about that made a smile spread across her face. A smile watched by those gorgeous dark eyes.

Suddenly, that feeling she'd had beside the fridge was back...that feeling that she was possibly about to be kissed!

'Dessert?' Alistair said, separating their hands as a rather grumpy waitress came to clear their plates.

Gosh, she thought as she helped herself to ice-cream at the dessert bar, never in a million years could she have imagined that her difficult day would turn out to be so promising.

So very promising.

He made the rather noisy surroundings melt away into nothing, so she could imagine they were the only two people in the world. Alistair made a pub dinner exciting.

Special.

It was as if Libby had chosen the most romantic restaurant in existence.

Still, even with dessert they couldn't stay at the table for three hours when the pub was this busy. They got up to leave, but both were happy not to part ways as they stepped out into the night.

In fact, with no plates or grumpy waitresses hurrying them on, they freely held hands. As naturally as if they'd been together a hundred years and held hands every day.

Libby went into the off-licence next door and bought Brendan a nice bottle of wine in a bag with a bow as his reward for helping with the fridge. Since she'd bought dinner for Alistair, they were even now.

Then they walked to a small corner shop, and Libby bought a couple of essentials for her new fridge—milk, butter, cheese...

'It'll be nice to have milk in my coffee in the morning,' Libby said, and then pressed her lips together, because everything she said sounded as if she was flirting.

He didn't answer that.

She selected two chocolate treats at the checkout.

Well, she selected one easily and then dithered over her second choice, her hand hesitating between a bar of hazelnut chocolate and one of chocolate-covered nougat.

'Sorry,' she said, glancing up to the shopkeeper, who she caught smothering a smile, and then looking to Alistair, who stood patiently behind her. 'This one,' she said, choosing the nougat, instantly regretting it, but trying not to show it.

She paid for her purchases and then Alistair bought a fondant-filled chocolate egg. 'I'll have it when I get home.'

Libby pouted as they walked out the store. 'Now *I* want a chocolate egg.'

He didn't answer—just looked up at the sky, which had turned to black as large drops of rain started to splash down.

'I've got my umbrella,' Libby said, opening up her vast bag. 'I think...'

She didn't have her umbrella.

'I must have left it at home,' she said, rummaging in it even as he steered them into a covered doorway. 'Typical. The one time...'

She looked up, and suddenly umbrellas really didn't matter because he was pulling her close.

'Are we going to wait it out here?' Libby asked.

'It's been almost three hours since we left the fridge,' he said. 'Aside from that, I don't think the rain's going anywhere.' As she reached for her phone, to summon a cab, his hand gently caught her fingers to stop her calling. 'I said it's been *almost* three hours. Can't risk you turning that fridge on...'

'Oh...' She happily put her phone back in her bag. 'Well, it's true that I don't have any patience.'

'Exactly,' he agreed, and pulled her into him.

She gave in then. She had waited three hours, after all, and when it came to it she found she had never known a kiss like it.

God, he was so sexy—because there wasn't any awkwardness. It was just a thorough rainy night kiss.

She was suddenly mindful that at any moment the little handles on Brendan's wine bag might break, so they stopped kissing for a second so she could put it carefully into her shoulder bag, and then got back to their deep kiss.

His lips were divine—firm and incredibly thorough—and he held her so firmly she didn't even have to lean on the wall for support.

He even took care of the carrier bag with her fridge food in it, grabbing it and lowering it to the floor.

'Luckily no glass in that one,' she said, and then his hands slid inside her coat and they got back to kissing again. She had never—not once in her life—wanted someone so badly, so urgently. It felt as if she'd been wanting him since this morning—and she undoubtedly had.

She was pressed against him, and it was very clear he wanted her too. But just when she was going to suggest they make a run for the flat—because it felt imperative that they must not part—it was he who pulled her hips and his mouth back.

'We're going to stop,' Alistair said. 'Because I have to strip off tomorrow during my assessment and I don't think we're going to be gentle, do you?'

Libby gulped, because usually she was so boring at sex. She didn't think it was anything special, if past experience was anything to go by. But she wanted to pinch him, and taste him, and just…

He brought out something in her that no one ever had before.

'I think you're being very sensible,' she said.

'Sometimes,' Alistair said, caressing her hips and looking at her with a hunger that had nothing to do with food, 'I wish I wasn't so sensible…'

'So do I,' Libby agreed. 'But you're completely right.' She was practically hanging off his neck. 'Thank you for all your help today. When did you change your mind about coming to help with the fridge?'

'I'm not telling you,' he said, kissing her neck and cupping her breast through her jumper.

She leant against him and realised that she had never been so consumed by desire for someone. So instantly attracted to another person. And the best part was that it was clearly entirely reciprocated.

'Please tell me…' she whispered. 'When did you change your mind?'

'I was always going to come.'

'Were you?' She smiled and could feel the pressure of his hands as he resisted pulling her back in.

'Call for your cab…' he said, and she reluctantly did so.

Unfortunately, her car was all of two minutes away,

which left time for just one more kiss before her phone bleeped again. 'It's approaching... Damn!'

He laughed at her angry hiss. 'Thank you for dinner.'

'You're very welcome.' She looked at the torrential rain. 'How will you get home?'

'I'm used to it,' he said, zipping up his jacket.

She stared out onto the street and watched a zillion headlights glaring, then a silver car pulled up. 'I'm going to go and plug in my fridge now.'

'Hold on.' He halted her, pulling her back into the doorway. He took her phone and checked the registration of the arriving car against the one she had ordered. 'Yes, it's good. Always check!'

'Okay!'

'I mean it. Don't just jump into some random car...'

'Yes, Alistair.'

'And remember—next time you buy a fridge, or whatever, measure twice, cut once...'

Libby laughed and made a dash for it in the pelting rain.

As she sat in the car for the short drive home she felt an unexpected bulge in her pocket. She reached her hand in and found a shiny foil-wrapped fondant-filled egg...and let out a happy sigh of surprise.

She was still wearing a smile as she let herself into her teeny-tiny flat. She immediately plugged in the fridge and turned on the switch, admiring her own restraint as she waited before opening the door.

'Let there be light!' Libby said.

And there was.

And also, suddenly, a booming clap of thunder.

More sheets of rain had started to fall, and if she'd had Alistair's number she'd have texted him to make sure he'd got home okay—and not just because she was a worrier.

It was filthy weather out there.

And while eating her lovely chocolate egg, she peered out at the storm-laden night and worried about him on his motorbike.

Worried a lot.

CHAPTER TWO

ALISTAIR HAD MADE it safely home.

Well, Libby assumed that to be the case, because all the paramedics the next day seemed to be in a good mood, and pleasant, so presumably he hadn't died.

Libby was seesawing between feeling dreadfully loose, because of the nature of that kiss, while simultaneously trying to reel herself in and dismiss it as just a kiss—because of course he would have kissed many women…

But the memory of it was perfect.

So perfect that she almost didn't want to take her upcoming days off, because it meant there would be no chance of seeing him.

In truth, she had no idea about the paramedics' shift rotas and days on and off or such things. She tried to ask Rory, who was back from his sick leave, but he seemed to infer that she was angling to go out with him and said, 'I finish around seven, if you want to catch up?'

'No, no!' Libby quickly declined—perhaps a little too emphatically. And then wished she had been more polite. 'I've got so much to do…with the move and everything.'

Phew.

Still, from what she *had* managed to gather from Rory, paramedics worked four long shifts, a mixture of days and nights, and swapped partners a lot—not in the swinging sense, of course.

By her next shift she'd worked out that Alistair was presumably now on nights, and the thought that she wouldn't see him had her sagging a little as she checked the equipment in Resus.

'Did you ever get your fridge sorted?' asked May.

'I did,' Libby said, nodding. 'Brendan and Alistair helped.'

'That's nice.'

'Yes,' Libby said. 'At first I didn't think they'd help…'

'Oh, Brendan's like that.'

While Brendan was indeed nice, she had been trying to steer the conversation onto Alistair, but no matter how much Libby tried she could not glean a thing from any of her colleagues.

And there were so many things she wanted to glean!

'Speak of the devil,' May said, and Libby started when she saw Brendan and Alistair wheeling in a patient who was hidden under a silver foil blanket. 'Shouldn't you be at home?' May asked the two unshaven paramedics, who looked more than a little bleary-eyed.

They must be at the tail-end of their night shift, Libby thought.

'We've been on scene for a while,' Alistair explained, 'and now we're well into overtime. This is Mrs Anna Dalton,' he went on. 'Eighty-seven years old, suspected fracture neck of the femur. She had a fall on her way to bed around eleven last night and has been on the floor ever since. Her daughter was unable to get her up and called for help at five a.m.'

That was a long time to wait before asking for help, Libby thought, briefly meeting Alistair's eyes. She guessed she might get a more detailed handover away from the bedside.

'It was a difficult extraction,' Alistair said, and then directed his next words to his patient. 'I'm just telling the nurse we had some trouble getting you out to the ambulance.'

Libby knew there must be more to it, because Mrs Dalton was like a tiny bird and they would have had little trouble moving her, but the reason for their difficulties would have to wait for now.

'Hello, Mrs Dalton.' Libby pulled back the foil blanket and looked at the frail lady as Alistair listed the drugs that had been given on scene, then reported that she was hypothermic and had a past history of mild dementia.

Her temperature was worryingly low, so Libby took her through to Resus, where they could keep a much closer eye on her. 'Where's her daughter?'

'She wanted to stay at home,' Alistair said. 'The daughter's name is Rosemary.'

Mrs Dalton spoke for the first time. 'Where's my Rosemary?'

'Rosemary's at home, Mrs Dalton,' Alistair said, then added to Libby, 'Rosemary has MS and isn't very mobile, but I said someone would call and update her.'

'Of course.'

When Libby had got Mrs Dalton on to a Resus bed, May came over and started setting up the warming blanket as Huba examined the diminutive lady and Alistair went through the handover again. Then he nodded his head at Libby, and then towards the door, to indicate he wanted to talk. Even though he was pulling her away, she knew there would be no flirting at work with Alistair—no departure from perfect protocol and procedure.

'The set-up at home isn't good,' he told her. 'There's a

hoarding issue—just stuff *everywhere*. We could barely get through to the lounge. Mrs Dalton gets upset if it's mentioned. Rosemary's doing her best, but she's barely able to take care of herself, let alone her mother. From what I can make out they really don't have any support.'

'None?' Libby frowned.

'The place is unkempt and freezing. There were a few cans of soup in the kitchen, but apart from that there was nothing I could see. Just tea and long-life milk. And Rosemary didn't want to come in with her mother. She said she was worried about how she'd get home, but I don't think she's actually been out of the house in a very long time. I've called their GP and asked him to do a home visit.'

Libby recalled what Alistair had said about a lot of his job being social work.

'The home situation really isn't safe,' he finished.

'Okay.'

The daughter wasn't their patient, and didn't want help, but it was clear the paramedics had been concerned enough to have requested that the GP intervene.

'I'll call her myself,' Libby said. 'What's her surname?'

'The same—Dalton.'

As May fussed over Mrs Dalton, Libby managed to duck out to the changing rooms and to her locker. Catching the paramedics as they left, she gave Brendan his bottle of wine in the gift bag with the bow on it.

'Thank you so much for moving my fridge,' she said.

'That's great, Libby, thank you,' Brendan said, and then held it out to Alistair. 'I should give this to you, seeing how last-minute it was…'

'Brendan, it's for you,' Libby said, frowning. And then it dawned on her that Brendan thought she'd bought one bottle of wine between them. 'I've got one for…' She stopped and glanced at Alistair. 'Well, I…'

She was stuck, because they all knew he'd been at his physical yesterday, so she couldn't say she'd already given him one, and she didn't want to admit they'd been out to dinner.

'I thought Alistair was off today.' She risked a glance at Alistair's impassive features and could see the twinkle in his eyes that told her he was laughing inside at her little dilemma. 'I'll bring yours in, Alistair, and keep it in my locker for next time I see you.'

'Thanks!' Alistair said carefully. 'That's very thoughtful of you.'

'Thanks very much,' Brendan said as the duo headed off. 'Alison will be thrilled.'

Libby guessed Alison must be his wife. 'Have a good sleep!' she called to them both, although her words were really aimed at Alistair.

So now she'd have to buy another bottle of wine, when she was as broke as a church mouse after the move, the new sofa-bed and fridge, and having to pay for the storage of her own furniture. And then there was that dinner… There had been no manly protest that he would pay instead.

Ha-ha!

She liked him far too much. Not that she had time to think about dark-haired sexy paramedics, because the day was shaping up to be a busy one.

A lot of Libby's morning was taken up with Mrs Dalton, and also speaking with her daughter over the telephone.

'What's happening with Mum?' That was naturally the main question she had.

'She's doing better,' Libby said, knowing Mrs Dalton was back from X-Ray. 'Thankfully her hip isn't broken, but there is an old fracture there.'

'That was ages ago.'

'How does she usually get around?'

'We manage.'

Alistair had been right. From all Libby could make out Rosemary had been struggling to take care of her mother, especially as her own health had declined. She was too scared to go out in case she caught anything and brought it back to her mother, and too nervous to let anyone into their home because of her mother's accumulation of stuff. On top of that, she was worried about putting the heating on, and had a nasty cough herself.

'Have you heard from your GP?' Libby asked.

'He called, but I told him I'm fine. I only called the ambulance because I couldn't get Mum up by myself.'

Gosh, she was stubborn. And she really didn't want anyone coming into her home.

'How do you manage for shopping?' Libby tried to get more details.

'My brother takes care of it.'

'How often is that?'

'When he can.'

In the end, it all took more than a morning.

Eventually a social worker came down and called the GP surgery himself. Fortunately Alistair's referral had been comprehensive enough that they had planned a home visit despite Rosemary's assurances that all was fine.

Mrs Dalton was still awaiting a bed on the geriatric ward by the time the end of Libby's shift rolled around. Libby was just helping her to open some sandwiches and add sugar to her tea when May came in and smiled at their patient.

'How are you doing, Mrs Dalton?'

She was more interested in the sandwiches than answering, and Libby explained that the wait for a bed on the ward was going to be another hour. 'I promised Mrs Dalton's daughter I'd call her when she was moved.'

'I've just come off the phone with her GP,' May said. 'He's done a home visit and Rosemary is going to be admitted to a medical ward.'

'Oh!' Libby was relieved to hear it. From her own conversations with Rosemary it had been clear that there was a lot going on, but her reluctance to go out or let anyone in to her home meant nothing had been addressed.

'She's coming via Emergency for a chest X-ray.'

May gave Libby a wink. Usually a direct admission went straight to the ward, but this way perhaps Rosemary would be able to manage a brief visit with her mother.

May smiled over to the patient. 'You're getting a visitor soon, Mrs Dalton.'

Mrs Dalton just peeled open her sandwich and peered inside before nibbling on it. She looked so much better than she had this morning. Her cheeks were pink and she'd chatted a little with Libby. She'd even walked to the toilet, but she had required considerable help.

'Go home,' May said to Libby, and Libby nodded.

After wishing Mrs Dalton goodnight, she headed out, walking with May to the changing rooms.

'I don't know how they've managed for so long,' she said.

'Barely,' May said. 'The GP said she was very reluctant to let him in. Apparently there's a hoarding problem at the house.'

'The paramedics said the same.' Libby told her. 'Hopefully now they'll get the help they need.'

'Let's hope,' May agreed. 'You're on days off now?'

Libby nodded again and wished May a good evening, before gathering her things and going home.

She was so tired that she almost dozed on the Tube, and she wondered if she might just sleep her way through every stop until the end of the line. But she jolted awake just in time, and gradually made her rather listless way home, where she had a shower and then wrapped herself up in her dressing gown and flopped onto the sofa, almost too tired to open it up and make the bed.

Why hadn't she gone shopping on the way home from work? she scolded herself. Now she was clean and cosy she didn't want to get dressed and go back out.

Tomorrow she would do a massive shop and get organised. Four days off in a row meant she could finally get on top of things. But that didn't help her grumbling stomach tonight!

You are not getting food delivered, Libby told herself.

There had been far too much of that since she'd arrived in the city. As well as moving, finding out her flat was missing a bedroom, putting a hold on her furniture delivery and sorting out storage, she had also started a new job, so there had barely been time to breathe, let alone shop for healthy, balanced meals.

She really ought to get up, get dressed and go out in search of something better than delivery food.

But then she'd have to cook it as well.

Bleh...

Suddenly then she heard—or rather *felt*—the throbbing purr of an engine in the driveway beneath her window. It sounded like a motorbike... *His* motorbike, maybe?

Libby found she was holding her breath.

It wasn't.

It couldn't be.

Yet she lay on her sofa-bed, resisting peeking and desperately trying not to get her hopes up.

If she looked out of the window then it wouldn't be him.

If she got up and ran a comb through her hair, quickly slicked on some mascara and pulled on something more attractive than her ancient robe, it wouldn't be him.

Of course it isn't him, she told her rapidly beating heart.

Yet as she lay there, ears on elastic, biting her bottom lip as she heard footsteps on the stairs outside, Libby found herself relishing the anticipation.

There was a smile spreading across her face as she listened to the sound of heavy footsteps getting nearer and nearer. There was a pause, and then a firm knock on her door, and hope shot like a flare into the night sky.

Oh, why hadn't she put on mascara or changed…?

Because it was probably a delivery for another flat in the building, Libby reminded herself as she jumped from the couch and walked to her door.

She opened it, bracing for disappointment while still hoping all the same. There were plenty of other residents who might have decided to order food in rather than go out into the cold winter's night.

Hope won!

'Alistair!' She grinned like an idiot. 'Did you drop another glove?'

'No,' he said. 'And, just so you know, I deliberately dropped it before, so I could come back.'

'Oh!' Libby's heart turned over in her chest.

She loved it that he didn't lie or play games…that he admitted his attraction up front.

It thrilled her.

As well as that, he had the unfair advantage of having spent the day in bed, and he was looking all refreshed and lethal to her senses in his leather biker gear.

And, even better, he came bearing gifts!

He handed her a tall paper bag with a red foil rosette attached to the top. Peeking in, she could see it was a bottle of wine.

'That's for you to give to me at work,' he said. 'Put it in your bag now, so you don't forget.'

'Thank you!'

'And this is for both of us for now.'

He held up a white carry-out bag, from which she caught delectable wafts of curry and spice. From under his arm peeked a bottle of icy bubbly wine.

'Just what I wanted!'

She had to fight not to leap forward and kiss him, and instead stepped back to let him in. *Play it cool, Libby*, she warned herself.

'You've rescued me from going shopping.'

'In your dressing gown?' he enquired.

'I was about to get dressed and…' She gave in. 'You're right. I was never going to go shopping tonight, but I was trying not to get food delivered—again.'

'Why not? You've been working all week,' he pointed out as he put all the goodies onto her kitchen bench. 'Anyway, it's cold out there.'

It was exceedingly warm in here…

Well, not technically, since the heater didn't spread its warmth very far. It was more that she was burning up inside.

He unzipped his jacket to reveal a thin black jumper beneath. He looked around for somewhere to put the jacket.

'There's a hanger on the back of my front door.'

'Thanks.'

He went to hang up his jacket and she heard the sound of his boots being unzipped. It made her feel fluttery and perturbed—but in a good way—and she looked up quickly as he returned.

Gosh, he was very big for her little kitchen, and she'd realised the grumble in her stomach had nothing to do with the cartons he was pulling out of the take-out bag.

'How was your physical?' Libby asked as she took out two plates and put them on the bench.

'I'm a fine specimen, apparently.'

'They didn't say that…' Libby grinned.

'They might have,' Alistair replied. 'It was very thorough.'

She bit down on her lip, resisting asking, *How thorough?* Resisting provoking him.

Except, when it came to Alistair, she simply could not resist.

She peeled open a corner of one of the lids, even though she didn't really want to—because how could she possibly be thinking of food with Alistair standing behind her? She wanted to turn to him, or at least turn her head, and she felt her breath hitch.

She didn't want to resist.

'How thorough?' Libby asked, in a voice that was a little bit croaky.

'Oh, you know…' Alistair said. 'They checked my back…'

'Really?' she squeaked, as he ran a finger down the length of her spine and the light touch almost shot her into orbit.

'My neck…' he added, as he lifted her hair and breathed on her neck, and then gave her skin the bliss of his mouth, making her ache—actually *ache*—for more contact.

'My ears…' he said, as he licked one of hers. It made her feel so faint that she spun around just to seek his mouth.

He didn't give it to her, though.

Instead, he went over to her little kitchen window and closed the blind, and then to the living area, and she heard the blinds being closed in there. Finally, he returned to the kitchen.

'We don't want to offend the neighbours,' Alistair said, with a look in his eye that made her blood start to sing.

'No…'

It would not be accidental sex, Libby knew.

Nor would it be just a kiss that went too far, or touches that got out of hand.

It was going to be absolutely, thoroughly, deliciously premeditated—on both sides.

In response, she slipped off her robe as easily as if she were alone and about to step into the shower.

Just slipped it off. Because it hindered what was to come.

Alistair took out a packet of condoms from his pocket and placed them on the bench, his dark eyes so intense in their hold on hers that she felt as if they had already had sex, or were having sex, or had known each other intimately before…many, many times.

'Come here,' he said, even though she was barely a step away.

She went gladly, wrapping her arms around his neck, and drank him in—actually *inhaled* his scent as she slid her hands inside his jumper in order to feel his skin.

And then she pulled the fine fabric of his jumper up, and he continued the motion to strip it off. Libby caught sight of a fan of black hair, and never had she been so bold or so desperate for a man.

She stood on tiptoes to revel in the sensation of his chest against hers, his warm skin on her naked breasts. His kiss was rough, and so thorough, so direct. And the turn-on was so instant that it felt as if they were resuming where they had left things the other night.

Only this time Libby was naked. And from the hips up so was he.

He reached down to unzip himself and she felt dizzy with lust as she held him, impatient to feel him, to have him inside her, in a way she had never anticipated such pleasure before.

Ever.

'Alistair…'

She was urgent, almost climbing up him in her desperation to coil herself around him, but thank goodness for his Mr Sensible side, because he was taking out a condom from the packet.

Libby watched as he slid it on and found herself panting a little, reaching to touch him.

'You *really* have no patience,' Alistair said, brushing her hand away, making her wait.

She sobbed in relief when he lifted her—but not onto the bench. He carried her over to the fridge that had somehow introduced them.

Certainly it was introducing her to a whole new world—because she was *not* a sex in the kitchen kind of girl.

Nor had she known herself to plead before, but the cold metal on her back as he took her, and the warmth of him against her skin, and the urgency of them together, was a cocktail of sensations that stripped bare all her inhibitions.

'Oh, God…' she said as he ground into her, taking her fast. So fast that it was breathtaking.

And then there were no more words. And there was not a thing she had to do but hold on.

'I'm going to come,' Alistair warned.

'Me…' she said, unable to precede it with *and*.

But he knew what she meant anyway, because he could feel how taut she was in his arms, how close to the edge she was.

'And then I'm going to take you again, so slow…'

Alistair held her so firmly that there was no thought in her head that she might slip, no discomfort, just sheer luxury. That he could bring her to the edge of orgasm like that…as if he already knew every inch of her skin…

Then he moaned, and she arched as he shot into her.

She came at his summons, deep and urgent, and then felt a weak relief as it receded. As if it had been essential...

He was breathing hard, and she was panting and resting her head on his shoulder, and then she gave a soft laugh and so did he—a happy, soft laugh, as if to say, *Thank goodness!*

She was glad they hadn't eaten first, because now they had the prospect of a delicious curry waiting for them.

He lowered her down and kissed her, long and slow.

And Libby felt...right.

So right.

As if the move to London made sense now. Because if she hadn't moved then she would never have known him.

That was how right she felt.

'I'm hungry,' Libby said.

'We won't even need to microwave it,' Alistair replied.

No, because it had been so deliciously fast.

'Go and make up the bed,' he suggested. 'We can eat there.'

How could those words make her so happy when making up the sofa-bed was surely the worst job in the world?

But she couldn't stop smiling while he served up dinner, anticipating the pleasure of him climbing in with her.

Alistair gave the naans a little spin in the microwave, and while he did, brought her through a mug of bubbly wine.

'I do have nice glasses,' she told him as she sipped on it, 'but they're in storage.' And then she couldn't help adding, 'You're so sexy...'

'*We* are,' he said, and headed back into the kitchen, giving her a view of his very nice bum.

Oh, she'd wake up in a moment, Libby thought as she lay there. She'd wake up and be in her dressing gown, lying on the sofa, starving hungry and contemplating whether to head to the shops...

Instead, her sexy paramedic returned with dinner and climbed in beside her.

'What are you doing?' he asked, when she pinched his arm.

'Just making sure.'

'Me too…' Alistair said, and he lightly pinched her back, his warm fingers on her breast.

The curry was spicier than she was used to—so much so that she had to reach for the box of tissues and blow her nose.

'Have you slept all day?' Libby asked as they ate.

'A couple of hours this morning.'

They chatted a bit about work, but eventually brought the conversation naturally around to talking about them.

'Perfect Peter?' Libby said. 'I can see where you got your nickname.'

He gave her a curious look.

'So beautiful…' she sighed, looking at his lovely mouth and tracing his features with her fingers, wanting to imprint the shape of him on her soul.

'Libby,' he said, removing her fingers and holding her hand, 'they're being sarcastic.' He frowned, as if he thought she must surely be joking. 'They call me that because I'm so pedantic.'

'Pedantic?'

'Yes—and I'm big on following protocol. Believe me when I say it's not a term of endearment.'

'Well, I think it is,' Libby said. 'I like my paramedics pedantic.'

She thought back to the way he always made his notes, and how he had told her he liked to study rather than chat during breaks.

'I take it all very seriously—maybe too seriously,' he said. 'But I didn't give up law to make friends.'

'You studied law?'

'More than studied. I worked in contract law.'

'How old are you?' Libby asked.

'Thirty-three. You?'

'I told you—twenty-eight.'

'And a half,' he said. 'That's right, you did.'

'That's quite a career change.'

'Yes.'

She looked over at him, waiting for him to elaborate, but he said no more. There was a slight strain in the silence, which felt unusual after the way they communicated together.

'Was being a paramedic something you always wanted to do, or…?' Her voice faded into another stretch of silence.

'No,' Alistair said finally. 'I'd never considered paramedicine. But someone close to me died and I was there…'

'I'm sorry.'

'Asthma,' he added. 'There was nothing I could do. I didn't know what to do. I've never felt so helpless. In truth, I think I had a bit of a meltdown afterwards. We were…' He stopped.

'Tell me,' Libby said.

But he remained silent.

'You were…?' she persisted. 'Married, or engaged, or…? Honestly,' she said, 'I won't mind.'

'Won't mind what?'

'Well, if she was the love of your life. I mean…'

'*He* was my best friend,' Alistair said.

'Oh! Gosh, I'm sorry. How dreadful.'

'It was. It turned out that he hadn't been using his inhalers and had ignored all the signs. There was a group of us. Middle of nowhere.'

'Alistair!' She felt tears in her eyes at the awful thought of what it must have been like.

'Oh, you don't mind now, do you?' Alistair said, and then he surprised her with a smile. 'You jealous little shrew!'

'I am not,' Libby said as he leaned over her and kissed her jealous lips.

But she was one big burning blush, because she had been caught out—one bonk in—for liking him so much. For liking him so, so much…

'Yes.' He took her wrists and held them up, and she squirmed under his scrutiny even as they both smiled. 'Why did you assume it was a woman who had died? The love of my life?'

'I just wanted to know what I was up against,' she admitted. 'Any big relationships before?'

'No,' Alistair said, 'not really. I'm not romantic enough, apparently. I just want sex, sex and more sex…'

'Poor thing,' Libby said, smiling as he kissed her breast.

'How about you?' he asked.

'No big ones either. Well, maybe one…'

She took a breath. She didn't know how to start talking about the details of her recent break-up. And it was surely too soon to be discussing her malfunctioning ovaries! But her troubles had certainly shown Vince in his true colours, so Libby attempted to explain sans details.

'I tend to go for bastards—well, present company excepted, of course…'

'Thank you very much.'

She didn't really know how to describe her ex, because even the longest, most serious relationship of her life had never felt as vital as what she was feeling now for Alistair.

But in the end she didn't have to say anything. His lips were too busy for her own to form words, and his mouth was trailing down her torso and kissing her stomach, first with tenderness, and then with such passion that she whimpered for him to move lower.

* * *

Libby and Alistair fell ridiculously fast.

Yet it felt necessarily so.

They didn't leave her sofa-bed for four days.

Only to collect the food they ordered to be delivered.

When she quickly dressed one day, and video called her mother, he stayed well away in the kitchen.

They chatted for a while, mainly about her mother's up-coming birthday, and Alistair could tell they were close. In fact, hearing Libby talking with her parents made him wistful for his own family, and how good he had once believed his relationship with them had been.

Only, it had turned out that the closeness he'd had with his father had been contingent upon him toeing the family line.

Leaving a successful career in law had cost Alistair a lot—and not just financially. The real hit had been the reaction of his family.

It was lonely at the bottom...

'I have to go, Mum,' Libby was saying. 'Kisses...'

They also left the sofa-bed to shower—unfortunately not together, because the cubicle was so tiny, though they did try. Several times.

On the last night before they returned to work Alistair unashamedly watched as Libby showered and told him about the acting lessons she wanted to take.

'Don't laugh.'

'I'm not laughing.' He smiled as, head down, she started to shave her legs. 'I want a front row seat when you perform, though...'

He saw the razor in her hand pause mid-stroke, above her calf, as he referenced the future, but then she sighed and made light of the situation.

'I might never get a part.'

Oh she'd be leading lady, Alistair thought, lost in visions of himself sitting through some dreadful amateur production... And yet, bizarrely, he couldn't pretend he wasn't looking forward to doing just that.

Then it was his turn to shower, and when he came out she told him he looked incredible—even with her lemon-coloured daisy-embroidered towel wrapped around his hips.

The towel that covered her entire torso was like a hand towel on him, thought Libby, and she didn't want this magical time to be ending.

She'd wanted to look up when he'd spoken about front row seats—to say that she'd make sure he got them and she wanted flowers in her dressing room too...

Was she being ridiculous and reading too much into his words?

Or was Alistair feeling the same?

'I don't want to go to work tomorrow,' Libby admitted.

She was kneeling behind him, drying his shoulders, but she stopped what she was doing and proceeded to wet them again with her mouth.

'We're going,' he said, and turned his head to meet her lips. Then he turned around more completely and pressed her down, so she lay beneath him.

It would have been far more comfortable for them to have relocated to his home for this four-day period, because he had a bigger bed—and a bigger shower, for that matter—but as he stared down at Libby, Alistair knew why they hadn't.

His practical mind was bewildered, because he had the feeling that if he ever took her back to his—well, they would return to Libby's flat for the sole purpose of collecting her things.

It terrified him that moving her into his place actually felt as if it might be the sensible thing to do.

He was usually so closed to others. He thought things through…

But, looking down at her now, Alistair felt as if he had Libby's dizzy, impulsive head on his shoulders—and he wanted nothing more than to take her back to his home and keep her there.

To be swept up in such a tide both unnerved and thrilled him. The feelings she provoked in him were so new, so unfamiliar, that he felt it would be necessary to examine them in more detail when he was alone.

And yet at the same time he did not want to come up for air.

Did not want to leave, nor for normal services to resume.

He liked this new normal.

No—he *loved* this new normal.

Libby felt the burn of his stare and saw something she had never seen in a lover's eyes before—something so deep that it felt almost like the L word.

She was not going to ruin things by blurting that out, so she just put her hand to his head and pulled his face down to hers.

He kissed her deeply, and she squirmed beneath him, because he was rough and unshaven after four days away from his razor.

One more kiss, she thought. Just one more…

But it was already one kiss too many, because they were in over their heads. Neither wanted their four-day sex-fest to end—and it was temptation at its purest to try to extend their time away from reality, to pretend that outside pressures didn't exist, that nothing bad could ever happen as long as they were together…

Alistair was reaching for the box of condoms.

'Last one,' he told her.

'Poor you,' Libby said.

'Why?' he asked as she slid it on.

'You'll have to go to the petrol station on such a cold night…'

They really were in trouble, she thought. They were both so close to tearing up the rule book…to saying no more condoms and moving in together…to succumbing to desire and moving from the *crazy about you* phase to the *I love you* one.

Don't spoil it, Libby told herself and closed her eyes.

Then she moaned as he filled her.

'Oh, God,' Alistair said on an exhale.

'There,' Libby said—unnecessarily, because he already knew.

They couldn't even part long enough for him to go to the petrol station when they were ready again, and so, in the absence of supplies, Libby woke him intimately with her mouth.

It was complete and utter bliss…

But of course paradise had to come to an end eventually.

'I don't want to go work,' Libby said again, at six-thirty the next morning.

She had just showered, and had come out of the bathroom to the sight of him sexy and unshaven and pulling on his clothes.

Extremely reluctantly she dressed too. 'And you're on till when?' she asked, pouting.

'Midnight,' Alistair said. 'Well, depending on what time we get our last job.'

'The off-duty rota hates us.'

'It's been pretty good to us, really,' he said, dunking

tea bags into two mugs. 'We haven't left your sofa-bed in four days.'

'Why did I say I'd go home to my parents on my next days off?'

'Because it's your mother's sixtieth!' Alistair smiled.

'Oh, yes…' *And those bloody tests.*

He gave her one last lingering kiss.

'Drop your glove so you have to come back,' she said into his sexy mouth.

'No.'

'Please can we call in sick?'

'No!'

He was by far too responsible, Libby thought, as he peeled her off him and with a smile headed off.

Well, he was by far too responsible *except* for that damn bike, Libby amended when she heard the engine, and no doubt he was annoying all her neighbours with the noise.

It was a ten-minute walk to work—twenty when it was freezing and you stopped for coffee and a doughnut on the way. Actually, a *bag* of doughnuts, because May had sulked last time when Libby had mentioned she'd had one and not got some for everyone.

'Good morning, Libby.' May smiled. 'Is it snowing outside?'

'No…' Libby frowned, but when she got to the changing room she laughed as she understood May's little joke. Taking off her coat, she saw that it was covered in icing sugar and, when she looked in the mirror, so was her face. She rinsed herself off and changed into scrubs. She was all floaty, floaty, happy, happy…

'Filthy morning out there. We're going to be snowed under.' May rolled her eyes and pulled her cardigan around her. 'Did you see the icing sugar?'

'I did!' Libby laughed. 'Don't worry, I bought a whole bag of doughnuts to share.'

'Good lass! You're learning.'

'Yes—either hide the evidence or buy plenty for all...'

'You're very chipper this morning,' May said as they waited for handover.

'Chipper?'

'Cheery,' May translated.

Indeed Libby was.

At least until the Bat Phone interrupted handover.

'Car versus motorbike...'

It was the cyclist they were being alerted about, and the mobile intensive care unit was attending.

'No ETA yet,' said May, summoning the trauma team, and Libby found herself in Resus, trying to tame her irrational mind.

Because Alistair had left her place ages ago.

She looked at the time and worked out that it must have been thirty or forty minutes ago.

Oh, God, it actually could be him.

It really could be Alistair involved in the accident.

Libby felt sick to her stomach as she set up for their incoming guest.

The trauma team came in, asking for more information, and May told them the little she knew as Libby ran through an IV, her heart hammering in her chest.

It remained hammering when the phone buzzed again.

'Okay,' May said. 'Thank you for letting us know.' She replaced the receiver and turned to the awaiting team. 'We've been stood down,' she told them. 'Declared dead on scene.'

It was horrible. Watching the trauma team disperse... looking down at all the equipment that had been set up and now would not be used because the patient hadn't made it in.

Libby's heart was still hammering.

She'd always hated motorbikes—well, since the start of her nursing days—but never more so than now.

'How old was the patient?' Libby asked.

'They didn't say.'

She felt sick.

Truly.

She kept wanting to text Alistair, to ask if he was okay, but she thought of her mother, who always did just that, and how much it annoyed her.

She refused to be like that, even though her heart felt as if it were in her throat.

It wasn't long before the driver of the car was brought in, and the poor lady was beside herself. 'I didn't see him,' she sobbed over and over. 'I didn't see him…'

'Vera,' Libby said, 'let us take care of you.'

She was trying to calm the patient, and at the same time attempting to undress her and complete a set of observations on the shocked lady.

She held her arm as they got IV access. 'Try and stay still. Your husband's on his way.'

'I'm not even hurt.'

'You *are* hurt,' Libby said.

Though her injuries were relatively minor, Vera herself was broken inside. She lay on her back with a hard collar around her neck, choking on tears of shock and regret. Libby wiped the lady's tears away and did her best to be there with her patient's emotions. Vera's world had changed for ever.

May put her head in and nudged Libby to come out. 'The police are here. And Huba's going to assess her. I need you over in Resus.'

May was correct with her prediction—it did turn out to be a very busy morning. When May suggested she go for coffee, Libby glanced at the time, surprised to see that it was almost eleven.

'Are you okay, Libby?' May checked.

'Of course.'

'Only, you look like a little ghost.'

She felt like one.

She had a horrible, haunted feeling that she couldn't shake.

The coffee didn't help, and nor did a slice of dark chocolate cake.

Part of her knew that it hadn't been him.

Surely word would have come from one of the other paramedics by now.

Of course it would have.

The morning had given her such a fright—and not just because of the motorcycle accident. It was more that her sense of panic had been so intense.

She had never fallen this hard for anyone.

Not even close.

It was scary, actually.

She honestly hadn't come up for air since they'd met. One minute she'd been crying over her ovaries, and then...

He'd revved into her life.

Claimed her with a kiss.

When she'd left work the other day she had known she fancied him, wanted him, and that much she'd thought she could handle. But now she had returned to work with her feelings in a completely new order.

Alistair Lloyd had shot straight to the top.

Libby felt as if a thief had been in and taken her heart, stamped *Alistair* upon it and then put it back in her chest.

He'd be perfect if it weren't for that bike.

Seriously perfect.

So perfect that it troubled her.

Don't fall too hard, she warned herself as she headed back to the department.

But it felt like closing the stable door four days after the horse had bolted—actually, six days, given how incredible their first kiss had been the night of the fridge-moving.

It had been a long day, and Libby felt exhausted, but suddenly there Alistair was, making up the stretcher as Brendan handed their patient over to May. Libby did an abrupt about-turn—and not just to get the wine Alistair had so thoughtfully bought for her to give back to him.

She needed to calm herself.

She'd felt such a flood of relief to see for herself that he was okay, and an even bigger flood of relief that she hadn't texted him with her fears.

Get a grip, she told herself, before heading back out there with the wine.

'Alistair!' she called, and made her way over. 'This is for you,' she said, handing it over. She hoped she sounded casual enough. 'Thank you so much for your help with the fridge.'

'You didn't have to do that,' Alistair said. 'That's very considerate of you.'

'What's going on?' Brendan was all cheery as he walked over with a blanket. 'Oh, you got your wine.'

'Yes,' Alistair said.

'Have you invited Libby to your leaving drinks?'

'I'm not having any leaving drinks,' Alistair said, rolling his eyes as he took the blanket and Brendan headed down to Reception to register the patient. 'He's trying to give me a helping hand.'

'How so?' Libby frowned, a little confused.

'Brendan's got it into his head that I like you, and because I don't tell him all the details of my private life he's trying to matchmake.'

'Oh!'

'He thinks I'm shy.'

'Boy, have I got news for Brendan!' Libby chuckled. 'So, what's this about a leaving do?'

'I got a call just a moment ago. I've been accepted into HART.'

'Is that…?' She swallowed. 'Is that the hazardous incident response thing?'

Brendan returned and happily answered her question. 'He's aiming to get into tactical response.'

'Eventually,' Alistair amended.

'Terrorism, guns…'

Brendan was like a kid, making a gun with two fingers and pretending to shoot like a cowboy. Usually Libby would have laughed. Not today.

'Alistair will be right in the thick of it, lucky bugger.'

'Seriously?' Libby tried to hide the look of horror that she knew must have swept over her features, but Alistair was still making up the stretcher so he didn't notice. 'How's that lucky?'

'I'd do it if I could—not that I'd pass the physical,' Brendan sighed. 'But if I were ten years younger…'

'When do you start?' Libby asked Alistair.

'Soon. They've got me on the next intake. Six weeks residential.'

'Oh.'

Libby just stood there and tried to push out an appropriate or normal-sounding response.

'Congratulations,' she managed.

She tried to remember that she wasn't supposed to know him well—at least in front of Brendan and other colleagues—because it was all just too new to share.

'Thanks,' Alistair said neutrally, as if she were just another co-worker.

Brendan, though, was persistent with his matchmaking. 'So, if I can persuade him to have leaving drinks, can we count you in?'

'Sure,' Libby said, even while thinking, *Not a chance in hell*.

No way would she celebrate this!

'Come on, Brendan. Time to go.' Alistair rolled his eyes at his matchmaker. 'Thanks for the wine, Libby.'

No, no, no, no, no...

It was like being in a nightmare. And it would be even more of a nightmare if she got involved with him.

She was already involved—she couldn't deny that. But if she became seriously involved it would actually be her worst nightmare to have the man she loved working in such a dangerous profession.

She'd be like her mother...constantly glued to the news.

This morning his motorbike had been her only problem, Libby thought as she took the Tube home and then forced herself to go to the shop.

After all the unhealthy food they'd eaten, she'd buy a salad for her supper. And some chicken parmigiana, because it came in a pack of two—but would that be enough for Alistair?

She stared at the chicken parmigiana for two and it scared her how easily she had factored him in...how her head, mind and body all wanted and craved his company tonight.

Usually, with other men, she'd be wondering whether he'd call when his shift ended, but instead she had assumed—or rather *knew*—that he would. She was confident that Alistair considered what they had found together as wonderful as she did.

But for sanity's sake she must end things with Alistair right now. Mustn't she? Wasn't that the best course of action?

Yet she bought dinner for two, while telling herself she would eat the spare chicken tomorrow night.

Then she bought soap.

And then she looked at the condoms and didn't know whether to throw a pack in.

And then she looked at the tampons—but she had plenty at home because it had been ages since her last period…

Oh, yes. That whole thing.

Libby took out her phone and looked at the GP app and then the texts asking her to confirm her tests. They felt frighteningly close.

Alistair had asked why she and Vince had broken up and she hadn't known what to say…knowing it was too soon to get into talking about her ovaries.

She had wanted to confide in him but had held back.

Libby wasn't sure she wanted such a conversation.

It all felt too much.

She felt too much.

She wanted to call him and beg him not to take the job with HART, beg him to get rid of the bike, and confide in him that she was scared about going home for these tests.

She was feeling things she had never experienced before.

The edge of love?

If that was the case…well, you don't try to change the person you love.

That much, Libby knew.

Please be my usual type of bastard and don't call, Libby thought as she trudged home. *Or, if you do call, please give me the sense to end things.*

When she arrived home her flat was in chaos. It had made her smile that morning, but now it made her heart ache as she tidied all evidence of *them* away, and then spent an hour researching the line of work he wished to pursue.

It made her feel rather ill.

Libby heated the chicken parmigiana, but couldn't even finish her single one, so it went into the fridge next to his. Then she pulled her sofa-bed out and made it.

The worst job in the world?

Not any more.

Alistair's new job was, for Libby, the worst job in the world.

For her.

She would be saved from making a decision tonight, Libby thought as time passed, midnight came and went, and she didn't hear from him.

She thought about his professional, neutral approach to her at work today. Perhaps he wasn't feeling it quite as much as she, after all?

Then, just before one a.m., her phone bleeped a message. She didn't open it, but it flashed up on her watch so it was impossible to ignore.

Are you up?

Of course she was up!

Furthermore, if she continued seeing Alistair then she'd be perpetually up...worrying.

She was her mother's daughter after all.

And that was why she couldn't get further involved.

She didn't answer his text.

She mustn't.

Instead, she lay in the dark and thought of another old saying, one she wished she'd heeded: *Look before you leap*...

Foolishly, she hadn't.

* * *

It was odd to break up with someone because you liked them too much—or so much that the knot in your chest was pulled tight at the thought of them on a bike or working at a dangerous job. So much, that you might have to tell them you were having fertility investigations, because the outcome might actually matter to them.

Thursday dawned, and as Libby made a chicken parmigiana sandwich to take for supper on her late shift, it was her mother, rather than Alistair, that called—all worried about something she'd seen on the news.

'I'm fine,' Libby told her. 'What are you talking about?' She held in a sigh as her mother told her about a missing person she'd heard about on the news. 'Mum, that's not even close to where I live. London's a pretty big place, you know...' She took a breath. 'Of course you had to be sure that I was fine...'

Libby, while weary of her mother's constant anxiety, perhaps better understood now. After all, she'd immediately panicked that Alistair might be the motorcyclist who had died...

At least her mother had a reason to live on her nerves. She had lost a child before Libby had been born and a catastrophising nature had ensued.

And Libby would do everything in her power not to live like that...

Just as she'd finished packing up her sandwiches Alistair called.

As she had known he would.

'Alistair...' she took a breath '...my phone's playing up. I just saw your text...' She was too good a liar.

'I'm at work, so I can't talk,' Alistair told her. 'But I should be finished by seven, if you want to come over to mine after work?'

'Alistair.' Libby halted him quickly, otherwise she knew that she would give in to temptation. Especially as he was inviting her to his home…pulling her closer when she was trying to break away before things got too intertwined. 'I can't tonight…' She took a breath. 'I'm wiped.'

She loathed confrontation of any sort—just avoided it at all costs—but, more importantly, she didn't want to do this. She *couldn't* do this right now.

'Is everything okay?' Alistair checked, perhaps hearing the strain in her voice.

'I guess, but… Look, you're going away soon, and…' She swallowed. 'I just don't think…' She didn't know what to say. 'I'm dreadful at long-distance relationships…'

That made her sound flaky, and incapable of effort—as if all she wanted was a good time. But it was better that he think that than know the real reason why she had to end things before they became any more serious.

Libby persisted with that line. 'I don't see the point when it's all just going to fizzle out.'

'I'm only going away for six weeks.'

'I know, but—'

'It's fine,' he clipped. 'You don't have to explain.' He was being supremely polite, but then suddenly he seemed confused, or perhaps cross. 'Are you *serious*, Libby?'

'Yes.' Libby said it with more conviction than she felt, and then, possibly already realising the utter error of her ways, she wanted to soften it…retract it, perhaps…

But the line had already gone dead.

He had ended the call.

She stared at his name on her phone for a very long time, fighting the urge to call him back, but then she took a breath and hit *Delete* on his name and number.

And then, because she knew she was weak, especially

where Alistair was concerned, she emptied the deleted items too.

It felt wrong.

So wrong that she was filled with a sudden vision of herself at the phone shop, pleading with them to work some magic to retrieve his number.

But it was already done.

And what was worse…

She regretted it already.

CHAPTER THREE

IT WAS AWFUL.

Far, far worse than any break-up she had known before.

Usually Libby phoned a friend, went out and had a glass of wine and bemoaned her situation, then came home and watched her favourite film in the world while working her way through a bar of chocolate.

Sometimes she had to use the friend, chocolate and film technique for several nights, but it didn't help here.

There was nothing to bemoan about Alistair, and she didn't feel as if her friends back in Norfolk would understand.

Still Libby tried. She was desperate for insight, and so confused by her feelings and her handling of things, that she called Olivia.

'How's London?' Olivia asked.

'Great,' Libby said. 'Well, actually…' She hesitated. 'I met someone and we've just broken up…'

'You've only just got there! It can't have been that serious…'

Libby heard Little Timothy, crying to be fed, and could almost feel Olivia's distraction.

'I really liked him,' she said.

'So what happened?'

'It's complicated,' Libby said, but then heard Timothy's screams quadruple. 'I've caught you at a bad time.'

'Hey, you're home in a few days…we can catch up then. Well, if I can get a babysitter…'

'Sure.'

'Or you could come over.'

A night with Olivia and her husband and new baby really wouldn't be the balm for a broken heart that she was after. Especially after she'd had a barrage of fertility tests…

She tried to read *Wuthering Heights*, because that always pulled her in, but, no, it wasn't working.

So she tried watching her favourite film version of it, but even that didn't spirit her away tonight; it just made her cry.

She also had a dreadful sick feeling, and she couldn't even make a cup of tea without thinking of him, because when she went to get milk from the fridge she felt as if she could see their reflection in the stainless steel.

Even her daisy-covered towel made her weep.

Work was…

Difficult.

Everything still felt incredibly new, with all the different consultants and registrars, and today, just when she felt she'd got a handle on who the junior doctors were, their rotation changed and a new intake started.

More new faces.

Then Brendan brought in a patient, but the leap of her heart was halted when she saw he was working with a woman.

Another new face.

'Lina!' May said to Brendan's partner, 'You're back!'

'Thank goodness,' Brendan said. 'Can you imagine a whole set of shifts with Perfect Peter endlessly quoting policy?'

'God love him,' May laughed. 'He *is* very thorough.'

Libby would have liked to shout at them, but of course she didn't. Not only because she and Alistair had remained a secret, but more because she loathed any sort of confrontation.

For herself, she loved how much care he took to do things right when it came to safe working procedures.

Worse than not seeing him, though, was the moment when she did.

He'd had his hair cut, and was so clean-shaven she wanted to put up her hand and feel his jaw.

Not here.

Maybe tonight?

But no, of course she couldn't. Because she had ended things.

If she hadn't messed up, she might even have felt it this morning.

Oh, what had she done?

Not that it seemed to have affected him in the least. Alistair was treating her exactly as he always had at work, and exactly as he treated everyone else.

No more, no less.

'Morning, Libby,' he greeted her. 'This is…'

And he introduced his patient and gave her a diligent handover, treating her exactly as he might have May or Dianne…

It was Libby who was one big burning blush and a stumbling mess.

'Alistair.' She caught him as he was heading out. 'Could I borrow you for a moment?' She smiled to the paramedic he was working with today—an apologetic smile that asked for a private word.

'What's this about?' Alistair asked.

'A patient you brought in last week…'

He frowned, but nodded to his colleague, who left them to it.

'What patient?' he asked.

'It's not about a patient,' she admitted.

'In that case…' Alistair shook his head. 'I'm at work, Libby,' he said. 'I don't bring my private life here.'

And he walked off. Just like that.

Libby had to fight not to run after him, to call him back, to plead with him to bring his private life to work so that she could admit she had made the most dreadful mistake.

Instead she just stood there and watched him leave.

There was no relief during her visit back home to her parents in Norfolk.

In the familiar streets she felt like a different person from the one who had left. The woman who had lived here hadn't known Alistair, or the bliss that had awaited her.

But she had to be happy and 'up, up, up' for her mother's sixtieth celebrations. It was quite a party, and Libby laughed and danced the night away.

On Sunday she went out with friends from her theatre group…yet she already felt out of the loop because, although it was great to see them, they mainly spoke about their new production.

Every day she felt worse about her decision to end things with Alistair rather than better.

Even so, there were confirmations that perhaps she had made the right choice, because on the Monday she had her detailed ultrasound and loads of blood tests.

Even though she was an emergency nurse, Libby couldn't stand the sight of blood when it was her own. She felt a bit faint, afterwards, and sat down outside and had a drink of water, deciding some chocolate might be required to replace all the iron. She was feeling so lightheaded that she came the closest yet to caving and calling the station Alistair was based at and asking him to contact her.

To say she was so sorry and had made a ridiculous mistake.

And please, don't take that job...

Oh, and can you get rid of your bike please?

And, in the interests of full disclosure, before you change your life because I ask you to, you should know I'm going to be a mess any day soon if I find out I can't get pregnant...

Her feelings couldn't survive the real word, Libby decided. And when she got home from the shopping trip she'd pretended to be on she found her mother was pacing because her father hadn't called her back.

Oh, heavens!

That would have been Libby's future if she had stayed with Alistair. She had already been like her that morning, when the motorcyclist had died before reaching A&E, and that had been enough of a glimpse into her possible future...

And Olivia was no help when they finally caught up—at her home, because she hadn't been able to get a babysitter.

'How long were you seeing him exactly?' she asked.

'Six days. Six perfect days.'

'So perfect that you ended it?' she said, sounding perplexed.

'I panicked,' Libby admitted. 'What with his new job and the motorbike and...' She paused. 'And I didn't know how to tell him about all these tests I'm having.'

'Isn't it a bit early for all that?' Olivia gently suggested. 'Look, I know that Vince was awful about it, but you haven't even seen the gynaecologist yet. There might not even be a problem.'

Said she, a woman who was holding her new baby in her arms...

It had been horrible, going through all those tests alone—as if her potential problem didn't count quite as much because she didn't have a partner in tow.

As if, because she wasn't actively trying to get pregnant, it was a problem for later and didn't matter much.

Yet to Libby it did.

And she couldn't talk to her mother about it, because she couldn't talk to her mother about anything problematic lest it upset her.

Then there came a different sort of lonely when, late the next afternoon, she stepped off the train in London and took the Tube, then walked down the high street, wondering if every passing ambulance might be him.

Instead of heading straight to her little flat, which just reminded her of Alistair, she stopped to get coffee and some doughnuts.

'There you go, Libby,' the barista said as he handed over her coffee.

'Oh, thank you.' She blinked in confusion because she'd been daydreaming.

'Two doughnuts today?' he checked.

'I'm starving!'

One now and one later.

Or one now and one straight after.

But then she realised why he was delaying her order.

'Do you want to go for a drink some time?' he asked.

No, she didn't. She wanted coffee and doughnuts and to cry all over again. But maybe she *should* go. Maybe a drink and a night out with...

Liam. That was his name. Or was it Leo?

'Sounds great,' she said.

He told her about a pub where the music was good— hopefully loud enough that he wouldn't notice if she got his name wrong, she thought.

It was just a drink.

A drink with someone who had a nice safe job.

Someone wouldn't leave her heart in knots and a crazed feeling in her brain.

So instead of spending the evening home alone, she pulled on a cheerful wraparound dress, strappy sandals with high heels and then, because that was a rather summery ensemble for February, added a coat.

It's just a drink, Libby told herself again as she sat on the Tube.

But not with Alistair.

She stepped off the Tube onto an unfamiliar platform and clipped her way along in her heels, all the time knowing it wasn't where she wanted to be…

She thought of their lovely, single date—the one time she had gone out with Alistair. Of how they'd had pepper steak and wedges, and he'd bought her a chocolate egg while she got bread and milk…and how utterly perfect he had been.

She got on the escalator to go up to the surface. It was steep, one of the old wooden ones, and for some reason that caused her eyes to fill with tears and she was momentarily blinded.

He'd probably left for his new job already—or he would be going next week.

Would Brendan and Lina even know where he was? And if she asked would they give her his number?

What the hell was she doing, going out with someone else when she was crying on an escalator over the most stupid mistake of her life?

She didn't for a second want things to be over with Alistair.

And she would tell him so. Yes, she would. Right now.

Libby turned to go back down the stairs—though of course she wasn't on stairs.

She was standing halfway up a very steep escalator…

It was odd to know no more than that.

CHAPTER FOUR

EVERYTHING REALLY WAS most odd, Libby thought.

'Alistair?'

He was here?

And in uniform?

Those chocolaty velvety eyes were staring down at her and she knew it was the only place she wanted to be—back in the path of his gaze.

Only she didn't know why she was…

'Alistair?'

She was starting to panic as it dawned on her that she was at work…but lying down. Actually, she was in Resus—and furthermore May was taking her blood pressure. And, just to confuse things even more, Alistair really was here.

It didn't make sense.

Nothing made sense.

'Hey,' he said. 'You're okay.'

'Why am I here?' She watched as he glanced over to May, who stood on the opposite side of her. 'Alistair, how come *you're* here?'

'Because I was bringing a patient in when you arrived,' he said patiently. 'Libby, do you know where you are?'

She looked at the white ceiling and the bright lights and heard all the monitors bleeping away. It really wasn't hard to guess. 'Work.'

'Do you remember what happened?'

Not really…

Yet as she lay there Libby found herself chasing wisps of a conversation she'd had with May—one during which she'd been trying to sit up and go home and May had been insisting that now wasn't the time.

'I fell?' Libby said hesitantly, unsure if the conversation with May had even taken place.

'Yes.'

'Are you the paramedic who brought me in?' Libby asked, and saw that he'd closed his eyes for a second, as if he was slightly frustrated by her question, even though she thought it was an obvious one.

She had no clue that she'd asked it many times before…

'No,' Alistair said. 'It wasn't me. I was here with a patient when they brought you in, and I came over to see if you were okay.'

'I'm fine,' Libby bristled, embarrassed and unsure as she looked up at May. 'I'd like to go home.'

'Not yet, Libby. Your parents are on their way.'

'My parents?' *Oh, for God's sake!* 'Why on earth have they been called? My mother will be beside herself…' She tried to sit up, but Alistair held her shoulder. 'Get off me!' she shouted uncharacteristically—not just to Alistair, but also to May, who was trying to get her to lie down as well. 'I want to go home.'

'Libby,' May said, 'you've had quite a fall. You're a bit confused…'

No. I'm not confused, Libby thought.

She was cross. Because someone had called her parents and her mother was going to freak.

'Why did you have to call them?' she demanded of May, and then she glared at Alistair. 'Why are you even here? I'm not your patient…' She knew she was being mean, and she wasn't a mean person. She was also being spiteful and that wasn't her. 'Perfect Peter?' she sneered. 'Not!'

'I'll leave,' Alistair said. 'I'm obviously upsetting her.'

'No, stay!' Libby was suddenly frantic, because it wasn't Alistair who was upsetting her, or May, but everything else—her confusion, her parents' imminent arrival, the fact that she was in Resus, with a huge collar around her neck, and absolutely no idea how she'd ended up here.

Or why.

Neither did she know why she was being horrible to Alistair when she wanted him to stay more than anything else.

The only certainty she knew was that she and Alistair had broken up and she did not deserve his concern—and yet it would seem that she had it anyway.

He was holding her hand gently, but she was gripping his, clinging on to it for dear life. '*Am* I confused?' she asked him. Because she trusted him. He was pedantic, and she knew he would tell her the truth.

'Yes,' he said. 'You are.'

'How do you know that?'

'Because you keep asking me the same questions and you've been quite combative...'

'Me?'

'Yes.' He offered her a kind smile. 'You're getting better though. You're more coherent now.'

'You should go back to your partner then,' Libby said, assuming that whoever he was working with this evening must be outside, waiting.

'It's fine. I've already signed off.'

'Why?'

'Because...' He closed his eyes and seemed to be battling to find a suitable response. He seemed upset.

'Why have you signed off?'

'I didn't want you to be on your own. I wanted to stay at least till your parents get here. I was worried about you…'

May cut in then. 'Libby, you were very distressed when you first came in to Resus.'

'How long have I been here?'

'An hour.'

'A whole *hour*?' She frowned.

Although now that she thought about it, it felt like a whole lot more than an hour was unaccounted for. She hadn't just lost her time in the department, but getting here, and the reason why she was here.

'What happened?'

He pressed his lips together and she realised that he *had* been frustrated by her question before.

'Have I already asked that?'

'It's fine.' He gave her hand a little squeeze and she squeezed him back. 'You had a fall on an escalator on the underground.'

That's right, she thought, slowly piecing things together. She'd been on one of the steep wooden ones.

'I was going on a date,' Libby told him. 'With someone who doesn't try to get themselves killed for a living.'

Had she really just said that out loud?

'Good for you,' Alistair said, as if the news wasn't a surprise.

Had he heard her say that before too?

'A date with someone who doesn't ride a motorbike,' she snapped.

'Well, it would seem one of those ridiculous heels you were wearing to impress your date might have got stuck in the escalator, or…'

'No,' she said.

Because that wasn't right. She knew she hadn't got her heel stuck, but she couldn't quite remember what *had* occurred—or rather, she was only remembering parts of it. She remembered lying on the escalator and wondering why it wasn't moving.

'They stopped the escalator…'

'They did.' May smiled and smoothed back her hair. 'You're starting to remember.'

'May?' She looked at her boss, and with little flashes of recall starting to ping in her mind she remembered fighting her off when she'd first arrived in the department. 'I'm sorry…'

'You've nothing to be sorry about,' May said. 'You're going to be fine. Garth wants you to have a head CT and…' She turned to Alistair. 'Could you excuse us a moment?'

Libby felt him let go of her hand. She was embarrassed to be seen like this, but at the same time so glad he was here in this swirly confusing world.

'Do you know the date of your LMP?' asked May, when he'd gone.

'No.' She shook her head. 'But I never do. I'm having some investigations…'

'It's okay,' May said. 'But is there any chance you could be pregnant?'

'I might not ever be,' she said, starting to cry. 'That's why I'm having the investigations.'

'Let's get a urine specimen…just to be sure. I've got a bedpan…'

'God, no.'

'Yes,' May said. 'This is no time to be shy.'

There really wasn't any opportunity to be shy.

Before Libby could insist that she was well enough to walk, a wave of nausea hit her. She tried to sit up and reach for the kidney dish, only the movement felt too violent, and the bay in Resus was so warm, and yet her skin seemed to have turned to ice.

'May…' She started retching and then her vision seemed to split, for there were two versions of everything—even when she closed her eyes.

She was both vomiting and half fainting, and she could feel the push of May's hands again—not just lying her down, but turning her onto her side.

Neither was there time to be embarrassed.

Libby was numbly aware that May was pressing the buzzer and summoning help.

'You're okay, Libby,' May told her. 'You just sat up too fast. Here's Garth now…'

Garth was the consultant on duty, and Libby lay, eyes closed, and heard herself being discussed as he peeled open each eye in turn and shone a torch in.

'Libby,' he said, 'do you know where you are?'

'The Primary.'

'And do you know what happened to you?'

'I fell.' She could remember that now.

'You certainly did,' Garth said, and then he asked her to push him away, and then to lift her legs. 'Is CT clear yet?' he asked May.

'Not yet,' she answered.

'Let's give her eight milligrams of Ondansetron…'

He also asked if she knew when her last period had been, or if there was any chance of pregnancy.

'No,' May answered for her. 'I was just about to get a urine sample…'

Libby could hear them talking over her, and about her, but she didn't have the energy to cut in—to explain that she and Alistair had been very careful. It was none of their damned business, her fuzzy mind wanted to shout. But instead she just listened as Garth changed his orders.

'Okay let's give metoclopramide…'

She heard Dianne's voice. 'Her mother's on the phone again.'

'No!' Libby knew she sounded like a drunken sailor. 'She gets so upset…' she tried to explain. 'Dramatic.'

'It's okay, Libby, I'll talk to her,' Garth said. 'May, call CT and see how long they'll be. We'll need to sedate her for the procedure.'

They didn't need to sedate her, Libby was sure, but she shakily signed the consent form. She no longer felt sick, but certainly she didn't want to move even an inch, so she lay there quietly, feeling the nausea receding. She was grateful when May and Dianne changed the bedding and her gown, and for the coolness of a wet cloth on her face.

'They're ready for her now,' Dianne said.

'Let's get her round.'

Alistair had seen the light flash over Resus, and heard the buzzer summoning staff, so he knew that something must be happening—he just hadn't known what or to whom. But then he had heard 'head injury', and Garth asking May to hurry along CT.

That was when he had felt the grip of panic that had hit him when Libby had first arrived tighten like a vice.

He'd just been finishing his notes on a patient when she'd arrived. Ironically, it was the patient who was holding up CT now, because he had been taken straight there.

Libby had been shouting, crying, terrified and confused when she'd arrived. He'd never heard her shout, and yet he had recognised her cries instantly and looked up.

She hadn't recognised him.

Or May, whom he'd assisted in holding Libby down as she'd attempted to flee.

She'd been in an alternative world when she'd arrived.

One where pelicans—which apparently she was terrified of—roamed the moors. And where her name was Cathy and she wanted to say things differently.

Slowly, over an hour, she'd started to return—but now, just when things had been looking better, those lights had flashed.

May came out. 'We're taking her round to CT…'

'Is she okay?'

'Alistair…' May hesitated.

He knew that there was little she could tell him, since he was not family and they were not a couple.

'We'll know more soon.' She paused mid-stride. 'Why don't you go and wait in the staffroom?'

He shook his head. He could not face the chatter in there. 'I'll just wait here, if that's okay.' But he knew that was impractical…him standing in the busy corridor. 'Or I can go and wait outside.'

'Tell you what—why don't you take a seat in Interview Room Three?' May suggested, but then she had no choice but to dash off to take Libby to CT.

It would be an awful wait, and since he wasn't next of kin or anything, he knew no one would be rushing to inform him of any updates to her condition.

They weren't even together any more, he reminded himself. He had no right to know. And yet he felt as if he needed to know, and he wished he had a right to know.

He had walked more relatives and friends into Interview Room Three than he could count, and it felt surreal to be heading there himself.

'Peter?' Lina said, walking towards him, smiling as she teased him with the use of his nickname. But then her expression changed when she saw his grim expression. 'What's going on?'

'I'm not sure,' he said, possibly sounding as disconnected as Libby had been for the past hour, because he gave no real explanation as he answered. 'She's just been taken for an urgent CT.'

'Are you okay?'

Alistair knew that Lina was as used as he was to having to work out a story from someone who wasn't able to articulate themselves clearly.

'I've been told to wait in here,' he said.

'Have you told Control?' Lina asked, and opened the door of the small, private waiting room.

'Yes, I was on with Rory—he's going out single.'

He didn't need to add that he was too upset to work. Certainly he hadn't told Libby that when she'd asked what he was doing there. But seeing her being wheeled in, dazed, confused and ranting, and not even knowing who he was, let alone where she was, had been more than distressing. He hadn't let that show to anyone, of course, but he had felt it all the same.

Brendan came over then, and the trio walked into the bland, joyless room. Brendan asked what was happening and Alistair told him his hunch had been right.

'Libby,' he said. 'We were seeing each other.'

'I knew it!' Brendan said, delighted to be proved right. 'So what's happened?'

Alistair told them the little he knew, and was grateful that they were waiting with him.

'We broke up,' he said, and then inexplicably found himself saying, 'I'm not sure why. I thought we were going great and then…'

He felt odd. He never confided in colleagues, or even his friends, really—he just didn't do that type of thing. Yet here he was, doing exactly that.

'She thought you called me Perfect Peter because I was, you know…'

'What?' Brendan asked.

'Good-looking.'

'Well, she *is* getting her head examined,' Brendan said, and somehow this made Alistair smile. Lina even held his hand and he let her.

'She was really confused at first,' he went on. 'But I thought she getting better. She'd been ranting about *Wuthering Heights* and pelicans when she arrived, but she became more lucid. And then something happened. They dashed her off. But I don't if she's had a seizure or blown a pupil…'

'Alistair.' Lina halted him. 'You can't know what's happened, so stop thinking the worst.'

'It's our job to think the worst.'

'The worst' was always amongst the list of possibilities in his head, so that he was prepared for any eventuality. Only this didn't feel like it did when he was at work.

Nothing like this.

It was a lot longer than an hour before May put her head around the door. They were all startled.

'Sorry to give you a fright,' May said, and then asked Brendan and Lina to excuse them for a moment. 'She's okay,' May told him. 'I can't give details, of course, but I can tell you that she's okay. We had to sedate her for the CT, but she's awake now and more lucid. Although she's still quite…' May looked for the right words. 'Out of sorts.'

Her confusion had been fading—he'd seen that for himself—but the frustration and short temper had increased, he was told, though that was common with a recent head injury. He'd seen the panic flare in her eyes as she'd tried to make sense of things, and he'd also seen her effort to remain in control.

'She's been admitted to our obs ward. She might be transferred to Neuro later, but Garth's keeping her here for now.' May looked at him. 'It sounds like you and Libby have quite a lot of unfinished business between you...'

He said nothing.

'Come on now, Heathcliff,' May said, because she'd been in there when Libby had been *really* ranting...

'What *was* she going on about?' he asked. 'Heathcliff's horrible; he's abusive. God—'

'No, no, no...' May tutted. 'Lord help me!' She took another breath. This was the woman who could deal with anything and who was rarely lost for words, Alistair found himself thinking. 'I don't think Libby finds Heathcliff to be so terrible,' she said. 'You have a logical brain, Alistair. Libby does not...'

'I know.' He nodded, and despite the seriousness of what had happened he couldn't help but smile when he thought of the time they'd shared together. But then the smile faded. 'She broke things off. We weren't seeing each other for long, but...'

Like a dam ready to burst, all that he'd held inside him since the break-up just had to come out.

'I even wrote to her—well, it was a card with my number on it, in case she'd deleted it and changed her mind, but I heard nothing back.'

'You didn't think to call her?'

'No, because I'd deleted *her* number.' He smiled wryly. 'I was so cross when she ended it. I just wiped her number straight away.'

'In case you drunk-dialled her?' May asked. 'Isn't that what you all call it now?'

'No.' He stared back. 'I don't do that kind of thing.'

'Hmmm...' May said, as if she didn't believe him. 'Now, she asked where you were and I said I'd come and get you. But remember, Alistair, Libby's not herself. She's improving, but she's still argumentative and is being quite con-frontational at the moment.'

'I'm not going to upset her,' Alistair said, but then he nodded, because he had given her a bit of a smart answer before, when she'd taunted him about going out on a date with someone else. 'I understand.'

'She needs to rest—and I mean that. I'll be asking all her visitors to bear that in mind,' May said, standing to take him around to the observation ward. 'I'll take you through. But her parents should be here soon.'

'Why does that sound like a warning?'

'Oh, I'm saying nothing,' May told him. 'I'm not get-ting involved in this.'

Alistair thanked Brendan and Lina for staying by his side, and then walked with May through to the observa-tion ward. There were a couple of patients that Alistair could see, though the curtains were drawn around what must be Libby's bed.

May peered around them before calling for Alistair to come in. 'Here he is!' May said to her very pale patient. 'I was just telling Alistair that your parents are almost here.'

'God...'

Libby closed her eyes. That was something she really didn't need right now. Her head felt like a pulsing rock under a desert sun, as if she'd been to a really wild party, and soon she'd have to pretend to be fine to her parents.

'I'm too tired for visitors,' she said, and then looked up at Alistair. 'I don't mean you...'

She paused. That sounded awful, and needy, and also as if she didn't like her parents when she absolutely did. It was all just too much to explain.

'I mean—'

'Shh...' Alistair said. 'It's fine. Nobody's going to stay

long. I'm sure they just need to see for themselves that you're okay.'

'I fell.'

'Yes.'

'And you were here, bringing a patient in?'

'Correct.' Alistair nodded. 'Do you know what day it is?'

She thought for a second. Actually, she did. It had been a week to the day since she'd made the most regrettable mistake of her life. She knew that because she'd been counting every single day and every single night.

'Thursday.'

'Yes. And do you know who the Prime Minister is?'

'Yes,' Libby lied.

She didn't have a clue. It was scary to know you weren't thinking properly. That there were big gaps in your thinking and your memory.

'An hour?' she checked. 'I lost an hour? I still don't feel right…'

'Libby, stop panicking.' Alistair was firm.

'But I feel all foggy.'

'You are so much better than you were. Every minute you're getting better.'

'Am I?'

'Yes.'

He smiled a very nice smile and she looked at the stubble on his jaw and remembered wanting to touch it. She tried to do so now, but he caught her hand before it got there, saving her from making a complete fool of herself. Libby knew he wouldn't be here if he hadn't been passing by, but somehow she had to keep that fact in a brain that didn't seem able to hold on to anything much at the moment.

'I am sorry about all this,' she said.

'Don't be,' Alistair said, and took a seat by the bed.

'I've got concussion, apparently. Nothing exciting at all. I've got to stay in overnight and then hopefully my confusion… I don't think I'm confused now.'

'Good,' Alistair said.

'But how did you find out I was here?'

Alistair told her yet again that he'd been bringing in a patient, only this time he could see it was sinking in.

'I'm sorry if I overshared,' she said.

'You mainly spoke gibberish about how if your name was Cathy—'

'Cathy?'

'Yes, and you talked about your pelican phobia.'

'I don't have a pelican phobia…'

'You said you did,' Alistair said, omitting to add that she'd also talked about hating his new job. And his bike. And said that she had been going on a date with someone new who didn't have a bike or a dangerous job.

He would have loved nothing more than to confront her with this information, but he'd only found out about her date by accident, so he chose to ignore it, even if it hurt. Even if it really hurt that she'd broken up with him over his job.

It had already cost him his family after all.

Well, not completely. But things were still very strained. He couldn't quite believe she'd let something so good go over his work, but he was too drained to think about it now. Just exhausted with relief.

'I might go and get a coffee and then—' He cut himself off as he heard May arriving with Libby's parents. She hadn't been exaggerating when she'd told Libby they were almost here.

Her mother was tiny, with huge mascara streaks on her face, and she was so loud!

'Oh, Libby!' she choked out, and then broke into noisy sobs.

Alistair was able to witness the exact effect her mother had on Libby, because her pulse shot up and as the blood pressure cuff was released it rang out a little alarm. And no wonder. Libby's mother stood sobbing on her husband as if their daughter lay dead in the bed.

'Mum,' Libby pleaded, 'it's just a concussion.'

'You had to be *sedated*!' she wailed. 'For a *CT*! We had to give consent!'

'Mum, please…'

Libby, Alistair noted, was actually the practical one.

'I signed my own consent form,' she told her mother. 'I do remember that!'

'I was so distressed that I had to get your father to pull over onto the emergency lane when they informed us!'

Libby's dad seemed very used to it all, and he patted his wife's shoulder with one hand while he shook Alistair's hand with the other. Brief introductions were made.

'A friend?' he checked. 'So you're not the paramedic who brought her in?'

'No.'

'Well, thanks for hanging around,' he said, rather curtly. 'We can take it from here.'

'Dad…' Libby warned, and Alistair watched as he turned to his daughter.

'Are you okay, darling?'

'Yes,' Libby said. 'And I'm sorry.'

Her father sat on the bed and took her hand, letting out a relieved sigh that Alistair completely understood—because that was what he kept doing. Every time she opened her green eyes and spoke more like the Libby he knew he wanted to sigh in relief, or let out an odd kind of half-laugh.

The same laugh that was bubbling out from her father right now—pure relief that she was fine. 'Are you sure you're okay?' he asked.

'Honestly. I'm just a bit foggy on details,' Libby said. 'And very, very tired.'

'I *knew* this would happen,' said Mrs Bennett. 'I knew that if you moved to London—'

'Come on now, Helen,' Mr Bennett said. 'London's not to blame for Libby tripping. She's always tripping.'

'I wasn't taking *drugs*!' Libby shouted. 'Why do you assume—?'

Alistair saw her father startle as his lovely Libby not only missed his meaning but also raised her voice.

'Libby!' Mr Bennett warned, and Alistair cut in.

'Your father meant falling, Libby,' he said gently, and he shot a look at her father that told Mr Bennett to remember that Libby wasn't herself.

'That's right. I meant falling,' Mr Bennett said, and then added, 'I'll bet she was wearing those heels…'

'It wasn't the heels,' Libby said, because it absolutely hadn't been her strappy sandals that had made her fall. At least, she thought not. In truth, Libby didn't actually know *what* had made her trip and fall. 'I can't remember…'

'That doesn't matter,' Alistair said.

'It does to me.' How she hated all these gaps! 'Anyway, I'm going home tomorrow,' Libby said. 'Probably…'

'We'll be right here with you until you do,' Mrs Bennett chimed in, looking around for a chair as if preparing to begin a bedside vigil.

'Helen…' Mr Bennett chided. 'She's not critically ill.

We're going to a hotel and then we'll find out what's happening in the morning.'

But Helen Bennett had other ideas. 'We can stay at her flat.'

'No!' Libby said hurriedly.

Alistair watched as Libby reeled back in horror, and he couldn't help but wonder what she might have left lying around in the flat that had so recently played host to their four-day sex-fest. She was burning in a blush, so he stepped in to ease her mind.

'Libby lost her keys when she fell.' Alistair rarely lied, but he thought he should make an exception, for Libby's sake. 'I think the paramedics might have located them, but it'll take a while to get them back.'

Her green eyes met his and he saw her rapid blink of relief. But then she frowned… '*All* my keys?'

'Don't worry, we'll get it sorted,' Alistair said.

Mrs Bennett came to a decision. 'We'll go to a hotel tonight, or for as long as you're staying in hospital, but once they discharge you you're coming back with us. The doctor said you'll be off for at least two weeks and—'

'Mum, can you please *stop*?'

'Libby!' her father warned.

'Now!' May interjected. She could clearly see the blood-pressure-raising effect the visitors were having on her patient. 'I'm going to borrow your parents for a couple of moments, Libby, to go over some details.'

Alistair knew May would explain things again to her parents. He wished they had been there and seen Libby when she had first come in. Not to upset them, more so they could know just how ill she had been and how much better she was now.

Libby just lay there, pressing her fingers into her eyes.

'Oh, my God,' Libby said thankfully, as May steered her parents away—no doubt to gently remind them that their daughter wasn't quite herself right now. 'She does this all the time. She has to turn everything into a drama.'

'Really?'

'Well, not always…' Libby sighed, removing her fingers and turning her teary eyes to him. 'But she's exhausting, isn't she?'

'She's you!' Alistair smiled.

'Me?'

'Completely.' He nodded. 'Although luckily I don't—'

He stopped himself from making a light joke about not fancying her mother. It was hard to remember that there was no longer a 'them'. That they weren't together. He hadn't been called as her emergency contact; he had just happened to be here. Thankfully Libby didn't notice his brief dilemma, because she was busy with one of her own.

'Now I've upset them…' she said.

'Libby…' He was firm. 'They're the ones who should not be upsetting *you*, okay?'

'I know.' She looked up at him. 'They lost my brother before they had me.'

'I'm sorry.'

'They'd bubble wrap me if they could.'

Right now, so too would he, Alistair thought.

'*Have* I lost my keys?' Libby asked him.

'No. At least I don't think so. May put your bag in her locker rather than the safe, so you could get access to it more easily.'

'That was nice of her.'

He so badly wanted to take her hand, but while it had felt right to do so before, when she'd been lost and struggling, it didn't feel right to do so now.

Although it felt necessary.

It felt as if it should be the most natural thing to do.

Yet she had broken them…she had undone them…and he had to remember that.

And Libby wasn't herself—he had to remember that too—so he resisted what was necessary and natural and didn't take her hand.

Then he heard her parents returning.

'I'm going to go,' Alistair said. 'I'm so pleased you're okay.'

'Thank you for everything tonight.'

'Get some rest,' Alistair said, and turned to leave.

'Alistair?'

He stood with his back to her for a second too long, and then turned. 'Yes?'

'I'm sorry for breaking us up. I made a dreadful mistake.'

'Libby, you are to rest and not get upset, so don't think about all that stuff.'

'But it's all I can think about.'

'Well, stop.'

'Will you come and see me tomorrow?'

'Get some sleep.'

That was the most important thing right now. It had to be.

Everything else could wait.

CHAPTER FIVE

ALISTAIR CAME TO see her the next day, after she had been transferred to the Neuro ward.

He was doing an extra shift, he explained when he came to visit, still wearing his uniform. 'How are you feeling?' he asked.

'Tired,' Libby admitted. 'Though that's probably because I've been woken up through the night for obs…'

'Or you could be tired because you've had a nasty fall.'

'Yes, maybe…'

She was starting to accept it, and really it was impossible not to, because as well as her head, the left side of her back and her left shoulder were tender, and on top of all that…

'I cried this morning because I didn't have a spoon on my breakfast tray. Unfortunately it coincided with the arrival of the consultant, so now they're keeping me in for an extra night. It's normal to be overly emotional after a fall, apparently, which isn't great when you're—'

'Already overly emotional?' Alistair suggested with a smile.

Libby gave a glum nod.

'Here.' He put a bar of hazelnut chocolate—the same as the one she *hadn't* chosen the night of the fridge saga—onto the hospital bed table.

'Thank you!' She pounced and opened it immediately.

'I keep trying to explain to them that my blood pressure's only up when my mother's here.'

'Libby, it's good they're here. And you're sounding better.'

She knew she wasn't looking it, though—her bruises were really starting to come out.

'Mum and Dad keep asking for the key to my flat. I've got my bag back, with the keys in it, but I haven't told them that.'

'What *is* the problem with your flat?'

'I just don't want them poking their noses in. There are tissues everywhere from my crying over you...'

He said nothing.

'And as well as that,' Libby further explained, as she broke off another piece of chocolate, 'I saved the empty box from our condoms.'

'Why would you do that?'

'Because I didn't have anything else from us that I could keep.'

He rolled his eyes, clearly unimpressed with her version of sentimentality, and then carried on being his practical self. 'I think it's wise that they're keeping you in for another night. Libby, you really were unwell yesterday.'

'I know.'

'I'm not sure that you do.'

'I do know. And thank you for staying with me when I was so confused.' She looked up at Alistair. He had put up with so much, and yet she desperately needed one thing more. 'Alistair, I know you're going to say no, but can I ask a favour?'

'No.'

Libby chose to ignore his response and forged on. 'Would you please say that you're going to look after me for a couple of days after I'm discharged?'

'In your tiny studio flat?'

'Yes.'

'And what do I say to your father about how long I've known you?'

'Say we're just friends…new friends. Please?'

'No.' He shook his head. 'I'm not prepared to do that. I will, however, go to your flat and get a change of clothes for you, and get rid of any damning evidence, if that helps.'

It wasn't the answer Libby had wanted, but it did help the situation, so she nodded and gingerly sat up as he went over to her bedside locker and pulled out her vast boho-style bag.

'What on earth have you got in here?' Alistair asked, because it weighed a ton.

'Everything,' she said. 'If I had lost this yesterday, I'd have died.'

'It's too soon for jokes, Libby,' he warned, but then seemed to check himself.

She looked up, hearing the strain of his voice, but he looked away, so she got back to wading through the previous tenants' mail, and her make-up bag and purse, and even pulled out her missing umbrella, before finally finding her keys.

'I've put red nail varnish on the one for the flat,' Libby informed him as she handed them over.

It was just as well that she had. For the occupier of such a small studio flat, Libby had the amount of keys of a prison warden, Alistair thought, taking the jangling bunch and finding himself wanting to know why she had so many.

He hadn't asked.

He was refusing to fall back under her spell.

Or rather refusing to let her know that he hadn't yet managed to escape it.

He wanted to guard himself from her.

It was odd, because he knew her parents were nice people, but yesterday he'd wanted them to take a step back and give her space and peace. He knew they were trying, because even he had struggled to deal with Libby's rollercoaster temper, lack of filter, and melodramatic emotional state.

Alistair was usually very controlled with his feelings. His emotions were his own and it felt even more imperative now that he keep it that way.

Even if she ran riot in his head.

The relief from yesterday was still there, but now the hurt was returning, and with it a quiet anger at just how readily she'd tossed away something so good.

They *had* been good, he thought as he located the red nail varnished key and let himself into her flat.

He felt as if it should be sealed off with tape—as if he were entering the scene of a crime.

Her flat was actually very tidy.

The sofa-bed was back to being a sofa, and there was a table beside it with lots of little balls of tissues. While he believed she'd cried, Alistair did not believe that it had been over him.

Not for a second.

There were a couple of chocolate wrappers too, and little balls of foil, but he doubted they were evidence of a broken heart. She'd brought chocolate the night they'd met, after all.

The box of condoms had been turned into a bookmark. He put her dog-eared copy of *Wuthering Heights* into her bedside drawer, with the 'bookmark' in place. If her parents snooped in there then it was their own damned fault what they found.

He tried to find some sensible shoes, but it would seem she didn't possess any. There wasn't even a pair of trainers.

The only flat shoes he could find were her nursing ones, so he collected them, as well as some jeans, and a few other bits she might need. He practically closed his eyes as he rummaged in her underwear drawer.

God, it killed him being her ex…

He dropped the bag of clothes and toiletries back at the hospital late in the evening, long after visiting hours.

Libby looked worse than she had that morning. There were dark rings under her eyes and her lips were pale. She was lying on the bed with no television on or anything, just dozing—but then she opened her eyes and smiled right at him, and relief came flooding back.

He wanted to do the same sighing thing that her father had. Instead, he settled for a nod and, 'Hello.'

'Hi.' She pulled herself to sit up. 'Thanks for this.'

'I couldn't find your trainers.'

'I don't have any,' Libby said.

'But I thought you were into fitness…what with the exercise ball and yoga mat…?'

'Oh, please!' Libby waved all mention of them away. 'I keep meaning to start yoga, and I was about to deflate the exercise ball and get a chair. I read that it was good for posture, but I hate the thing.'

'Are you still being discharged tomorrow?'

'Yes. Well, they'll decide for certain in the morning, but for now it looks like I'm headed home with Mum and Dad. I'm to come back for an outpatient appointment in two weeks.'

It was too soon for her to go home, Alistair thought. He was arrogant enough to believe he was right and the consultant was wrong. It was also too soon for a two-hour drive and the raining down of questions and overbearing concern from her mother.

He had given her dilemma some thought, because even

though he was cross, he still cared about her. And she really was alone in London.

'Look, it's not ideal, but you can tell them that you're coming back to mine.'

'No.' Libby shook her head, assuming he meant that she should lie to her parents and to the hospital in telling them that she'd be recovering at his place. 'It's kind of you to offer, but my mother calls all the time and she'll realise that I'm at my flat, given they helped me move in.'

'I meant,' Alistair corrected, 'that you can stay at mine, if you want.'

Libby's eyes widened in surprise. Oh, she desperately wanted to say yes, but...

'I wouldn't do that to you...'

It was hardly fair to land herself on him, given all that had passed between them, so she cast about in her bruised and shaken mind for a plausible reason to turn down his kind, albeit reluctant, offer.

'Anyway, I want to be around my own things. Please, will you just tell them you're staying with me?'

'Fine.'

And even though she could hear his supreme reluctance, Libby was simply relieved. Just so relieved that she would be able to rest and heal in peace without her mother watching her sleep, or peering in at her every five minutes.

Her father was less than impressed when she told him her plans on the morning of her discharge; her mother was appalled.

'Libby, you barely know him.'

'I do.' She closed her eyes, but her voice was adamant. 'Alistair's coming to collect me.'

Her parents were draining...and being in hospital itself was actually exhausting.

She'd had another mainly sleepless night.

But happily there had been a spoon with her cornflakes this morning, and all her obs were behaving; she'd even had a shower with a grad nurse hovering outside in case she felt unwell. She'd been fine. Ish... And so, when the consultant came around, it was agreed that she could go home.

Phew.

Getting dressed proved a little tricky. Alistair had chosen the ugliest pair of knickers in her drawer, and of all things a strapless bra! He'd brought jeans that were too tight after so many takeaways, and there was a formal shirt she wore for interviews and such. It took a lot of effort to do up the buttons. He'd also brought her nursing shoes for her to wear. She looked quite a sight once she'd managed to put it all on.

When her parents had checked out of their hotel, they came onto the ward to collect her, they now had to say their reluctant goodbyes. Libby was sitting on her bed, waiting for her outpatient appointment and her doctor's letter, and holding her head injury information leaflet. As soon as Alistair arrived and she had her documentation she would be able to go home.

'Where's this young man, then?' her dad asked.

'He's thirty-three,' Libby snapped. 'And he's very, very responsible.'

Apart from his motorbike and his choice of career.

Hopefully he wouldn't arrive with a crash helmet for her to squeeze on, but it didn't actually matter. She had her phone and would call a cab; she just needed him to sign her out of here.

And then, finally, there he was, wearing dark jeans and a black linen shirt and carrying her coat.

'At last,' snapped Mr Bennett.

'I was just getting some shopping in,' Alistair responded—with the patience of a saint, Libby thought. 'I thought it better to get organised now, rather than leave her alone once we get back to the flat.'

Her father gave an extremely reluctant nod.

'How are you today?' Alistair smiled his professional smile at Libby.

'Better. I'm just waiting for my outpatient appointment,' she said. 'And Mum and Dad are just about to go.'

Helen didn't want to leave, though. 'We'll wait until you're discharged.'

'Dad's working tonight,' Libby said. 'Please, stop making so much fuss.' She felt wretched and so on show, with her parents carrying on as if she were ten or even twenty years younger.

They were lovely, but complicated, and she was too tired for it all right now.

'Take care, Libby,' her father said, and she could tell he was more worried about leaving her than he had been when he'd arrived.

Oh, that was so unfair, when Alistair was beyond dependable. And, yes, she had only known him a short while—she could not lie—but he was a good guy and he didn't deserve suspicious looks.

Her father pulled Alistair aside and the two of them talked quietly. Libby cringed, sure her father was lecturing Alistair.

'I love you, darling,' Mrs Bennett said. 'I'll call you tonight.'

'I'll call *you*, Mum,' Libby said. 'Don't forget, I'm going to be sleeping a lot.'

'Fine!' she snapped tartly, and looked over to Alistair as if he was somehow causing this, rather than doing his best to fix things for her.

'I'm so sorry,' Libby said once they'd gone. 'They are actually lovely.'

'I can see that they are. They don't know me, and of course they're worried about you.'

'Yes.' Libby took a breath. 'We usually get on so well, but honestly…'

'I get it.' He took a seat by the bed she still sat on. 'You're lucky they care so much. I barely talk to my parents.'

'Really?'

'Their choice,' Alistair said.

'Why?' Libby asked.

'I don't want to discuss it.'

He drew such a firm line, closed down the conversation so completely, that Libby had no choice but to accept it.

She tried to make light of his rejection. 'I'd probably forget it even if you did discuss it…' she joked. 'Honestly, my head is like a sieve. I'm sure I'd missing some vital point or say the wrong thing…'

He gave a pale smile.

'I'm sorry you're not talking with your family.'

He nodded, but refused to be drawn.

'Do you have brothers or sisters?'

'Libby, why don't you lie down?'

'Because then they might keep me in,' Libby muttered. 'I just want to go home to my own bed and to sleep into next week.'

She forced a smile at the approaching nurse.

'I've got your appointment,' the nurse said, and then turned to Alistair. 'You're going to be taking care of her?'

'Yes.'

'Then I'll go through the head injury instructions with you.'

'He's a paramedic,' Libby snapped.

But Alistair ignored her. In fact, he said something that made the nurse smile, and then listened intently as she went through all the instructions with him as if he were five years old.

It made Libby grumbly, and she didn't quite know why. 'I bet you even watch flight attendants doing their demonstration,' Libby said as they walked down a very, very long corridor. 'Just to be polite.'

'Of course I watch,' Alistair said. 'And not just to be polite—every plane is different.' As she slowed her pace he glanced over at her. 'Are you okay?'

'I'm just tired.'

They had a little rest mid-corridor, and then he put an arm around her and led her the rest of the way to the end. They came to the ambulance bay where ambulances were lined up, waiting to offload their patients.

'They're waving to you,' Libby said.

Alistair ignored them and sorted out their taxi back to her flat.

Of course he matched the registration before getting in.

The world felt a little too fractured and the radio in the car too loud. Everything seemed somehow amplified. For the first time Libby felt a flutter of panic as to how she was going to manage, and questioned her decision to wave her parents off and send them home.

'Oh!' she said as they arrived inside her front door— because he hadn't just picked up her coat and clothes, he had also cleaned! The flat was gleaming, and when she opened her lovely fridge she saw that he really had been shopping for her. 'That's so kind. I really do appreciate it. I'll transfer the money...'

'It's fine. I'll be eating a lot of it.'

'Don't be daft. I don't expect you to *actually* take care of me. Just call, or pop in whenever. But really—'

'I'm not leaving you—at least for the first few days,' he said. 'The instructions are very clear.'

'Yes, but I've got one tiny sofa-bed.'

'And I shan't be getting into it,' he said.

'Where are you going to sit?'

On her exercise ball. That was apparently his plan. And later, when she woke from a doze and saw him stretched out on her yoga mat on the floor, she couldn't believe it.

He turned his head and looked at her. 'How do you feel?'

'Worse than I did at the hospital.'

'They said you'd feel like that. Have some water and try and go back to sleep.'

He was being lovely, but really she felt so dreadful that had she been on her own she'd have been scared.

Later still... 'I feel a bit nauseous,' she admitted.

'There's a bowl there if you have to vomit.'

And even later... 'I've got a really, really bad headache.'

'Because you've got a really, really big bruise. Would you like two headache tablets?'

Two headache tablets aren't going to fix this, Libby grumbled to herself.

But she took them anyway, and then suddenly it was dark outside. She realised she must have been asleep and the tablets might just have worked!

'What time is it?'

'Six,' Alistair said. 'I'll get you something to eat, shall I?'

'I'm not hungry.'

'Just something light?' he suggested. 'Why don't you call your parents?'

'I guess...' She sat up in bed and went through her bag for a comb. After she'd attacked her hair, she tried to look suitably bright as she reassured her mother on a video call for five minutes. And then she held the phone for her father, and Alistair gave him a wave from where he was sitting on her exercise ball.

'Don't worry,' Alistair said. 'I'm keeping a close eye.'

And he was.

'You can lie here,' Libby said, when she'd changed into fresh pyjamas and saw he was flicking out a sleeping bag onto her yoga mat.

'No,' he told her. 'You dumped me; you don't get to share a bed with me.'

'I didn't dump you,' Libby attempted. 'We fizzled out.'

'No, we didn't. And that's hardly an invitation to bed.'

There was very little dignity in her scrambled brain. 'I know we didn't fizzle out—well, I know it didn't fizzle out for me. I've missed you so very much…'

He gave her a tight, mirthless smile. 'Get some rest.'

'Alistair…'

'Libby, you need to rest.'

It was hard to rest, though, with him beside her. Admittedly, she felt better able to rest with him beside her than she would have at her family home or if she were alone, but…

'Alistair?'

'Go to sleep, Libby, or just lie quietly and relax. We are not getting into this.'

Not now, and nor the next day, apparently, because when she awoke Alistair was talking on his phone, and then he came out from her tiny kitchen and it seemed a decision had been made.

'You'll have to come to mine,' Alistair told her. 'I've got a spare room.'

'I really don't need taking care of…'

'You need to be watched,' Alistair said. 'And you need to rest or you could run into problems. Please take this seriously, Libby. I've already lost one friend because he chose not to follow medical advice.'

'I am taking this seriously,' Libby said. 'That's why I didn't want to go back to my parents'. I haven't lived at home since I was eighteen. And I know I need to be quiet and rest.'

'Then you also know you shouldn't be on your own. And I don't want to sleep on a yoga mat or sit on your exercise ball. If I've got to be stuck with you, then I'd at least like a little space and comfort.'

'Stuck?'

'Yes,' Alistair said. 'I landed myself in it, so I'm not blaming you, but I'm pretty much stuck with you for the next few days. Unless you want to call your parents to come and collect you, or unless you have a friend who doesn't mind dropping everything and coming here to stay.'

'Stuck?' she checked again, inviting him to change his choice of word, but he nodded. 'You're not a very nice nurse.'

'I'm not,' he agreed. 'And right now you're not a very nice patient. But that's because you're not yet yourself.'

'I am.'

'No,' he said, 'you are not. You're being a right little madam, in fact.' He looked directly at her. 'I'll pack a few things for you.'

'I need—'

'Libby, I do this all the time when I'm taking a patient into hospital. Phone, charger, laptop, charger, knickers, pyjamas, toothbrush, hairbrush or comb, shampoo, deodorant, tampons, pads… Any medication?'

'No.'

Good grief, he was efficient.

In mere minutes he had achieved what would have taken her an entire morning—and even then she'd have left something behind.

'Moisturiser,' Libby said as he came out of her bathroom.

'I've got it,' he said. 'I'll just take the perishables out of your fridge…'

'How long am I coming to yours for?'

'I'm not your doctor, Libby. How long would you have stayed at home? How long until you'd have been ready to take the train back down to London and get on the underground? Go shopping and look after your flat?'

'I am sorry,' she said. 'I wasn't really thinking straight when I suggested this.'

'No,' he said, 'but I was, and I agreed to it, so blame me if you want. Come on.'

It was a very bright winter morning, and everything was wet. The glare was a lot for her to take, so she sat on the wall with her eyes closed as they waited for a cab.

'You make me feel so incompetent.'

'I don't intend to; I'm trying to be practical,' he said, and sat on the wall beside her. 'And you're certainly not incompetent.'

She wasn't, Alistair knew, for she had very competently captured his very controlled heart.

Then tossed it away.

Then taken it back.

He was not going to get into a row with her now—of course not. But at the same time he was not going to let himself get drawn into this, or let her flirt with him.

She was still a bit… Not confused, but it was more she was just not quite herself. She was cross, teary, and still unaware of just how unwell she had been and how much time it would take her to heal.

He turned and looked at her, sitting on the wall with her eyes closed, and he felt that odd little sigh again.

His mouth closed into a grim line.

Her anger seemed to be fading.

Just as his was returning.

* * *

Libby definitely wasn't feeling herself, because she slept in the car. And she must trust him implicitly, because she didn't know the street he lived in—just that the front door of his house was cobalt blue, there was a pot of earth beside it and that it said number thirty-five.

'If you collapse,' Libby said, 'and I have to call an ambulance, I shan't know your address…'

'You can use the co-ordinates on your phone,' he said as he opened up the front door, but then he told her where she was.

'I'm none the wiser,' Libby said, because she really didn't know London at all.

'Come in.'

There was a staircase to one side of the hall, which was long and led to a kitchen.

'The lounge is through here,' Alistair said.

She peered in and glimpsed a large leather sofa and a chair by a fireplace, but then they carried on down the hall to the kitchen. It was small, but bright and modern, with large French doors that led out into a narrow garden. There was a high breakfast bar, and a kitchen table with pretty pot plants in quirky containers.

The washing machine was in the kitchen, and humming away—which confused her, because he'd been at her flat all night.

'Is there a delay button on that?' Libby asked.

Perhaps it was odd to be trying to make sense of his washing matching, when she wasn't quite sure of the month or who the Prime Minister was, but she couldn't stop fixating on it.

'Don't worry about that now,' Alistair said.

Perhaps he saw how droopy she was. It felt like too

much effort to pull out a chair, and the breakfast bar stools looked too high, so she just stood there, feeling a little overwhelmed.

'I'll show you the guest room.'

'How do you work and keep it so neat?' she asked as they climbed the stairs.

'I have a cleaner once a week,' Alistair said, showing her the bathroom, which was opposite the room where she would sleep. 'I asked her to come and sort out the guest room—that's why the washing machine is on.'

'Oh.'

She glanced down the hall and saw a half-open pale wooden door, which she guessed was his bedroom. Libby wanted to look behind that door so much that she tuned out of what he was saying about what Chloe, his cleaner, had bought for Libby's arrival.

'I asked her to buy sheets, a duvet and pillows, towels...'

'I'm an expensive person to be stuck with.'

'It's fine. I kept meaning to get round to buying all that anyway. The spare bed's never even been made up before.'

His cleaner had good taste, because the bed was dressed in white linen. She was thoughtful, too, because there was even a box of tissues by her bed. The room's walls were a lovely soft grey. Libby knew that if she'd risked grey walls they would have ended up looking like a prison cell. Instead they looked soft and pretty—it was a lovely guest room. She was surprised he'd never so much as made up the bed...

'Don't you have friends who stay over?'

'Libby, my overnight guests generally sleep in *my* bed.'

Ouch!

She screwed up her nose at the thought of his overnight guests and really, really hoped he wouldn't be having any while she was there.

Not that she could object, of course, but it would be torture.

As well as completely her own fault.

She sat on the edge of the pretty white bed and looked up at him, recalling how he'd invited her into his home once before, and her response had been to end things with him. She could have been in his bed, in his bedroom, but instead it was unseen and forbidden to her, hidden behind a pale wooden door.

'I'm sorry, Alistair…' There was no dignity in concussion, because she felt her face screw up and tears start tumbling out of her eyes. 'I made a mistake.'

'Please don't cry…'

'I don't usually,' Libby attempted. 'It's my head injury…'

'Libby, you were sobbing over a fridge the day we met.'

'It wasn't just the fridge I was crying about.'

'Okay…'

'The fridge was the final straw. I was having a bad day—at least I was until you showed up.'

'Okay,' he said again.

But Libby noticed that, unlike when they'd been together, he didn't ask her to elaborate, or try to find out more about her life. In fact, he was quietly and calmly putting away her things, unpacking her bag for her as she sat there, listless. She didn't mind. The contents were hardly private—he'd packed it after all.

'Why don't you try and get some rest?' he suggested, putting her pale blue pyjamas on the bed. 'Maybe get changed and get into bed and I'll bring you up some lunch.'

'Aren't I allowed downstairs?'

'Of course you are.'

She was just feeling so completely listless, though. Even the effort of relocating to his flat had depleted her.

She picked up her handbag and started to go through it.

'What are you looking for?' he asked.

'Headache tablets.'

'I'll bring you some up with your lunch,' Alistair said. 'Do you want to give me your toiletry bag and I'll put your things in the bathroom?' As she nodded he added, 'You're the white towels.'

It was such a little thing, to be the white towels, but it stung so very much.

She thought back to their time together…to Alistair with her lemon-coloured daisy towel around his hips.

Now she was relegated to newly bought guest towels.

She piled her clothes onto a chair and pulled on the pyjamas, even though they were more suitable for summer, and then padded over to the bathroom.

It was a very boldly decorated bathroom, with jade walls and towels and a huge white enamel bath that she would have loved to fill and sink into, but the doctor had warned her to avoid baths until after her outpatient appointment.

Over the bath was a shower, but she would tackle that tomorrow, Libby thought, peering at the lovely green towels that were forbidden to her.

Then she stopped sulking as she caught sight of herself in the mirror.

Gosh!

It was the first time she'd really seen herself since the accident.

There had been mirrors in the hospital bathrooms, of course, but it had taken all her mental energy just to wash her hands and dry them.

Or possibly she'd been avoiding looking at them.

Now she peered into his mirror.

The green décor could be to blame for giving her complexion such a sallow hue, but there was nothing to account for the dark shadows under her eyes.

Were they bruises?

They were so dark Libby actually considered it for a moment—but no, they were shadows.

There *were* bruises, though. Not just the one she couldn't see, on the back of her head, one on her hand, and one inside her elbow, where they'd put in drips.

Now, she took off her pyjama top and saw that her left shoulder looked as if it had been painted purple. And it was no wonder her back hurt, because as she turned around she saw not just bruising, but the actual imprint of the lines of the escalator on her skin.

She swallowed—it really had been some fall.

Her top went back on and she made her way to the guest room, where it was actually bliss to sink into very comfortable sheets and soft pillows and hear Alistair coming up the stairs.

'Here,' Alistair said, and came in carrying a tray. 'Have some lunch.'

Libby sat up and looked at the pretty tray, all dotted with poppies, and a rather delectable-looking lunch. 'Chicken soup?'

'Good for the soul, apparently,' Alistair said. 'Mind you, it's just from a tin.'

Ahh, but it had been warmed by him, and served with lovely buttery toast, two headache tablets and a big jug of water with a glass, which he put by the bed.

'I'm all bruised…'

'Yes.'

'Not just the back of my head. My shoulder and back are too.'

'I saw at the hospital.' Alistair nodded.

'I feel like you know more about me than I do,' Libby admitted. 'I hate missing that hour…'

'Listen…' he held the tray steady and then sat on the bed '…I helped turn you and get you off the spinal board…'

'What did I say?' She had an awful feeling she might have told him she loved him, or something embarrassing.

'You repeated yourself a lot,' Alistair said. 'Just asking where you were…'

'What else did I say?'

He took a breath. 'Once we'd got past the pelicans, and Cathy, you said you were cross about my job…'

'Yes.' Libby nodded. She remembered that.

'And my bike.'

'Yes.' She sort of remembered that. 'What else?'

He was quiet for a moment. 'Not much.'

'Alistair?'

'You said you were going on a date…'

'No.'

'What?'

'I mean, I *was* going on a date, but I changed my mind,' she said. 'I knew I'd made a mistake.'

'Stop!' he said, gently but firmly.

'But I did.'

She could remember now, turning around, knowing she had to see Alistair, but he was refusing to be drawn into her version of events.

'I changed my mind and turned to go back down the stairs.'

She remembered that moment now. And the moments leading up to her fall. Realising she was on the wooden escalator, not stairs, the blinding veil of her tears, the realisation that she had to see Alistair—had to tell him why she had ended things and that she didn't want it to be over between them.

'I knew I had to see you.'

'Okay,' he said, and moved to stand up from the bed. 'Have your lunch.'

'You don't believe me?'

His eyes met hers. 'No,' he said. 'I don't. But I'm not going to argue about it.'

'Talk to me about it, then.'

'I don't want to talk about it, Libby. You're here because right now you need someone to take care of you, and it would seem that person is me.'

He gave her no more than that.

Yes, Alistair was taking caring of her, but on *his* terms.

Meals were brought in on the poppy tray, and headache tablets too, and there was one awkward moment the next day when she didn't know how to turn on the hot water for the shower.

Wrapped in a white towel, she had no choice but to call out.

'Sorry…' Libby said.

'It's fine.'

He didn't give her so much as a look, just a practical lesson on the nuances of his hot water system.

'Thank you.'

He didn't respond, just headed out, closing the door behind him. 'Call if you need anything, or if you get dizzy.'

'Thank you.'

It wasn't even awkward to know that he was listening out for her in case she felt unwell.

It just made her feel sad.

And then irritable when she rinsed out her shampoo and couldn't find her conditioner. 'You didn't pack my conditioner,' she called. 'Can I use yours?'

'I don't have any!' he called back. 'I don't use it.'

Grumbling about dry hair and curls, she turned his odd hot water system off and wrapped herself in a guest towel. Then she sat on the edge of the bath, wondering how she could be complaining when he had done so much for her.

'Are you okay?' he called, and she guessed the silence was concerning him.

'Yes.'

'Good.'

With the water off she heard him leave his post and head down the stairs. Avoiding her, she was sure.

When she ventured downstairs a couple of evenings later, that thought was confirmed.

She was starting to feel better, more herself.

A little bored, actually!

He was sprawled on the sofa, his long legs spread along the length of it, his shirt loose and unbuttoned, exposing his chest. He was watching football on TV. His team, she knew, because in their dizzy four days of bliss he'd told her who he supported. And she'd heard him urging them on as she came down the stairs.

He glanced at her as she entered, but didn't move or make a space for her, so she sat on the chair next to the sofa.

'Good game?' she asked.

'Mmm…' He must have seen her looking at his bare chest, for he started buttoning his shirt. A few minutes later he stretched, rose from the couch and walked towards the stairs.

She glanced at him, puzzled. 'Are you leaving?'

The game had gone into extra time and promised a nail-biting finish.

He lifted an indifferent shoulder. 'I've got some studying to do.'

'But it's going to penalties,' Libby said, not quite understanding, because even with her zero interest in sport this game was clearly an exciting one. And it was his team.

'Here.' He handed her the remote. 'I'll say goodnight. Call out if you need anything.'

'You mean you're going to bed now?'

It was early.

'I'm going up now.' His voice was flat, uninterested.

'You're not making me feel very welcome, Alistair.'

He spun back round. Eyes that had once held hers so tenderly were angry, and they refused to meet hers, but his voice was, as always, was measured and calm.

'Listen, Libby, you've got the full run of the house, an on-call paramedic, meals, a bed…' He took a deep breath. 'I'm trying to be polite here…'

She bit her lip and fought her frustration—because this wasn't the Alistair she'd once known. 'But you're not as you were…'

'You didn't particularly like that version of me either, did you?' he reminded her. 'Now, I'm not arguing, and I'm not interested in discussing it. You're not supposed to be getting worked up and I'm trying to facilitate that as best I can. But smiling and pretending everything's fine…? Lying on the sofa together…?'

Oh, yes, he'd obviously seen her hovering, seen her hoping he'd make room for her.

He shook his head as he told her, 'That I can't and won't do.'

He walked out and left her holding the remote, staring blankly at a game she had no interest in play out its final desperate minutes.

Alistair's team won.

Libby knew it was she who had lost.

CHAPTER SIX

ALISTAIR MIGHT NOT be the cheeriest nurse, but he was incredibly efficient and Libby was very well looked after.

Several days and nights passed. She slept a great deal, and each day when she woke she felt a little better.

Slowly, she was healing.

The bruises on her back and shoulder were fading, her head felt much clearer, and she wasn't so snappy or teary any more.

Or so needy.

Every day she returned a little more to herself.

And every day Alistair distanced himself just a little bit more.

The hand-holding had stopped on the night of the accident and never returned.

And now there was no sitting on her bed and reassuring her, as he had on the day she'd arrived.

Alistair provided her with meals that tempted her appetite. He was taking good care of her, even if he hardly talked and barely looked at her. And when he did it was in a distant, almost professional way.

He was treating her as if she was his patient.

Not his lover.

Nor even his friend.

And the distance he placed between them reminded her of everything that might have been and all that she had lost.

She'd made such a mess of things, but she couldn't turn back the clock. She just had to live with the now and hope it would get better.

And even though he was cross—she knew that he was—Alistair was still a very soothing person to be around. So much so that each time she woke up she mentally located him. It was as if her heart had to know whether he was downstairs, or in his room, or in the bathroom.

He worked hard, even on his days off. She heard him listening to lectures, or tapping away on his computer. Sometimes she caught the low-pitched murmur of his voice on the phone, and tried not to wonder who he was talking to.

It was none of her business. He'd made that more than clear.

She was coming to know the sounds of the house and his routines. Each morning she heard the creak of the central heating that he only ever put on after he woke in the morning. Why didn't he set a timer?

This morning it was cold, and she heard his bare feet padding on the floorboards as he passed her room. He muttered something, cursing the bitter morning as he ran downstairs.

Did he sleep naked? It was her first one of *those* thoughts. She closed her eyes and tried not to imagine him sprinting down to the kettle, naked, his long legs taking the stairs two at a time, his strong, lean body once warm from his bed now shivering in the cold air.

But no, he wouldn't. She was his guest—an unwanted guest at that—and he wouldn't risk them bumping into each other on the landing. More was the pity!

She lay there, straining her ears to hear who he was speaking to on the phone and wishing he'd packed conditioner. Or lip balm. Or anything for her flirting arsenal. But no, she had nothing. Just her returning spirit, along with the pale blue summer pyjamas she was coming to loathe, and a second pair of ugly red tartan flannelette ones. She wore them on rotation, and handed him her washing each day, but today she was going to do it herself.

She didn't need him, Libby was sure.

'When are you back at work?' she asked, when he knocked and came in with a breakfast of cereal, toast and a mug of tea.

'Not for a couple more days. I've swapped some shifts around. How are you feeling?'

'A lot better,' Libby said.

'Good.'

'I think I can go home.'

'To your parents'?'

'No.' She shook her head. 'Back to my flat.'

'Okay,' Alistair said. 'When you've finished eating, take your tray down and do the dishes. Then, after your shower, your sheets will need to be changed. There's another set in the second drawer and you'll need to put the others in the washing machine.' He frowned. 'You don't have a washing machine at your place, do you? Why don't you try going to the laundromat today? It's not far, and you can use it as a trial—to see how well you can manage.'

'Of course I can manage,' she forced herself to say. That look in his eye was a challenge and she wasn't going to back down from it.

He raised a brow. 'Good. Well, in that case, on your way back you can buy some bread, cheese and lettuce—or whatever you fancy for lunch. Then, if you feel fine after all that, we'll talk about you going home.'

The prospect of all those normal daily tasks felt ridiculously daunting.

Impossibly so.

'I am joking, Libby,' he said, and she looked up. 'You're better, but…'

He'd been wonderful to her, she knew, but they couldn't go on like this.

She'd been promoted to the sofa by day, which meant he moved upstairs when she came down. It was as if he couldn't bear to be in the same room as her.

And he no longer hovered like a worried parent when she took her shower.

'I'll call my parents,' Libby said wearily. 'I really shouldn't have landed all this on you. I just wasn't thinking things through.'

'Of course you weren't. You were ill.'

'Even so, I didn't realise I'd be such a…' she cast around for the right word '…such a responsibility.' And he was so…well, *responsible*. 'I don't need a full-time carer now. Just…'

She sighed, thinking of her old bedroom and the drama of her mother, compared with the lovely soft grey walls and the sheer bliss of being with Alistair, even if he was being distant.

Even if he didn't like her any more.

His eyes still refused to meet hers.

'I spoke to Dad last night,' Libby said. 'I think he's off today. He could drive down…'

'Listen.' Alistair sounded practical. 'I'm going out for lunch, to give us both some space, and then if you're up to it we can go for a walk this afternoon.'

'A walk?'

'Just along the canal,' he said. 'Then tomorrow I've got a few things on, and we'll see how you are. After that I'm back at work—two day shifts and two nights—and by then you should be fine to go back to your flat. If not, you'll have to go to your parents' as I'll be on my course.'

'I'm taking up so much of your time…'

'Not really. I've got loads of studying done—I had to do it before the residential, so being housebound has had some advantages.'

'When do you leave?' Libby asked.

'At the end of the week. I've just got that one more block of shifts before I go.'

'You've taken time off, haven't you?'

'It's fine,' he said.

'I didn't want you to use up your leave on me.'

'I was going to have a week off before I left for the course, to do all the studying. I just moved things around and am having it now.'

'Hardly a holiday…' Libby sighed. 'Is Brendan still pushing for you to have leaving drinks?'

'A few of us are getting together, yes.'

There was a stretch of silence, but no invitation for her to join them. Of course not. Libby knew she had seen to that herself.

'Thank you for taking such good care of me. And I do mean that. It's far more than I deserve—'

He threw up a hand. 'Of course you deserve to be taken care of. Let's just get you well and then you can go home.'

His brisk, practical attitude showed Libby he was done with her drama—done with *them*—and as he left her to have her breakfast it was quite a feat to give him a polite thank-you and not give in to the distress that swamped her.

So hard to be in the house with the person she possibly loved. And so hard to face up to the fact—which he'd made more than clear—that he no longer wanted her.

She took a shower and came back to fresh sheets—he'd changed them for her. She sighed.

Libby decided the sofa could wait until he went out. She knew he'd only head upstairs if she went down, so she tried to give him the space he clearly needed.

She must have fallen asleep, because she woke to the stunning sight of Alistair in a dark suit with a white shirt and sliver-grey tie, freshly shaven and carrying her tray. Well, *his* tray—but it felt like hers now. On it was a cheese, pickle and lettuce sandwich, a packet of crisps, a mug of tea and two chocolate biscuits. He told her they were for later, as he was going out.

He was perfect…so perfect.

Except for the polite, distant smile.

'You look lovely,' Libby said, and then swallowed when he didn't respond. 'Sorry. I didn't realise I wasn't allowed to make personal observations.'

He almost—*almost*—smiled. 'I'm heading off. Text me if you need anything.'

'I will,' she lied, rather than tell him she no longer had his number. But he halted at the bedroom door and then turned around.

'Have you still got my number, Libby?'

She avoided his eyes. 'I'll be fine.'

There was no *almost* smile now. 'So you deleted it, then?'

She closed her eyes in shame as she nodded, then opened them to the sight of Alistair by the bedside table, taking out a pen and writing his number down. He was so close that she had to fight not to reach out for him.

'I was scared I'd give in and call you…'

'What? You mean you'd have called when you fancied a shag?'

It was his first display of bitterness and his cynical words cut into her. It had never been like that, but she wouldn't be able to convince him now.

'No! I ended things because I was upset about your job—'

He cut her off. 'You don't have to explain, Libby. I'm more than used to it. I'm going to lunch with my father. He too dumped me when I changed careers.' He gave her no time to ask for more on the subject. 'Call me if you need me,' he said, and then he was gone.

She had hurt him so very much, Libby knew. And he point-blank refused to talk about it.

When he got back from his lunch he didn't come up to see her.

'How are you?' he called up the stairs.

'Fine, thank you.'

There would be no gentle walk by the canal today.

CHAPTER SEVEN

SHE WOKE TO a reminder about her gynae appointment and called to reschedule. She dug in her bag for a pen. There she found the bundle of post that belonged to the previous occupant of her flat.

Not at this address, Libby wrote. *Not at this address... Not at this address...*

Even writing one phrase over and over was exhausting, but just as she was about to give up on the task she stilled, because there was a pale lilac envelope and it was addressed to her.

Oh! It was a sympathy card.

Thinking of you, it said on the front. And inside it said, *Wishing I could be there.*

Alistair.

He'd signed his name and beneath was a phone number. She checked it against the one he had written down by the bedside. It was his.

He came in then.

'Alistair...' She looked up. 'Why did you send me a sympathy card?'

'I didn't.'

'Yes, you did. It says, *"Thinking of you"*. And inside it says *"Wishing I could be there"*, and it has purple flowers on it. It's a sympathy card.'

'No,' he said. 'It's just…' He took the card and looked at it. 'I thought it was just a *thinking of you* card,' he said, blushing. 'Is this honestly a sympathy card?'

'Yes!' She smiled a watery smile.

'You must have thought I was a right jerk…'

'I've only just seen it. I've been getting the old tenant's mail and I haven't gone through it all yet. When did you send it?'

He shrugged, but didn't answer.

'I think it's lovely. And I'd have thought the same if I'd got it before. I'd have caved if I hadn't deleted your number. Actually, I was already caving. I was going to plead for help at the phone shop, to see if they could retrieve it…' She paused. 'You don't believe me?'

'I don't,' he stated, but without malice. 'I sent it a couple of days after you broke things off. I was on a night shift, getting petrol and buying a coffee…' He gave a wry smile. 'Lina asked if I was okay when she saw it. She must have thought I'd lost someone.'

Alistair thought back to that bleak night.

He *had* lost someone: Libby.

Stopping at the petrol station for a coffee, and seeing the card on a display rack by the coffee machine, he had been struck by how it stated exactly what he'd been feeling.

He'd bought the card and a stamp along with his coffee, written his number in it, and posted it before he could talk himself out of it.

Pride had kicked in since.

He was too proud for his own good, Alistair knew.

Too private, perhaps.

He didn't share his thoughts easily—unlike Libby, who had just blurted them out even before she'd had her accident.

Alistair wanted to believe her.

He wanted to believe that she'd changed her mind—that she'd missed him even a tenth as much as he'd missed her.

That she'd only just seen this card.

Only he didn't.

Oh, he believed she might regret it a bit—or was it more a case that he was now suddenly convenient?

They needed to talk. He knew that, although he had been putting it off. Because if they didn't there was the risk of falling into bed with each other again.

Not yet—but as her energy and health started to return there were moments, increasingly frequent moments of late, during which he had to ignore the memory of her body and the scent of her. Moments like now, when he had to deliberately *not* notice that the bottom button of her pyjama top was undone, and ignore the glimpse of pale stomach that he had once inhaled and deeply kissed, touched, lingered over…

Damn you, Libby Bennett.

He refused to fall in deeper, only to be spat out later, when Libby got bored again…

'Do you want to go for a walk?' he offered, because otherwise he might just move forward.

'A walk?' Libby said.

'Yes.'

For Alistair, it was a far safer bet.

Alistair gave her some sunglasses and watched as she put on her nursing shoes, jeans and one of his jumpers. Without conditioner, her curls were frizzy, and she must look such a fright.

But, even so, it was actually lovely to be out.

The canal was a very short walk from his house. It was a little frosty, though, and he suggested she take his arm—

but it wasn't for any reason other than to avoid her tripping over or fainting.

'Your father said you trip a lot,' he said.

'Not a lot. But I might have to retire my heels for a few weeks.'

'You were in a summer dress and sandals when you fell.'

'I had a coat on.' She suddenly laughed. 'I probably looked like a stripper!' She saw him smile. 'It was the most stupid thing ever. I was so very determined to prove you were just a crush, and then the guy at the doughnut shop asked if I wanted to go for a drink…' She felt helpless as she tried to explain. 'I mean, how dangerous can working in a coffee shop be?'

She'd wanted safe.

And yet Alistair, even with risk attached, made her feel safer than anyone ever had.

'I can't ever go back to that café now,' she said. 'And it's a shame because they did amazing doughnuts. But—'

'You could always tell him what happened.'

'God, no. I didn't even want to go. I'd changed my mind. Like I told you, I didn't get my heel caught. I turned around because I'd changed my mind, and I forgot, just for a second, that I wasn't on the stairs—you can't go *down* an up escalator…'

He didn't believe her. She could feel it in his silence and in the way he looked ahead as he walked.

'It's true,' Libby insisted into the silence. 'I knew I'd made a dreadful mistake. I missed you so much. And I just panicked. There had been a fatal motorbike accident the morning you left mine…'

Alistair turned and she felt his eyes on her.

'The rider didn't even make it into the department. We got stood down. For a while I thought it could be you. I knew I was overreacting, but…' She gave a hopeless shrug.

'Or perhaps I wasn't? I've hated motorbikes since I worked on an orthopaedic ward.'

'I've done advanced courses.'

'Good for you,' Libby said, a little sharply. 'And then that afternoon I heard you'd been accepted for a job that will place you right in the hot zones...'

'Yet you didn't think to talk to me about it?'

'What good was talking going to do?' she asked. 'You weren't going to change your job, or give up your bike, and I knew I had no right to ask. I didn't want you to change; it's me who has the issues.'

'Yes,' he said—but nicely. He smiled, and the arm she was leaning on felt a little more like a friend's arm than the support of a physiotherapist.

Not a lover's arm, though.

'I can't ask you not to take this job.'

'I wouldn't have given it up even if you had asked, but we could have spoken about it,' Alistair said. 'And may I point out that you're the one who's currently injured? *I'm* fine...'

'You've seen what my mother's like. I love her so much, but I swore I'd never get involved with a firefighter or anything dangerous because I've seen the toll her worrying takes on both her and my father.'

'Libby, your parents are very, very happy—well, they seem happy to me. Are you saying your mum wishes she'd never met him?'

'Of course not!'

'Your mother might worry all day if he were working in doughnut shop...'

Libby took a breath. What he was saying made perfect sense. Logical sense.

But it didn't factor in the leaping salmon in her chest that was disguised as a heart.

'It *is* a dangerous job you'll be doing, Alistair. And it

scares me. Or maybe it was how much I liked you that scared me. And I had this appointment coming up, and I felt all churned up—'

'Appointment?'

'My malfunctioning ovaries.' She took a breath. 'That one *"almost serious"* relationship I told you about? He didn't take it very well when I said I was going to have some investigations.'

'He broke off with you because of that?'

'No, I broke it off with him. I was already upset, and he just made it a thousand times worse.'

'What about your parents?' Alistair asked.

'I haven't told them. Can you imagine my mother?' He didn't answer, though she didn't really pause long enough for him to respond. 'I don't know... I was just confused, because I really liked you, and I didn't want to kick things off with my fertility issues, your career path issues, motorbike issues...'

Alistair spoke then. 'Do you want a coffee?'

'Please.'

They went into a lovely café and looked at the menu. 'You've put me off doughnuts...' he said. 'Although they're really good here too.'

'Why don't we both have one and just get over our doughnut issues?' Libby suggested. 'Because I don't want to live a doughnut-free life...'

He looked at her with his lovely brown eyes. 'Custard or jam?' he asked.

'Chocolate custard, please,' Libby said. 'How about you?'

'I think I'll have chocolate custard too.'

'And I'm getting this,' Libby told him once they'd given their orders. 'No arguments.'

'There'll be no arguments from me...but you didn't bring your bag.'

Libby laughed as she glanced down at the floor and then to the chair, where she'd usually put it and saw that he was completely right. 'God, I'm a liability. If I'd been on my own I'd have ordered...' She blew out a breath. 'I am *not* this totally teary, dippy person.'

'I know that. And you're not *totally* teary and dippy,' he smiled. 'You are a lot better. I can see it.'

'I'm going to be much more empathetic when I give out head injury instructions in the future. I would never have thought it could be like this.'

'That's why your parents were worried about leaving you with a stranger and why I was never going to leave you on your own. Your father video calls me every day for updates.'

'Does he?' She closed her eyes for a moment and let out a big sigh.

'I don't blame him,' Alistair said. 'You really haven't been well.'

'I know... We are close, and they're both great when things are going well.' She gave him a tight smile. 'You know how you've spent the last few days trying not to upset me...?'

He nodded.

'Well, that's my whole life. I love my mother, but she's so easily upset. I know you said that I'm like her...' She puffed out a breath of frustration. 'He really calls you every day?'

'I try and take it downstairs, so you don't find out just how closely you're being watched.'

'I thought you were running for the kettle.'

'I've got an app for my kettle,' Alistair said. 'I can turn it on from my bed.'

Libby looked out at the glittering canal, because it was

easier than looking at him and trying not to offer a flirty reply about what else he could turn on from his bed.

Perhaps the one ounce of self-restraint she possessed where Alistair was concerned was finally returning.

And so, rather than flirt, she watched the cold ducks. The drakes were looking spectacular, with their glossy plumage, all ready to dazzle the females come mating time.

'What are female ducks called?' Libby asked.

'Ducks, I think.'

She snorted. In that moment, Libby felt like a duck, drab and unimpressive, while he sat there so effortlessly gorgeous and glossy.

For a while there she'd been the luckiest duck in the world.

She just wished she hadn't stuffed things up so badly.

Or possibly it was for the best that she had?

She thought back to that dreadful morning and the fear that had clutched at her heart when the alert had come in that the motorcyclist had been killed.

She knew there were accidents all the time—though thankfully not always with such dire consequences. But then on top of that had come the news of his new job.

She had been trying to get used to the feelings he provoked in her—to the lurch in her heart, to the impact of Alistair on her life.

Such an impact…

'Yes, females are called ducks,' Alistair said, putting down his phone.

'My own personal fact-checker.' Libby smiled, but then it wavered, because she knew she didn't have him for much longer—this walk was another step closer to her going home and being out of his life, only for good this time.

'Why are you fighting with your parents?' Libby ventured.

'It's not that dramatic. We're not arguing or anything. Well, not any more.'

He stirred some more sugar into his coffee, though to her it looked as if it was more for something to do as he considered how much to reveal.

'I come a family of high achievers and my father simply could not get that I didn't want the same thing. Especially as I was enjoying working in corporate law, and the life it afforded and all that. But then my friend died and I took stock. Do you know what my father said when I told him I wanted to be a paramedic?'

'What?'

'He said, "Well, that was a waste of a good education."'

'I'm so sorry.'

'I love him. He's an arrogant prick, but I love my parents. We're at a stalemate, though. I went to lunch with him and one of his clients yesterday. I used to keep my hand in, but that's finishing up now. Once this project concludes I don't see anything to keep us seeing each other.'

'What about your mother?'

'I have coffee with her now and then, but it's tense. We don't talk about my work. We don't talk about a lot of things. I've kept my hours up—for now—because I agreed to do that when I told them I was training as a paramedic. But I know they're just waiting for me to change my mind. I haven't.' He looked over to her then, and she knew the next words were also for her. 'I won't.'

'I've never asked you to change your mind,' Libby pointed out.

'I know. You just decided someone doing my new job wasn't for you.'

'It could be…' She blinked.

Only, it was no longer just his work that was the issue.

'In a couple of days I'm going away for six weeks, and then I'll be busy in a new job.'

She had broken his trust, Libby knew.

He shook his head, then said, 'Maybe we're just not suited.'

He got up to pay and she sat there, staring into space, with tears gathering in her eyes. They left the café and walked under grey skies.

'It's started to rain,' Libby said, and was terribly grateful for it, because it meant her tears would go unnoticed.

She took his lovely arm again, all the while hating herself for all that she'd lost when she ended things with Alistair. Even if he didn't think so, she thought they were very suited. She thought he was perfect.

'It's for the best,' he said, trying to make light in the gloom as they walked along the canal. 'You'd be a nervous wreck.'

'I could stop watching the news…'

He smiled.

'I could turn off my phone, practise meditation…' She looked up to his smile. 'And be all calm and serene and *How was your day, dear?* when you get home.'

'You wouldn't last five minutes…' Alistair sighed. 'Look, we went out once, and then shared four incredible days on your sofa-bed. It was great and then…not. That's okay. There's no need for a row or whatever.'

'I'd like a row,' Libby said. Because she wanted to shout out that she had made a mistake, and that she wished for him to go back to being upset at how much she'd hurt him. 'I want you to believe me.'

'But I don't, though,' he said. 'And that's not the best basis to start anything, is it?'

'No…' Libby had to concede. She did hate his job, his bike… He didn't believe that she'd changed her mind…

Alistair was right. It wasn't a great place to start.

'The thing is—' Libby stopped herself. Not because of pride, but because she just didn't know how to explain things—and it had nothing to do with the bang to her head.

It was simply that she didn't know how to explain that she didn't feel as if they were at the start of anything. She felt as if the start had been a very long time ago, and now they were in the *middle* of something.

She *had* fallen.

But not just down an escalator.

Libby was rather certain she had fallen straight in love.

That was what had terrified her.

And now it saddened her—more than she knew how to deal with.

'Alistair, I've been very spoilt, and I'm incredibly grateful, but I'm so much better that I feel like a bit of a fraud now.'

'You're not a fraud,' Alistair said. 'But you definitely seem better today. Look, you don't have to rush off. If you want to have a couple of days here while you're feeling better—a practice run, if you will—then you're welcome to stay. I'll be working twelve-hour shifts, so you won't even see me. Maybe go before I start my nights? Whatever works for you...'

'I could go shopping for you,' Libby offered. 'On my practice run.'

'No need. I've got a delivery coming tomorrow.'

'Well, I'll put it away.'

'It's all taken care of. Chloe does all that when I'm working.'

'Chloe?'

'The cleaner who went shopping for bed linen and such.'

'Oh.'

While she had known that his life was ordered, Libby

felt she was being kept at arm's length—being silently told that he really didn't need or want her in his life.

At all.

The conversation had become strained, so his cobalt blue door was welcoming when it appeared.

And the little pot of earth by his door had tiny shoots emerging.

'Oh, look!' Libby said.

'Daffodils.'

Spring was around the corner, only it didn't feel like it for Libby.

The creak in the stairs as she walked up had grown familiar and it made her smile sadly. She was intending to change out of her damp jeans and his huge jumper, but as she headed for her room she turned and saw the door to his was open.

A suitcase was on the floor, and it was clear he was getting ready for his training course.

It made her feel hollow and empty, rather than scared as to the nature of his work.

She pulled on her tartan pyjamas and then went down to the kitchen and peered into his cupboards, wondering if she should offer to cook.

'Hungry?' he asked as he came into the room and found her staring into his fridge.

'I was about to offer to make dinner.'

'Well, good luck with that, because I haven't got anything in.'

'That's not very efficient of you,' she teased, because he was the most organised person in the world. 'What happened to your system?'

'You did,' Alistair said. 'We can order something in. What do you fancy?'

You, she was so tempted to say. But instead she pouted as she remembered no flirting was allowed.

Not standing by the fridge. *Especially* not standing by the fridge.

'Let me get dinner,' Libby said, taking her phone from her pyjama pocket.

And because it was Alistair, there were no arguments.

She ordered curry and extra garlic naans—because she didn't have to worry about end-of-the-night kisses and such.

It was a lazy evening, and there was a good film on television. Unfortunately, all too soon, it showed a couple making love on-screen.

'Awkward!' Libby gave a little laugh.

Alistair smiled, and Libby knew it was because she tended to mention the things most people would politely ignore.

But it was extremely awkward—watching a sex scene on TV whilst you were sitting next to the person you wanted to have sex with, but who no longer wanted to have sex with you.

He took up their plates.

'I'll do it,' Libby offered.

'It's fine,' Alistair said. 'I'm going to load the dishwasher, then I've got one more lecture to watch.'

'What time are you working tomorrow?'

'Midday to midnight...'

'I'll see you in the morning, then.'

Libby smiled, but it wavered as he turned without responding and went through to the kitchen.

They were over.

They were completely and utterly over.

Libby knew it, but she wished desperately that it wasn't so.

CHAPTER EIGHT

SHE WOKE TO the sound of Alistair in the shower.

It was late—almost eleven! She'd slept for twelve hours straight, but it felt worth it because, aside from a broken heart, she felt well. She felt so well, in fact, that she no longer suited her invalid status.

Really, it was time to pack her things and go…and get past the first day of really missing him.

Seriously missing him.

For. The. Rest. Of. Her. Life.

She didn't want to go.

Was it love? Libby pondered, wishing he'd hurry up so she could go to the loo. And, if it was, shouldn't she therefore fight for it? Shouldn't she force that row so they could move past it?

Only he didn't want one—and now neither did she.

She just wanted to touch him and say sorry with her body.

And thank you.

Just one kiss and they'd go back to the way they were, she was sure.

Shouldn't she at least try?

The old Libby would have.

And the old Libby, she decided, was back.

She and Alistair had an unvoiced agreement. After the

first couple of days, when he'd waited outside, he now went downstairs and remained down there while she showered, and Libby did the same for him. Also, if she was in her bedroom when he showered, she remained in there.

But not this morning!

Perhaps she should be grateful for the ugly tartan pyjamas, given that the house was freezing, but they weren't exactly seductive. Very deliberately she avoided the mirror, not wanting to see her fluffy hair and lose confidence in herself…

She opened up the bedroom door and glanced down the hall. She wanted to slip into his bed and surprise him, but she decided that might be a bit much.

She started as the bathroom door opened.

He was naked except for a towel wrapped around his slim hips, and he paused at the unexpected sight of her.

Her eyes drank him in. Fresh from the shower. His thick, dark hair was damp, and a few drops of water still clung to his skin.

She wanted to lick them off.

His jaw was so smooth. There was a little bit of shaving cream by his ear, and she wanted to kiss that off too!

She looked at the sexy mouth that had had her blushing since it had mouthed *Long fall* at her. Her face felt as if it was on fire now.

Her whole body was.

Cotton wool hair or not, she knew there was sex in the air. She could feel it as she lifted her eyes from his mouth and finally, *finally*, met his.

He gave her one slow, searing glance that almost burned her skin and had her about to stumble over to him, but then, a second later, an indifferent expression shuttered his eyes. He gave her a curt nod, then strode down the hall, heading for the privacy of his bedroom.

He didn't say a word—just turned when he reached his room and gave her a stark warning look. It was an accusatory glare that sent her stumbling into the bathroom, as if that had been her intention all along.

They both knew it hadn't been.

She heard him close his door firmly behind him. Shutting her out. As if she hadn't already got the message.

God, but he wanted her.

He had all along.

He'd wanted to give in on holding back, but he had told himself when he'd brought her to his home that he would not be taking advantage of their forced proximity, nor of the fact that Libby had been unwell.

Only, she was better now.

That had been no accidental bump into each other in the hall, Alistair thought as he sprayed deodorant and pulled on his uniform.

He had felt her longing fighting and tangling with his own from down the hall.

'Damn you, Libby,' he cussed, because he wanted her out of his home so he had space to think.

It was hard to think clearly when the person you needed to think about was in your home, sitting on your floor eating curry, lying in bed in the room next to you, relaxing on your sofa…

The woman who'd dumped him…who'd not even replied to his card… Of *course* she'd seen it before; he was not going to fall for that one. She'd turned his life inside out and upside down, and she was everywhere, and he needed her to be gone so he could think.

Yet he wanted her here.

Here, Alistair thought as he sat on his bed and did up his boots.

He wanted her here in his bed.

Aside from all that, he was late for work!

For her sins, there was no breakfast in bed for Libby.

In fact, she rather had the feeling he'd gone to work without having breakfast himself, because just a few moments later he'd gone down the stairs and she'd heard the front door close and then the sound of his bike.

His rejection stung—but she had seen desire in his eyes. Such desire that it somehow inspired her. Made her feel a little bit of hope that they maybe weren't quite done.

Was there still a chance?

Libby pondered the question as she made her bed, unsure whether she should strip it and pack.

She was well enough to go—she felt much more like her normal self now. Well, apart from the fact she was making her bed on rising, which she rarely did at home!

She was upset to find the kettle cold, because that meant that he hadn't even had a cup of tea in his haste to get out of there.

Time to go, Libby.

It was nice, though, to have a little practice run of being alone and doing normal things. She made a bowl of cornflakes, and some toast and tea, and wondered if he'd mind if she pinched the poppy tray, because it was so pretty and so feminine…

Yikes. She'd bet it was one of his exes who had bought it.

She ate at the table and looked out onto his garden—which, unlike the house, looked a little neglected.

Perhaps she could offer to take his daffodils while he was away, Libby thought. It seemed such a shame that they would flower unseen.

Though of course really she was just trying to come up with an excuse to see him after he'd completed his course.

Returning his daffodils would be a good excuse…

But surely she could come up with something better than that?

She was rinsing her plate when she was startled by the sound of a key in the door. She jumped, in the hope that he was home, and then sagged when she recalled that he'd said Chloe, his cleaner, was coming.

'Hi, I'm just in here,' Libby called, and then smiled as Chloe came into the kitchen. 'I didn't want to startle you.'

Although it was actually Libby who felt startled—because Chloe was completely stunning.

Her caramel hair was tied high in a messy bun. She had legs right up to her neck, and she wore black tights with shorts over them and a jumper cinched with a belt. If Libby wore the same outfit she'd look as if she was playing dress-up, but it looked fantastic on Chloe.

'Startle me?' Chloe frowned at Libby's choice of words. 'Why would you?'

And with that she made it clear to Libby that she wasn't the first overnight guest to be found rinsing her plate in Alistair's kitchen.

'Anyway,' Chole said, 'I never know if he's on nights, so I don't call out…'

She stomped upstairs and returned a short while later with armfuls of navy linen—presumably from Alistair's bed, though Libby had never so much as seen it—and threw them into the washing machine, then slammed the door closed.

Disconcertingly, for Libby, Chloe made no further attempt at conversation.

She discarded the scarf, jumper and belt quite quickly, and was soon wearing just a very little vest top. She began emptying the dishwasher.

'How long have you worked—?' Libby tried.

Chloe turned and pointed to her headphones. 'I'm listening to my music.' She took one bud out. 'What did you want?'

'Nothing…'

Libby felt awkward, so she went through to the lounge, but Chloe soon came in there so that didn't help. She really was the sexiest cleaner ever. But she scowled at Libby as she vacuumed—so much so that Libby went and hid in the bedroom while the online shopping was delivered.

Her phone pinged, and her heart leapt when she discovered it was a text from Alistair. Despite rejecting her this morning, Alistair had dutifully texted to ask how she was, because it was her first day alone. He really was perfect.

She quickly replied.

Hiding from Chloe. She hates me.

Alistair called her. 'What's wrong?'

'I was joking—well, sort of. But she doesn't like me. It makes me think that she might like *you*.'

'Chloe?' he checked. 'No. That was ages ago—we were never serious.'

'So you two *have* been on with each other?' Libby's mouth gaped and she knelt up on the bed. 'Jesus, Alistair, you could have warned me. I'd have gone out, or…'

She was indignant, jealous and embarrassed all at the same time—even if it wasn't actually her place to be. It felt like her place, though.

'You're cross with me over Doughnut Man, yet you're sleeping with your cleaner.'

'It was a couple of times last summer. Look, I've got to go. I'm not discussing my private life while I'm at work.'

'Have you got a patient with you?'

'No.'

'Then you can answer my question. If we had made it back to your house as lovers, would you have warned me then?'

'Warned you?'

'Warned me that your sexy cleaner gets between your sheets. No wonder she doesn't shout out when she arrives. Does she just slip into your bed?'

'You don't get to ask that, Libby.'

'The one time I make my bed…' Libby knew that Chloe had assumed Libby was sleeping with Alistair. 'I'm really, *really* cross, Alistair.'

'Then you're being ridiculous!'

'Not on this occasion! And my anger has nothing to do with my injury. You're an arrogant, insensitive prick—and when I say that I can pretty much guarantee I'm speaking on behalf of Chloe too.'

This time it was *she* who hung up on *him*. Then Libby got dressed and grabbed her bag and his spare key.

As she headed out, Chloe was sulkily pulling the sheets out of the washing machine, and Libby knew she wasn't misreading the situation. She was cross again, for both herself and Chloe, and so she went out.

She would come back once Chloe was gone, and then she would pack her things and leave, Libby decided as she walked down the street. She would like to have stomped, like Chloe, but she was too scared of slipping, so instead she took a few cleansing breaths and found they actually helped.

God, she was jealous.

What had gone on between him and Chloe wasn't any of her business, and that was a horrible thing to know.

When she got to the canal she managed a small laugh as the green-eyed monster faded into a blush and then cooled, and when she got to the café she caught her reflection in the mirror and saw she was back to her normal pink colour rather than pale.

After first checking that she had her bag and purse with her, Libby went in. The table she and Alistair had shared previously was taken by a couple far more loving couple than they had been when seated there. They were feeding each other pancakes and holding hands.

She wanted Alistair to hold her hand again.

'What can I get you?' the waiter asked.

There was actually nothing on the menu that she fancied, but she ordered anyway. 'Could I have a cheese and pickle sandwich...with lettuce, please?'

'Sure.'

'And crisps.'

She ordered tea too.

The same lovely lunch Alistair had made her.

It was soon served, and it was absolutely beautiful, with a glass teapot, and crisps on a plate rather than in a bag. But there were no chocolate biscuits for her to enjoy later.

Gosh, he had taken such care of her, even while feeling hurt and angry.

He had taken such care of her at every turn.

So, no, she wasn't leaving in a temper—but she would still pack this evening and be in bed by the time he got home. Tomorrow she would thank him, and then she would go back to her own flat.

The hardest part? How to say goodbye? With grace?

It was no one's fault but hers, Libby was sure.

Alistair wasn't so sure that everything was Libby's fault, though. After she hung up on him, it was he who was doubting *his* part in all this.

He wasn't even sleeping with Chloe. That had been over ages ago.

It wasn't the same as Doughnut Man, he thought angrily. Libby had gone out on a date a week after their break-up.

But she had never made it there, he reminded himself.

Had Libby really changed her mind about seeing him?

Did it even matter whether she had or not?

He stared at the phone, thinking of his own refusal to see her side of things.

'Hey,' Brendan said as he came over. 'What's up?'

'Nothing,' Alistair snapped.

Certainly he would not be discussing this with Brendan.

Later in the afternoon, he saw Brendan glance at him. 'How's Libby doing?' he asked.

'They kept her in for a couple of nights. Concussion.'

'I know that,' Brendan said. 'I meant, how has she been since discharge?'

'How the hell would I know?' Alistair said, still refusing to bring his private life in to work.

But it was a hopeless task. They all knew. The pick-up point for the cab home when Libby had been discharged from The Primary had been near the ambulance bay, and half the station seemed to have been lined up there.

Watching.

No doubt later gossiping.

Brendan soon confirmed that fact. 'I thought that was why you moved your leave? Because she went home with you?'

'No, I took her back to her flat,' Alistair corrected.

'Really?' Brendan checked as he started up the ambulance's engine. 'You left her there alone?'

Alistair said nothing.

'That's not like you…'

Alistair stared ahead.

'That was a pretty nasty head injury,' Brendan persisted. 'I would have thought that you, of all people—'

'She wanted to go home,' Alistair interjected—and then gave in. 'But obviously that couldn't work. She's staying at mine for now.'

Brendan said nothing, but Alistair could feel his questions hanging in the silence.

'In the guest room,' he added.

They did a couple of straightforward jobs, but Alistair would have far preferred they'd been complex and something he could have really got lost in, because the evening dragged on slowly. There was just too much time to think.

'Are you looking forward to your course?' Brendan asked.

'I am.' Alistair nodded, but then thought for a moment. 'Although there's a lot to sort out before I head off...'

'Yeah, I heard there's a lot of pre-study.'

Alistair had done all the pre-study, and the lectures, and his packing would take no time at all. Yet it still felt as if there was an awful lot to sort out before he disappeared for six weeks.

Away from Libby's witchery, and the spell she had cast, he was able to think clearly for the first time in a while.

It wasn't just her angry words this afternoon that were replaying in his mind, but their conversation by the canal. She'd told him about the motorbike fatality that morning, and how it had scared her. Then she'd found out about his new job... As well as worrying about the medical investigations she was going through.

He'd been so cross about her method of getting over him—had felt so let down that she'd been going out on a date when she'd had her accident—that he hadn't really addressed *why* she had ended things in the first place.

It *wasn't* the same as his father rejecting him because of his career-change.

Libby had run in fear.

Fear of losing him.

He'd had that same sense of fear on the night she'd fallen. It had overridden everything—so much so that he'd done his best to put aside the hurt and anger…so much so that she was currently in his home.

'I was watching a lecture last night,' he said, looking over to Brendan and lying through his teeth.

He hadn't been watching a lecture last night. He'd been eating curry and resisting Libby. He just wanted, possibly needed, Brendan's thoughts. The man was in a brilliant marriage after all.

'It was called *Fight, Flight, Freeze…*'

'There's plenty more Fs,' Brendan said, and glanced over as if assessing him. 'You fight…you face things…'

'Not always.'

He looked out at the dark, gloomy streets. Libby, Alistair knew, always went into flight mode. Not at work—there she dealt with things with her own brand of humour—but in her private life she ran. And who could blame her?

He'd said she was like her mother, and in all the nice ways she was, but Helen Bennett just fell apart…

No wonder Libby found it difficult to talk about the problems in her private life.

Perhaps they did need to talk about it?

Or should he wait until after the course…when she was completely better?

It was odd, because he'd spent all this week thinking they wouldn't be able to last a single night apart. Now he knew that those feelings would still be there at the end of his course.

He didn't want to leave without sorting this out.

They were heading back to base and it was nearing midnight when Alistair decided he might need a bit more advice from Brendan—because he was actually considering knocking on Libby's bedroom door and asking to discuss things with her when he got home.

Fat chance of discussing things, though, he thought, as he recalled the burn of their chemistry this morning.

If she was still at his home.

If she hadn't returned to her flat in anger.

Libby had been so angry when he'd called, and he knew she was well enough to go home.

God, he hoped she was still at his place.

He'd wanted her to stay. He'd wanted her to finally be well enough so that they could speak about what had happened between them. Only the days seemed to have raced away, and now there was the drama of Chloe—who had never felt like a drama until now. Alistair held himself to high standards and had never cheated in his life.

A text came through from Chloe, telling him she wouldn't be working for him any more.

Damn.

Then a call came in, and it was clear there would be no getting home just after midnight. Instead of signing off, they were being dispatched to a gentleman with back pain who had been waiting for an ambulance for some considerable time.

As Brendan turned at a roundabout, Alistair looked over to his colleague. 'Hey, Brendan, if you occasionally slept with someone…'

'I've only ever slept with my wife,' Brendan said proudly.

'You're no help, then.'

'Try me.'

'Okay.'

Unfortunately, he'd barely got past the description of his casual relationship with Chloe, and how that had been over ages ago, when the radio started to get busy.

They were just pulling in to their patient's house when Control contacted them again.

'Have you made patient contact?' they were asked—which was perhaps the first ominous sign that there was something big going on, because once contact had been made they couldn't be pulled from a job.

They hadn't made contact, though, and neither would they—for they were needed elsewhere.

Another call came over the radio then, and another, and another…

'Doesn't sound good,' Brendan said.

There was no more personal talk. Instead, they listened to the unfolding horror as they turned on the siren and made their way rapidly to the scene.

There would be no getting home on time and no talking to Libby tonight.

Alistair glanced at the time and saw it was almost midnight. He hoped to God that she was already in bed…hoped that Libby was oblivious to the hell he and Brendan were approaching.

It was one of those nights when people were just turning the television off before heading to bed, or closing down their computers, or hitting the *Do Not Disturb* button when a breaking news alert halted them. In Libby's case, she had packed all her things into her bag—although it had taken her far longer to do so than it had taken Alistair.

She wanted to be safely in bed, asleep, when he got home, as she knew he'd be worn out, and she wasn't sure she could manage to say she was leaving tomorrow and thank him without bursting into tears, or something equally pathetic.

She was still working on that graceful goodbye.

Her brain was back in worry mode, and it felt good to be herself again.

Perhaps she could leave a note? Though it might be better to wait until she was home, and from there send a present and card.

Send it to where, though? He would be away on his course for the next six weeks.

Or should she put her heart on the line and tell Alistair that she loved him?

Libby stood in the guest room—when she really wanted to be in his—and looked at her bag which she had so reluctantly packed.

Everything about tonight felt wrong.

Go to bed, Libby, she told herself, changing into her tartan pyjamas.

Alistair's laundry service had stopped a couple of days ago—she was well enough to do her own laundry now.

They were the same clothes she'd been wearing this morning.

Reject me again, then! Libby thought, as she buttoned them up. *But I am going to tell you I love you!*

Or should she go to bed instead?

Remembering she'd left the heating on, Libby padded down the stairs and turned it off—but now she was back to worrying about everything! Should she turn it back on and keep the house warm for him?

She was trying to decide when her phone pinged and she frowned at the news alert.

She tried to discard it, telling herself it must be wrong.

An exaggeration.

Probably nothing.

But then another alert chimed, and it was more specific this time.

Reports Confirmed...

City of London...

He'd be nowhere near there, Libby told herself, as she saw that it was just after midnight. His shift was over and he was probably on his way home.

Even so, she turned on the television and had to then work out how to operate his remote to get to the news.

And straight away she knew that the situation wasn't being exaggerated.

London was in trouble tonight.

Her hands were shaking so much that she couldn't work out how to adjust the volume for quite a while.

No.

Oh, no.

No, no, no.

Yes.

It was one of those awful nights where you don't go to bed. Instead you watch and feel ill and really kind of hate the world—or rather its inhabitants, and the awful things they do to each other at times.

Libby sat on the edge of sofa or paced, watching in horror while also keeping one ear open, hoping for the purr of his motorbike as it turned into the street and no doubt annoyed the neighbours.

As much as she hated his bike, she'd give anything to hear it right now.

But it never arrived.

A major incident had been declared, and if she hadn't been off sick she might well have been called in to work. Instead, she flicked through the channels and tried to get more news on her phone. She read that there were now unconfirmed reports of two emergency personnel injured.

She tried to keep calm and drank tea.

An awful lot of tea.

Then she burst into tears, remembering the cold kettle this morning and how Alistair had gone to work without tea.

'That'll be you…' Brendan said to Alistair as they arrived on scene and watched the Tactical Response Vehicles moving into the warm zone

They were being held back in the cold zone, as it was an extremely active crime scene and casualties would be brought out to them.

'There's a way to go before that,' Alistair said.

Their conversation was not stilted, but there were large gaps between sentences as they listened to the radio and watched the unfolding scene in silence.

'Will Alison be waiting up?' Alistair asked.

'Yes.'

'Should you call her?'

'No need,' Brendan said, pausing as the police moved a barricade and they inched their ambulance a few feet ahead.

'She'll be worried if she's up, though…' Alistair frowned.

'Of course she will be,' Brendan said. 'That's part of the job, isn't it?'

He said it so matter-of-factly, as if it was simply a matter of course, and it dawned on Alistair then that he'd never had a significant other to worry about.

He'd never had to do this job with someone worrying about him at home.

'Libby's probably asleep,' Alistair said, and realised he had named her to Brendan as the one person he was thinking of tonight. 'Otherwise there'd be a hundred missed calls.'

He looked at his phone and hoped to God that he was right and Libby had no idea what was going on.

They sat for hours, watching and waiting to help. Alistair just wanted to be in there—right in the thick of it—because it was hell being held back. Instead, he kept thinking of himself and Libby walking along the canal, and how he'd dismissed her concerns for his safety.

'We had a bit of a disagreement,' Alistair said, thinking back to this afternoon and how cross she had been. 'I was going to talk to her about it when I got home...' He looked at his phone, still debating whether to text and risk waking her.

'Alison and I have a deal,' Brendan said.

'What's that?'

'I never leave for work on a row.'

Alistair stared ahead, less than soothed by the fact that he and Libby had never had that row. Oh, at first it had been for all the right reasons, but in recent days it had been nothing but wounded pride holding him back.

He thought back to this morning.

They could have made love, and instead he'd walked away and closed the door on her.

'I don't need to call her because nothing's been left unsaid,' Brendan nattered on, and where he once might have sounded smug in his marital bliss, to Alistair right now Brendan sounded wise.

Everything between him and Libby had been left unsaid.

But Brendan didn't get to finish his recipe for wedded bliss, because there was the sudden sound of rapid gunfire, followed by a pounding on the ambulance, and it took a second for them both to register that their vehicle was under attack.

'Get back!'

The police were waving their arms and shouting, and the bricks or bottles that were hammering the vehicle disappeared as Brendan swiftly reversed. Then the rear doors opened, and for split-second Alistair did not know whether or not they were being invaded.

'GSW to the neck!' he heard.

It was a female police officer, literally dragging in a colleague, and Alistair got straight to work.

'Good man,' he said, as the young policeman pressed a cloth to his own wound while his colleague did all she could to assist.

That his bleeding wasn't arterial was the only reason the patient was alive.

New crime scenes were being established, and their ambulance was now considered part of the hot zone. It was the most volatile situation Alistair had ever been in. There were still missiles being aimed at the ambulance, even as Brendan skilfully backed them further out. The policewoman pressed on her colleague's wound now, as Alistair administered oxygen and secured an IV. She helped squeeze through fluids as Alistair did all he could to keep his patient alive while Brendan alerted the nearest hospital.

'Gunshot wound to neck,' Brendan told them. 'GCS?' he called to Alistair, wanting more information.

'Was twelve—now nine,' Alistair called back, and relayed the young policeman's deteriorating vials.

In the moments just preceding his limbs had become flaccid, his eyes were no longer opening, and he was making no attempt to vocalise now. The only sound coming from the patient was the ringing of his phone in his jacket— a loved one, Alistair was sure, desperate to know he was safe.

When they arrived, the hospital was in full major incident mode, and the patient was rushed through to the experts waiting to receive him. But there was no time to follow this patient. They were already being summoned back...

* * *

As Libby waited for the kettle to boil, she tried to tell herself that Alistair was surely fine—and that what was happening tonight was the reason she could not let herself love him.

Except it was a ridiculous argument because she already did.

She already loved him.

It was like a baptism of fire, Libby told herself.

Excuse the dreadful pun, she told herself as she walked into the lounge and an awful image came on the screen.

'In further developments,' the reporter said, 'emergency vehicles are now coming under attack…'

Oh, God…stay calm, stay calm.

They all had to.

Alistair had to.

So she would too.

But when she wasn't at work she was dreadful at it, and she watched in horror as the news got worse and worse…

It would be unfair to call him with her hysterics now—though of course she'd be directed to leave a voicemail.

Would it be too much to text him? Just so she could have the opportunity to say *I love you*? Libby pondered. Or rather *I love you, I love you, I love you, I love you, I love you, I love you, I love you, I love you…* Maybe five hundred times over—which was strange because she hadn't yet said it once…

All that tea meant a lot of dashes upstairs to the loo. And on one trip came the dreadful thought that she hadn't even seen inside his bedroom.

It was wrong, perhaps, but given the scary circumstances Libby decided she was going to cross boundaries.

She pushed open the pale wooden door and turned on the light.

Dark curtains were closed and the navy sheets that had

in part caused their row this afternoon had been replaced by willow-green ones and a matching cover.

The wooden floorboards were softened by a dark rug, and the suitcase she had only seen from the hall still lay on the floor, one side filled with folders and manuals, the other waiting to be filled with clothes.

Lucky the patients who had him, Libby thought.

Why, oh, why hadn't she waited until she'd calmed down when she'd found out about his new work?

Why had she raced in and ended things?

Because she was as impulsive as he was sensible…

So impulsive that she was tempted again to peel off her tartan pyjamas and climb into his bed and wait for him there.

Hardly a dignified exit!

And not the graceful goodbye she had been practising all afternoon.

And anyway, she had denied them both her right to do that.

Now she was a guest in his home.

An inconvenience foisted upon him.

The user of newly bought guest towels.

She thought of his words on the night he'd brought her back to her flat after her stay in the hospital. *'You dumped me. You don't get to share a bed with me.'*

And how he'd rather miss a nail-biting football match to load the dishwasher and head upstairs than get cosy with her.

Tears threatened to come. So she did the right thing and turned off the light and walked out. She padded downstairs and watched as the police stormed a building and shattering noises caused the tears to come tumbling from her eyes.

She felt a desperate need to get fresh air, despite being in no danger herself.

She opened up the front door and gulped in icy lungsful of fresh, cold air. She peered up at the dark sky and then down to the pot of daffodils that were still only shoots. She could not bear it that they might flower unseen, and that had a far darker meaning now, as she forced herself to face the stark reality that he might never return.

She scanned the street for the lights of his bike, willing him to come home.

Nothing.

Then finally it was over.

Libby stood in the lounge as the reporter informed her that the situation was now under control, though the breaking dawn would be met with breaking hearts for too many. The world was a crueller place, and London was grey in the silence of the morning.

And still she didn't know how he was, or whether she was overreacting, or how she was even supposed to be...

All Libby knew was that she loved him.

Then she jumped as she saw there was a police car pulling up outside. She gave a cry of relief when she saw Alistair getting out.

She fled upstairs to her bed and still did not know how to be.

Was it even her place to be upset?

Should she pretend to be asleep, as if she hadn't seen it and been up all night worrying? Or should she smile and casually enquire, *How was your night?* Or should she wish him good morning and pack her bags and walk out?

Because maybe she'd been right all along and she simply wasn't up to being in love with someone who did this kind of job? Someone who was actively trying to be present at this type of scenario on every scale.

She heard his footsteps on the stairs and did not know if he would head straight for his bedroom or not. Did he even know there was frantic love burning behind the door of the guest room of his home?

She wanted to shout out to him, to run to him, to drape herself around him in relief. But perhaps that wasn't what he needed after such a night.

Then the door to her room was pushed open without a warning knock, and she was too late to close her eyes and pretend to be asleep.

'Hey.'

He was at the door, and though he was often pale after a long shift, this morning he was as white as a ghost.

'How are you?' he asked.

'Fine,' Libby said in a rather high voice. 'How are you?'

'Fine,' Alistair said.

'That's good.'

She stared at his drained, exhausted face and knew she did not want to foist her tumbled emotions on him.

'What did you do last night?' he asked.

'Me?' Libby said. 'Oh, the usual. I watched a film on my laptop with a bar of chocolate and then I dozed off...' she lied, playing for time as she floated in sheer relief that he was safely home.

'What film did you watch?'

It was such an odd thing to ask, given the night he had surely had, but perhaps he just wanted to speak about something normal. Or possibly he was testing her, seeing if she'd had the mettle to stay calm or had instead been frantically pacing the floor.

Which she had been, of course.

'*Wuthering Heights.*' Another lie, of course, but it was a very safe lie, given that she knew the film back to front and inside out as she had watched it so very many times—not that Alistair could possibly know.

'Oh?'

'It was actually quite good.'

'Quite good?' he enquired.

'Mmm…' she said. 'I remember reading the book at school.'

Alistair loved how hard she was trying to lie.

He loved everything about getting to come home to her: the mugs on the coffee table in the lounge…the balls of tissues too.

He knew that she must have leapt into bed when he'd arrived home. Not only had he seen the twitch of the lounge curtains, he had also felt the warmth of her being downstairs, while it was cold up here. There was no silver foil from a chocolate bar, and her bed was far too neat for a night spent beneath its covers. The curtains hadn't even been closed…

'Although,' Libby mused, elaborating upon her lie, as if she really had been tucked up in bed with chocolate and watching the film on her computer last night, 'there was a part that wasn't quite as I'd have played it…'

His lips wanted to twitch into a smile. After a night spent in hell it was so nice to step out of it for a moment, to be here rather than out there. So he lingered in her will-o'-the-wisp world for a moment longer. He wanted more of the light she brought to his life.

'What do you mean, it wasn't how you'd have played it? I'm not with you.'

'I mean, if I were the actress playing Cathy I'd have done it differently…' Her green eyes met his.

'How so?' he asked.

'You know the part when Cathy says, "I am Heathcliff"?'

'No,' he said. 'Not off-hand. What about it?'

'When I read the book at school—*ages* ago—I seem to

remember that I imagined Cathy declaring it loudly, but in the film she says it quietly.'

'The film you were watching last night?'

'Yes.'

'How would you have played it?'

He was dying to know, and of course Libby obliged.

She leant forward. 'This is how she went…' Libby dropped her voice so she was soft-spoken. '"I am Heath-cliff…" Whereas I think it should have been more…' she knelt up and spread out her arms '…more adamant. "I *am* Heathcliff…"'

It was a burst of pure emotion and it was aimed only at him.

'Actually, I think she should have risen to stand…' she did the very same, '…and loudly declared, *"I. Am. Heath-cliff!"*'

Libby almost toppled over with the effort of her own performance and he caught her.

'I believe you,' he said, and pulled her off the bed and into his arms.

'Please don't. Because I'm lying…'

And then she was kissing his cold, cold face, and he was holding her so tight, and he didn't seem to mind the kisses she rained upon him.

'I haven't been watching the film! I just know it back to front, inside out…'

'I meant, I believe you that you would be foolish enough to turn around and try to walk down an escalator—and, yes, I believe you that you don't check your post. I mean, clearly you do stand on the bed…'

'I do!' She was guilty as charged, and happily so, now that he finally believed her. 'I'm so, so glad you're home.'

She rested her head on his wide shoulder and breathed

him in, just nestled her head there in the best place to be, as he turned and kissed her cheek. It was a small, tender kiss that tasted of the tears she'd been crying, which she had tried not to reveal.

'I'm so relieved you're home.'

'I know,' Alistair said as he held her. 'Last night I thought a lot about how you were feeling, and I decided that I'm a selfish bastard to do this job and not consider the impact—'

'No, no, no! I'm neurotic.'

'Never change,' he said.

'Nor you.'

'Do you want to see my bedroom?'

'I peeked last night.'

He carried her into his bedroom and pulled back the sheet and placed her in his bed. But she had so many questions.

'Why did the police bring you home, Alistair?'

'Because I asked them to,' he said as he undid his boots. It seemed to her a very long time since he'd put them on. 'I went to check on a patient I'd brought in…a colleague of theirs.'

'How were they?'

'Just out of Theatre,' Alistair said. 'Alive. To be honest, I didn't think he would be, and nor did his partner.' He was quiet for a moment. 'Anyway, I said to her it would be so stupid to get killed on my way home after a shift like that and she gave me a lift.'

He turned and looked at Libby.

'Why do you have so many keys?'

Libby blinked. It seemed like such an odd question. 'I have Mum and Dad's. My car. My friend Olivia's, in case she gets locked out. The theatre at home…' She grimaced. 'I ought to give those back. Why do you want to know?'

'Because I want to know *you*.' He didn't look at her directly. 'I'll give up the bike, but not the job.'

'You don't have to—but thank you very much if you do,' Libby said. 'The only thing I *will* ask you to give up is your cleaner.'

'Done. Last night Chloe fired me,' he said. 'Although she texted this morning to check I was okay.'

'Grr…' Libby said, and then took a breath. 'Fair enough.' Then she looked at him, standing there, and her voice was serious. '*Are* you all right?'

'Yes.'

'Is Brendan?'

'He's okay. A few of us went for breakfast and had a bit of a debrief. Brendan's been great, actually. He gives good advice.'

'I'm pleased you can talk to him.' Libby took another breath, unsure if he wanted to discuss last night now. 'Do you want to—?'

'Not now,' he cut in. 'I want to sleep.' Then he looked at her. 'How about you? Are you okay?'

'Yes,' Libby said.

She looked at him standing there. He seemed a bit stunned, really. She thought of the toll his job must take on him. Yet he took it so willingly. As well as that, he loved it—and she loved him, so that was that.

So, yes, she was okay, too, because she would far rather be here than anywhere else in the world.

And then he changed her world all over again.

'We're getting married,' Alistair said as he took off his uniform.

'Are we?' Libby smiled, not believing him for a moment, certain he must just be on some sort of post-dramatic night duty high.

'We are,' he affirmed, and his tone was so absolute, and

his eyes so intent, that everything that had been shaking inside Libby since that first news alert had pinged in suddenly stilled.

'Married?' she checked.

'If you'll have me.'

She would marry him this second, right now, if she could, without hesitation or doubt.

It was Alistair's certainty she was scared to believe in.

Which was odd, because it was his very certainty that she relied upon.

She was scared of him retracting it later, when his common sense had invaded and he'd thought it through.

'Alistair...' She flailed, attempting to be the sensible one even when she didn't want to be! 'We've known each other...what? Three weeks? What happened to measure twice, cut once? Or look before you leap?'

'Is that a no?'

'Of course not. It's a complete yes from me. But what if I can't get pregnant? Or what if you're just feeling all messed up from last night...?'

'I'm incredibly clear *thanks* to last night,' Alistair corrected. 'I thought we had time on our side—that I'd find out about your jangly prison warder keys and such. I was hoping that we could maybe pick things up in six weeks... sort it out once you were well. I was starting to realise we'd still be feeling the same. And then last night showed me we might not have time, and also that this is love.'

Libby swallowed. His love was everything she craved— but not if it was just a knee-jerk response to last night's events. Not if it was just words that he might later come to regret.

'Alistair, I'm worried that you're—'

'Libby,' he cut in, 'whether or not I love you is one thing you *never* have to worry about.'

To a constant worrier, that was the nicest thing he could possibly say.

'When they rushed you off for your head CT I hated not being your next of kin. And I think, last night, you kind of *were* my next of kin…'

'I was. I am…' Not legally, perhaps, but they were the closest person to each other in the world, and she had held him in her heart all night.

He was the person she first and foremost needed to know, because his heart was beating in time with hers, because he would be there beside her even when he was physically distant.

This love took nothing from your love for others—it simply elevated one person to The One.

And the one she loved was climbing into bed, where he lay with his eyes closed as she slipped off her pyjamas and they rolled into each other. He felt like a block of ice, so cold that he made her thighs jerk when one of his legs slid in between hers and the other wrapped around her.

'Ow,' she said, because he really was cold, but she clamped her thighs around his all the same. Then, wrapped in each other, they let the horror of the night recede and return, then recede again, like the tide going out.

'Can you believe,' Alistair said sleepily, with his eyes closed, 'while all this was going on some bastard swiped my daffodils…?'

'Oh, that was me,' Libby readily admitted. 'I thought that if anything happened to you… Well, a condom box isn't much to show for things, so I decided I would be keeper of your daffodils.'

He gave a low laugh and opened his beautiful brown eyes to meet hers. 'You took them?'

'They're by my packed bag, in the wardrobe in the guest room.'

'You actually packed?'

'Extremely reluctantly.' Libby nodded. 'I've also stolen your poppy tray.'

'We'll unpack it all later,' Alistair said. 'And we'll sort out your flat…' He couldn't think of all the logistics right now. 'I don't know when…' He looked at her then. 'Are you going to be lonely for the next few weeks?'

'No,' Libby said, 'so long as I can sleep here.'

'Of course.'

And then she was serious, her heart still beating a little too wildly in an odd mixture of fears glimpsed and elation. And how lucky she was to be here.

'I wanted to text you last night and tell you I love you, but I didn't want to add to the strain of what was going on…'

'Thank you,' he said. 'I wanted to do the same, while at the same time I was hoping you were asleep.'

'No.' Libby shook her head. 'I think the fact that I love you has been my problem all along.'

'Loving me was the problem?'

'Yes.' It was hard to explain, but she tried. 'I didn't just fall in love with you, Alistair, I crashed into it. I dived into it. And when I came up for air, I didn't know what had happened. I couldn't explain it to myself, let alone to my friends. I don't expect you to understand—'

'Oh, but I do. Do you know why we stayed at yours for four days?' Alistair asked.

'Because we were too happy to move?'

'In part. But I had a feeling that once I brought you to

my place, you would only ever go back to that flat to pack up your things and bring them here. For good. I needed to think. But being in your sofa-bed was too nice for me to do that. Then, when I got home, I still felt the same. So I called, asking you to come over. I knew how I felt about you. And then you dumped me.' He smiled a smile that told her all was forgiven. 'Seems I was right. You're here and you're not leaving.'

'Never,' Libby said as his hand moved down past her ribs to her hips, stroking her skin.

The warmth and togetherness of them was restorative. His touch sent a delicious shiver through her and her touching him did the same. His forearms, his flat stomach... She touched him lightly, so relieved he was there. She held him, stroked him, as they explored each other without haste. They stared at each other in the false night they had created by closing out the world.

The glitter in his eyes, the intensity of his stare, was something she had seen before, of that she was certain. And Libby knew she had been bathed in that same glow before. They really had loved each other, even then...

Their mouths met softly and they kissed in a slow kiss, huddled beneath the covers, their tongues teasing. His hand slid under her and then he pulled her right into him, his kiss rougher and more thorough.

And deeper too.

He rolled her, his kisses chasing her onto her back, and Libby relished the weight of him and how it felt to be pinned down by love. There was no need to hold back their constant desire and no feelings to resist.

And they really were tearing up their rulebooks, because she parted for him readily, and he didn't even attempt to reach for protection.

Libby was so ready that when he squeezed in she moaned with bliss, her stomach curling as she arched her back.

His breath was hot in her ear. 'You feel so good...' he told her, moving slowly.

'So do you.'

Oh, he did. He felt so, so good.

He moved up on his forearms and his face was over hers. Libby reached with her mouth for his, but found his strong shoulder instead, and she tasted his salty skin as he glided and moved within her, taking her, driving her on, ever closer.

They moved together in a slow, deep rhythm and Libby tried to keep her eyes open, so she could see how he looked with his eyes closed in pleasure.

Then she felt a spread of heat the length of her spine, which he'd traced that first time, and it was Libby who closed her eyes. Even her hands tightened in tension. And then came the final swell of him, and his breathless shout that brought her home.

'Oh, Alistair...'

Her orgasm was fading, but the heat and the love and the emotion remained, and she cried on him just a little, in giddy relief that he was here.

'It's okay,' he said.

'I know it is.'

These were happy tears, and so they lay together, catching their breath, his hand stroking her arm. Coming back to the world together...

Alistair's phone was ringing, again and again.

'Turn it off,' Libby said.

He went to do so, but then he must have changed his mind because he started texting.

'Alistair!' She was affronted. 'How can you be on your phone when—?'

'It's from my father.' He showed her the message.

He had texted to say that he was proud of him.

'Oh…' She felt her eyes well with tears. 'Call him!'

'I've already spoken to him. He saw the news when he woke up and called me.'

'I'm so pleased.' Libby smiled, thinking how sometimes it took something terrible to happen, or almost happen, to wake people up and make them realise what was truly important in life.

'They want to meet you,' he said.

'Ooh…' Libby said. 'We really are doing this, aren't we?'

'We really are.'

And now poor Alistair really was having a time of it. Because when the phone rang, instead of checking the caller ID or the number, as he usually would, he answered it—only to find himself naked in bed and on a video call with her father.

'I've been trying to call Libby,' he said. 'You weren't caught up in that mess last night, were you?'

Then he must have recognised the curls on the pillow next to Alistair.

'What the hell…?'

It was Libby who rescued the situation. 'Dad!' She took the phone. 'Alistair and I are getting married, so you don't have to kill him. I love you and Mum so much, but he's had a dreadful night, so I have to go now…'

'But, Libby, you hardly know him.'

'I know that I love him,' Libby said. 'Kisses!' She turned off his phone. 'You have to marry me now.'

'I do.'

'I'm going to make you a cup of tea,' she said. 'Then

we're going to sleep, and I might even go and get doughnuts later. How does that sound?'

'Perfect.'

Indeed it did.

EPILOGUE

'I THINK I'M in labour.'

Unusually, Alistair was running late for work, but of course he halted and turned around, even though Libby had said this *many* times before.

'Why do you think that?'

'I've got backache,' Libby told him, although admittedly she always thought that. 'Maybe the sex triggered it.'

'Could you perhaps have backache because you're thirty-six weeks pregnant?' Alistair suggested, stroking her very pregnant belly for a full ten minutes and feeling a couple of kicks but no contractions. 'Backache is normal, Libby.'

'I know it is, but...'

It had taken three years of trying, and now that their baby was soon to be here every day apart from it felt a day too long. Maybe her conviction that she was in labour really was just wishful thinking.

She looked up at him. 'Do you have to go to work?'

Of course he did.

She was the girl who cried wolf. Libby knew that as he gave her a kiss and headed off to dive into the underground.

This felt different, though.

Except the midwife at the hospital didn't sound concerned when she called a couple of hours later.

'No contractions?' the midwife checked.

'No.'

'And baby's moving?'

'A lot,' Libby agreed, watching a tiny foot push at her stomach.

'Your waters are intact?'

'They are.'

Given that in recent days she had called the hospital rather a lot, Libby already knew the questions the midwife would ask.

Everything was fine, she was reassured. In fact, the midwife pretty much said the same as Alistair had—that backache was normal, she had an antenatal appointment tomorrow, and she was to call back if anything changed.

Nothing changed.

Her mum called, and Libby airily said that all was well. 'I'm not due for another four weeks,' Libby said. She certainly didn't tell her about her backache.

Olivia called and patiently listened to her symptoms.

'We can't wait to come and see you when the baby is here,' she said.

Olivia had visited them only last week, with little Timothy. They'd stayed in the guest room and Alistair had happily babysat when she and Olivia went out. Possibly he'd agreed to it to get an evening's relative peace! Libby's new theatre group had decided on their next production…and it was *that* one. *The* one. And if Libby didn't get the leading lady part—well, she'd possibly die.

This morning, Libby updated her friend on the new production.

'They've announced the auditions,' she told Olivia. 'And they're holding them on the baby's due date. I'm sure it was done deliberately, so that I couldn't be there.'

'Libby!'

'No, I'm quite sure. Well, I don't care if I give birth mid-audition. I'm going to be there.'

'Oh, I'm sure you are!' Olivia laughed.

Libby found that she was pacing and unsettled, so she had a lovely long bath and wrapped herself in jade-green towels… Ha-ha! And then she thought about a morning snack, because apart from the baby and the auditions she thought about food more than anything else.

She got on with setting up her poppy tray, and caught sight of her reflection in the French windows. She was back to feeling like a duck again. Not because she felt drab and plain, just because of the way she was waddling around.

Libby thought back to the last time she'd compared herself to a duck—sitting in that café by the canal, so certain she'd blown things. So certain that it was all down to her, not knowing that Alistair was working it out too.

Always.

And then she stopped thinking about ducks and fond memories as her stomach tightened into a rock and pulled at her back.

If this was the start of labour, then she was getting an epidural.

'Does Libby think she's in labour again?' asked Trent, because Alistair's phone was buzzing *again*.

Alistair might be the new guy in the Tactical Response Unit, but they all knew about Libby and the upcoming birth!

Alistair listened to her symptoms.

'*One* contraction?' he checked.

'You can be *so* condescending,' Libby snarled, and hung up on him.

Her tone left him frowning.

Libby didn't snarl. Well, not often. Only when something serious was going on…

He called her straight back and was met with a shaky announcement.

'I'm in labour.'

'Okay,' he said. 'Tell me what's happening.'

'Alistair, my waters have just broken…' She started groaning.

'What?'

'You have to go because I need to call an ambulance. I want to push…'

'I'll call it in,' Alistair said. 'Libby, try not to push…' he attempted, but she'd already gone.

Oh, God…

Libby was thinking exactly the same!

Well, a slightly more exaggerated version!

Oh. My. God!

Another contraction gripped her, even stronger than the one before. So much so that she wasn't even able to make it into the hall to open the front door. Instead, she dropped to the floor by the washing machine.

But Alistair had called it in, and Libby got more than an ambulance.

She got Lina coming round the back via the gate, then entering through the French doors of the kitchen.

'Hi, Libby.' Lina crouched down beside her and did a sweeping assessment. 'I'm going to open the front door and Brendan's getting all the equipment. Okay?'

Libby nodded.

And it wasn't just Brendan—there was the sound of a back-up crew arriving too.

As well as that, all the neighbours had come out to see what on earth was going on at number thirty-five!

And then Libby got a Tactical Response Vehicle too!

Alistair came charging down the hall and was treated to the sight of Brendan's back, in his kitchen, and Lina on her knees with Libby against the washing machine.

There was no delay button for this—Alistair could see the dark hair of his baby's head, already crowning!

'Told you I was in labour!' Libby accused, even as her arms simultaneously reached for him.

'You did,' Alistair agreed as he crouched down by her side.

'She's going to make you pay for this, mate,' Brendan said, 'for the rest of your life.'

'I know,' Alistair said, and kissed her very red face.

He looked over to Lina, who was about to deliver his baby, and she looked up at him with a quiet offer. Did he want to take over? But no… He was needed at the other end.

'Libby, listen to Lina,' he said. 'You're amazing…'

'Please can we call him—?'

'We are *not* calling him Heathcliff,' Alistair said. 'No matter how much you cry.'

'You really don't know what you're having?' Brendan enquired.

'We don't,' Libby said through gritted teeth.

Alistair did.

He'd cheated, and was very quietly confident that there would no need to deny Libby her dreadful choice of name for a boy…

'I'm scared,' Libby admitted through chattering teeth.

She was terrified, and yet so excited and so pleased that Alistair was there, holding her tight as she did her very best not to push, so their baby could make a slightly slower entrance than the one it wanted.

'Okay,' Lina said. 'Well done. The head's out…'

She was shivering, and too scared to look, so she just breathed in Alistair's scent, and heard his heart thumping as fast as hers in his chest, and he didn't show, not for a second, that he was anything other than completely calm.

And then Libby gave a little sob as their baby was delivered.

She looked down at the beautiful dark-haired baby who lay sprawled on her stomach like a little washed-up frog.

'She's here!' Alistair said.

And Libby watched her baby turn pink as she stroked her stunned little face, then turned to Alistair and kissed the proud husband and father.

'She is…'

It hadn't been easy to get to this day—not easy at all. Some miracles took time. But finally here was their baby.

Libby heard a sound that she never had before—a single sob from Alistair.

He attempted recovery with a sniff, but then had to press his fingers in his eyes as his colleagues and friends all congratulated them.

'Catherine,' Alistair said, and very deftly cut the cord, enabling Libby to scoop their long-awaited and so very gorgeous baby right up to her.

Together they welcomed her to the world, touching her fingers and watching the curl of her toes, gazing into milky blue eyes as they blinked their first blinks and her rosebud mouth pursed.

'Is she breathing okay?' Libby asked, ever anxious.

It was their little girl who answered that.

Tiny, pink, squirmy and now cross, she opened her mouth and started letting out indignant screams, already searching to be fed.

'Cathy!' Libby cooed as she gazed upon her daughter.

'Catherine,' Alistair corrected again, and everyone else, including Libby, suppressed a smile.

All present knew that Alistair didn't have a hope of winning that one…

* * * * *

HEALED BY THEIR DOLPHIN ISLAND BABY

MARION LENNOX

MILLS & BOON

This book is dedicated to Lorraine
and to Bill and Mandy and Scott, who were with
David and me on our first ever tropical island escapade.
We had the most glorious time.
Thank you for the most glorious friendship.

PROLOGUE

'BEN, THIS IS my fiancée, Dr Anya Greer.'

Mathew's chest puffed up with satisfaction. All was well in his world, and he was pleased to let his colleague from university days know it.

'Anya, this is Dr Ben Duncan, who's kindly agreed to act as locum for us during our honeymoon.'

Dr Ben Duncan had had little to do with Dr Mathew Cummins since they'd trained together, but he knew him to be a skilled, if slightly pompous, clinician and he was interested in meeting the woman he was about to marry.

But why did the realisation that Mathew's bride was gorgeous surprise him?

The woman smiling a greeting had, he gathered, just come from performing a minor procedure in Theatre and she was dressed in green hospital scrubs. She was almost a head shorter than him. Her shiny black hair was caught back in a sensible knot but curls were wisping outward. Her skin was warmly honey-coloured, her smile was wide and her eyes twinkled at him as she held out her hand.

'I'm very pleased to meet you.' Her voice was soft and welcoming. 'I hope Merriwood doesn't give you too much trouble while we're away.'

And as he took her hand he was caught by the last thing he'd expected. A stab of...jealousy?

What the…? Where had that come from?

Mathew could keep marriage, he thought, jerking himself back from unwanted sensations, almost in shock. He wanted nothing to do with relationships. The ache in his back, the weakness in his left leg—surely they were enough to remind him of the disaster emotional connections caused. The tragedy of his marriage had been the result of just such instant attraction. A moment's impulse. A lifetime of regret.

Mathew was doing it much better, he told himself. Apparently he'd known Anya since childhood and they'd been friends for ever. This marriage, Mathew had told Ben—and yep, there'd been pomposity in this statement as well—was based on sense and a shared commitment to the good of the town.

Wow. To marry a woman this gorgeous because of sense and a commitment to the town…

Um, stupid thought. No doubt there'd be hot sex in there as well, and years of kids and fun and family.

Meanwhile he'd held Anya's hand for just a bit too long. He released it and backed away, leaning heavily on his cane.

'Congratulations,' he said, somewhat inanely. 'I wish you both joy.'

'Thank you,' she said, still smiling. But had the twinkle faded a little as she glanced at Mathew? 'I'm sure we'll have it. In spades.'

Joy.

Anya had finished work for the day—well, for three weeks, until she and Mathew returned from their honeymoon. The staff had waved her off with excitement. When she reached the car park someone had wrapped her little sedan in streamers and tied tin cans to the back. She considered removing them, but then decided people would love seeing her car tootle through the town wrapped like this, jangling loudly enough to bring them all out to see.

The town would love this.

Wasn't that what this was all about?

No, she told herself firmly. It was about a wedding. Joy. She and Mathew, for ever and ever.

So why, as she drove home, was she thinking of a tall, lean, dark-eyed guy leaning heavily on a cane, smiling at her with warmth, holding her hand as he'd smiled? She could still almost feel that hold.

Was this last moment panic, a stupid, fleeting thought that there were more men out there? Other men than Mathew?

Oh, get a grip. She turned the corner of her street and her mum was out on the lawn waiting for her. Someone must have warned her that her daughter would be driving home in style. Neighbours were out, too, laughing and cheering as she emerged from her decorated car.

Everyone was so happy about this wedding.

And so was she, she told herself.

Joy. It was there for the asking. A happy ever after with Mathew.

The feel of a strange doctor's hand in hers…

That was last-minute nerves, she told herself. Forget it. She had a wedding to prepare for.

And back at the hospital…

'Come out with us tonight,' Mathew urged Ben. 'It won't be a wild buck's night, just Dad and my uncles and a couple of mates I can depend on not to try and get me drunk.' He glanced at Ben's cane. 'I figure you're the same. If you're still on painkillers you won't be drinking.'

'I'm not,' Ben said shortly. 'But thanks, no.'

'Oh, I understand,' Mathew said, suddenly contrite. 'It's

only been twelve months since you lost Rihanna. You'll hardly be wanting to think about weddings. You go to bed, mate. Your apartment kitchen has the basics, but I can ask Beth, our hospital cook, to send something more substantial.'

'I'm okay.' Ben's face tightened. 'I can look after myself.'

'Yeah, but…you know you only have to ask. One thing I've prided myself on, the staff here are trained to be kind. Anything you need…'

'Thanks, but no,' Ben said, and managed to swallow the rest of his thoughts.

Anything he needed?

He did *not* need kindness.

CHAPTER ONE

'IT'S TIME TO GO, sweetheart.'

Twenty-four hours later it was, indeed, time to go. Anya took one last look at the reflection in her mirror, and it was all she could do not to grimace.

This wasn't her. Her dress was a mass of white satin, with a glittering overlay of silver toile. Her curls had been skilfully arranged to cascade from a central silver tiara, loaned by her future mother-in-law, and the cosmetics applied by the local beautician—free of charge—were making her face feel—and look—as if it might crack at any minute.

The whole image made her feel like a picture in a birthday cake book she'd been shown before her seventh birthday.

'Choose a cake, sweetheart,' her mother had told her. *'You can have any cake you like, but Mrs Olsen says she's aching to make Ballroom Beauty.'*

Mrs Olsen was the lady who'd organised discreet dropoffs of secondhand clothes whenever they were needed. Anya had longed for the fire engine cake in the 'For Boys' section' of the book, but even at seven she'd known her duty. Her birthday cake had therefore been a gorgeous sugary version of Ballroom Beauty, complete with plastic doll's head sticking out the top.

And Anya had been…grateful.

Life, for Anya, had been a long exercise in being grateful. She'd wanted to join the Sea Scouts, but 'Mrs Grayson says you can join her ballet class for free and it's on the same night'. She'd ached for a puppy for her twelfth birthday, but Mayor Cummins and his son Mathew had turned up a week before, bearing a kitten. 'Our Tabby's had a litter of six, and we knew your littlie wanted a pet.'

Anya's mother, Reyna, had been an 'outsider', a bride from the Philippines. Mike Greer, Australian tourist, had meet her when she was halfway through her university course, and their unplanned pregnancy had seen Mike bring a shocked, disoriented bride back to Merriwood. Reyna had been madly in love, but she'd known no one and she'd spoken little English.

The community, however, had rallied to the cause, and when Mike went back to his job as a long-distance truck driver the town had embraced her. When Mike had died in a fiery highway crash, leaving a financially destitute wife and small daughter, that support had magnified tenfold.

Anya had thus been raised to be unendingly grateful. Even her medical degree was cause for gratitude. She'd had the marks, she'd won a scholarship, but her mother's distress at Anya's need to study in Sydney meant that she'd still needed support.

Once again, the town had rallied, assuring Reyna they'd be there for her. Her teachers had assured Reyna that university holidays were long, that Anya would sail through medicine and be home in no time. She could come home, practice medicine in Merriwood and live happily ever after. Plus that nice boy Mathew Cummins—son of the kitten-giver—had left town to study medicine three years before and he'd look out for her.

He had, indeed, looked out for her.

Mathew had been super-kind, Anya conceded. He'd

made that first frightening year as a cash-strapped country kid into a success.

She'd loved medicine, and when Mathew invited her to come home to Merriwood to join him at Merriwood Hospital, when her mother, when Mathew's parents, when practically every person in Merriwood had assumed both Mathew and Anya would practice medicine together here—well, why not?

Plus her mother's health was failing. A type one diabetic since childhood, Reyna's one pregnancy had almost been a disaster, and long-term complications meant she was coping with dialysis three times a week. A kidney transplant had failed and she now also had heart issues. The community was caring for her, however, as they'd always cared for her, and Anya was endlessly grateful.

So why not agree? Come home and be a doctor in Merriwood? Yes, she would.

And she'd marry Mathew.

It was funny how she'd never split those options in her head, though. It was only now, staring at the billowing folds of the gown the town's sewing bee had made for her, that she was thinking suddenly, stupidly—sadly?—of that fire engine cake. Of the load of obligations she owed Mathew.

And weirdly…still of that handshake. A doctor called Ben?

Um…no. Ridiculous.

'Sweetheart, you can be ten minutes late but no more.' Her mother's arm was around her waist. She was beaming into the mirror. For her mum this was a dream come true. 'Let's go.'

Her mother deserved this day, Anya thought, and mentally squared her shoulders. Right, let's get this over with.

And then she wondered if a bride should be thinking

such thoughts on her wedding day. And why was she thinking them now?

It wasn't as if she didn't want to marry Mathew. He was
a nice man, endlessly kind. He was a great country doctor. They'd set up the best practice and her mum would be
so proud.

So would the whole town.

This wedding itself was yet another act of kindness.
Mathew's sister had done the flowers—and wow, Anya's
bouquet was gorgeous. His mum's friends were decorating
the church and hall, and Mathew's best friend from school,
Jeanie Ray, was doing the catering.

That was a bit of a risk, though, Anya thought. Jeanie
had just opened her own catering business and Anya wasn't
too sure of her capabilities. With Mathew's parents inviting
almost the whole town to a pre-wedding lunch, with the reception to follow, the catering needs were huge.

'But it's such a great opportunity,' Mathew had told
her, reproachful that she should question his decision. 'It'll
launch her business like nothing else can, and she's giving
us a cut rate. We should be grateful.'

How many times had Anya heard that line? It had been
all she could do not to wince.

And Anna had thought…if you weren't marrying the
charity kid, would you want your inexperienced friend to
do the catering?

But Anya *was* the charity kid, and she couldn't argue.

That was what this wedding was all about, Anya decided as she saw trouble in her mother's face and gave her
a reassuring hug. Somehow it seemed a thank you for this
whole community, and Mathew was a part of it. He loved
her—she knew he did—but she'd long ago realised there
was a part of him that revelled in do-gooding.

Well, so what? It was good to be marrying someone who was kind, and the thought of not marrying him…the reproach that'd follow…her mother's devastation…

For heaven's sake, what was she thinking? She took a deep breath, steadied and smiled down into her mother's face. And then she hesitated. Reyna looked…pale? Washed out?

'Mum, are you okay?'

Reyna glanced into the mirror and winced. 'I'm okay,' she assured her daughter. 'My tummy has butterflies, but why wouldn't it? My only daughter, marrying. I'm so proud. But I shouldn't have agreed to let Myra Stevens do my make-up. She's made me look pale.'

Hmm. The doctor in Anya looked a little longer at her mum, thinking, yes, she was wearing unaccustomed make-up, but her eyes seemed shadowed and a bit too big for her face. But then, her mum had been so nervous about today. So happy.

As she was. She was marrying Mathew. She was heading for happy ever after.

Do it!

'Okay, Mum, let's go.'

'You know I want grandbabies,' Reyna said as they settled into the limousine Mathew's dad had organised. 'Do you think you might start trying straight away?'

'Straight away!'

'Well, you know, my kidneys,' her mum said diffidently, fussing over the arrangement of her daughter's Cinderella-type gown. There was even a hoop under it! 'Oh, Anya, you're making me so happy.'

But Anya's attention was caught. 'What about your kidneys? Everything's stable, isn't it? That visit to the specialist while I was away… You told me everything was fine. Mum…'

'I *am* fine,' her mother said resolutely. 'Everything's fine. Everything's wonderful. Now, let's go get you married!'

Ben was having a lazy Saturday afternoon—and he wasn't enjoying it one bit.

Merriwood's hospital was in a very nice setting. Some might even say gorgeous. Nestled in a valley overlooking the New South Wales south coast, he was looking down through bushland to the long stretch of beach and the sapphire glint of the ocean in the distance. From the grounds of the church along the headland he could hear music— Pachelbel's *Canon*? The music was mixing with the birdsong in the eucalypts overhead. The day was perfect. It was a great day for a wedding.

In the hospital behind him were sixteen not very sick patients, and Ben had nothing to do.

Ben was second on call and he was feeling useless. 'I can't have a honeymoon without you, mate,' Mathew had pleaded. 'Anya's a doctor too. That means instead of three doctors, Merriwood will only have one, and Mary's elderly. She won't be able to cope.'

But it had turned out Dr Mary Carmichael was a mere sixty, fighting fit and aching to have the hospital to herself. She'd also bristled when Ben had arrived and been introduced.

'I can manage alone here, and Mathew's organised the doctors in the next town to do the routine clinics. Unless there's an emergency, I have no idea how you'll make yourself useful. What was Mathew thinking?'

She'd reluctantly let him check on two of the nursing home patients this morning, and at lunchtime she'd handed him an application for funding for a new CT scanner to fill out. 'If you must work then you can do this.'

The paperwork for the application was sitting beside him. He'd looked at it, but he had no idea of the financial or practical requirements of this hospital.

He should leave. Mathew had persuaded him to come to be kind, and he should have known. He'd endured over a year of unending kindness. Enough!

The sounds of the distant music faded and Ben thought, *They'll be making their vows now.* That took him back to a place he didn't want to go. A cathedral in central Sydney, with a crowd of Sydney's fashionable set in attendance. Rihanna, a television presenter, had looked almost ethereal as she'd made vows that, in retrospect, she'd had no intention of keeping.

They'd only been dating for four months when she'd told him she was pregnant, and her devastation had seemed overwhelming. She'd said her career, even her life, would be over if they didn't marry. He'd believed her. He'd also believed her, two weeks after the wedding, when she told him she'd miscarried. It was only later that the doubts had edged their way in. Ben's parents were old money with links to British aristocracy. They'd represented something Rihanna wanted.

And she'd wanted it right to the moment their car had smashed at speed, killing her instantly.

It had taken a while to regain his memory, but he now had flashbacks to their last night together. There'd been a society dinner. He'd arrived late after a hospital emergency, to find Rihanna in a secluded alcove with one of her colleagues. He'd seen the intimate body language, the guilty start when he'd approached. Suspicions had turned to certainty, and on the way home he'd finally confronted her.

Her anger had blown him away. She was no longer the

vivacious society beauty he'd fallen for, but a woman vituperative in her anger.

'Yes, I'm having an affair, but what do you expect? All you ever do is work. Derek knows how to have a good time.'

'Then go to Derek,' he'd said heavily. 'And slow down.' He'd gone to the function in a taxi, straight from the hospital, and she was driving him home. It was raining, the roads were slippery and she was well over the speed limit. 'Rihanna…'

'What do you mean, go to Derek?' she'd snapped, and her foot had firmed on the accelerator.

'I want a divorce.'

'You can't divorce me,' she'd said in a high-pitched voice that had him suddenly wondering how much she'd been drinking before he'd joined her. 'Because guess what? I'm pregnant again. I'm carrying the Duncan family heir. Your mummy and daddy will be so pleased…'

And then oncoming lights, a screech of brakes…and nothing until he'd woken what turned out to be weeks later, to see his mother standing over him. And crying.

'Ben, I'm so sorry. Your back…you've crushed two vertebrae. They're doing their best but they're not sure you're going to be able to walk again.'

'Rihanna?' He remembered struggling to get the word out.

'She's dead. Oh, Ben…'

What followed then had been surgeries, more surgeries, pain, months of intense rehabilitation.

Somewhere in there he'd been faced with the coroner's report on Rihanna. Alcohol. Drugs.

But this time she had been speaking the truth. She'd been weeks pregnant, but he didn't want to know who to.

Block it out. It didn't matter. There was only months of pain—and kindness, kindness and more kindness.

He'd kept up with his medical skills. He'd used the time to read, study, listen in on online conferences, determined to get his life back.

And through it all he'd endured the unending sympathy of family and friends.

That sounded ungrateful, but by now he'd had kindness and sympathy up to his ears. He was still walking with a cane, his back still ached, but it was time to get his life back. Returning to hands-on medicine was to have been the final step back into work, and when Mathew had come to see him he'd thought this could be step one.

'A three-week locum, mate, you'll be doing me a huge favour.' Great. He'd do this, and then a couple more before returning to full-time work.

But now here he was, sitting in the sun, realising that Mathew would have been able to get a hundred locums to work in this place and knowing also that Mary could well cope without him. What was the town doing with three doctors anyway? Why had Mathew even employed Anya, when surely Mary and Mathew could have coped? More kindness?

One of the nurses had told him Anya's background— the daughter of a widow, a life of poverty and need. 'It's so lovely that Mathew's marrying her. Her mum wants her at home so much, and he's so kind.'

And that was causing another niggle. As students he'd grown to know Mathew well—with surnames starting with C and D, they'd been in the same tutorial groups at medical school. He'd seen Mathew preen when he'd had his professor's approval—and the memory of that was creating the niggle now. The way Mathew had looked at Anya when he'd introduced them…he'd seen no adoration in Mathew's eyes, just the same self-satisfaction that he'd done the right thing.

He was being kind? *Bleurgh.*

Cut it out, he told himself. Mathew's marriage was none of his business, and why a pair of smiling eyes had set him worrying… It was dumb.

He grabbed his stick and pulled himself to his feet. Dammit, there had to be something he could do.

And then Mary appeared at the door.

'Dr Duncan, can you hold the fort?' she said briskly. 'I've had a call. One of the wedding guests seems to be ill and they want me to go over.' She grimaced. 'Bertha Mayne's always one to make mountains out of molehills, but her husband's taken her out of church. He says he doesn't want to disturb Mathew. Well, I should think not, breaking up a wedding because she has gastro? But I wouldn't put it past her, so I'll go. Are you okay on your own?' And she looked—pointedly—at his cane.

'I can manage,' he said, trying hard not to grit his teeth. The hospital currently held long-term, nursing home care patients, plus two mums with newborns and three others who, in Ben's opinion, could have been discharged yesterday. Yep, he might just possibly be able to manage.

'Excellent,' Mary said briskly. 'Good luck,' she added as if she was leaving him with an emergency ward full of accident victims—and left him to it.

The church was crowded. Every one of Mathew's relations was here. Every person who'd ever helped Reyna through those long, difficult years. Every person who'd cared. There were smiles everywhere as Anya made her way down the aisle.

Her mother was by her side, and Reyna's smile was the broadest of all. Her Anya was finally settling into this community who'd cared for her. Her Anya was becoming a doctor for this town. This was her mother's happy ending, Anya thought, focusing on keeping her feet in time with the music.

She also needed to smile.

There was Mathew in his dinner suit, beaming with a smile that sometimes she thought was a trifle too self-satisfied. She tried a smile back—she should have been smiling all the way down the aisle.

'A bit slower,' her mother whispered, and suddenly the hand on her arm became heavy. Anya glanced at her and saw a sheen of sweat on her face beneath the smile.

There was a place in the front row waiting for her mum, and they were nearly there. Mathew's dad was already standing, waiting to assist her to her place. So much kindness.

And then Mathew's mum rose as well. That wasn't in the plan, surely.

'S…sorry,' she gasped, and she pushed past her husband, edged past Anya and Reyna—and she bolted for the door.

And it was as if her departure had been a signal. Others were standing, muttering apologies, pushing along the rows to reach the aisle and then almost running.

And, beside her, Reyna's knees buckled. She sank to the floor and she started to retch.

The phone was ringing at the nurses' station, but the nurses, Mike and Janet, were having tea and scones on the lawn. They'd invited him to share, but the thought had made Ben flinch. He'd wanted this locum to be a way to ease back into medicine, and tea and scones wasn't what he'd had in mind.

Ben had trained in emergency medicine. The city hospital where he'd been based before the accident was usually frantic on a Saturday afternoon. Here…not so much. But one of the nurses should be on phone duty.

The phone was on its eighth ring before he reached it, and that made him flinch again. What if it was an emergency?

Did emergencies ever happen in Merriwood?

He lifted the receiver. 'Merriwood Hospital?'

'Ben?'

It was Mary, and she sounded panicked. More than panicked. Terrified. 'You'd better get over here. Food poisoning? Norovirus? Whatever, they're going down like flies.'

'Who?'

'Half the church,' she wailed, and as if on cue one of the nurses—Mike—came striding through from outside. Striding? More like running.

'Sorry, mate,' he gasped as he headed for the bathroom. 'Something I ate?'

'Mum?' Anya was stooped over her mother, instinctively feeling for her pulse, looking at the grey of her face.

'S…sorry.' Reyna was fighting for control. 'Oh, love… Just help me outside. Please…don't let me stop you from getting married.'

They left the hospital unmanned—or almost. Beth, the hospital cook, had just started preparation for dinner when Ben limped into the kitchen.

'Beth, we have an emergency over at the church. Possible multiple food poisoning. Are you feeling okay?'

'Never better,' Beth said. She was middle-aged, portly and unflappable. '*Food* poisoning?'

'We don't know for sure. Mike's unwell as well, and Janet and I are heading for the church. Can you cope for a bit, answer bells? Ring me if you need me.'

'Well,' Beth said, wiping her hands on her apron. 'What a to-do. Off you go, then. I can answer bells and provide bed pans with the best of them. It'll have to be cold meat and salad for tea tonight, but no one will get food poisoning on my watch.' And then she sniffed.

'It'll be that Jeanie and her *catering*,' she said with dour satisfaction, saying the word *catering* as if it were a joke. 'Her mum said she was making sushi for the pre-wedding lunch, and I'm betting that's what it is. Lorna was proud as punch that her daughter was making something exotic, but it's cooked rice. I thought where was she going to store sushi when every fridge at the hall was packed with stuff for the reception? She'll have left it out overnight, that's what I'm betting. What's wrong with sandwiches and sausage rolls? I thought, though she'd probably have found some way to stuff that up too. She's a ding-a-ling, but Mathew feels sorry for her and this is the result.'

'Beth…'

She waved her hands in dismissal. 'I know, you're in a hurry and here I am hypothesising instead of helping. Go on, get over there and fix it. Oh, my heavens, what a disaster.'

It was indeed a disaster. He and Janet took the hospital car, and as they pulled up they saw clusters of wedding guests in the church gardens, each gathered around someone kneeling or prone. There were more guests further out, where garden turned into bushland.

Beth's words were echoing in Ben's head. Sushi. Cooked rice.

She could well be right.

Bacillus cereus was one of the most common causes of food poisoning. Ben had seen it often in his work in the Emergency Department at Sydney Central. The nickname for it among the staff there was Fried Rice Syndrome. Cooked rice was one of its favourite breeding grounds.

Janet was out of the car almost before it stopped. 'Oh, my… That's my dad over there,' she threw at him. 'I'll just make sure he's okay before I…' She didn't finish the sentence before she started running.

Ben took a little more time. Initial appraisal—triage, as comprehensive as time allowed—had been drilled into him since first year medical school. *Unless someone's actively dying, don't jump in before you have a clear picture of the whole situation.* Often attention could be caught by the person screaming the loudest, when the quiet ones were the persons in most need.

So his gaze moved from group to group. At a guess, he thought, maybe one in three or four was actively ill, and they were generally being supported by those who weren't. Maybe they hadn't been at the lunch or hadn't eaten sushi.

What he needed right now was a megaphone. He didn't have one. Okay, channel your inner football coach.

'People, I need your attention.' He made his voice as booming as he could manage, and was reasonably satisfied as heads swivelled.

'I'm Dr Duncan,' he told them. 'I'm standing in for Dr Cummins.' Where was Mathew? Still getting married? And was Doc Mary inside the church? 'My first thought here is that we're dealing with food poisoning, maybe food that wasn't refrigerated properly.' He was using Beth's untested hypothesis, but it could help. People would be familiar with tummy bugs caused by off food, and an explanation could ease panic.

'So it's unpleasant but it'll pass,' he continued, still in his booming voice. 'And those who didn't eat whatever it was can't catch it. What I want you all to do is look out for each and every one of our sufferers. The most important thing is to make sure no one's breathing is blocked—every one of you, that's your biggest job. Also reassure everyone that it's just something they ate, and it'll pass. Janet'll be moving around outside. I'll check those inside the church and then come out to help. I assume Dr Carmichael's in there? I'm not sure if Dr Cummins is...'

'If it is food poisoning it'll have come from lunch,' someone called. 'And Mathew was somewhere with his mates and Anya was having her hair done.'

'Great, that means we'll have every medic able to help,' he said. 'Okay, people, take care of everyone else, and if you're worried, call for help. Loudly. One of us will be with you in moments.'

And in the church...

All around her was chaos. Guests were sitting white-faced in the pews clutching their stomachs while their companions hovered, wondering how to help. A beefy farmer was roaring at someone to get out of the bathroom leading off the vestry, hammering on the door. Mary Carmichael was trying to help eight months pregnant Louise Hoffman. Anya could hear her over the noise—'Jim, lift her up, we'll get her across to the hospital but I'm pretty sure these cramps will be from the tummy bug, not the baby coming.'

And on the carpeted floor of the aisle lay her mother.

Reyna had retched once, and then slumped. Her face had lost all colour. Anya had caught her as she'd fallen, lowered her, glanced up and seen others leave clutching their stomachs.

And then Reyna's face had changed to another colour. A deathly blue.

'Mum!' She didn't scream out loud, but she screamed inside. She was a doctor. She knew this colour.

Where was her pulse? Where?

She was hauling her mother's pretty scarf from around her neck, fighting to clear her mouth, searching for any signs of breathing. Her breathing wasn't blocked. It was just…not there.

Mum!

Her heart. CPR! Dear heaven, she needed help. She was trying to rip her mum's blouse, fighting to be a doctor, fighting not to be a terrified daughter. Please, no! Why didn't this blouse rip?

And then another figure was standing over her—and then crouching. Ben.

'There's no…she's not breathing.' It was all she could do to say it.

'You're sure?'

'Yes.'

'Then clear her airways and breathe for her,' he snapped. 'Leave the compressions to me.' He was grabbing the sides of her mum's blouse and ripping with one sharp pull. 'Breathe, Anya, do it.' His hands were already cupped and pushing down.

The rest of the world had to be blocked out. Even if this wasn't her mum, this was first priority. Cardiac arrest…

It *was* her mum.

Block it out.

Two breaths every fifteen compressions. Breathe. Count. Breathe. Count.

Mum, breathe yourself. Please…

'Mary!' Ben's voice reverberated up to the rafters of the church, cutting through the chaos as he yelled to Dr Carmichael. His hands didn't stop their rhythmic pumping. 'You have your phone? Ring the hospital and get a defibrillator over here, fast. Tell Beth to leave what she's doing and break the speed limit. Cardiac arrest!'

That caused a sudden shocked hush in the little church. Even those actively retching seemed to stop, mid retch.

'I've killed everyone. I've killed everyone!' It was an appalled scream from the middle of the church, followed by hysterical sobs. Jeanie. Mathew's friend. Wedding caterer.

But Anya wasn't focusing on Jeanie. Thirteen, fourteen, fifteen, breathe…

The sounds in the church were becoming a muted buzz. All she could hear was the counting in her head. Mum!

It was too long. Far too long with no response.

Someone—Beth?—came flying in with the defibrillator. Pads.

Attach. Shock. Repeat.

Nothing. Nothing worked.

She'd lost her mum.

CHAPTER TWO

THE REST OF the day passed in a blur of medical necessity. And grief.

And Mathew was nowhere.

Not that Anya noticed. She was beyond noticing anything but what was in front of her.

In those first few minutes Ben cleared everything from her way. She accompanied her mother's body back to the hospital. She sat beside her for a numb half an hour or so, when her mind simply wouldn't function, and then somehow she emerged. She closed her mind to shock and horror, she pulled off the stupid wedding gown and left it in a heap in the hospital laundry, she donned theatre scrubs and somehow she pulled her mind back into medical mode.

Both Mary and Ben were working at full pace—or faster. So was Janet. The nurse glanced at Anya's face, flinched, gave her a swift, hard hug and then asked the question.

'Sweetheart, can you work? This is beyond awful, but Ben and Mary are up against it. It's definitely gastro, though. Everyone ill seems to have eaten the sushi.'

Anya took a deep breath and somehow fought back all thoughts of her mother. That had to wait. For now, she had to be what she was. A doctor.

'What needs doing?'

'The younger ones have mostly headed to their own bathrooms,' Janet told her. 'But Ben's said no one's to go home alone. If there's no one to care for them then they stay here. He's co-opted people to do one-on-one care, yelling if they need us. Ben's worried about...' She faltered and then continued.

'Well, he's worried about someone else collapsing like your mum. We've set up a supervision area on the veranda and Mary's setting up drips. But it's Louise Hoffman who's the most concern. The cramps seem to have pushed her into full labour and she's ill as well. There's signs the baby's stressed...the heart rate's dropping. Ben wants to do an emergency Caesarean, but Mary's also nauseous. Apparently Jeanie dropped sushi off at the staffroom and Mary had a taste for lunch. Not much, she says, and she's only queasy, but giving an anaesthetic to someone liable to retch is... Well, Mary says she needs total focus and if she's nauseous she doesn't trust herself to do it. We wondered...can you...could you possibly act as anaesthetist?'

'Where's Mathew?' Anya stared at Janet in bewilderment.

'We think he took Jeanie home,' Janet said in a voice carefully devoid of judgement. 'Someone said...she's not ill but she's upset. Mathew's not answering his phone.'

The two women stared at each other. Said nothing.

'I see,' Anya said at last. She closed her eyes for one brief moment. She regrouped.

And then she went to help Ben deliver a baby.

Half an hour ago Ben had left her at her mother's side, in full bridal wear, crumpled and sobbing, gutted to the core by the shock of her mother's fatal infarct. Now she entered Theatre and she was already dressed in scrubs.

Her face was swollen from weeping, but it was washed,

devoid of bridal make-up. A simple band held her soft, dark curls away from her face. Her face was drained of colour. She looked almost haggard, but her expression was set.

'Louise.' She went straight to the table and took the young mum's hands in hers, ignoring everything around her in the face of Louise's distress. 'I'm here to help, as backup to Dr Duncan. I'm so sorry you've copped this. A tummy upset and a baby all in the one day—wow!' And then, somehow, she managed to recreate that smile he'd seen when he'd first met her, the smile that was as reassuring as it was warm.

'The good thing is though, Louise, that by the time your tummy settles you'll have your gorgeous baby to cuddle while you recover. It's a little girl, isn't it? How lovely. And Jim…' She turned to the big man sitting, white-faced and silent, in a corner of Theatre. 'No tummy bug problems for you?'

'I never eat sushi,' Louise's husband said in a voice that was tight with strain. 'Louise ate heaps.'

'Don't talk about sushi,' Louise moaned.

'No, let's talk about babies,' Ben said, glancing again at Anya and thinking this woman must have courage in spades. The transformation from grief-stricken bride to efficient and reassuring doctor was astonishing. 'Anya, I assume you're here to give the anaesthetic?'

'If I can't get married today, next best thing is delivering a baby,' she said, and there was that smile again. Dear heaven, the courage of the woman.

Neither Louise nor Jim could have heard about Anya's mother, Ben thought, and Anya would realise that this needed to be a birth scene, where death had no place. Cheer, therefore, had to be summoned, and confidence, and Ben watched in awe as Anya almost visibly pulled those two together.

'Janet's told me why the Caesarean,' Anya was saying. She cast a glance at Ben as she talked, and he saw in that glance that she knew the urgency. The baby's heart rate was dropping to a dangerous level and Janet must have briefed her before she'd entered Theatre. 'I assume you're already scrubbed?'

'I have.'

Janet was moving into gear, setting up the screen so Louise—and Jim—would have no vision of the preparation for incision. An incubation crib was ready at the side. He had everything at hand. He'd already briefed Janet on how to handle the newborn if it was distressed.

'Right, give me three minutes to wash up and we're ready to go,' Anya told him, still with her eyes on his. All sorts of medical questions were being asked and answered in that look. Like how bad was it? Like was there anything else she needed to know?

'We've given metoclopramide a few minutes ago,' Ben told her, meeting her look full-on. 'That should stop the retching. We're under control as long as you're happy giving a general. We'll be ready—if you are?' And that was a question he had to ask.

'I'm ready,' Anya told him, their gazes still locked, and then she looked back at Louise. 'Is it okay if I pop you to sleep for just a few minutes? I know you'd like to stay awake, and I get that, but it's such a bad look—your little one wants to greet a warm, smiley mum, not one with her head in a bucket.'

And Louise gave her a shaky smile. 'Please, keep my head out of the bucket,' she whispered. 'Just give me my baby.'

He was good. He was very good.

Performing an urgent Caesarean on a mum who was

compromised with gastro was a hard call. What Anya would have preferred—what she desperately wanted—was a full theatre of trained staff. A gynaecologist with surgical skills, with more surgical backup behind. A neonatal paediatrician to receive the baby. A fully trained anaesthetist who could cope with a mother who was liable to vomit at any moment.

Her training had included this, but Caesars were rarely performed in Merriwood—a bigger hospital with a full complement of specialists was only an hour away. So her skills were rusty, but she had no choice.

Given her druthers, light sedation and a spinal block might have been the preferred option, but for a vomiting patient it could have resulted in a messy disaster. What was needed was a general anaesthetic—but a light one—with the insertion of an endotracheal tube to prevent aspiration of any vomit. This level of anaesthesia was normally outside Anya's professional comfort zone, but with Ben she felt fully in control.

Ben was in control.

She knew his background was emergency medicine, not obstetrics, but there was no hesitation in his work, no hint that he didn't perform Caesars every day of his working life.

Many obstetric surgeons asked dads to stay outside during a general anaesthetic, but Jim was given the option to remain. Outside there was no staff member to offer a cup of tea, to make sure panic didn't set in, and Jim had already coped with vomit, with mess. When Ben offered him the option to wait outside he knocked them back with grim determination. 'I'm staying with my girls!'

So he stayed, white-faced and silent, while Ben worked swiftly, expertly, surely.

And he was an expert. His fingers were fast and sure,

and he worked with total confidence that all would be well. And as he worked he kept up a running commentary for Jim. Steady, professional words that resounded around the theatre, that promised all would be well.

And finally…

'Two minutes and she'll be all yours,' Ben said at last and then, 'Hey, little girl, welcome to the world.'

And instead of panic there was a happiness. A happiness that flooded the theatre, as one healthy little girl was raised from her mum and even managed a glorious, healthy mew of protest.

Anya didn't have time to weep, but if she had the tears would have been from mixed emotions.

Something good had come of this night. No, something great. A new little life.

The anaesthetic was reversed. The intubation tube was removed. The thing was done.

'Th…thank you,' Louise quavered as she surfaced, as a now beaming Jim proudly placed their daughter into her arms, as their world settled.

But Ben shook his head. 'No thanks required,' he told them. 'This has been an absolute joy.'

And Anya could only agree.

The night settled. The drama was over, for the whole town. The gastro attacks had been sharp and short. Whatever it was that had caused the reaction seemed to have faded by nightfall.

Louise's baby was perfect, her heart rate settling almost the moment she was born. Baby Elizabeth was currently asleep in Jim's arms, and Louise was asleep as well. Jim wasn't sleeping—he wasn't even thinking of being tired. He was sitting in an armchair at his wife's bedside, holding his daughter and gazing at his little family with awed bliss. Tomorrow the drama of gastro would simply be part of the birth story.

And Anya returned to say goodbye to her mother.

Reyna's body hadn't been shifted to the morgue. Someone—it must have been Ben, because somehow he'd become doctor in charge—had decreed that she shouldn't be moved until Anya had had all the time she needed to sit with her. Finally Anya was able to weep as she needed to, and to let the events of the day replay in her head.

The awfulness of losing her mum. That was the worst, and it needed to be faced, but it was too big a grief to take in completely. Instead, as she sat by her mum, as she felt Reyna's presence slowly slip away, what had happened during the rest of the day settled in her confused mind.

Her mum's joy as she'd helped her dress. That was a memory that would last for ever.

Then the church. Seeing Mathew at the end of the aisle. Strangely also she remembered…the doubts.

But then she remembered the feel of her mum's hand in hers, the quiet pressure to walk forward. Her mum's happiness.

The expectant faces of the wedding guests.

And then the chaos.

Ben, taking charge. The awful emptiness as realisation of her mum's death had sunk in.

But then glimmers of something else. A tiny baby. The look of joy on the new parents' faces. The way they'd looked at each other.

Their love.

Ben's gentleness. Janet's hug as they'd stood back and watched the new little family come together.

So many emotions. Everything was out of kilter. It was like a kaleidoscope, image after image superimposed on each other.

Trying to distract herself, she picked up the chart some-one had put on the bedside table—as if it could still matter. Reyna's medical history.

She leafed through it—and then she froze.

No.

It was too much to take in. She would not—*could not*—think about it.

She focused again on her mum. She held that cooling hand and let herself weep as much as her body demanded.

Finally she rose to leave, but before she left she had one final thing to tell her mother.

'I can't marry Mathew, Mum,' she said, softly but surely. 'I'm sorry, but I'm over being grateful. I know he was kind to us, the whole town was kind to us—but you and I have more than repaid our debt. I'm glad you saw me being the bride you wanted me to be, but from now on… Mum, I'm on my own and I don't want to be indebted ever again. Thank you, Mum, for giving me so much. I'll love you for ever.'

Then she bent and kissed her mother's face. She blinked back the tears she was determined to no longer shed until she was safely home, and then she walked from the room and closed the door.

What next? She was having trouble focusing but she needed to make sure things were done for the night, that Mary and Ben were safely in charge.

Ben. His presence today had been a godsend. She'd been incredulous when Mathew had hired him—'Why do we need a locum when Mary's more than willing to take over?' but right now she was overwhelmingly glad he had.

Where was he? She turned and headed for the nurses' station, and there he was.

'Anya.' He turned from the front desk, looking calmly professional, setting down a chart he'd been reading. 'All's well in the wards,' he told her. 'Mary's gone home to bed but she's okay. I'm on call during the night and Mary's capable of backup if needed, but everything's quiet.'

'Where's…where's Mathew?' She didn't actually want to know, but she had to ask.

'He's still not answering his phone. It doesn't matter. We have things covered.' He hesitated. 'Can I drive you home?'

And then her phone pinged with an incoming text. She lifted it and saw Mathew's name.

For a moment her gut instinct was to toss the phone into the wall. The events of the day had been overwhelming, the chart she'd just read had left her feeling sick to her stomach, and her reaction now was an almost visceral revulsion.

Ben was watching her. Smashing her phone would achieve nothing. She forced herself to read.

With Jeanie. She's so upset I'm having to medicate her. But I've just heard about your mum. I'm so sorry. I'll be with you as soon as I can.

She stared blindly at the screen—and then she stared up at Ben. He gazed back, looking concerned. Was he reading another disaster in her expression?

No. This wasn't a disaster. This was just the end of a very long day.

The end of…a lot.

'I need to make a call,' she told him.

'I'll leave you to it.'

'No.' On impulse she stopped his instinctive retreat. 'Ben, please…if you will… I know this sounds dumb, but for some reason…will you listen? I think… I just need someone to be here while I do this.'

'Sure,' he said, sounding confused but still concerned.

It was dumb to hold him here. She knew that, but her

knees seemed like jelly and maybe...maybe Ben's presence might help her say the words that needed to be said.

Mathew answered on the second ring. She'd turned the phone to speaker, so his voice rang out in the corridor as if he were here in person. 'Love...'

She cut him off. The last thing she needed right now was sympathy.

'Mathew, why didn't you tell me Mum's heart problem was worsening?'

That was followed by silence—and Anya let it hang. The silence helped her as well, settling what she needed to do. In her mind was the information on the chart in Reyna's room, the chart she'd picked up almost automatically.

She'd been three things today, a bride, a grieving daughter and a doctor, and of all of those things, medicine was what gave her time out. So she'd read the chart.

And now she stood and waited for Mathew's answer. Which was taking a long time coming.

'Her history's there,' she said. 'Ben must have asked for it, or maybe one of the nurses grabbed it. I don't know. But I just read it. You sent her to a specialist three weeks ago—it must have been while I was at the conference in Sydney. Did your mum take her? I guess she did, your mum's always kind. But the report's there. Recommendation, immediate cardiac bypass surgery. And the report came to you. Did you tell her, Mathew? Did you? Because you sure as hell didn't tell me.'

And she could no longer hold it back. Anger, deep within, was coiled so tight it felt like a hard, tangible ball.

'Of course I told her. But we thought...'

'Who thought?' She was vaguely aware of—and somehow held steady by—Ben's presence. He was still with her, leaning against the wall, his hands in his pockets, calmly watching.

Strangely, it helped, to have this dispassionate bystander as mute witness. Or as quiet support? That was what it felt like, and it was the one crumb of comfort in this whole mess. That Ben hadn't turned his back on her.

Was he, too, being kind? No, she decided. He was being professional. Grieving daughter in the hospital corridor, ready to explode with anger. Professionally, he was probably mentally loading a syringe with tranquilliser. Wondering which hospital bed he could put her in tonight.

'We thought it was best,' Mathew said at last, sounding miserable. But then he seemed to regroup, and his voice took on a trace of belligerence. 'She and I discussed it, but it didn't seem so urgent that she needed surgery straight away. I told her it could probably wait until after the wedding.'

'Probably?'

'It was a joint decision. Your mum agreed it wouldn't have been kind to worry you when we were about to leave on our honeymoon.'

'And so she died.' Her voice sounded weird.

'Love, I know it's awful, but long-term…you know your mum had end stage renal failure. Everything was starting to shut down. Your mum was so happy to see you married, so maybe…maybe this quick death was a blessing. I know you can't see it now—you must be devastated. I feel your pain.'

'You don't feel my pain,' she whispered, and for some reason she glanced at Ben. Amazingly, Ben nodded, as if he approved. How could he? But that nod…somehow it helped her find the strength to say what had to be said.

'Mathew, I don't want to marry you.'

Another silence. He'd be incredulous, Anya thought, in the small space in her head that was capable of considering what he'd be feeling. Mathew was the town's biggest prize, the golden boy, the guy who'd taken an impoverished kid and given her so much…

'Why not?' he said at last.

And somehow she had to suppress her fury, to make herself say the words that had been forming in her heart… for how long? Maybe for ever.

'Because you're kind,' she managed at last. 'You've been kind to me for most of my life, but Mathew, from now on you can take me off your list of charitable causes. I'm not marrying you. It's over.'

And before he could say another word she disconnected. Then she stood, staring at the floor, trying to figure what came next. She needed to go home, she thought. Home—without her mum?

Finally, she looked up at Ben again and found him still calmly watching.

'I'm sorry,' he said gently but she shook her head.

'Don't be. Telling him that has been the one good outcome of a horrible day. I should have done it years ago but… but it would have hurt too many people.'

'I can see that,' he said, and she met his gaze and thought that somehow he did.

'Can I drive you home?' he asked, and she made her fuzzy mind consider. It was a kindness that he'd offered, and right now she wanted kindness like a hole in the head, but she could accept this.

'Mum… Mum and I arrived here in the wedding limo,' she told him. 'My car's at home, so yes, please, I'd like you to drive me home. I'm… I'm done here.'

CHAPTER THREE

BEN DROVE ANYA home in silence. Apart from terse directions, she said nothing, just stared rigidly ahead. When they
reached the house, he pulled up and watched her stare out
of the car window and almost visibly brace.

The moon was full and the front yard was almost as
well-lit as in daylight. He could see stuff sitting on her front
porch. Bunches of flowers. What else?

'They'll be casseroles,' she said dully, staring out at
them. 'Multiple tuna bakes. Already.'

'In the middle of such chaos?'

He couldn't believe it. A wedding abandoned, half the
town with food poisoning, and there were still those who'd
thought of Anya and dashed home and cooked a casserole.

'People are…' She hesitated.

'Kind. I get it. But so fast?'

'Kindness is an involuntary reflex in this town. It's always been that way. I'm…'

'Grateful?' He looked out at the pile of casseroles and
then looked back at her face. The closed look. The pain.

'You want me to cart them away and ditch them in the
river?'

There was a moment's silence and then she swivelled in
the car to stare at him—as if she were looking at a patient

who'd taken a few too many drugs and she was assessing where on the scale of crazy he was sitting. And then her face cracked a little and she choked out something very like laughter. Which sort of ended in tears.

But the tears weren't permitted to flow. She swiped her hand across her eyes and when she spoke she seemed to have herself under control. Sort of.

'Thank you, but no,' she told him, and she almost managed to suppress the wobble in her voice. 'I'll need to give all the containers back, carefully washed, with thank you notes attached. The locals would be offended if they saw their beloved Tupperware containers floating downstream.'

'It might, though,' he suggested thoughtfully, 'give you some satisfaction, setting them free.'

'I couldn't be so...' he heard the strain as she almost forced herself to say the word '...ungrateful.'

There was a moment's silence while he thought about saying something. But then he gave an inward shrug. The strain on her face... He could hardly make things worse.

'Janet told me a little about your background,' he said softly. 'She told me how good Mathew's been to you. She added a few more facts while we were assessing baby Elizabeth. Janet thinks Mathew's been oppressively good.'

'Does Janet think that?' She shook her head, looking dazed. She hardly saw him, he thought. 'I guess,' she whispered. 'Janet's an outsider as well,' she whispered. 'She's a single mum of teenage boys. She came home ten years ago to nurse her ageing parents. Maybe she's been the recipient of Mathew's kindness too.'

'Haven't we all?' Ben said grimly. 'You don't really think Mathew needed a locum.' It was okay to talk about this, he thought. Anything to give her a break from the overwhelming grief. 'Did he tell you I was in a car crash twelve months back? I've been out of medicine since, while

I've struggled with my wife's death and rehab from spinal injuries. Mathew thought this would be a kind way to break me back into medicine.'

'He didn't tell me,' she whispered. 'But… I'm so sorry.'

'Don't you dare be sorry,' he said, suddenly harsh. 'I'm over *sorry*, like you're over *grateful*.'

'I…yes. I guess.' There was another silence. She stared at him and then closed her eyes for a millisecond, before turning again to the car door. Ready to go into that silent house alone.

And he couldn't bear it.

He looked again out at the pile of casseroles and winced. She didn't want him to be kind, he thought. He got that— he knew too well how unbearable continual charity could seem. So he understood, but he was also remembering a silent house, an aching void, and he knew he had to do something.

'So what say we head to the river and feed all these casseroles to the fish?' he said.

The car door stilled, half open. 'We can't.' She sounded bewildered.

'Yes, we can.' Then, as she turned to stare at him again, he tried a smile. What he wanted was to make things okay for her, but there was no way he would—or could. Her grief was her own, not to be intruded on. But this way…

'Maybe tossing casseroles would be cathartic for both of us,' he suggested, thinking of logistics. 'It's a full moon so we should be able to see, and with the chaos in this town there'll be no one around. I have a prescription pad in my bag. We can feed the fish, then pop a script, with descriptions, into each container, so you can write thank-you notes at your leisure. If I'd thought, I'd have pre-purchased some flowery notepaper so we could have done thank-you letters on the spot, but we'll just have to make do.'

There was a moment's stunned silence while she thought about it. While he stayed silent, hoping that appalling look of grief might ease just a little.

'You're crazy,' she said at last.

'Maybe we both are a little,' he agreed. 'Mine's a back-burner of crazy. Yours…a catastrophe of a wedding and your mum's death. Anya, if you can't be crazy tonight, then when can you be?'

'Thank you, but I…can't,' she said and then she turned and stared back out at the casseroles. 'There must be a dozen or more casseroles out there.'

Ha! He had her. This was a moment's thought of something besides confusion and grief. 'Will there be any good ones?' he asked.

And the moment expanded. 'The tuna bakes, not so much,' she admitted. 'There's a generic recipe everyone seems to use, and who really likes pineapple with tuna? But I'm betting Mrs Hornby will have produced her lasagne. That's been voted by the town as the best this side of Italy.'

'Then if you don't want it, I'll take it,' he said promptly. 'Or we'll share. I'm living in hospital accommodation, with only a microwave for company.'

Amazingly, that was enough to produce a gurgle of choked laughter. It sounded…good. It sounded free.

'Should I add that in my thank you note to Mrs Hornby?' she managed. 'That Dr Duncan was grateful as well as me?'

'No,' he said, suddenly very, very serious. 'Dr Duncan is done being grateful, and by the sound of it so are you. Now, let's get things moving. We have a river full of hungry fish, just waiting for a tuna bake.' And then he paused as a discordant thought hit him. 'Hang on. Tuna bakes… Fish… We're not encouraging them to be cannibals, are we? Or doing something environmentally appalling?'

She shook her head, suddenly determined. 'How can

we be? Big fish have been eating little fish from time im-memorial. Besides, most of the fish upstream are carp, and they're taking over from native fish. There's a station downstream to catch and remove them. It'll make them slower and fatter, easier for the Fisheries people to catch.'

'How excellent!' Then, as he saw the strain behind the attempt to smile, because he didn't seem to be able to help himself, he reached out and touched her cheek. It was a feather touch, the merest trace of human contact, but he wondered as he touched her why he seemed to need it as much as he sensed she did.

'There you go,' he said in a voice that was suddenly a bit unsteady. 'The casseroles won't have been baked in vain. Let's go do a community service. Do you think anyone will be grateful?'

'They'd better not be,' Anya managed. 'Because like you said, I'm done.'

'Yep, grateful is so last week,' he agreed. 'Let's move right on.'

It was the weirdest night.

Her wedding was off.

Her mother was dead.

By rights, she should be curled up in bed, huddled in a cocoon of shock and grief. Instead, she was standing knee-deep in the pebbly shallows in the midst of the Mer-riwood river.

Ben was on the bank. He'd produced a lantern from the boot of his gorgeous vintage Morgan. 'You drive a car like mine, you need to be prepared for running repairs in the dark,' he'd told her. He was now carefully inspecting cas-seroles, writing details in his pad and then bringing them out to where she stood in the shallows.

Her job was to scrape them out, making sure they didn't

drop into the water in a lump, but scattering their contents, so the fish could easily feed and there was no way a Merriwood local could come upon a hearty wedge of tuna bake washed up on the bank the next morning.

The water she stood in was cold—icy in fact. She'd grabbed a jogging suit before she'd left home. Her sweatshirt was warm but her rolled-up pants left her feet freezing.

She hardly noticed. She and Ben weren't talking. They were simply acting automatically.

It was almost like operating, she thought, like standing in Theatre. If she was the surgeon, Ben would be the assistant, providing what she needed without having to be asked.

And maybe he *was* providing what she needed. He'd offered to be the one out in the water, but his offer had been tentative. Maybe he'd guessed that standing knee-deep in the shallows, listening to the water ripple gently over the stones, letting the moonlight glimmer through the eucalypts and play on her face…after the chaos of the day, this was balm.

No, not balm, she thought as she let the latest casserole disintegrate in her fingers. Her mother's death was still there, real and dreadful. Reality would slam back soon enough. This was simply time out, a breathing space she desperately needed.

Ben was wading out to her now, his pants rolled up as well. He was limping but he'd left his cane on the bank. She could see a band of scarring on his left arm as well as on his leg—how badly had he been hurt in that car accident? Should he even be here? His feet must be as cold as hers, but he didn't seem to notice. He took the empty container from her and replaced it with a full one.

'Yep, it's another tuna bake,' he said morosely. 'I'm thinking we have about an eighty percent hit rate.'

'I read a murder mystery once,' she managed, and was

astonished to hear a touch of lightness in her voice. 'A widow was finally nailed for murder when her freezer broke down and defrosted. For ten years her husband's body had lain undiscovered, covered with layer upon layer of tuna bakes.'

He chuckled, a rumbly, deep chuckle that added to the strange sensations of the night. And with it…a sliver of something unrecognisable pierced through her grief and shock. For some dumb reason Ben seemed to be enjoying himself, and that enjoyment let her feel lighter.

How could this man's smile make her feel…make her feel…?

That she had no idea how she was feeling.

But she had little time for introspection. He was examining the empty container, swishing it under the water again to make sure there were no remains. Finally, he waded out and went to fetch the next. Then the next.

Finally, he called out, 'That's it. All done until tomorrow's batch. Now, what are you planning on doing with the flowers?'

The flowers. They'd been piled by the door as well. She'd have to cope with them when she got home.

She had a sudden visceral memory of the days after her father had died. She'd been five years old and her memories were blurred, but she did remember the flowers, so many their smell was overpowering. She remembered her mother, almost shadow-like, walking from loaned vase to loaned vase, carefully topping up the water of all of them.

'People have been so generous,' she remembered her mother saying, over and over, like a mantra. 'We can't just let them die.'

Why was she thinking of that now? Regardless, she was, and her silence must have lasted too long.

'You know, when my wife died people brought flowers to our home,' Ben said into the stillness. The rippling water was a murmuring backdrop which seemed to make everything less personal. 'I was unconscious at the time—three weeks in an induced coma and even plastic flowers would have been tempted to wilt. But apparently there were flowers a mile high piled up at our front door. So finally a few of my mates decided to collect them and they had a memorial service of their own.'

'A memorial service...?'

'Well, sort of,' he told her. 'They waited for a decent surf and an outgoing tide, then headed to the cliffs off Coogee Beach. They got rid of every piece of wrapping and then set them all free. They made a video for me to see when I was well enough, and that's how I remember them—a wash of flowers flowing out to sea.'

And then, when she didn't answer—she didn't know how—he looked thoughtfully at the rippling water. 'Maybe not here,' he said. 'They'd wash back through the town—not a good look. But we could check the tide. If it's outgoing, we could release them from the headland and they'd be out to sea and gone. Only if you're interested, of course, but it's an option.'

'But...' She stared. 'All of them?'

'Why not?'

'I... Visitors.'

Her mother's words came back to her. *People have been so generous.*

'People will come,' she whispered. 'If their flowers aren't there...'

'Are you really thinking of entertaining visitors over the next few days?' he asked. 'Do you want them? You could play the jilted bride as well as the bereaved daughter. Miss Havisham has nothing on you when it comes to having the right for isolation to be respected.'

'I...' She stared at him, stunned. 'How...?'

'Easy,' he said lightly, but there was empathy behind the lightness. Warmth. An understanding of the bewilderment this day's events had caused? 'We can paint a cross on your front door—didn't they do that in the olden days? Along with a brief note—something like *Intruders Will Be Shot!*—and no one will dare darken your door. They'll therefore assume you're grieving in a home awash with floral tributes, with their bunch front and centre.'

And up it bubbled again, a choke of laughter that was surely absolutely inappropriate. How could she be laughing on such a night? But as the laughter settled she thought again of her mum, her face set and grim, carrying her watering can from vase to vase.

Why was that memory so strong?

'Let's do it,' she whispered.

He looked at her for a long, long moment, giving her time.

'Anya, I need you to be sure,' he said softly. 'Don't let me put my ideas above what you think is the right thing. I'll help you find enough jam jars to hold every flower if you want. I'm the last person to bully you into doing something you don't want. Or to guilt you. You have no need to do anything out of obligation to me.'

There it was again, that flicker of something she didn't understand. Recognition? That didn't make sense.

But he was waiting for her to decide and, whatever strange sensations she was feeling, her way was suddenly clear. 'Mum'd love it,' she said softly. 'I know I sound ungrateful. These flowers, these casseroles, they've all been given with love and I'm incredibly grateful to have such support—Mum and I have always been grateful—but when I think of this night... We could...let the flowers go as... as maybe I need to let Mum go?'

And then, as her voice thickened with tears, she forced herself to continue.

'I need to remember this night with peace,' she told him. She looked across at the riverbank, at this man, surrounded by empty casserole containers, who was smiling gently, encouragingly at her to make her own decision—no judgement here—and suddenly she found herself smiling back.

'Today was a nightmare,' she whispered. 'Right now I can feel Mum's approval in what we're doing, and maybe even…in time…maybe she'd finally understand my decision to ditch Mathew. And who knows? I might eventually even remember tonight with a touch of laughter.'

They released the flowers from the headland beyond the town. Ben stood back and watched, a silent sentinel as the flowers scattered on the moonlit surf, then drifted outward and off to the open sea. Anya watched them go, saying nothing.

She must be overwhelmed, he thought, but there was nothing more he could do. He simply waited until the last flower was gone. Finally, she seemed to brace herself and then turned to him.

'That was…okay,' she said simply. 'I'm ready to go.'

He drove her home. He walked her to her front door, she inserted her key and then she turned back to him. 'Thank…'

'No,' he said, cutting her off, and once more he touched her face, a feather touch, a gesture of contact that he seemed to need as much as she did. 'No thank you. No gratitude. Tonight was almost as much for me as it was for you. Mathew invited me to be locum here out of sympathy, and for some reason tonight I finally felt that I've moved on.' And in a way he suddenly realised that it was true.

Releasing the casseroles, releasing the flowers—he hadn't been able to do anything like that when Rihanna had died. But tonight, strangely, it had felt as if they were doing more than farewelling Anya's mother.

'I'll be leaving as soon as things settle down at the hospital,' he told her. 'Or sooner. Mathew can surely cope with the aftermath of this on his own.'

'I'll be leaving too,' she whispered.

'No decisions,' he told her. 'Not tonight. Give yourself time.'

'I think,' she said slowly, 'that I've had enough time. Tonight was…right.'

'It was, wasn't it?' he said, smiling down at her. 'And if you wake tomorrow hungering for tuna bake, don't blame me.'

'There'll be more tomorrow.'

'You want me to come back tomorrow night?'

And at that she seemed to straighten. 'I can cope on my own.'

'You know, I'm very sure you can.' He touched her face again. 'Goodnight, Anya. It's been a privilege to share part of this night with you.'

And his eyes met hers for a long moment. He wasn't sure what was happening, what strange sensation was passing between them. He only knew there was no need for further words.

She gave a tiny nod, then reached up and touched his face in turn.

'Ditto,' she told him and then she turned and walked into her empty house and closed the door.

He returned to the car, drove back towards the hospital and then he slowed. Almost of its own volition the car turned towards the headland. He parked, then sat and looked out over the moonlit surf.

What now?

Something new, he thought. Enough of waiting for others to help. He should never have accepted Mathew's generous offer of this superfluous locum job. He needed to do something that was for him, where he didn't need to thank anyone and no one had to thank him.

Yeah, right. He was a doctor. Patients inevitably thanked him.

But even that, right now, felt as if it'd set his teeth on edge.

So what? Give up medicine? Go find a beach bum type of job, pouring cocktails in some fancy beach resort?

He smiled at the thought, thinking the chances of getting such a job would be pretty remote. His CV—fully trained doctor with solid experience in emergency medicine—would hardly cut it as a barman.

But what if…?

An idea was stirring. Cocktails. Surf. Sun. There must be a job somewhere…

The locum position at Merriwood was supposed to have been for three weeks—a low-pressure job to ease himself back into his high-powered position as Emergency Physician at Sydney Central. A position where he coped with catastrophe after catastrophe. Where lives were saved. Where people were endlessly grateful for what he did.

Why was the thought of that gratitude strangely unsettling? Would something like…cocktails, surf, sun…be a way to escape the dark thoughts that still haunted him?

Was it wrong to think of escaping?

Enough. His head was all over the place, and his leg and back ached. He needed to sleep. He'd head back to the hospital, make sure all was secure, and then he'd think about what came next.

But in his thoughts was still… Anya.

He couldn't help her, though. She didn't want more help and he got that. She'd cope. She was one strong woman.

But as he finally turned from the sea, the vision of her stayed with him. Anya, standing bare-legged in the river, spooning out the casseroles, her face still blotched with tears.

Anya.

'She's nothing to do with you, mate,' he said fiercely into the night, but as the ocean disappeared behind him the memory stayed.

Anya.

CHAPTER FOUR

DID ANYONE EVER remember the details of the funerals of those they'd truly loved? Anya surely wouldn't. It was all a blur. What she'd remember would be snippets—and the way she'd felt.

The day was extraordinary. The town had pulled out all the stops to give Reyna a magnificent send-off. The church was crowded. There were flowers—so many flowers. Strangely, instead of making her feel oppressed, she loved them. They made her remember farewelling her mum down by the river, the tuna bakes, the wash of flowers heading out to sea. The true funeral?

Her mum had played the piano, and in times of deep contentment or of celebration she'd played the piece she loved best, the second movement of Beethoven's fifth concerto. For the funeral the local school band and their best piano player made an awesome attempt to get it right. Anya had asked for it, and it felt good.

The rest of the details she'd left to others. They didn't matter. Nothing seemed to matter.

She'd move on, she thought. People had told her not to make fast decisions but one was clear. The thought of staying here in her mum's house, of staying working beside Mathew…she couldn't. So maybe this funeral was more than a memorial for her mum. Maybe it was a goodbye.

Meanwhile she greeted everyone and she thanked, she thanked and she thanked. She even managed to eat two of the tiny pink jelly cakes that Jeanie produced—yes, Jeanie was doing the catering, although there wasn't any sushi in sight.

'I've saved you some,' Jeanie whispered, and when, finally, she headed for her car, Jeanie pressed a box of them into her hands. Clearly labelled 'Jeanie's Jelly Cakes'.

It was almost enough to make her smile. When she reached home she carried them to her front door, then stood, holding the box in her hands, fighting back a ridiculous longing to phone Ben. 'Hey, Ben, we have jelly cakes for the carp.'

He'd left almost a week ago. The idea was ridiculous.

But then, as the thought faded, a car door slammed and she looked out towards the street. She half expected to see Mathew. He'd been at the funeral but she'd refused to have him drive her, or sit by her. He'd been desperate to explain, to atone, to do something, but her decision was final—it had to be.

And now…it wasn't Mathew. It was someone in a gorgeous green vintage Morgan.

It was Ben—and for some reason her heart seemed to miss a beat.

'Hey.' He climbed out of the car and limped towards her, but he stopped at the front gate, as if unsure of his welcome. Or suddenly realising that it was dusk and she was alone?

She stared at him, confused. He was dressed casually, in jeans and an old leather jacket. She'd been surrounded by funeral-goers in sombre formality all afternoon. He looked good in comparison.

Actually he looked great, but that was no reason why her heart should do this weird, missing-a-beat thing.

'Before you ask, I come bearing no tuna bake,' he said

before she could speak. 'Nor flowers, nor even my presence if you need to be alone. If you want, you can tell me to come back next week—or maybe never if you don't like what I'm going to suggest.' And then, as she didn't respond—she didn't know how to—he forged on.

'Anya, it seems a crazy time to approach you with such an idea, but then I thought…what better time to throw you a distraction? Regardless, like it or not, I'm here to offer you a job.'

This day was getting away from her. Carefully, as if they were infinitely fragile, she set down Jeanie's jelly cakes on the front step. 'A job?' she managed blankly.

'I know it's out of left field,' he said, and still he hadn't moved through the gate. 'But I rang Janet to find out how you were, and she tells me you've tossed in your job. So here's something to think about. I'm here to throw the prospect of a position you might enjoy, with no strings, no thanks, no gratitude attached. As a doctor on the Dolphin Isles.'

'Dolphin Isles!' She knew the place, but by reputation only. No one she knew had ever gone there.

Dolphin Isles was a gorgeous coral quay on the outer edge of Queensland's Great Barrier Reef. The biggest landmass was Dolphin Island, home to an internationally renowned luxury resort. It was too far from the mainland for day-trippers and the cost of staying in the resort was reputed to be eye-watering. A luxury resort for squillionaires.

'The job's at the island resort,' Ben was saying, while she stared at him incredulously. 'Dolphin Isles Resort. Island population three hundred. There's a small marine research centre focusing on coral rehabilitation, but the population's mostly tourists. *Rich* tourists. Because the resort's so expensive and exclusive they offer a twenty-four-hour medical service, so they're asking for a partnership. Two doctors. Once you know how much it costs to stay there, you'll know they can afford it.'

'A partnership?' Did she sound as stupid as she felt? Luckily he didn't appear to notice.

'There's been a husband-and-wife team there for the past few years,' he told her. 'An older couple who saw it as an easy lifestyle but who've finally decided to retire. So the island's used to two doctors and it wants two. With rich tourists doing what rich tourists tend to do, there'll always be swimming accidents, sunburn, overdoses—you can guess the type of thing. Plus the needs of the staff at the resort and research centre. It seems the guests the resort attracts tend to demand attention for the least scratch, and as they pander to every need someone has to be on call twenty-four-seven.'

He spread his hands. 'Anya, I'm almost ready to go back to work but I still need time to get my physical fitness back. I crushed two vertebrae in the accident and it's taking time to get myself right. I need to swim, I need a decent gym and I can't take on so much work that I can't stay focused on healing. This job sounds as if it'd suit me, and I'm applying for it. But they want two doctors, and it'd be great to find someone compatible to work with—so I thought of you.'

Her brain was struggling to take this in. She remembered, suddenly and stupidly, a cartoon she'd seen somewhere years back. A kid asking his teacher, 'Please, miss, can I go home now? My brain's full.'

Right now, her brain felt as if it might burst.

'Why...why me?' she managed.

'Why not?' he said easily. 'I've talked to the current doctors, and it sounds a doddle. You want to go live on a tropical island, lie in the sun with a little medicine on the side? There will be some genuine need, but we'll be over-paid for what we do—a population of three hundred surely can't keep two doctors frantic. Anya, best of all, we won't be doing anyone any favours. They won't be doing us any, and there should be no gratitude in sight.'

'I don't want…'

'Gratitude? Who knows that better than me?'

'But…me?' The idea made her feel dizzy. The whole day had made her feel dizzy and maybe he knew, because his voice gentled.

'Hey, I know, this is a crazy time to throw this at you, but I figured you probably wouldn't sleep anyway. And for some reason I thought it might suit us both. Why not grant yourself thoughts of tropical islands and piña coladas in between your waves of grief?'

He hesitated and his voice changed. 'Look, this is only an idea,' he told her. 'I can't work at full pace yet—this leg is still damnably weak. I also need space, and I suspect you do too. So here are the details.' And there came that smile again, gentle, beguiling—understanding?

'Think about it if you can,' he told her, and he held out a bundle of literature. 'I'm heading back to Sydney now, and I won't pressure you further. If you're interested, call me. It's only an idea, Anya. No pressure.'

'I…thank…'

'And you can cut that out.' His voice was suddenly al-most savage. 'I don't like the idea of a medical partnership with someone I've never met—it'd be a downside of tak-ing this job—so the benefits of you joining me would be mutual. But I'm applying anyway, with or without you, so there's not the least need for gratitude. This is all selfish on my part and it needs to be the same for you.'

And with that he laid the package of brochures on top of the mailbox—and he turned and limped back to his car.

* * *

Why had he done that?

Ben drove slowly back to Sydney, taking the slow coast road, roof down, enjoying the breeze on this warm night, the sense of freedom this gorgeous little car was giving him.

If he went to Dolphin Island he'd have to leave it behind.

He'd leave a lot else behind too, he thought. His parents' almost overwhelming concern. His mates' sympathy and kindness. His position at Sydney Central—they'd held it open until now, but he couldn't expect them to hold it for ever. There were bright young doctors aching to take his place.

He should mind, but he didn't. Once upon a time he'd have fought to get a position in this prestigious hospital, but right now it left him cold.

As most things left him cold.

He still wasn't sure why he was applying for Dolphin Island. He'd intended to take a couple more locum jobs before returning to Sydney Central, but Dolphin Island was a permanent position.

Was that what he wanted? A long-term career with little responsibility?

A job with Anya?

That was only a possibility, he told himself, and it was a slim one. She surely wouldn't be interested. He could have rung and asked, but the idea of taking a day and doing the lovely drive to Merriwood had been appealing.

Liar. He'd wanted to see her again. See her face. See how she was coping.

He thought of the advertisement he'd read for the job he'd told her about. *Medical Partnership on Dolphin Isles*. He'd thought of Anya working to deliver little Elizabeth Hoffman, of the way she'd thrust her grief and shock aside and worked with pure professional skill. She'd seemed an awesome doctor, compassionate and clever, and Janet had reinforced his impression of her competence. Once Janet had told him that Anya intended to leave Merriwood, it had therefore seemed logical to ask her if she was interested. It was surely much better to work with someone he knew.

But it wasn't all sense. The memory of Anya in the river, in the moonlight... The thought of her grief, her anger, her skill and her strength... The memory of the look on her face as she'd watched her mother's flowers wash out to sea... They'd merged into an image he couldn't forget.

Yeah, he'd like to work with her. He'd like to get to know her better.

Because?

Because nothing, he told himself almost savagely. It wasn't much more than twelve months since Rihanna had died. The last thing he needed was more...entanglement?

Was that what this was? More entanglement?

It was no such thing. And Anya would hardly be likely to accept, he told himself as he drove on through the night. Maybe it'd be a good thing if she didn't.

Right. Except why did that prospect feel...bleak?

CHAPTER FIVE

THE THOUGHT OF a job on Dolphin Island was so unexpected, so out of left field, so…almost crazy…that a stunned Anya, almost without thinking, rang Ben the next morning and accepted. Which was why, six weeks later, she found herself sitting in the bow of a gorgeous turquoise and gold cruiser with 'Dolphin Isles Resort' emblazoned on the side, heading to the outer rim of Queensland's Great Barrier Reef.

There'd been brochures for the resort in the information pack Ben had given her. Dolphin Island was maybe ten kilometres wide at the most, with wide sandy beaches, a centre of magnificent rainforest and a resort hidden discreetly among the trees. Its gorgeously furnished bungalows had been designed to catch the views out over the coral quays surrounding the island. A vast swimming pool, designed to look like a natural lagoon, meandered through the resort.

But as they neared the jetty she thought, as enticing as the brochure had been, it still hadn't shown this breathtaking magnificence. As the ferry drew closer, Anya was looking out at miles of turquoise water and sandy cays. A kayak was drifting outward from the island, a man and a woman on board with paddles stilled, seemingly entranced. She could see why. A pod of dolphins was cruising around them, bodies glistening in the crystal-clear water.

She glanced around and Ben was watching her, and he was grinning.

'Great, huh?'

He'd been here. The island's management had flown him over for the interview, but she gathered with his credentials and with hers, the job had almost been theirs from the start. Doctors generally looked for this type of job early, wanting a couple of years of little stress before starting their career progression. Or later when they were winding down, wanting a quiet life. For two experienced, capable doctors to apply together…

'How long did you imply that we'd stay?' she breathed, and Ben's smile widened.

'There's a three-month cooling-off period. I've left my gorgeous Morgan garaged in Sydney, just in case it doesn't work out, but of course I implied for ever.'

Why did that give her a jolt? To make her think…for ever?

It was nothing, she told herself. That was always what happened in job interviews—total commitment to the proposed position. But as he smiled at her…

For ever?

Get a grip, she told herself.

The last few weeks had been an emotional roller coaster, her grief at her mother's death overlain with the practicalities of packing a house full of memories, of saying goodbye to a town that truly had been good to them, of cutting lifetime ties.

But underneath the grief and organisational needs there'd been an undercurrent of anticipation, which right now was swelling to almost epic proportions. That first phone call to Ben to accept had been made almost without thinking, but right now she didn't regret it. She was about to land on a gorgeous tropical island with a doctor-cum-partner who seemed as kind as he was good-looking. And whose smile was…

Um…no. As the thought crossed her mind, she hauled herself back to reality with a start. Ben had just lost his wife. She'd just ditched her fiancé. They both needed time out. She needed to think of him as a medical partner, nothing else.

Meanwhile there was a guy driving a turquoise and gold luggage cart towards the jetty to meet them, and her new life was about to start.

No more ties, she told herself. No more indebtedness. She realised she was grinning back at Ben, and her smile was probably a mile wide.

'How soon for the piña coladas?' she managed, and he chuckled.

'Let's go meet the locals first,' he told her. 'It's probably not the wisest look for us to get off the boat and demand the quickest path to the bar.'

'Fair enough,' she managed but they were both grinning, two conspirators who'd pulled off something magical. 'Let's put indulgence aside for the moment—but not for long.'

The guy driving the upmarket luggage buggy introduced himself as Joe. 'I'm carter of baggage, greeter of guests, sorter of problems, general dogsbody. Anything you need, I'm your first port of call.'

Wearing shorts and polo shirt in the turquoise and gold colours of the resort, with 'Dolphin Isles Resort' emblazoned on his chest, he looked to be in his sixties, but he was wrinkled enough to seem older. Anya couldn't decide if he had indigenous heritage or if he'd simply spent a lifetime in the sun. If he had Anglo Saxon skin under that deeply tanned outer layer, she hoped he'd been checked every two minutes for skin cancers.

For some dumb reason that pleased her. Hey, I must still be a doctor, she told herself, reassured to find a sliver of professionalism inserting itself into what seemed a fantasy world.

And then they pulled up outside a bungalow, set apart from the rest of the resort accommodation. It looked gorgeous—but Joe was apologising. Its location meant if they wanted a morning swim they'd have to walk a whole hundred metres.

Oh, the hardship.

'The clinic's right next door.' Joe pointed a weathered thumb at a discreet building set to the rear of the bungalow, with a sign directing guests to Dolphin Isles Medical Centre. 'Access is coded—codes are all in your info book. I can show you through if you like, or maybe you'd like to explore yourself. Martin—our resort manager,' he explained to Anya, 'is caught up with a film crew at the other end of the island. All hush-hush of course, but you'll probably recognise the actors. That's in your contracts though, you shut up about anyone you see here. If you ask for an autograph or a selfie you'll be kicked off the island in minutes. You stay out of their faces, they stay out of yours.'

Hooray, not a chance of a tuna bake in sight, Anya thought, and she caught Ben's glance and he was looking as pleased as she was.

Joe was heaving the luggage out onto the veranda. Now he opened the door with a flourish and gestured them to come in.

'Nice place, this,' he told them. 'Nice big living room. Bathroom's the same as the resort's—outside waterfall shower but there's an inside one as well if the insect life gets a bit much. Last docs said they'd have liked a study but there's heaps of space over at the clinic if you need to work. The bedroom's just through there. Martin'll be back before dinner—he said he'll meet you in the bar at six. Meanwhile the refrigerator's stocked, make yourself at home.'

But Anya wasn't listening. She was staring at the bedroom door.

One bedroom door.

'Only one bedroom?' she asked faintly, and Joe glanced at her with doubt, maybe hearing the note of caution.

'Well, yeah. Big, though, great king-sized bed. Guess it has its problems. Doc Brenda, she's one of the docs that just left, well, she and Doc Craig had a tiff a couple of years back and Brenda slept for a whole week in the clinic. Martin reckons if he'd provided them with two bedrooms they'd still be fighting, so I guess you two need to get on. Still,' he said and grinned, 'if you can't get on here, I don't know where you can. Welcome to paradise, guys. I'll leave you to it.'

And he walked out, closing the door behind him.

Silence.

Anya walked slowly across the magnificent living room, filled with gorgeous cane furnishings, mountains of bright cushions and rugs. A vast wooden fan whirred gently overhead. There were potted plants that looked as if they'd grown there for ever, and she could see glimpses of the ocean through the palms outside. It was an awesome room—but she was focused on the bedroom door.

She walked forward and opened it. It, too, was awesome. Huge. Old-fashioned style. Another whirring fan. Gorgeous thick rugs, old-style wardrobes with Oriental carvings etched into the doors. Through the door she could see an en suite bathroom, with a stand-alone clawfoot bath, his and hers washbasins—and a door to what looked like a fernery: a shower room under the stars.

But she hardly looked at these things either. She stared

instead at the truly massive bed which took up three-quarters of the room.

One bed.

'Did you see this house,' she said in a voice she hardly recognised, 'when you came for the interview?'

'I saw it from the outside,' Ben told her, sounding cautious. He obviously saw the problem. 'Brenda and Craig had their family staying from England.' He looked a bit abashed. 'Martin referred to it as the doctors' quarters, and Brenda's sister and brother-in-law were staying here as well. I guess I assumed multiple bedrooms, but maybe… they must have been using camp beds in the living room.'

'You didn't actually count the bedrooms?'

'Um…maybe not.'

There was a moment's silence while she thought this through. And then thought a little deeper. 'Did you imply to this… Martin,' she asked at last, 'that we were…married?'

'I did not.' He'd come into the bedroom behind her but there was something in his tone, something in the emphatic way he spoke, that made her wheel around to face him.

'So how exactly did you describe our relationship?'

'I did imply,' he said cautiously—very cautiously indeed—maybe sensing her loaded question, 'that we were a medical partnership. That we've been working together at Merriwood.'

She stared at him for a long moment, her mind whirling. 'Did you mention,' she said carefully, 'how long we actually worked together?'

'They didn't ask for specifics.'

'They'll surely have rung Mathew. To check on our credentials.'

There was another silence. And then, 'Mathew might,' Ben admitted, 'have been persuaded to gloss over the timing. I've told him how great this job would be for you, and he does owe you.'

'You're kidding.' The silence continued while he met her eyes, unapologetic, innocence personified.

'So,' she said at last, trying to get over the idea of Mathew's arm being twisted to deceive. Mathew, who'd probably never told a white lie in his life. 'The advertisement for the job stated a partnership, yes? Did you check that partnership meant medical only?'

'Possibly…not.' He'd rearranged his expression and she was reminded of an ancient dog she'd fallen for on a television show she'd seen as a kid—Boris used to pinch his owner's socks and then convey—with eyes alone—that he was innocence personified.

Boris had been the reason why she'd wanted a dog.

She'd got a kitten instead.

What had she got…*instead*…now?

She had a dumb desire to laugh—but this was serious!

'So… I let you do the interview, all the arranging.' Her gaze fell to his left hand. 'And you're wearing a wedding ring.'

He glanced down at his hand. Why he still wore it he didn't know. Respect for Rihanna's parents? More protection from the truth? Whatever, this was something else he had to move on from. He twisted it off now and tossed it onto the dresser. 'I…yes.'

'Did they actually ask if we were married?'

'Maybe not,' he admitted. 'But…' his tone became virtuous again '…we have different names.'

'How many female doctors do you know who've changed their professional names after marriage?'

'Anya…'

'Did you know?' she demanded. 'Did you suspect they thought of us as a couple?'

'I…'

'Don't you dare lie.' She glowered and his expression changed. He spread his hands. Admitting all?

'I thought this job seemed great,' he told her. 'Just what we both need. Okay, maybe I suspected they assume it, but no, I didn't lie.'

'That's so noble of you.'

'It is, isn't it?' he said, and there was that look of virtue again.

For some reason she badly wanted to giggle—but giggling was Not Appropriate.

'I'm sorry,' he said, Boris-like again, and she fought to regain her indignation.

'Yeah, that's helpful,' she said acerbically. 'So get us out of this mess. You'll explain to this Martin—and whoever else is even vaguely interested—that we're not romantically, emotionally, sexually involved. Not the tiniest, least bit. And tell them how long we actually worked together.'

He raked his fingers through his hair. It was a very ordinary gesture but it didn't seem so ordinary. It made him look…vulnerable. That and the cane he still carried.

Vulnerable? She narrowed her eyes and looked at his penitent expression and she hardened her heart. Manipulative, more like. And, sure enough, here it came.

'Why?' he asked.

'What, why tell the truth?'

'Anya, I didn't lie,' he told her. 'If they didn't want to do their homework that's up to them. I told them I'd only been at Merriwood for a short time as a stage in my recovery, but they should check my reputation at Sydney Central. In fact, they mostly talked to Mary about your time in Merriwood.'

'Mary.' She thought about it. 'Not Mathew.'

'In the end Mary and Janet and I thought Mathew wasn't

the best placed to give an overview. I checked that he'd confirm things but that was all.'

'You talked to Mary and Janet…'

'They really wanted you to take this job.'

'You're kidding.' She glowered. 'So my friends have landed me with this?' She motioned to the ridiculously vast bed. 'Now what? You want to build a fence down the middle?'

'No need. I promise I'll keep to my side. We can share.'

'In your dreams.'

'Well…' He considered. 'I can sleep in the clinic.'

'You heard Joe. What sort of impression does that give? A warring couple? No, thanks. You can tell this Martin, whoever he is, the truth and arrange separate accommodation.'

'I doubt if there is any,' he said, his expression still hangdog. 'He told me there was a shortage of staff accommodation—too many staff and not enough rooms. And after I saw this place… Anya, I really wanted this job and I thought you would too.'

She glared at him. Then, because a glare wasn't big enough, she put her hands on her hips and assumed a megawatt glower.

'Sorry,' he said.

But there was something about that sorry. That glint behind it. A trace of laughter?

She opened her mouth to tell him where he could shove this job, this island, this whole set-up—but that twinkle gave her pause. It was almost a challenge.

She was standing in a dream house, a dream island. She had the dream job in front of her. Was she planning to walk away because this man was devious? Where would she go? Certainly not back to Merriwood.

Somewhere else as good as this?

She glowered a bit more, but her brain was suddenly suggesting practicalities. And she was also casting a surreptitious glance out of the window at the gorgeous sparkling ocean she could see through the palms. She was thinking of the kayak she'd seen. Of the dolphins.

Practicalities, she told herself. Her indignation was still full-on, but remnants of sense were intruding. Also, this view was fantastic. So…

She looked carefully around the bedroom, at the lavish but tasteful furnishings. This bed was huge—how on earth had they ever got it through the door?

On impulse she stalked forward and tugged one side of the bed. Pleasingly, it did what she'd noticed was the norm in many of the hotels she'd stayed in as a solitary medical delegate at professional conferences. The bed was on wheels but it didn't move smoothly as a single unit. She hauled off the bedlinen—and found two normal-sized double beds.

'Ha!'

'So…' Ben said cautiously, watching from the sidelines. 'Um… You're thinking we can move a bed into the living room?'

'No.' She directed another glower at him—and his dratted twinkle. 'I'm not intending to live in the bedroom while you reign supreme in the living room—and neither do I intend sleeping in the living room, with you traipsing through every time you need to go in and out. Help me separate this—and then help me move the wardrobes.'

'Wardrobes?'

'In case you hadn't noticed, we have two huge wardrobes,' she said with exaggerated patience. 'We shift them both into the middle to make a divider. One will be facing my side of the room—that'll be the side with the big window facing the ocean and with the door to the en suite—

because you owe me, Ben Duncan. The other side will be yours, the side with the sliver of window up the top. You can use that dinky little bathroom off the living room. We'll have to come to some agreement over the settings of the central ceiling fan—I'm prepared to negotiate on that, but nothing else.'

'You're very…' he paused, considering '…bossy?'

'Too right, I'm bossy,' she told him and for the first time she allowed herself to smile. 'What other arrangement can work? If I meekly let you give me the best side I'd need to be grateful, and gratitude is *not* in my contract. This way you don't get to sleep in the clinic, but I'll overlook your need to be grateful. Okay, Dr Duncan, let's get on with this.'

'And Martin?' he asked cautiously. 'What do we tell him?'

'Nothing,' she said. 'I'll concede that. He doesn't get to see our bedroom. He didn't ask particulars about our relationship and it's none of his business.'

'I think housekeeping is included in our contract,' he said, still cautious.

'Then it gets taken out. You clean one week, I clean the next. We like our privacy. Right?'

'Right.' He looked at her, fascinated. 'Does that mean problems are solved?'

'For the moment,' she told him. 'Any more questions? If not, I intend to go find a piña colada. We can cope with furniture-moving later.'

And she grinned and tossed her bag on the bed—*her* bed. 'Join me if you want, but I'm heading for a drink.'

She headed for the bar. He stayed behind and did some furniture reorganisation. It was the least he could do, he decided, but also he needed a bit of space.

At the interview he'd suspected the island authorities had

assumed—maybe wanted to assume—that there was a romantic link between the two of them, but he'd never been
asked outright. He'd thought if it caused problems it'd be
a matter of simply saying, whoops, no, professional only,
to Martin and whoever else needed to be told. They could
hardly sack them for not being married.

So the whoops was in reserve if anyone asked—but what
was there in the sensible fallback that gave him pause?

Was it that, watching Anya's eyes flash fire, watching
her incredulity and then the tiny glimmer of laughter edg-
ing in at the sides, had made him think that sharing a bedroom with her would be okay by him?

It was her laughter that had caught him. It was six weeks
since her mother's death, six weeks since the catastrophe
of her wedding, and yet she'd looked at this set-up, she'd
listened to his pathetic excuses—yeah, he hadn't really
thought this through—and he'd just known there'd been
the niggle of an urge to giggle.

The woman had spirit.

He was thinking again of the night at the river, of Anya
standing up to her knees in the water, of the beauty of the
night, of the beauty of… Anya.

He'd wedged a mat under one of the wardrobes and was
now sliding it into position. It was a decent-sized wardrobe.
Two of them would make a good-sized barrier—there'd be
no way they could see each other.

But there'd be no door. They could hear each other, and
if…

Um…no. No, no, no. She was six weeks bereaved, plus
six weeks from a disastrous non wedding. He'd put her in
an invidious position by letting everyone on this island
think they were a couple. One stupid move from him and
he knew she'd have no choice but to walk away from this

job, and this job looked like being just what she needed. And what he needed.

More, it looked like being fun.

So keep it light, he told himself, assuming a schoolmasterly tone inside his head. You're here to enjoy yourself, and that means...not enjoying yourself.

He grinned. Okay, this was dumb, tugging wardrobes was dumb, but if that was what it took he'd behave.

The bar was waiting. Anya was waiting.

He tugged the second wardrobe into place and headed out to the veranda.

To find Joe striding along the path towards him—fast. One look at his face and he knew there was trouble.

Bad trouble?

'Anya?' It was a dumb thing to think, but that was where his mind went. Anya had headed over to the bar fifteen minutes ago. What could have happened to her in that short time?

Surely nothing. But Joe was grabbing the veranda post and struggling to get his breath. He'd run?

'You gotta come, Doc,' he gasped, and made a wide gesture towards the beach. 'Coupla silly buggers on the beach...jet-skis...playing chicken, would you believe? Head-on crash. Doc Anya saw it from the bar—she's already gone. Said to get you fast, plus first aid stuff, then ring the mainland for evac. One of the kids is taking the kit down to the beach, but Doc, it looks bad. We're gonna need you.'

CHAPTER SIX

ONE MINUTE SHE'D been sitting in the bar, piña colada in hand, admiring the reflected glow of the setting sun over the sea. The next Anya was standing chest-deep in the surf, directing frightened lifeguards to help a tattooed hunk of an accident victim. At the same time she was applying pressure to try and stop catastrophic bleeding from another man's knee.

Two jet-skis had crashed headlong into each other at high speed. One man had been thrown backwards into the water; the other's leg seemed to have been smashed almost into the machine itself.

She'd seen it from the bar, two idiots doing high speed loops just out from the resort. She'd watched in dismay as a couple of young lifeguards had started yelling, waving, desperate for them to stop. She'd seen one of the riders raise what was surely a beer can at his mate, signalling… one last race?

His mate had waved in reply. The yelling from the beach had been ignored. They'd raced in tight circles, right into the shallows, surely at impossible speeds—and then they'd ridden straight at each other.

An appalling game of chicken…

And neither side had won. Neither jet-ski had swerved.

There'd been the smash of crunching metal, a scream—and then silence.

Dear God…

'Get Ben,' she'd snapped at the barman, who was staring out at the beach with surely as much horror as she was feeling.

'Ben?'

'The other doctor. My…partner. Joe knows. Go!'

She'd been running even before she'd finished speaking. Down across the beach, through a cluster of horrified onlookers, past a couple of bikini-clad beauties standing knee-deep in the water and screaming.

A couple of kids in resort-coloured lifeguard uniforms had headed out towards the guys on the smashed machines. The jet-skis were a mangled mess. One man was in the water, the other still on what was left of his jet-ski. Blood was already clouding the water.

Thankfully—if one could be thankful for such a tiny mercy—the beach sloped at such a gentle angle that even where the jet-skis had crashed, the water was still only chest-deep.

The lifeguards had headed to the guy in the water. She was pushing her way out through the shallows, figuring where she was most needed. The crimson stain spreading around the guy still on the jet-ski made her choice for her.

From his knee down was a bloody, pulpy mess. The crimson bloom in the water suggested an artery must surely be severed. The blood was pumping. He might already have bled out.

Every second counted. She was shoving her way through the small waves, hauling her shirt off as she went. Then her pants too—even from here she knew she'd need some sort of pressure pad.

He wasn't dead, at least not yet. Slumped across the bars

of his machine, he looked almost lifeless, but as she reached him he managed to stir a little.

'W...won,' he said stupidly, thickly. 'Troy's...an idiot.'

'So are you,' she said grimly, but he didn't reply. He couldn't. This amount of blood loss...

He was lying sideways across the wreck of his machine, and his oozing, bloody leg was almost clear of the water. She had no choice but to tug it upward, resting his foot on her upper arm. Then she twisted her soaked pants into a pad and shoved it as hard as she could against the source of the bleeding, fighting to find the pressure point where artery neared the bone.

The spurting flow decreased. The blood was still oozing from under her fingers but the worst of the flow seemed to have ceased.

Enough to save his life? How much blood had he lost already?

But the pad was in place. She shoved downward even harder—and then took a moment to see what was happening around her.

The two lifeguards, surely only kids, were trying to support the other guy in the water, who looked to be unconscious.

'Use a surfboard!' she yelled across at them. 'Put the board under him in the water, moving him as little as possible. I don't want his back or neck moved.' But both kids looked terrified almost to immobility. Surely they'd done this in training? They were holding the guy's head out of the water, stopping him from drowning at least, but they needed direction.

And suddenly they had it.

'Priority?' The deep call cut across the chaos, across the women's screams. And blessedly, thankfully, here was Ben, striding out through the shallows towards them. How had he got here so fast, with his bad leg? It didn't matter. He was here, he was demanding a fast update from her, his medical colleague—and she could have wept with relief.

'You go there!' she yelled. He'd be seeing the wash of crimson, which was why he was heading straight for her. 'I haven't assessed that one. But send one of the lifeguards to me.' She had to have help—she was using all her strength to keep the pad in position. One hand was under what was left of his calf, the other was pressing down, but she needed extra hands to twist tie a tourniquet.

She saw Ben pause, realising how caught up she was, and that he still needed to be in first responder mode. He cast a fast appraising glance around the scene, taking in the mess, the young kids in lifeguard gear, the huddle of shocked bystanders who'd backed off…

And then he transformed into doctor in charge.

'Apart from the lifeguards, is there anyone here with first aid training?' His voice boomed out towards the crowd of resort guests, the horrified onlookers on the shore.

A sun-wrinkled elderly woman stepped forward into the shallows. She was wearing a floral swim skirt, a matching hibiscus-covered bikini top and a gorgeous flowery swim-cap which didn't quite cover her snow-white curls.

'In between raising children I've spent thirty years as a nurse in ER,' she called, her accent markedly American. 'Retired for years, but if I can be of use…'

'Welcome back to the workforce,' Ben snapped and motioned towards Anya. 'Can you help Dr Greer? Anyone else? I need strong volunteers to get these guys to the beach. You, you and you.' He pointed as people stepped forward. 'Dr Greer's in charge at that side, I'm on the other. Take orders from either of us, we're the island medics.'

And, just like that, instead of a crowd of frightened on-lookers and a couple of terrified kid lifeguards, he had a team. He was heading for the guy in the water as he spoke, and by the time people stepped forward he was already assessing.

Ben was in charge. She could focus.

The lady in the amazing swim cap had waded to her side. She was elderly, short and plump, she was up to her armpits in water, but when she spoke she sounded immediately competent.

'Dorothy Vanson,' she said briskly. 'If I can't cope with what you want me to do, I'll yell. Tell me what needs doing.'

'Ruptured artery,' Anya said, taking her at her word. 'This pad's stopping spurting but I've assessed no further. Can you check his airway?'

'Would it be better if I take over the pad?' the woman said, obviously doing her own assessment and figuring how best she could help. 'I may look old and dotty but I'm as strong as a horse. I'll push, you do the rest. You want my bikini top as a tourniquet?'

Anya blinked. 'Um...no. I think my shirt should be enough.'

'Probably for the best,' Dorothy said serenely. 'We don't want to add shock to the injuries. Okay, his foot can go on my shoulder, my hand's coming in now.'

And a millisecond later Dorothy's sun-wrinkled hand was pressing as hard as Anya had been, and Anya was free to check the guy's breathing. No obstruction there, but the breaths were fast and shallow. How much blood had he lost? Certainly enough to drop his blood pressure to dangerous levels.

What else was wrong? She couldn't assess for much else while she was in the water, but now, blessedly, she had her hands free. She could take her time to rip her shirt and make it long enough to twist into a decent tourniquet.

There were others in the water now, resort staff wading in to help, waiting for orders.

Ben was working on his guy. His makeshift team had him on a board and were carrying him towards the shore. She glanced towards the beach and saw Joe opening a massive box. A huge red cross on the side denoted it a medical kit. Equipment. Once they had these guys back on the beach their chances would increase exponentially.

But to get this guy off the jet-ski...

'I need a surfboard here too,' she called to Ben, and Ben shouted to the people on shore.

'You heard the doc, a surfboard there now, and half a dozen people to hold it steady.' And Joe himself was heading into the water, a surfboard breaking the small waves in front of him.

But his first reaction when he reached them was shock at the sight of the little lady helping. 'Mrs Vanson! You're a guest! You shouldn't be doing this.'

'So who else is going to do it?' Dorothy retorted. 'You men leave all the hard work to the women. Are you ready to shift him, Doctor?'

Anya wasn't. The last thing she wanted was to unravel him from his wreck of a jet-ski, to risk crushing a possibly injured spine, to risk opening more unexposed wounds. She couldn't stand back enough to get an overview of how he was positioned.

And then Ben was there, heading back to them but still watching the guy they were carrying towards the beach. 'Roll the whole jet-ski onto its side,' he ordered. 'Let's set the board up beside him so he slips straight on. All of you, look at the position he's in now and that's the position we want him on the board. Do it!' He glanced at Anya. 'The guy on the beach needs a trachy. Can you manage here?'

'Of course we can manage,' Dorothy said indignantly. 'You go play hero somewhere else.'

And despite the adrenalin, despite the desperate emergency, Anya found herself close to a chuckle.

Half an hour after the call they had both men stabilised. Almost. They had a tracheostomy tube in place and secure. They had drips set up, and Anya's patient's blood pressure was finally starting to rise. There were multiple fractures of face, ribs and limbs, but there were no outward signs of pierced lungs. Even better, both men were stirring into consciousness—a major indicator that they weren't facing brain damage. The problem they now faced was pain management, which was fraught when both men were obviously well affected by alcohol.

But finally, blessedly, the medical evacuation chopper appeared, swooping in fast and landing on the beach. On board was an emergency physician, two paramedics and a pilot. They took charge with competence and speed, intent on transferring the patients to the facilities of a major mainland hospital. Thus, twenty minutes after it had landed, Anya and Ben were left standing side by side, staring up at the disappearing chopper and trying to come to terms with what had just happened.

The beach had been cleared of onlookers. The resort staff were clearing the mess. Joe was escorting Dorothy and her husband back to their bungalow, apologising as he went. Obviously the Vansons were Very Important Guests and Joe was clearly horrified at their involvement.

'Oh, for heaven's sake,' Anya heard her say. 'I can't spend all my holiday lying in the sun. Henry knows I like to be busy.'

'Holiday?' Anya said faintly as they disappeared. She

was still soaking wet, she was disgustingly bloodstained and she was wearing knickers plus an oversized Hawaiian shirt one of the tourists had kindly offered as soon as she'd had a chance to be aware of what she was—or wasn't—wearing. And then she added for good measure, 'Wasn't that what we were supposed to be having? A doddle? Isn't that what you offered, Dr Duncan?'

He sent her a lopsided smile. 'Whom do we sue?'

'You for a start.' She looked down at her disgusting self. 'I hope our luxury villa has plenty of hot water.'

'I hope so too.' And then his smile faded. 'Anya, you did great.'

She paused and looked at him, met his gaze and tried to figure what to say. Something flippant, she thought. Keep it light. Instead, she heard her voice wobble as the words came out.

'So did you. I can't believe you did a trachy on the beach. Awesome, Dr Duncan.'

'He looks like he has spinal damage. It'll be a long road back.'

'Yeah, and the other guy's likely to lose that leg. They won't be playing chicken again any time soon.'

'They were drunk.' Ben's voice became grim. 'And these were resort jet-skis they were using.'

'The brochure says alcohol's all-inclusive in the hotel rate.' She stared out to the shore where the remains of the wrecked jet-skis were being hauled onto a trailer. 'Those lifeguards didn't stand a chance keeping drunken idiots under control. I'm thinking…compulsory breath tests before use? The punters may not like it, but I can't see any choice.'

And then they were distracted. A short, dapper man

in a navy business suit was hurrying across the sand towards them.

'Martin,' Ben said as the man approached. The resort manager?

'Ben!' The guy held out his hand in welcome—and then got near enough to see the state of them. The hand was smartly withdrawn.

'I wouldn't touch me either,' Ben said. 'Martin, this is Anya.'

'Pleased to meet you, Dr Greer,' Martin said, as if there was nothing unusual about standing on the beach with two soaked, bloodstained doctors. 'It's good to meet you at last. Your husband's told me all about you.'

'He's not my husband,' Anya said shortly.

'No? Sorry.' Despite his urbanity, the guy was clearly distracted. 'Joe tells me you did great. We'll have a drink later, but not now. There's so much…'

He hesitated and then grimaced. 'First things first. Troy and Nathan are part of the film crew, here to shoot the latest Gerry Boyne thriller. When news gets out I'll have every media outlet trying to get on the island, and the last thing I want is aerial shots that look as gruesome as this.' He motioned to the staff trying to haul the wreck of the jet-skis to shore, and to the bloodstained gear still on the beach. 'Ugh.'

'Does that include us?' Ben queried, and Martin had the grace to give an apologetic smile.

'If you wouldn't mind…'

'We're clearing off,' Ben told him. 'But Martin, first thing…that was a disaster that could have been avoided. Those men were so drunk it made medical treatment almost impossible. So our first condition as incoming resort doctors is that no guest gets on a recreational motorised vehicle without a breath test. Starting now.'

Martin stared at him for a long moment, seemingly considering, but then shook his head. 'There's no way we can refuse what the superstars want—but I will ask the staff to give warnings.'

'No warnings. Just the rule.'

'Look, I don't have time to talk about this now.'

Ben's face hardened. 'A rule or we leave—and we tell the media why we're leaving.'

Simple as that.

'Ben…'

'Those guys almost killed each other,' Ben said harshly. 'And it could have been worse. They were using jet-skis in the swimming area, in shallow water. Your lifeguards didn't seem to have any control. They could have slammed into kids, into other guests, or maybe into the dolphins out there, which would have upset everyone who saw. This is non-negotiable, mate. Take it or leave it.'

The men stared at each other. This was a side of Ben that Anya hadn't seen before, uncompromising, grim—ready to walk away.

Walk her away? This was her job too. But she was already moving closer to Ben, facing Martin down as well. They might not be married but in this they were a partnership. As one.

'We'll talk about it later,' Martin tried.

'Now. Or we walk. This whole mess was avoidable.'

'You can't leave.'

'So make the decision.'

Finally the man shrugged. 'Fine,' he said, almost pettishly. 'Will you talk to the press, after you've cleaned up, of course? They'll want to know the extent of the injuries.'

'Tell them to contact the hospital in Cairns,' Ben said. 'I can't imagine you'll want us to release confidential patient information.'

The man's face paled. 'No!' he muttered. 'Of all the things to happen… This could well crash the resort if they shift the blame to us.'

'You might,' Ben suggested diffidently, 'like to send a report to the mainland police, with a possible suggestion. Driving water craft when intoxicated is illegal, isn't it? National laws are national laws, and people are responsible for their own behaviour. The doctors in Cairns will do blood tests if the police request it. I'll write suspected intoxication in a report if you wish.'

There was a moment's silence and then Martin's face cleared. 'Good. I'll do that. Dammit, I can't let the movie lot blame us.' His panic seemed to ease and he regarded them almost benignly. 'You're heading off now?'

'We're taking our disgusting selves out of sight of any marauding cameras,' Ben said promptly. 'Come on, Anya. Let's go.'

They walked back to their bungalow in silence, each intent on their own thoughts. But Anya got halfway there and had to stop. She was shaking, she realised. The adrenalin of the catastrophe had dissipated and shock was setting in.

She was a competent doctor, she'd coped with emergency situations in the past, but never before had she come so close to losing a life in such circumstances.

She was filthy. Her body was still sticky with dried blood. She was wearing someone else's dumb Hawaiian shirt and even that was bloodstained.

Suddenly her body didn't want to move.

'Give me a minute,' she said, standing still and taking deep breaths. If she didn't know better she'd say she was heading for a panic attack—but surely doctors didn't have panic attacks. The two women on the beach, girlfriends of the guys who'd been airlifted to Brisbane, had both had full-blown ones and they'd been distractions she and Ben could have done without.

She stood absolutely still, she focused on breathing and waited for this to pass.

Ben stood back and waited. He stayed by her side, a tiny bit distant, with her but not. Giving her space. She was aware that he was there, she was almost grateful for his presence, but she needed to focus only on herself.

Breathe, breathe, breathe...

And finally it eased. The sense of overwhelming catastrophe, the feeling that the world was crushing her, that she was totally out of control, there was nothing she could do, nowhere she could go, finally it backed off. She let it subside a little more and then sighed.

'Sorry,' she muttered, and Ben's voice answered gently.

'Don't be. You did great, Dr Greer.'

'Yeah, but...'

'No buts.' He reached out and took her hand in his, his fingers laced through hers, and there was the gentlest of pressure. 'Your mum died six weeks back, your fiancé turned out to be a louse, you've packed up your home and you've travelled to another state, another job. This afternoon you saved a guy from bleeding out, all the while stopping him from drowning. You want to take twenty-four hours to focus on your breathing, that's okay by me. Totally justifiable.'

She nodded. Said like that, it put things in perspective.

'You did a great job too,' she ventured. 'You want to breathe a little as well?'

'I'd rather have a shower.' He tugged her round so she was facing the path. 'Good idea?'

'Yeah.' But as his hand tugged her forward, as they headed for the bungalow again, the memory of his words to Martin started replaying in her mind. His anger had almost matched her panic attack, she thought, and she knew that if Martin hadn't caved he would have left the island. Right now.

'Ben,' she said carefully into the stillness. They were walking again, hand in hand. It was a strange sensation of familiarity, but it felt okay.

More than okay. It felt right.

'Yep?' They were speeding up now, in the home stretch, hot showers beckoning like a siren song.

'When you told me your wife was killed in an accident... was that caused by a drunk driver?'

'Yes,' he said shortly, and his hand was withdrawn as if she'd stuck something sharp into his palm.

'I'm sorry. It's none of my business. I just thought...it did seem personal back there.'

'A bloody waste,' he muttered. 'Two guys who're going to regret this day for the rest of their lives.'

'At least they did it to themselves, not to others,' she ventured. 'If they'd crashed into swimmers...'

'That would have been much worse.' But there was something in his voice—it was loaded with bitterness? She cast a curious glance at him, her own shock and nerves subsiding into the background.

Should she shut up? She didn't. Maybe it was her medical training—ask the hard questions, you'll never figure what's really wrong if you don't ask. Like asking someone who seemed depressed or too quiet or maybe agitated, 'Are you thinking of suicide?' She'd been trained always to ask.

Maybe that was the reason she opened her mouth again.

'A drunken driver killing your wife, injuring you so badly...is today bringing that back for you?'

There was another silence then, a long one. Maybe he wouldn't answer, she thought. They walked on but as they neared the bungalow he paused.

'You go ahead,' he told her. 'Two people using the hot water at the same time'll probably strain the system anyway. I need to walk things off. I'll head up to Reception and do that report for Martin.'

'In those clothes?'

'I assume they have a back door. And the worst has already washed off.'

'You're not exactly respectable,' she told him and then paused. 'Ben, is there any way I can help?'

'No,' he said shortly and then he exhaled.

'You can't,' he told her. 'It's just…a drunken driver did kill Rihanna and injure me. Only that drunken driver was Rihanna.'

CHAPTER SEVEN

WHY HAD HE told her that?

Left with his thoughts, they weren't exactly comforting. It felt almost a betrayal.

He'd told no one.

The speed. The white lines blurring in front of him. His voice, demanding Rihanna slow down…

After that, a merciful blank.

But he'd woken after a few days to pain, to endless medical treatment, to never-ending sympathy and kindness. He'd been surrounded by eulogies for a beloved wife and daughter, a woman who, according to the police, could have ended up driving straight into the path of an oncoming car.

A burly police sergeant had come to see him in hospital, driven by, what, sympathy?

'Mate, there's CCTV along that stretch of road. Your car was turning into that bend way too fast, and in the end it looked to be heading straight for the other sedan. Mum and Dad and three little kiddies were in that car. Now, I dunno for sure what happened, but the view on the CCTV looked pretty clear—you seemed to lean over and wrench the wheel. You hit a tree instead of the oncoming car. Mate, if you're prepared to let people know just how drunk your wife was, I'd be backing you. In my book you're a bloody hero.'

A hero. Great. What was the use of that? No. Let people

think Rihanna was the angelic wife and mother the eulogy said she was.

But he would get the Breath Test Before Use rule enforced on the beach. Anya would back him up, he knew she would. And why was he thinking of this now, of Rihanna, of his marriage, of a time he desperately wanted to put behind him?

Because of the blood, the chaos, the fear of this afternoon, he thought. He'd been away from medicine for so long. Was this post-traumatic stress? Was one accident making him think of another?

Or was it Anya, looking ghastly in her bloodstained borrowed clothes? Anya, coping with chaos, waiting until it was all over to allow herself the luxury of personal reaction. Anya… Was she what a real hero should look like?

Yes, it was, he thought, and his pacing feet slowed. Anya, who'd be back in the bungalow now, showering— in what should have been their en suite bathroom but was now firmly labelled *her* bathroom.

Was she shaking again?

What was he doing, walking aimlessly around the island when Anya might be needing him?

Anya didn't need him. He thought of those two wardrobes and he found himself grinning. He knew deep down that the reaction that had made her cling to him, that had let him grasp her hand, that had forced her to hold it as if it was there to save her, was an aberration.

Anya. One strong woman.

Wardrobes. Two separate beds.

They were now colleagues. There was a whole new future to think about.

Um…think about what? She was still in the midst of shock and grief. Back away, he told himself, but even as he did he was turning back to the bungalow.

Home? Back to Anya?

She'd be in the shower. He could imagine her there, maybe shaking again as the events of the afternoon replayed in her head.

She was his colleague. He needed to support her.

Yes, he needed to go home.

She stood under the shower for a long, long time, and it was wonderful. The bungalow's 'en suite' was so much more than just a bathroom. The tiny courtyard was netted overhead to keep the bugs at bay, but it looked almost like a slice of rainforest. Its floor was made of roughly hewn stone and its walls were covered with some sort of flowering vine—mandevilla?—a mass of deep pink, pale pink and white blooms. Palms leaned overhead and the squawks of lorikeets made her feel as if she were almost in a menagerie.

Along the edges of the stone floor, out of range of hot water but close enough to enjoy the steam, she could see at least half a dozen bright green tree frogs. The sweet-smelling soaps and hair products lined up for use had discreet labels—'not harmful for wildlife'—and the frogs looked as if they were even enjoying them.

This was okay. More than okay.

She stood under the stream of luscious warm water, she used meditation techniques she'd learned during medical training to let the nightmare of the afternoon dissipate and she let herself think that this job…might even be good. This afternoon's drama had taught her that she and Ben were needed, but such incidents must surely be rare. The job must be as promised. Rich tourists doing stupid things, patients who'd be evacuated if they needed real medical help, this place…

Ben.

The thought of him cut into her deliberately peaceful

thoughts. Ben. She'd thought she was escaping emotional ties by coming to Dolphin Island. What she'd learned today was that Ben had just as much emotional baggage as she did.

No, she thought fairly. More. She'd lost her mum, but her mum's health had been precarious and they'd both known her time was limited. And somehow she'd escaped from a marriage that, looking at it in hindsight after a whole six weeks, she knew would have been disastrous if it had gone ahead.

A door banged from outside and she heard footsteps treading across the wooden floor. She thought of Ben, going to his side of the bedroom, collecting what he needed, heading to the small bathroom off the living room. A plain, ordinary bathroom, not the tropical splendour she was savouring.

'He deserves no less,' she told the frogs who were sitting on their respective rocks, savouring the steam she was creating. 'Letting people even think we're a couple.'

And then the water pressure dipped a bit and she thought, Fair's fair. She'd had a gorgeous soak, her head was together again, and Ben deserved as much water pressure as she could give him.

And more. On the beach… The tracheostomy… 'I don't think I could have done it,' she told the frogs. Now the stream of hot water had ceased, they were off their rocks and hopping through the puddles on the shower room floor.

'You could get trodden on,' she told them, but she was suddenly no longer thinking about frogs. Her mind had been caught by the vision of Ben in his own shower. That long, lithe body, water streaming down his back, his hair slick and wet, his eyes closed, maybe lifting his arms to savour the sensation.

Naked. Ben.

'Well, that goes to show how shattered you are at losing Mathew,' she said, speaking to herself now and speaking sternly. 'Or not. Out of the frying pan, into the fire? I don't think so. Don't even think about going there.'

And with that she wrapped one of the resort's luscious towels around her body and headed back to her bedroom. *Their* bedroom?

She dressed fast, conscious that Ben could finish in the shower soon—he'd have no frogs to play with. It didn't matter if he came in, she told herself. The rooms were well divided, and she was on the far side. Nevertheless, she dressed fast, donning a crop top and sarong—two things she'd bought on a whim from the airport shop. Okay, she thought, staring at herself in the mirror. Surely now it's time for a piña colada. Or even two.

Almost as she thought it, she heard Ben walk into his side of the bedroom.

And then she heard a knock on the outside door.

It was actually quite hard to answer the door. She needed to walk past Ben's side of the bedroom to get there.

'Are you respectable?' she called, feeling silly.

'Always respectable,' he called back, and she metaphorically girded her loins and marched past. Eyes straight in front.

Maybe only a tiny glance to the left to see a bare chest being towelled dry.

Dear heaven, that body was hot.

'Says the devastated bride,' she muttered to herself and, thrusting aside the desire to take a longer glance, she marched to the door and opened it.

A woman was standing under the porch. She looked very like the two women who'd been screaming on the beach as their boyfriends were being treated. Another of the movie set? Sleek, blonde, gorgeous, the woman was manicured and made-up to within an inch of her life, and from the moment she opened her mouth she oozed entitlement.

'Is the doctor here?' Her tone pretty much said, Stand aside, servant, lead me to someone important.

'I'm a doctor,' Anya said mildly, and the woman blinked in disbelief.

'They said it was a man. Dr Duncan.'

'That would be me.' And Ben was behind her, naked except for a towel draped round his waist.

The woman took a step back. 'You don't look like doctors.' It was an accusation.

'Whoops,' Ben said and smiled and turned to the medical kit which had been lugged back from the beach and dumped inside the door. He reached down—dangerous when his towel didn't look all that securely fastened, grabbed a stethoscope and fastened it round his neck. 'Is this better?'

'We really are doctors,' Anya said quickly, frowning him down. 'Just in off-duty clothes. How can we help?'

'My…my boyfriend.'

'Is he ill?'

'Yeah. He keeps moaning. He got a bit sunburned today and you'd think he'd been dipped in hot oil, the fuss he's making. Not,' she added quickly. 'that he's not entitled to make a fuss. He's Ricardo de Silva.'

She obviously expected them to know the name, and Anya did. Ricardo de Silva was the latest media sensation, a hot young movie star. He'd obviously be on the island for the making of the film.

'Can you ask him to come to the clinic?' she said, casting a dubious glance next door. Neither she nor Ben had had a chance to check the clinic out yet, but she assumed there were facilities.

But the woman had stiffened. 'You come to him,' she said, sounding shocked. 'He's ill. The contract says twenty-four-hour medical care. You can't expect him to walk over here.'

'Which bungalow are you in?' Ben asked before she could respond.

'Number one,' the woman said, as if it was obvious. 'The one with its own horizon pool. And hurry. I don't know why I had to come myself, there was no one answering on Reception.'

'I guess they're busy,' Anya said, figuring she might do a bit of damage control on the island's behalf. 'Every media outlet in Australia and a whole lot overseas will be searching for news about this afternoon's accident.'

'Look, I don't care about them,' the woman said hotly. 'They're not stars. Ricardo needs attention now. Are you coming or not?'

'Give us five minutes,' Ben said. 'Sunburn, you think. I gather you think he'll survive that long?'

'Don't be funny,' she snapped and turned on her heel and stalked away.

'I can do this myself,' she told Ben as they watched the woman depart. He surely didn't look like an efficient, clinical doctor.

'Um…look at yourself,' he told her. 'Sarong? Crop top? Do you know this guy's reputation? How tightly tied is that sarong?'

'Don't be ridiculous. He's got a girlfriend.'

'Reports are it's never stopped him in the past.'

'Well, reports are that you're as likely to be at risk as I am,' she retorted. 'And your towel looks more precarious than my sarong.'

He grinned. 'I reckon we're okay. There's nothing like a little sunburn to dampen testosterone.'

'A little sunburn?' She assumed mock outrage. 'Didn't you hear the woman? He's in agony.'

'Then let's go see if we can fix the agony. You reckon we should don full theatre gear?'

'Not a snowball's chance in a bushfire,' she said briskly. 'I have a piña colada with my name on it waiting in the bar, and His Lordship's bungalow is almost in a direct line.'

'And I'm thinking there might be a hamburger attached to said piña colada, I'm starving. Okay, let's go treat a sunburn fast—though maybe we should put on clothes that look a bit more professional.'

'What, take this job seriously, you mean?'

'I guess,' he said reluctantly. 'But I'm starting to worry. This job seems to be getting in the way of its job description.'

They did change, into decent trousers and shirt and demure trousers and blouse respectively, but as they walked down towards the beach their mood was strangely lighter. Ben had put together a bag of what they might need, and the walk through the discreetly lit, ever so carefully natural, bush path towards the movie star's bungalow was a lovely one. Ben's limp was a little more pronounced than usual—it had been quite some day.

This afternoon had been as shocking a scene as Anya had ever encountered, she thought. It wasn't only that Ben's leg was giving him trouble. She was also having trouble keeping her thoughts under control. The adrenalin, her emotion afterwards, Ben's frank admission of his wife's death, they'd left her reeling.

So break the moment.

Time and time again after drama, medics could be found

reacting with a humour that outsiders sometimes found shocking. But it worked. Often humour could break the appalling tension of what had gone before.

So try.

'You know,' she said thoughtfully as they walked under the palms in the warm dusk breeze, 'this is a great spot for drop bears.'

The legendary and entirely mythical Australian drop bear had been referred to since time immemorial to scare newcomers in this type of situation. The story was that the bears hung high in just such places, only to drop when least expected on the unwary folk underneath. And suddenly she had an urge to share her own drop bear story with Ben.

'You can't scare me with drop bears,' Ben told her, smiling. 'I was brought up on drop bear stories.'

She grinned. 'Rats. But here's a story. My mum told me that Dad terrified her as a new bride. He ended up carrying her all the way home from the local pub "in order to protect her from the bears". "It was the most romantic thing," Mum told me, and she giggled every time she thought about it. I think she was almost disappointed when she found out they didn't exist.'

Ben chuckled—and the deep chuckle sounded good. The tension of the day dissipated still further.

'So are you absolutely sure they don't exist?' she asked Ben. 'You know, if you don't believe in them it's been statistically proven you have a seventy-nine percent higher chance of being dropped on.' She had a sudden ridiculous vision of her picking him up and lugging him home. And the thought made *her* giggle.

'What?' he demanded, and she told him and he grinned.

'I'd like to see you try.'

'Hey, I've chopped wood since I was ten years old. Arms like oaks.'

'Try it,' he said and stopped dead and spread his arms, willing for her to lift.

'If a drop bear descends, I will,' she said with dignity. 'So are you absolutely sure they're not here?'

'Impossible,' he said firmly. 'I've been through the items we can claim for government rebate on this island, and bites and bruises from drop bears doesn't appear once. Though,' he said thoughtfully, 'I can't say Martin won't have collared every drop bear and had them held captive at the far end of the island, in order to keep his precious film crew safe.'

She chuckled, but medicine had to intrude again. They'd reached the bungalow—if it could be called that. This was a more impressive building than anything they'd seen on the island, a mini mansion set right on the beach. The lights were on over massive Balinese-style doors and when Ben lifted the huge knocker and let it fall, the thud on the thick wood—complete with echo—made Anya start.

And then she pretty much jumped again. The guy who opened the door was huge. He was wearing black jeans, black T-shirt, black sunglasses, his arms were like tree trunks and his neck…well, gorilla sprang to mind as a comparison. He was also wearing the sort of welcoming expression a gorilla might be proud of.

'Yeah?' It was a deep, guttural growl, a warning all on its own.

'We're the doctors, here to see Mr de Silva.'

'You don't look like doctors.' So much for their neat clothes, Anya thought. What did he want, white coats?

'They are.' The girl appeared in the background, sounding sulky. 'Let 'em in, Rod.'

'You sure?'

'They're all this crappy island has,' she snapped, and led the way into the living room.

Ricardo de Silva was lying stretched out on a vast leopard-skin couch and he was everything a movie star should be. Anya stopped in the doorway, stunned, and only Ben prodding her in the small of her back made her recover.

The movie star looked…amazing. He was tanned to a deep, deep gold, his shoulder-length blond hair was tumbling to his shoulders and he was naked, apart from what looked to be little more than a loincloth. He looked up at them with startling blue eyes and a mouth already pursed in anger.

'You took your time,' he snarled. 'I'm in pain here. I need some decent drugs, and fast. And why do I need two of you?'

'We're a partnership,' Ben said smoothly, but Anya heard a faint tremor in his voice. This set-up was ludicrous, almost comical. The gorilla bodyguard, the manicured beauty, the he-man alpha hero, lying on his faux fur settee… It looked like a movie scene all by itself. 'We work together. Your… partner…tells me you're sunburned.'

'She's not my partner,' he growled, scowling at the unfortunate woman. 'Mia's an idiot. Why didn't she get burned? I told her to get sun stuff and whatever she used, it didn't work.'

'Honey, it was coconut oil,' the unfortunate Mia wailed. 'When you're as tanned as we are, you don't need kids-type sunscreen.'

Uh-oh. Anya edged a little closer to the man on the sofa. He certainly looked tanned—but was that inflammation underneath?

'Is that tan real?' Ben asked conversationally, and Ricardo flashed him a look of pure filth. 'Piss off.'

'Maybe we could ask your bodyguard and your…friend

to leave for a moment,' Ben said smoothly. 'If we're to examine…'

'We're going,' the woman said hastily and practically pushed the gorilla out of the door, slamming it behind them.

Leaving Ben and Anya looking down at their patient.

'You have blisters on your shoulders,' Anya said, softly now and sympathetically. This really did look painful. 'How long were you out in the sun?'

'Most of the day.' He glowered. 'We were supposed to have the day off and then do a dusk and night scene tonight. So we caught some rays.'

'You surely did.'

'I told her to bring the lotion,' he growled. 'Stupid b…'

'Did you specify sunscreen?' Ben said mildly. 'Fifty plus protection? Waterproof?'

'She should have known.'

'If she has brown skin already and has a decent natural tan, she might think you just wanted to get darker,' Ben said. 'The tan…it's fake, isn't it?' He too had walked forward.

And winced.

From the door the man had looked absurdly, impossibly handsome—impossibly tanned—but up close the tan was underlaid by vicious red. All over. There were blisters on his shoulders and his stomach. Were there blisters on his head?

'Could I check?' Ben asked.

'Don't you dare hurt me.'

'I won't,' Ben said but he tentatively lifted a lock of the blond hair.

The scalp underneath was red as well.

'No hat?' he asked mildly.

'It must have come off.' It was a sullen mutter. 'And I told you, she was supposed to cream me up.'

'Does she know how fair-skinned you really are?'

There was no answer.

'How are you feeling?' Ben asked. 'Headache? Any dizziness?'

'Just damn pain.'

'That's reassuring,' Ben told him. 'I know the pain's an issue but you're lucky to have avoided a major case of sunstroke. There are a few things that'll help. First is to drink fluids, lots of fluids. A cool bath will help—you might need to hop in and out a few times overnight when you feel your body overheating. There's a king-sized tub of aloe vera in our kit—sunburn is something seen a lot in this climate. Lather it on everywhere, it really does work. Then anti-inflammatories, aspirin's probably the best. Do you have any, or will we leave you some?'

'I don't want blasted aspirin. I want something with grunt. Morphine. This pain's crazy.'

'Have you had morphine before?' Ben asked mildly and Anya nodded silently to herself. The way he'd asked for morphine…

'Just for damn pain.'

'Do you have any on hand now?'

'I'm out,' the guy said sulkily. 'Sore throat last week. I can't work with a sore throat.'

'Could you give me the contact details of the doctor who prescribed you the last lot?'

There was a moment's stillness and then the guy's eyes narrowed. 'You think I'm an addict.'

'I don't,' Ben said quietly. 'But morphine for a sore throat, morphine for sunburn when I don't know you? I can't in good faith prescribe you any tonight. Aspirin, aloe vera and cold baths…'

'What the…? Mia!' he roared and as the woman reappeared, looking scared, he yelled, 'Get me the island manager. Get me Sven!'

'Sven's caught up with the fuss from the two guys who were hurt this afternoon,' Mia said apologetically. 'Sven's our director,' she explained to Ben, her eyes not leaving Ricardo's face. 'And he's up to his ears, trying to figure how to shoot tomorrow without Troy and Nathan.'

'That's unfortunate,' Ben said sympathetically. 'But now there might be more trouble. Aloe vera and aspirin will cope with the pain, but you're going to peel,' he told Ricardo. 'All over. The skin underneath will be raw. I'd advise no cosmetics until you completely heal. Your tan's going to disappear too,' he added. 'You might need to make plans.'

'What the…? Fix it!' the man screamed, and Ben turned to Mia.

'We're leaving you anti-inflammatories and aloe vera,' he told her, 'but that's all we can do. I'm sorry but you seem to be in for an uncomfortable night.' And the look he gave her was one of pure sympathy.

'You can't just leave!' Ricardo yelled, but Ben shook his head.

'There's nothing else we can do. Do you concur, Dr Greer?'

'Absolutely,' Anya said unsteadily, taking one last look at the ridiculous setting—and at the panic in the eyes of the unfortunate Mia. And then she hesitated, glancing across at Ricardo and then back at the woman.

And Ben got it almost before she did.

'Mia, if you need anything else for yourself, any support, we're available twenty-four-seven,' he said, watching the girl's face.

'What, if he hits me, do you mean?'

Bang. She hadn't imagined it then, that flash of fear, and Ben had obviously seen it too.

'I can't imagine that will happen,' Ben said smoothly, and he gave Ricardo a long, considering stare. 'But Mia, you know where we are, and the resort's security guys are always on hand.'

'I'm not going to hit her!' Ricardo roared.

'I'm sure you won't,' Ben said.

She hadn't been aware that she'd been holding her breath, but it was released in a rush. Now that it had been said out loud, now the guy knew Ben was wary, she was pretty sure there'd be no physical assault.

'Mia, we'll contact you in the morning and see how things are going,' Ben was saying. 'Now, if you'll excuse us, Dr Greer and I have another urgent case to attend.'

'I… I will come to see you tomorrow, if that's all right,' Mia muttered, with another nervous glance at her boyfriend. 'Just…just to let you know how Ricardo is.'

'That'll be fine,' Anya told her, taking up Ben's cues. 'I'll book you in for a consultation at nine.'

CHAPTER EIGHT

THEY LEFT, THEIR steps automatically turning towards the bar.

'Urgent case?' Anya said once they were out of earshot of the goon watching them go from the bungalow's portico.

'Malnutrition plus dehydration,' he said. 'And urgent's too mild a description.

'Symptoms?'

'Extreme crabbiness. This job was supposed to be a walk in the park. We appear to be working overtime already. Though we do appear to have done good.'

'Treating sunburn?'

'We did save two lives. Plus,' he added softly, 'I suspect we've stopped a woman being bashed tonight.'

'You guessed. Good call, Dr Duncan.'

'I saw your face. You guessed it, too. I'm willing to bet you'll have her in the clinic tomorrow, weeping buckets.'

'I hope I do,' she said, her voice softening. 'What a to-erag. She might be the epitome of dumb blonde, but to treat her like that…'

'Will you advise her to go home?'

'The whole movie crowd might go home,' she said thoughtfully. 'They've lost two minor actors and now, having a leading man who's alternately itching, peeling and swearing… Problematic, wouldn't you say?'

'Martin's not going to thank us when we break the news.'

'He's not, is he?' she said, suddenly cheerful again. They'd almost reached the bar and she could smell food. Was that fried onions? 'And you know the one great thing about today?'

'What's that?' He was watching her, a curious look on his face. As if he didn't quite get her.

Maybe she had no reason to be smiling, she thought, but suddenly she couldn't help it. Yes, the day had been horrific, but she'd been a doctor for long enough to know she could normally block things out. A hamburger with crispy bun oozing with butter and fried onions was surely therapy of the best kind, and *surely* it was time for her piña colada now?

And this place was fabulous. The twinkling lights over the vast veranda of the bar. The soft wash of the tiny waves on the nearby beach. The moonlight over the water...

And added to that...the thing that made her smile most...

'You know,' she said, her smile getting wider. 'We've worked our butts off today, Dr Duncan, and no one, not one single person, has said thank you.'

'They won't either,' Ben said morosely. 'We've stuffed their movie.'

'Not us, Dick the Duck,' she said lightly. They'd arrived at the terrace and a waiter was coming forward to greet them—and surely that was a drinks menu in his hand. 'They did it all by themselves. Not a thank you in sight, and here comes my piña colada. Welcome to our brand-new world, Dr Duncan. Let's dive straight in.'

They were late to the bar. The movie crowd, who, they were told, represented almost half the island's guests, was noticeably absent. Maybe they were too shocked to be out drinking in such a public place or maybe they were gathered somewhere changing plans. After the news of Ricardo broke, there'd be an even greater need to replan.

There was thus a minimal wait on service. Ten minutes after they arrived they were sitting in gorgeous, plushly cushioned cane armchairs, wrapping themselves around hamburgers that were everything Anya could wish for. There was also a piña colada for Anya and a large, ice-cold beer for Ben. Anya finished her cocktail fast—and then looked regretfully at the empty glass.

'Go on,' Ben told her, grinning. 'I'll be the on-call doctor tonight.'

'There'd better not be another call,' she told him. 'Being busy seems a serious breach of our contract.'

Then Martin arrived with a man and a woman they hadn't met before, all of them looking practically bug-eyed.

'What's this I hear about Ricardo?' Martin demanded. 'Sunburn? His girlfriend's been onto Sven here saying he won't be able to work. Surely you can fix sunburn?' His tone was pure challenge.

'We don't have to,' Ben said mildly. 'It'll fix itself. He's been lucky to escape sunstroke. He'll be itchy for a while but he's okay.'

'But he says he'll peel!' The plump little man beside him—introduced as Sven, the film director—was looking as if he was about to have kittens. 'And Serena here says she can't do make-up on sunburned skin.'

'It would look awful,' the woman said. Martin's introduction had been sketchy—'This is Serena, our make-up artist'—and it was clear both regarded her as a minion. 'But there are worse problems. If the skin's peeling…'

'There must be a way,' Sven snapped.

'The make-up will peel off with the skin,' Serena said miserably. 'Unless I cake it so thick it can't look natural.'

'If you put thick make-up on skin so severely sunburned you run an almost certain risk of infection,' Ben told them.

'But he's essential,' Sven snapped. 'Sunburn! It's nothing. Surely we can manage. I can get by without two yahoos this afternoon, but not Ricardo.'

It seemed major injury to two actors was a minor inconvenience, but the effect of sunburn was a potential disaster. There was a moment's silence while Anya and Ben mutually and silently decided to let that go through to the keeper.

'So you'd be prepared to risk someone as high profile as Ricardo getting a major infection on your watch?' Ben asked at last.

'There are antibiotics...'

'We strongly advise against it,' he said flatly. The realisation that, for this man, the two severely injured actors were of no account in the face of a case of sunburn had turned Ben's attitude to grim. 'And I'm afraid it'll need to be written up in the medical notes, there for possible legal subpoena. That's all we can say.'

'But...'

'I'm sorry but my hamburger's getting cold,' Anya interjected as her second piña colada arrived. She really was hungry. 'Would you mind if we eat?'

She got a glower from both Martin and Sven, and a shy smile from the make-up artist.

'Go right ahead,' Martin snapped—and the party retreated.

Anya munched on her burger and watched them go, her expression speculative.

'You realise you just annoyed our boss,' Ben said, but he was watching her with a faint twinkle in his eyes.

'Couldn't be helped.' She was on her third bite. 'This is delicious!'

'You could be sacked.'

'And I just figured that I don't care. There are other tropical islands. They're not grateful to me and I'm not grateful to them. I can walk away in a heartbeat. How good is that?'

'It's not bad at all,' Ben said slowly, watching her turn her attention back to her piña colada.

'These have to be the best piña coladas I've ever had,' she said happily. 'Not that I've had many. Maybe two max, until now. Are you sure you don't want one?'

'One of us needs to stay sober tonight. Professional ethics.'

'Then I'm glad it's you,' she told him. 'And I swear I won't even say thank you.'

For all she'd intended to make a night of it, it didn't happen. Hamburger consumed, halfway into her second cocktail weariness hit like a tsunami. One moment she was high on the adrenalin of this afternoon's rescue, the ridiculousness of the night's sunburn victim, the realisation that she could walk away with no compunction if anyone wanted to sack her. The next it was almost too much effort to raise her glass.

She put her glass down on the table and noticed, with some annoyance, that her hand was suddenly shaking.

'Had enough?' Ben asked mildly, and she flashed him a look of annoyance. That was the type of comment Mathew would have made.

'I can drink more if I want to.'

'I wasn't talking about alcohol. I was talking about you. Today. These past weeks. This whole set-up.'

She looked at him uncertainly, not sure whether to take offence or not. But his eyes were kind.

As Mathew's had been, she thought, but Mathew being *kind* was different. Mathew being *kind* was smothering. Mathew thought he knew what was best for her.

The whole town had thought they knew what was best for Anya and her mother.

Why was she thinking about that now? Why was she suddenly feeling…odd?

'I guess I have had enough of today,' she said, but her mind was still intent on this puzzle. Why did it feel so different, the way this man asked how she was feeling? 'I… It's probably time for bed,' she managed but her sense of confusion was growing.

'I might be headed that way too,' he told her in a voice that said her decision was just that—*her* decision. 'It didn't do my back or leg any good at all, hauling an idiot out from under a jet-ski. What I really need right now is a massage. I bet there are scores of masseurs on this island. Should I ring for room service? How do you think that'd go down?'

And that made her grin. 'So…the new doctor on the island would be calling for the island masseur at midnight on his first day on the job…'

'Hardly a good look?'

She chuckled. 'Possibly not.'

But… *I could give you a massage.* The thought was there in her head, almost bursting to be said out loud. She'd done a massage course. Her mother had had arthritis along with everything else, and she'd loved doing that for her. She was actually pretty good.

But not here. Not with this man. Despite her weariness, alarms were sounding all over the place.

'You'll just have to sleep it off,' she said instead, and pushed the remains of her cocktail aside. 'Bedtime for the island doctors.'

'For the new roomies,' he said and rose and held out a hand to help her up. 'I hope you don't snore.'

'The feeling's mutual, Dr Duncan,' she told him. 'But, even if you do, I reckon sleep is only minutes away.'

* * *

Except it wasn't. They walked home in silence, but it wasn't a comfortable silence. Something had happened.

The day had happened. Last-minute packing. Frantic goodbyes. Janet driving her to Sydney and then a flight to Cairns. The ferry ride to the island, cruising across the breathtaking waters of Australia's Great Barrier Reef. Being transported from one world to another. She'd walked—or rushed—out of the world she knew, and suddenly she was a doctor in surely one of the most beautiful places on earth.

Then there'd been the shock of the shared house, the discussion of pretend marriage, the unnerving knowledge that she'd be sleeping metres from this man, with not even a wall between them. But she'd not even had time to let that sink in before they'd been thrown into a life-threatening medical trauma.

That had made her realise just how good Ben was—how skilled. She'd spent so little time with him back in Merriwood that, apart from the fast Caesarean, she hadn't had time to properly assess his medical skills. But she'd thought there'd be little use for extensive medical skills here.

One afternoon had taught her how wrong that thought had been, and one afternoon had shown her the breadth of Ben's abilities. What he'd done on the beach... The memory of it still took her breath away.

Then there was the gut-lurch when he'd told her about his wife. She'd been trying to block it out—it was surely none of her business—but it refused to be blocked. It had stayed in the back of her mind during the stupidity of the sunburn incident. While she'd seen the way he'd handled it. His...kindness? Wrong word maybe.

Mathew had been kind. Ben was nothing like Mathew.

She was suddenly—and inappropriately—thinking of

the way he'd smiled at her over the table as she'd tackled her hamburger and her cocktail.

Her two cocktails, she corrected herself. It was no wonder she was feeling a bit…fuzzy. Warm.

Why was his hand holding hers?

How had that happened? He'd held out a hand to help her from the table—she remembered that—and then the steps down from the terrace had been dimly lit, and he certainly wouldn't want his medical partner falling.

He was using a cane. She should be taking his hand.

Well, she was holding it, she told herself. Maybe that was how it had happened. Maybe his injured leg was the reason she wasn't pulling away.

Liar, liar, pants on fire.

'Tell me about your wife,' she asked suddenly and a bit too fast. Why had she asked? To break this sense of intimacy? To find out more about this man who was holding her hand? It was definitely none of her business, she had no right to ask, but the question was out there now.

He stopped walking. The question hung, waiting for an answer.

It didn't get one.

'I'm sorry.' She broke the silence, speaking a bit too fast. 'Ben… I had no business asking. It was just…'

'That I told you about Rihanna's drinking?'

'I guess, but I had no right. It just…came out. I'm sorry,' she repeated.

'There's no need to be sorry.' Their linked hands had somehow disconnected. He stood in the dim light, leaning heavily on his cane and his voice was heavy to match.

'Just don't see me as a grieving widower,' he said at last. 'I wasn't much more than a kid when I met Rihanna. I was a med student with my head in my books. Rihanna had just got a job as a junior television presenter and she was so glamorous. She was also intent on one thing—promoting Rihanna—but of course I didn't see that.'

That was followed by a long pause. Anya tried to think of something to say and then decided nothing was the only option. Finally, he seemed to force himself to continue.

'Anyway, we dated for a few months—I thought fairly casually—and then she fell pregnant. At least she told me she was pregnant. And I know this sounds callous but, looking back, I don't know what to believe. Rihanna… Well, my parents are old money, part of the Sydney *Who's Who*, with all the right connections. They're also incredibly social, and Rihanna loved being part of that. I didn't realise how much until…after. Anyway, there was no baby. Our marriage was empty almost from the start, and when she died she was pregnant to another man.'

'Oh, Ben…'

'Don't you dare say you're sorry,' he said, savagely now. 'I've had enough sympathy to last a lifetime. Like your gratitude, I've had enough.'

Whoa.

Where to go from here? She took a deep breath and tried to get her thoughts in order. They wouldn't…order. She thought suddenly of the tissue box she kept in her consulting rooms. A big one. Sometimes she needed to hand over tissues and delve into a patient's grief. Sometimes it was better to retreat and be practical.

Right now, tissues didn't seem the way to go.

'Well,' she said at last, 'I thought *I* needed a tropical island and piña coladas. I reckon your need is double, yet you ordered only a single beer tonight! Surely you can do better than that. What's the saying? Physician, heal thyself. You need to pull your act together.'

And to her relief he gave a grunt of something that

could almost have been laughter. 'You're prescribing *me* piña coladas?'

'If you won't prescribe them for yourself then someone should. Plus as much self-indulgence as you can manage—this job really does need to be a doddle.'

'It does, doesn't it?' he said, and his smile reappeared. There was a moment's pause while he seemed to gather himself back into the persona he presented to the world. Physician in charge of his world? 'Meanwhile, let's go home.' And his hand reached out and caught hers again.

The linking was a relief. It eased things. It helped…her as well as him? They walked on, slowly, in deference to his stiff leg—but also slowly because her thoughts were whirling—and maybe his too. As they walked, the linking of their hands seemed to grow…more important?

Not something to be tugged back from.

Maybe it was the cocktails. Maybe it was the night. Maybe it was the knowledge of each other, a realisation of vulnerability, of pain.

Or something deeper?

They reached their bungalow and it was time for her to pull away, but as they paused on the veranda there seemed no impetus to go inside. The moonlight glimmered across the ocean, a bush turkey was shuffling in the undergrowth, but the feel of Ben's hand holding hers was suddenly…everything. The warmth, the strength, the solidity of his body.

His vulnerability? Why did that feel so important?

She was standing too close to him. She was feeling…

As she had no right to be feeling.

It was less than two months since she'd walked away from Mathew, less than two months since her mother had died. Ben had just talked to her of his dead wife. There was surely no room in this moment for these sensations.

But the sensations were present.

Ben's eyes were smiling but his smile looked uncertain. Was he feeling…what she was feeling?

They were two sensible, mature people, she told herself a little bit desperately. They had every reason to back away.

Except those good, sensible reasons were suddenly like threads of gossamer, fragile, impossible to grasp even if she wanted.

What was it about this night? This woman?

Maybe it wasn't Anya, Ben thought. Maybe tonight had just been the culmination of things that had been building for ever.

Tonight was the first time he'd ever spoken honestly about his marriage. It was the first time he'd ever let someone glimpse the emptiness, the sadness, the betrayal, and the way he felt now was almost indescribable.

He'd never wanted to talk about his marriage. His time with Rihanna was his personal grief, his load to carry, but for some reason telling Anya seemed to have lifted something he'd hardly acknowledged was there.

Maybe it was this place, he thought, or was it what had happened today? This night out of time, this tropical paradise, the tensions and medical urgency of the afternoon, the unreal situation with Ricardo…they'd somehow jerked him out of his grey past.

Or was it being with Anya?

Whatever, the sensations he was feeling now were suddenly almost overwhelming. Heaviness had lifted, to be replaced by a lightness that made him feel almost dizzy. He was flooded with a vast feeling of freedom, of moving on. Of…the future? Anything was possible, he thought, feeling dazed. His time of bleakness was done.

And now… He was standing in the moonlight with a

woman who was as beautiful as she was skilled, as kind as she was smart.

As desirable as…

As Anya.

He didn't have to move on. Anya was right here.

Anya was watching Ben's face, wondering what he was thinking. Watching the flood of emotions. Half-expecting him to back away, say goodnight, move on.

But then his uncertainty seemed to fade and his smile changed. Tenderness. Wonder. Need?

'Anya…' When he said her name there was a hoarseness in his voice, a depth that made something in her stomach clench. Something that made every thread of sense cut loose from its moorings and drift away.

'Anya,' he said again, and her other hand was held. And then he said it for the third time.

'Anya?'

And, with that, qualms, sense, the past, everything seemed to dissolve and there was no choice what to say.

'Yes,' she said, because a question had been asked and it had been answered.

The warmth of the night in this tropical paradise, the drama of the past day, weariness…or plain old-fashioned lust…were they reason enough for what she was feeling? Maybe she no longer needed a reason. What did matter was that his mouth was on hers and she was being kissed. Ruthlessly, deeply, magically, she was being kissed—or maybe *he* was being kissed.

Who'd instigated it? She didn't have a clue. Maybe she'd raised her mouth to his. She must have. If she had, it was entirely instinctive. She shouldn't want to make love with this man—surely she didn't?

But her body had different ideas. For whatever reason,

she was standing at the entrance to a bungalow where the single bedroom had been divided in two—and every fibre of her being was flooded with the knowledge that there'd be no divider tonight.

Her mouth was under his, his tongue was tasting her, savouring, and she was taking the same sensations from him. Heat, want, pure animal desire.

All day as she'd worked with this man, this feeling had been building. She wanted him so much, but it was more than that. His confessions about his past marriage had made no difference—or maybe they'd added to what she was feeling. It was as if in this moment he was somehow…almost a part of her. And joining in any way they could seemed inevitable.

Her arms were around him, feeling the strength of him. Her hands slid under his shirt, feeling the breadth of his shoulders. Feeling the heat…

Oh, she wanted him.

His hands were under her blouse and the feeling was exquisite. She felt her breasts firm. She was crushed against him. His lovely long fingers were slipping into her bra and the feeling was…as if this was where she was meant to be.

Like two halves of a whole. Like a perfect solution.

It was no solution. She was surely sensible enough, aware enough, to know that this was—well, not sensible at all. But they were two mature adults, well past thinking a moment's passion meant a lifetime commitment. So surely…surely…

Oh, but she couldn't think. His hands… The feel of his body. The way her breasts were crushed against him, the way her feet seemed to arch upward so she could deepen the kiss…

And then he was pulling away, holding her at arm's

length, but this was no finality. She could see desire in his eyes, a desire that matched hers.

And a touch of desperation that she understood.

'We can't,' she managed before he said it, but she knew—they both knew—that this break, this moment of intruding sense, was all about practicalities.

'We have a medical clinic next door.' His voice was unsteady, thick with desire. 'A ready-made pharmacy. Surely it'll stock…'

Of course it would. Her body almost seemed to sag in relief.

Practicalities. She was using no protection—her engagement was over, why should she? Ben didn't seem like a guy who carried condoms in his wallet just in case.

And neither of them was stupid.

Or maybe they were, just not stupid enough to have sex without any protection at all. But a ready stocked pharmacy…

'Wait here,' Ben growled, but she shook her head.

'You don't know where to look. Two of us can search much faster than one.'

'Anya…' She heard laughter in his voice, but she also heard something else she hadn't heard before. Happiness. Lightness. As if he was suddenly letting go of shadows.

As was she, she thought as Ben searched the information book for the access code to the clinic and they both headed through the adjoining door. So fast they almost blocked each other—the doorway was too narrow!

For heaven's sake, they were like two horny teenagers, in lust, aching for each other's bodies. But that was what she felt like—a kid again. This night was out of time. A crazy night where they were both in another world.

A world where, thankfully, they found a beautifully ordered clinic with everything clearly labelled. And in the bottom drawer of a medical supplies chest they found what they were looking for.

Ben held them up in triumph and they whooped like idiotic kids. And kissed.

And melted.

It was a miracle they didn't end up naked on the clinic floor. Somehow they ended up back in one of the beds.

Somehow they ended up exactly where they wanted to be.

Somehow they ended up together.

She woke and reality hit her like a sledgehammer.

What had she done? Was she nuts?

She wasn't nuts. She was exquisitely, wonderfully sated and if her fairy godmother was hovering to grant a wish, she'd wish she could spend the rest of her life in this man's arms.

Protected. Loved. Cherished.

But, almost as she woke, the first tentacles of doubt crept in as another word slammed into her head.

Grateful. Was she grateful for last night?

She was—she felt incredibly, deliriously grateful, but for some dumb reason the word was suddenly front and centre and it felt like a clang of warning. Maybe it *was* dumb, but it was there all the same. She'd had almost two months of independence, two months of not being grateful, two months of being…her.

She lay in the almost magical warmth of Ben's arms and she thought of letting this moment continue. She could continue this 'mock marriage'. They could take away the wardrobes, push the beds together and fall into the future.

But I don't even know who Anya is yet, she thought, suddenly panicked. I'm me, and I need to find out about me. Make love to this guy? Yes, because it was fabulous, it was the best feeling. It *is* the best feeling.

Except now she couldn't get up and head home to her place, to her independence, to a place where any decision about her future was taken by *her*.

It was too soon. Too fast.

And Ben… She thought of what he'd told her the night before. His marriage. His tragedy. Where did that leave him?

She'd hardly got her own life together. How could she help him?

Her heart seemed to be racing, and the medically trained side of her thought suddenly, Am I heading for more panic? She forced herself to breathe slowly, deeply. She closed her eyes, but all she could feel was the warmth of him, the strength. The need…

She wasn't panicking, she thought. These thoughts were realistic. They'd had an amazing night. Emotions had blasted away any semblance of sense, and now it was time for reality to reassert itself.

But not yet. His arms were still holding her. She could give herself these last few minutes, she thought. She could lie here and think…what if?

There was no future in *what if?*

Except…colleagues had become lovers before. If they gave themselves time…space.

Space? Somehow she had to regain it.

Somehow she would, but not quite yet. She'd take a couple more moments of feeling as if she was in the best place in the world.

A couple more moments of imagining life could be perfect.

He had Anya in his arms. She was spooned against his chest, gloriously naked, her skin warm against his. Her body was beautiful.

She was the most beautiful woman he'd ever met. This was where he wanted to be for the rest of his life.

Which was a crazy thing to think, and as he thought it his arms must have tightened. For she murmured and stirred and he felt her body shift a little.

His arms had been holding her, but he let her go. She twisted in the bed, his gaze met hers and he saw the expression in her eyes.

Dismay?

Sadness!

It was so far from what he was feeling that his gut lurched. He raised a hand to touch her face but she flinched.

'No.'

'No?'

'I've… I've been thinking. We can't. Ben, that was stupid.'

'It didn't feel stupid.'

That brought a glimmer of a smile into her eyes, but it was squashed fast.

'They already think we're married,' she said, and he could hear traces of panic.

'So we push the beds together.' He made his voice deliberately prosaic.

'And put rings on our fingers and get on with it?'

That made him pause. Like the lack of a condom the night before, sense raised its ugly head.

Once upon a time he'd fallen into lust and ended up married. No. This was way too soon. Too fast. Had he learned no lessons from the past?

And he saw the same flinch reflected in her eyes.

'No,' she said, softly now. 'Ben, this isn't going to work. I've been beholden all my life, and marriage for me… Well, it was just something that everyone expected. The inevitable. What's happened with us is different, but there's the same risk that we're falling for what's expected. We work together, we push the beds together, we…'

'Enjoy each other's bodies?'

'We both know we can't do that without…without an emotional connection.'

She was so beautiful. Her body was still touching his. She'd pulled away, but this bed was too narrow—and every part of him that touched her was screaming for more.

But the look in her eyes… It was almost desperation.

And he got it. Of course he got it. This was an impossible situation—to want her, for her to be so close and yet…

For sense to prevail. He needed to be sensible as well.

'I'll talk to Martin,' she was saying, softly but implacably. 'If there's no other accommodation and it's impossible for us to work here except as a practically married couple, then I'll resign.'

'No!'

'I suspect I won't need to. We saw yesterday how much they need two doctors, and we haven't broken our contract. Accommodation is provided in our contract and there was nothing there that said that meant a shared bedroom. They've made assumptions…'

'We let them make them.'

'You let them make them, and that assumption has to stop.' She took a deep breath and then slipped out of bed, and the wrench he felt was like physical pain. 'Ben, we know we need to be sensible.'

She tugged the top quilt from the bed and draped it around herself, cutting herself off from him even further. 'Ben, I need space. Martin must have a spare room somewhere on this island.'

She was talking sense—he knew she was. He thought of Rihanna all those years ago, smiling at him like the cat that had got the cream. *Darling, I'm pregnant. Surely it doesn't matter, though. It must means we'll have to get married faster.'*

Of all the stupid things to be thinking now…except he was thinking it.

'I'll find a room,' he told her, accepting the inevitable. 'You stay here.'

'Nope.' And here came that smile again, a trifle rueful but gorgeous all the same. 'Ben, I don't trust myself. There's no way I'm sleeping in a room that's one door away from a whole drawer full of condoms.'

'And me?'

'You can do what you like with them,' she said, and there was a wobble in her voice, but also defiant certainty. 'Ben, we're free and we need to stay that way.'

And that was that. She disappeared to her side of the wardrobes, to her ensuite bathroom, to her independence.

He headed for the other shower, he stood under steaming water and forced himself to think.

She was right. He knew she was. This had happened too fast. Yesterday had been fraught, but for Anya the last two months had been a roller coaster.

And for him?

Yesterday he'd been a doctor again. A true medic, performing at the top of his game.

He'd hardly practised medicine since the accident. The locum post at Merriwood had been planned to ease him back into his career, and this island job had been meant to be more of the same. An island retreat with a little easy medicine on the side. A way to slowly regain his medical confidence and give his body more time to recover.

But yesterday had demanded all his medical skills, and there'd been the same demand on his recovering body. What he'd managed…it had felt deeply satisfying.

And maybe what had happened last night had been more of the same. The old Ben resurfacing. A man in charge of his world. A man with a gorgeous woman.

But that woman needed even more time to recover than he did.

She was right. Falling into what the island would see almost as a formal relationship was impossible. Neither of them wanted it.

Really?

Cut it out, he told himself as his body stirred again. Get dressed, go see Martin, organise separate living arrangements.

Right.

Moving on.

Anya saw a tearful Mia in the clinic at nine, and by nine-thirty they had plans in place for her to leave the island.

'He's been hitting me for ever,' Mia admitted. 'But he's so gorgeous and so rich, and people think I'm so lucky.'

'Do you think you're lucky?' Anya asked gently, and got sobs in reply.

'I guess not,' she admitted at last. 'Not any more.'

'Then it's time to leave,' Anya told her. And then, looking at the woman in front of her, she softened. 'Hey, you'll be known as Ricardo's ex, a woman who walked away from him rather than the other way around. How much social cachet will that give you?'

'I guess,' she sniffed. 'But I'm scared.'

'Scared of leaving?'

'He'll be so angry.'

'We'll have Security with you until you leave the island,' Anya told her. 'Starting now. And believe me, it's so much better to walk away. There are so many other lovely guys out there—it's time you found a kind one.'

'Kind as well as gorgeous?' Mia said, her chin firming a little. 'Do they exist?'

'Yes, they do,' Anya told her—and tried very hard not to think of the guy she'd just spent the night with.

Enough. It was time to put that aside and figure how to move forward.

She organised one of the female security officers to meet them and help Mia pack, and then she went to find Ben. Then they walked silently across to the administration buildings to meet Martin.

But as she walked she kept thinking of Mia, silently packing and leaving.

It's for the best for me too, she told herself. But there's no comparison. I'm not exactly leaving the island—and Ben... Well, Mathew was kind too.

Mathew's kindness had felt very, very different.

Why?

She didn't understand, but she didn't have to. Get over it, she told herself. Just…make yourself separate.

They found Martin still reeling from the events of the day before, and he seemed almost confused at this new complication. In the face of the delay to the movie, with the associated mass cancellation, this must have seemed almost trivial. He listened, seemingly almost bemused, as Ben apologised for the misunderstanding, blaming himself.

Then Anya told him they'd wondered if splitting the bedroom would work but one night had convinced her it wouldn't.

'He snores,' Anya said blandly, and Martin looked at them for a long moment and maybe came to his own conclusions.

But the bottom line was that the jet-ski incident had shaken him badly, he was in damage control mode and this was a minor hiccup he needed to deal with fast.

At another time he might have objected, knowing that allocating more accommodation would hurt his bottom line. But without these two doctors he might well have been explaining deaths to the circling media, rather than admittedly horrific injuries.

'The island's two doctors were on the scene within minutes...' It had sounded okay in the piece the island's publicity officer had released. If one of those doctors walked away this morning it would look bad.

The delay in filming meant that the resort was no longer fully booked. There was a studio apartment empty, and thus Anya could move straight in.

Sorted. They came out and stood in the sunshine and Ben smiled ruefully down at her.

'Done. Now for that "walk in the park" future we promised ourselves. I'm heading for a swim. What about you?'

'Not with you,' she said, and then tempered it. 'Sorry. That sounded...ungrateful.'

'But I never wanted you to be grateful,' he told her. 'In fact, it's the last thing I want. So separate everything?'

'Apart from medicine.'

'And the odd piña colada on the terrace at night?'

'Not me,' she replied, and managed a smile to match his. 'After last night...piña coladas seem very dangerous indeed.'

CHAPTER NINE

No!

What had followed was six weeks of letting her world settle. It had also been six weeks of working side by side with Ben. That had involved initial strain, but their jobs had continued to be more demanding than they'd expected. They'd needed to work both separately and in partnership and, as they had, the sexual tension between them had finally faded.

But it hadn't disappeared, Anya conceded, and when she woke six weeks after their arrival she decided it must be tension that was making her so exhausted.

It couldn't be anything else. Her little studio was perfect. The workload might be greater than they'd expected but it wasn't huge. She'd had time to swim, to snooze in the sun, to get to know the resort staff. To think that this job was actually pretty awesome.

But for some reason she couldn't relax when Ben was around. Every time he was near, her body seemed to tingle. To demand that she be closer.

She'd worked late with him the night before, treating an asthmatic guest whose husband had been so terrified Ben had called for her to back him up.

He'd walked her back to her studio in the moonlight,

and there were those nerve-endings again, all pointing in the one direction, screaming at her to...

To do nothing, she'd told herself harshly, but it had taken her ages to go to sleep. She still felt tired and when she'd made herself toast she'd thought, Do I really want to eat it?

And then, as she stared at her uneaten toast, she'd thought... *No!*

Appalled, she'd slipped across to the clinic, found what she needed—and now she was staring at a double blue line.

No, no and no!

And then, as her world seemed to turn into a dizzy maelstrom of emotion, Joe arrived—holding a turtle. A small one, its shell not much bigger than a dinner plate, its shell cracked, its neck extended and oozing blood.

'Reckon it's been hit by one of the buggies,' Joe said while she stood at the door and tried to make her mind focus. 'I found it on the track coming up from the beach. Ben's out having his morning swim so I brought him to you. You reckon there's anything you can do?'

Okay. Somehow she pulled herself together, back into medical mode. Everything else—or just one thing else—had to be put on the backburner.

She and Ben spilt their workload as much as they could so they could work separately, but she looked at the little turtle and knew it needed them both.

This was another aspect of her job she hadn't counted on. It seemed Medical Officer meant coping with injured wildlife as well, and where was that in the small print of their contract? It wasn't there, but there was no way the resort would pay for helicopter transfer for a damaged turtle.

'In the past we've put them down,' Joe had said the first time he'd presented them with a sad, dehydrated possum. 'The last docs wouldn't have anything to do with anything that wasn't human, but I'm hoping you're different. If you can fix this guy so he can survive till the next ferry run, I can organise a wildlife carer on the mainland to take over. There's a vet on the mainland, Rob Lewis, who'll talk you through anything you need to know. He's sent me a great handbook but it's too complicated for me to follow anything more than "Keep 'em quiet, keep 'em warm". So what about it, docs? Can we occasionally give you a different kind of patient?'

And that was what this turtle was. A *very* different kind of patient.

She looked down at the broken shell and the lacerated neck, and her distracted mind settled in the face of medical need. A vet was surely the way to go, but the next ferry to the mainland wasn't scheduled until Friday, and the little creature's odds of surviving until then were minimal.

'Let's get him to the clinic. I'll get him warm while you let Ben know what's happening,' she told Joe.

Her shock, her emotions needed to be put aside, but… now she'd be operating with Ben. Did she need to tell him?

The thought made her dizzy.

Whatever.

Shock was still making her numb, but she had work to do, she told herself as she carried the little turtle across to the clinic. She needed to phone their friendly vet and get some advice, and then set up their mini theatre.

In the last weeks Martin had agreed to them buying equipment to cope with such situations—it was a good look for the island, he'd conceded, to have a wildlife first aid station he could brag about. One of their first patients had been a goanna with an injured leg and that had meant heating was required.

Reptiles, including goannas and turtles, were coldblooded. That meant their blood was the same temperature as the atmosphere, and if they were cold everything slowed. Normally that was okay, but anaesthetics depended on a reasonable blood flow to make them effective. So while she made her call to the mainland vet, writing down everything she needed to know about surgery on turtles—or all the information she could get in one phone call—she was also pushing up the clinic's heating, and then pumping up the hot pad.

By the time Ben arrived she had the place cosy warm—or a bit too warm. Okay for a turtle, but for her...

'Are you okay?' Ben asked. He'd walked in the door and stopped and looked at her.

She shrugged. 'I think so.' She managed a smile. 'I usually wear make-up, but Joe handing me a turtle when I was still mid-breakfast put paid to that.' No need to tell him that her breakfast hadn't been touched.

He smiled back, but gave her a long look. 'You're up to this?'

'Hey, it's not brain surgery. I've designated you as surgeon. I'm on breathing. Our instructions are here. Right to go?'

Another searching look. Disconcerting.

He was disconcerting. He'd also obviously dressed in a hurry—Joe must have met him at the beach. Island gear. Shorts, sandals, an open-necked shirt, tousled damp hair.

Six weeks on the island had seen his already tanned skin turn a deep golden. The swimming had also improved the strength of his leg. He often abandoned his cane, and his limp was becoming less pronounced.

He looked...

No! Don't go there!

He was flicking through the sheets she'd written. Most of the instructions were on how to intubate a turtle, which would be her job. Then he was checking the little turtle, examining the cracked shell.

'If we took that piece off…' he said, considering. 'It's not huge and, according to your notes, it should regrow. It'll spoil his beauty, though.'

'We'll tell him to stop looking in mirrors,' she managed, cutting off thoughts that were spinning in every direction other than where they needed to go. 'Ready when you are.'

'Right,' he said, but he cast her another long look. 'Let's go.'

Intubating a turtle was like intubating a newborn. Tricky. It should feel far less stressful, she thought, as she set up the hose and taped the airway into position, but the turtle's head was tiny, maybe less than ten centimetres wide. So maybe it was even harder than intubating a newborn. But the vet manual had pictures, the instructions had been clear, and luckily her fingers stayed steady enough to cope.

And once she had everything in place, once the anaesthetic took effect—heavens, they'd had to make the place warm!—it was a matter of monitoring and watching Ben work.

He was good. Really good.

The tiny head had a deep laceration along the side and the rough, leathery skin was grazed and filthy. 'Someone driving too fast,' Joe had growled. 'Our buggies are only supposed to go at ten kilometres an hour but they'll push faster downhill, and that's where we found this little guy. I like to think the idiot who hit him didn't realise, otherwise I'd be pushing Martin to kick him off the island.'

Me too, Anya thought, but her concentration was almost solely on Ben.

He was gently, carefully probing the wound, removing tiny bits of gravel, making sure the lesion was completely clean before he closed. That was easier said than done when the gravel was the same colour as the turtle. But he had all the patience in the world, and with the wound cleaned he stitched it closed and then looked at the shell.

'I reckon we can do this too,' he said. 'It could wait for a vet, but it'd mean another anaesthetic. You up for another twenty minutes or so?'

Why was he asking? Did she look that wobbly?

'Cut it out,' she growled. 'I'll stop wearing make-up entirely if losing it has this effect on my colleagues.'

That resulted in another searching look, but he nodded then turned his attention back to the shell.

A piece almost as big as a small egg had cracked, and Ben had folded it away while he tended to the neck wound.

'Rob assured me it'll regrow,' she told Ben. 'Not as smoothly, but eventually. He'll need to stay in a wildlife refuge until it does.'

'Well, he'll be a quiet little guest and I'm guessing he won't eat much.' He looked again at the shell. 'This isn't a clean break—see how the edges are shattered and the piece itself is broken? We'll keep what we can in case the wildlife vets want to wire and cement it together, but if we leave it like it is those edges are likely to pierce his skin. I can cut away the piece that'll lie over the wound itself, and the damage isn't so big that it'll leave him exposed where it matters.'

She nodded and went back to checking the airway, then figuring what was needed to keep the little creature anaesthetised for longer. And trying not to think about the searching look Ben had just given her.

And trying not to think…how to tell him. The prospect was pretty close to blindsiding her.

It was just as well she needed to focus on the job at hand, she decided, otherwise she might well have fainted, and it wasn't just the heat that was doing it to her. She stayed fiercely concentrating as Ben carefully removed the broken part of the shell, debrided the edges, swabbed, dressed and finally said, 'Right, we're done. He might even live because of us.'

He stood back from the table and watched as she checked and rechecked, then removed the intubation gear, as she cleared her stuff away, as she carried the heated pad into a little enclosure they'd set up in the storeroom for the wildlife they'd already treated, as she finally had no excuse but to stop being busy.

'Anya,' he said as she came back into the clinic, and she met his gaze and she knew exactly what was coming.

'I… Yes?'

'Is there any chance you could be pregnant?'

Pregnant. The word seemed to explode in her head. *Pregnant!*

How had he guessed?

'Anya?' He was on the far side of the operating table. He was watching her with concern, but also…what else?

Horror?

That was too strong a word, she thought. It was too strong a word for what she was feeling, too.

Or was it?

There was a seat by the desk. She pulled it out and sat down, hard. There was no way she could avoid this. No way she couldn't tell the truth.

'I just did a test,' she whispered. 'I…yes.'

There was a moment's appalled silence.

She was forcing her fuzzy mind to think…the unthinkable. It was six weeks since they'd had sex. Six weeks! And two months before that since her abandoned wedding.

Her cycle…

'I had an IUD.' She was stammering. 'After the wedding… I removed it, there was no use for it, but it's taken a while for things to settle. It often does.'

'So you haven't had a period?'

'You're not my doctor,' she flashed, suddenly angry. Surely this wasn't a conversation she should be having with him.

It was a conversation she should be having with herself.

She was already having it.

'We used a condom.' She said it out loud, almost defiantly. 'We're not stupid.'

He didn't answer. Instead, with an expression on his face she couldn't read, he rounded the table and pulled open one of the drawers that held pharmaceutical supplies.

Right down the bottom was a box containing what they'd found that night. Condoms, all in their original wrappers.

'I didn't think.' His tone was blank, hollow. 'It was our first night here. I didn't check…'

'You didn't check what?'

'You know that they sell these in the resort gift shop,' he said, still in that empty voice. 'I've seen them there. They sell basic things like paracetamol, sticking plasters, antiseptic. Maybe when the resort first opened they put everything here, but the doctors would have fast become tired of being woken to supply such things. How long's the gift shop been open? If these have been sitting here since then…'

He held one up, he read the label—and then he blenched.

'Wh…what?' she stammered.

There was a long, loaded silence. And then, in a voice she hardly recognised, he said, 'Anya, their expiry date is over ten years ago.'

Her thoughts suddenly veered, strangely, to her mother. Telling her of how she'd come to live in Australia.

'Anya, I was pregnant. I didn't have a choice but to follow your father.'

Choice.

Her mother had wanted to be a teacher. She'd just won a scholarship to one of the Philippines' top universities.

But then she'd met Anya's father, a visiting tourist, and that had been that. Pregnancy, marriage, leaving everything she knew to travel to a life of isolation—and the endless need for gratitude.

Maybe even the fact that her father had offered to marry her had been cause for gratitude.

But this was different, Anya told herself frantically. Far, far different.

So why was she instinctively touching her belly and thinking…of tuna bakes?

There were so many emotions, he couldn't get them in any sort of order.

He was looking at Anya's face, seeing her instinctive move to touch her belly, realising she was as shocked as he was. Looking at her hand on her belly, he accepted it as absolute truth.

But he'd been down this road before. *'Ben, I'm pregnant.'*

The shock.

Years seemed to fall away. Once again he was that nerdy kid, staring in horror as Rihanna made her announcement. He was back seeing the sophisticated woman he thought he knew, sobbing in what he'd realised afterwards was well acted terror and knowing without doubt there was only one road to follow.

And now… His world seemed to fade into some sort of mindless fog and, before he even realised he was about to say it, the words were out of his mouth.

'I… We'll have to get married.'

Why…*why* had he said that? It was crazy, stupidly inappropriate, completely out of kilter with everything that should be said. It was a gut reaction, a repeat of what had gone before, and he knew how wrong it was the moment the words were out of his mouth. And Anya's face reflected it. She stared up at him and flinched as if she'd been struck, and then she stood and faced him with horror.

'Don't you dare,' she managed.

'Dare?'

'No! What are you saying? Marriage? Are you out of your mind? What the…? Am I supposed to fall at your feet in gratitude for such an offer? This isn't the last century, Ben. This is my body, my life.'

'But I…'

'You what? Impregnated me? So you're the noble guy who'll do his duty? Because of what? Guilt? Go jump.'

'Anya…'

'No.' She caught herself and her hands flew to her cheeks, as if she was trying to somehow keep her head steady on her shoulders. 'This is crazy, but I need to think.'

'We do. Anya, this is our decision.'

He was trying to say it was a shared responsibility, that he wouldn't walk away, that this wasn't all on her shoulders, but she read it wrong. Okay, he'd said it wrong.

'I think we both know that's not true,' she said, and she closed her eyes. And when she opened them her face was set.

'Look after the turtle,' she managed. 'I only… I only realised myself this morning. You're on call and I need time to get my head in order. Ben, I need to be by myself.'

And without another word she walked out.

He felt as if he'd been punched. No, this sensation was bigger than any punch could be. It was overwhelming.

The memory of Rihanna was all around him, her two declarations of pregnancy, the way he'd felt.

This was different. It had to be.

But still, the feeling of entrapment was inescapable. One stupid mistake, a night of overblown emotion, and now consequences.

He remembered his student self, looking at the gorgeous Rihanna in horror as she'd announced her pregnancy. Those emotions had surged to the fore as he'd realised Anya was pregnant.

They were wrong.

Still, though, they'd been inescapable—they were almost a muscle memory.

This *was* different, though, he told himself. Anya didn't want him. She didn't expect anything. It was only his honour…

Was it?

The memory of Anya's face was still with him, blanched with shock. He'd wanted to hold her, to comfort her, to say…

We'll have to get married?

Stupid, stupid, stupid.

But what had been the alternative? Go down on one knee and propose? Pretend marriage had been in his mind before?

She was right, he thought as he checked the heating pad under the little turtle and watched it resurface to a bewildering new reality.

That was what he was facing, he thought. A new reality. It was just as bewildering.

Anya was right, he decided. They both needed time to get their heads in order. They needed to be…by themselves?

Maybe they did. He was in unchartered territory and the kaleidoscope of conflicting emotions was refusing to settle.

Nothing had to be settled today, he told himself. Life could go on as normal.

Anya was pregnant.

They were pregnant.

Suddenly there seemed no such thing as normal.

CHAPTER TEN

THEY MANAGED TO stay apart for nearly three days.

As long as there were no crises that was possible, even on an island the size of Dolphin. They alternated clinic duty, and they also alternated call-outs to the individual villas. Over the last six weeks they'd often gone together, but now, unless it was imperative, they worked alone.

Because they needed to get their heads around…

Pregnancy. The future. Ties that neither of them wanted. Or did they?

Realisation of the pregnancy had seemed to hit Anya like a blow to the side of her head. One part of her was busy castigating herself for being unbelievably stupid. Another was railing at Ben for his insensitivity, his crass proposal.

The biggest part of her was responding with panic.

But three days was a long time in the life of a woman who'd just learned she was pregnant, and by the end of the third day she'd reached a few conclusions. Which, she decided on that third afternoon, was only fair she share.

She knew Ben had received a call to the marine research centre—someone with chest pain. She'd heard the call come in on the receivers they both carried. She'd offered to go with him—their need for solitude didn't extend to medical emergencies—but Ben had knocked her back.

'The manager's pretty sure it's a panic attack—the guy's

had them before and he has a research paper that's overdue. I'll contact you if I need you.'

So she knew where he was, and she knew he'd be coming home. To *his* home next to the clinic. Her home was two pathways away. Her studio apartment was small enough for most tourists to turn their noses up, but it was perfect for her. As she closed the door behind her and headed towards Ben's she thought, I want to stay here.

Which was pretty much what she wanted to say to Ben.

When Ben returned Anya was sitting on the front steps of his bungalow. The sun was sinking behind the island. Lorikeets were coming in to roost, and their raucous calls filled the night. The island was settling to sleep.

The setting was lovely. And the woman on the step was lovely. Dressed in shorts and an oversized shirt tied at the waist, her hair tumbling to her shoulders, she looked relaxed and calm, a million miles from the woman he'd met only a few months before.

But as he got nearer he saw the look of tension in her eyes. She was here to say something important—he knew it—and he felt his own tension surge to match.

'Hey,' he said warily.

'Hey yourself. It was a panic attack, then?'

He nodded. 'Apparently his research paper—differential wave motion affecting specific coral spawning...' He smiled but it was an effort. He could almost taste the tension between them.

'I know, I can't wait to read it too,' he managed. 'But I gather it has to be submitted by tomorrow or it'll miss the publication schedule, which means missing out on funding. His pride hasn't let him ask for help, but once he admitted it we organised colleagues to help. They'll stay up until midnight or longer or until it's done.'

'So heart attack fixed?'

'I wish they were all that easy.' He reached the base of the steps and looked down at her. 'I'd offer you a drink but I see you already have one.'

'Iced water,' she told him, raising her glass. 'Isn't it lucky I swore off piña coladas on that first night and haven't had an alcoholic drink since? It's as if I knew.'

'I can't believe you didn't.'

Her face froze, and once again he thought, What am I, an idiot?

'I didn't know,' she said flatly.

'Anya, I'm sorry. That was a crass thing to say. Of course I believe you.'

'It doesn't matter.'

'It does matter,' he said and sat down beside her. 'Anya…'

'I'm going to keep it.'

He was silent, letting her statement settle, not game to open his mouth unless something else stupid came out. So it was Anya who spoke next.

'And I'd like to stay on this island,' she said, almost defiantly.

'Anya…' Why wasn't his brain engaging his mouth?

'This place is perfect.' She was speaking in a rush, as if she had to get the words out fast. 'It's early days but if…if my pregnancy stays…viable…my little studio will be big enough for me and a baby, at least for a couple of years. I can use the island creche. I'll need to take a few weeks off after the birth, but if you're still here you can cover for me. If not… If you decide to leave… Hannah—you've met Martin's wife?—she told me scores of doctors applied for the position. It'll be easy enough to get someone else. They *did* want a couple, but they like us, they've accepted our arrangement, so nothing will change.'

Nothing will change? He thought…baby? Everything would change.

But all he said was, 'You talked to Hannah?'

'I had to talk to someone,' she told him. 'Their kids are older now, of course, but she said this is an idyllic spot to raise them. You know there's a little school here for the kids of the resort and the research station, and as they get older the resort subsidises boarding school fees on the mainland. Apparently, they need that to attract permanent staff. And Hannah will support me.'

I had to talk to someone. Hannah will support me.

Why was his stomach clenching at those words?

He remembered the overwhelming feeling of being trapped when Rihanna had announced her pregnancy. That feeling had flooded back three days ago but now Anya's calm words had dispelled it completely.

He missed it? Did he want to be trapped?

This wasn't a trap. This was just…what happened when people were stupid. It was what happened when people were in lust.

Or in love.

Love. Where had that word come from?

'So where do I fit in all this?' he asked slowly.

'I guess…wherever you want to fit—short of marriage,' she added hastily. 'I thought, initially, not at all. The last thing I want is commitment because you feel obligated. But if you'd like to be a part-time dad…if you stay on the island…maybe we could work things out. Or even if you don't stay…other people have worked co-parenting. But only if you want it, Ben. This baby might like a father, but not one who's doing it from guilt—or for me. I don't need it. Be very clear, I don't need you.'

It was like a slap.

It was so different from Rihanna's announcement of pregnancy that he was having trouble taking it in.

But suddenly he knew what he wanted to say. What he had to say.

'I'd like to share.'

This time his words went down better. The tension in her eyes seemed to soften. There was a long silence and then she nodded.

'Sharing might be good,' she said softly. 'But Ben, it's early days yet. We both know nothing's settled. Even if it does... I mean...' Her hands automatically seemed to move to her tummy. Protectively? 'There's plenty of time to organise access, formal agreements.'

'Would we want formal agreements?'

'I don't know.' She gave another decisive nod, as if she'd covered everything she needed to cover, and stood up. 'We'll figure it out, but that's all I wanted to say tonight. I'll leave you to come to terms with it.'

'You don't want to have dinner with me?'

She stared down at him, and her face closed again. 'In preparation for you to tell me again we need to get married?'

'That was stupid.'

'Yes, it was,' she said, briskly now. 'This baby's nothing to do with...well, with obligation. Let's figure things out formally. There's no other way.'

CHAPTER ELEVEN

IT SEEMED SHE had a village.

Where had this come from? During her first weeks on the island almost all her attention had been on the resort and its guests, but behind the scenes was a working community. The research centre had permanent staff, many with families, and most of the resort staff were permanent as well.

When Anya had first learned she was pregnant she'd hardly known them, but that one conversation with Martin's wife had been taken by Hannah as a need for support. Hannah had asked if Anya wanted the news kept secret. Anya had wondered whether there was any point. The news had thus spread, and almost within minutes the other mums on the island had collectively gathered her into their 'tribe'.

She was astute enough to realise, though, that their friendship, their support, their offers of help, weren't made out of charity. She was now their local doctor, the one they called when little Ollie had earache, or little Joey broke his toe. She wasn't an outsider who needed help, she was accepted as one of them.

She was thankful but she didn't need to thank. The sensation was great.

Strangely, though, it was Ben who now seemed the outsider. Because she wouldn't let him in? Or because he didn't want to be…in.

She hadn't told Hannah it was Ben who was the father. She hadn't told anyone. She'd also been deliberately vague about dates, and the islanders had decided on an alternative all by themselves. Apparently, someone knew someone who lived at Merriwood. Rumours of her disastrous wedding had thus spread, and her pregnancy was assumed to be part of the same disaster.

Regardless, the locals seemed to have collectively decided to respect her privacy, and she figured if Ben wanted to announce impending fatherhood it was up to him.

Which left them in a strange type of limbo.

She'd half-expected him to plan on leaving the island. This was a great place for him—his leg was strengthening almost daily—but surely he could soon go back to his career as an emergency medicine specialist.

But he gave no indication of leaving.

They therefore worked together. As the weeks went by they relaxed enough to figure a way to get by, but the future was uncharted and undiscussed.

He seemed to think talking about her pregnancy was off-limits, and maybe it was.

How much did he want to be involved?

How much did she want him to be involved?

As the weeks rolled on, she came to terms with the stupidity of his crazy proposal. She accepted that it had been about Rihanna, a reaction to his appalling marriage. They both needed time to come to terms with this new normal.

She didn't need him, though, she continued to tell herself. She had her life on track and one moment's stupidity should surely not keep Ben from his own path.

At twelve weeks she took the ferry over to Cairns and had her first scan. That was a bit weird, a bit confronting, a bit…lonely? Maybe she should have asked Hannah to go with her. Or Ben? He'd offered, but the thought had made something inside her cringe. Wanting that of him…it'd be demanding responsibility and she wouldn't do it.

But as she looked at the scan, at the grainy image on the screen, for the first time she felt a pang of something that had nothing to do with either herself or Ben. This was a new little…person.

And with it came the realisation that this new little person had rights as well.

Like it or not, she had to let Ben closer.

'I brought you the ultrasound image. If…if you're interested.'

It was late afternoon. Ben had been sitting on the bungalow steps watching the light slowly turn golden over the sea. Anya approached looking…nervous.

He'd known where she'd been—of course he had—and he'd hated the thought that she was going alone. But she'd been adamant, as she'd been for weeks, answering every query about her pregnancy factually but with any offer of help being met with, 'Ben, I don't need you.'

'Is everything okay?' he asked now. He was watching her face as she came nearer. Dammit, he should have insisted on going.

He hated that she wouldn't let him.

'Everything's fine.'

That's…great.' He could have been anyone, he thought. A friend. A colleague. Even a casual acquaintance asking if she was well.

If *their* baby was well.

He guessed most couples would be super excited right now, but he and Anya most definitely weren't *most couples*.

Anya was wearing her normal work gear, casual trousers and blouse. Her hair was tied tightly back and she look almost businesslike. Maybe that was deliberate, he thought. What was between them—should it be business-like for ever?

This woman made him feel so conflicted.

The last few weeks had seen him flooded with emotions so confusing they were impossible to get his head around. One part of him wanted to be with her, support her, do… well, what he'd suggested the moment he'd learned of the pregnancy. Protect, cherish, take on full responsibility for the child she was carrying. But there was another part that maybe she understood better than he did.

She stepped forward but she didn't climb the steps to the veranda. Instead, she handed the print up to him.

He looked at the grainy black and white image and he didn't say a word.

So many emotions. What he was feeling…how could he even begin to understand? *His child.*

He looked to Anya and her face looked almost wooden.

'Ten fingers, ten toes, but tricky to tell the sex yet,' she said, her voice almost emotionless. 'We tried to figure it out but couldn't.'

'We?'

'The sonographer and I.'

And again that cut deep. It should have been him.

'Anya, I do want to be involved.'

'That's your right.'

'I mean…' How to say this? How to even mean something he didn't understand himself? 'With you,' he ventured. 'With us and our…our baby. Anya, what's between you and me…'

'There's nothing.' Was that a defence?

'It doesn't feel like nothing. Underneath all the baggage…'

'Yeah, the baggage,' she said, grimly now. 'There's way too much baggage. I would never, ever want you to think you were forced into another relationship—and I can see by your face that that's exactly what you're feeling.'

'I'm not.'

But was he? Honestly, he didn't have a clue. He and Rihanna had been together for so long that the feeling of obligation, of entrapment, was almost bone-deep. How to tell Anya that it wasn't obligation or guilt that made him want to take this relationship forward?

That made him want Anya for herself?

He couldn't, because he wasn't sure himself. And he met her gaze now and he could see that she knew it.

'Leave it, Ben,' she said, her voice gentling. 'You're an honourable man, and this baby will be lucky to have you as a dad. That's a pretty big step to take without…the rest. There's no need to force things.'

'I'd never force things.'

'I know you wouldn't.'

'But I do want more involvement.' He stared down at the picture again and something inside him twisted. *His baby.* 'The next scan…' he said, trying to think forward. 'The normal scheduling's five months. Yes?'

'I…yes.'

'So in eight weeks, would you let me come?'

'I don't need…'

'I know you don't need, but maybe I need. Please, Anya.'

And her reply came fast, almost a gut reaction. 'Ben, I'm scared of letting you close.'

She said it too loud, too fast, and it was as if the words had been forced out. They hung between them, loaded.

'I guess the same might be said for me,' he said at last, and reluctantly he handed back the photograph. 'But we're doing a pretty good job of being independent now. Just, can you let me be involved? I accept you don't need me, but I can surely be involved with our baby without either of us needing each other.'

But was that even true? His thoughts were jumbling again. The way she looked, standing in the fading light, the honesty in her gaze, the tinge of fear...

What he wanted right now was to walk down the steps between them and gather her into his arms. To hold her against his body. To hold her against his heart?

Because she was vulnerable? Because he could see the fear in her eyes?

Because she was lovely?

It was all of those things, but strangely it was fear that held him back. But her fear or his? What she'd gone through... What they'd both gone through... He knew it was too soon, for Anya and for him.

So somehow he made himself hand back the photograph and smile.

'Thank you for showing me this. I'd like a copy.'

'To stick on your fridge?' She managed a rueful smile in return. 'I'll have it on *my* fridge, but if you put up a matching one the whole island will know.'

'I wouldn't mind.'

'But I would,' she said, hurriedly now. 'I know we'll eventually have to admit our...connection...but please Ben, not yet.'

'But the five-month scan...'

'Okay, I'd like you to come.' Her chin came up, semi-defiant. 'To be honest, it felt a bit lonely today. And I'll tell you...when...when I feel the first kick. Whenever I'm worried. I will keep you informed.'

'Informed doesn't mean involved.'

'I can't help that,' she managed. 'That's as far as I'm brave enough to go. Goodnight, Ben.'

The flash of fear on her face was unmistakable and,

without another word, she turned and walked away. He was left on the step, looking after her.

He wanted...

No.

Emotional baggage was still there in spades, for both of them. He didn't know what he wanted.

Or maybe deep down he did, but he didn't have a clue how to get it.

Eight weeks later she was due to have her mid-pregnancy check-up and ultrasound. She made the appointment on the resort's changeover day. The ferry took guests to the mainland, then docked for a few hours, restocking supplies before bringing the next batch of guests back. That'd be plenty of time to have her check-up and do a little shopping—her clothes were now being stretched to the limit. Everything was sorted.

Except she had to tell Ben. With hardly any guests on the island it should be safe for both of them to leave, but they'd hardly talked about her pregnancy over the past eight weeks. Would he still want to come?

He'd been almost deliberately distant for the last few weeks. When he wasn't working, he'd been fiercely focusing on rebuilding his fitness. They acted as colleagues only, providing a great medical service, working together as needed but at all other times being completely separate.

And Ben was more separate than she was. While she seemed to be fitting into island life, making friends, Ben was more and more a loner. She watched him swimming endless laps of the cove, driving himself to exhaustion. She saw him through the huge plate glass windows of the resort gym, pitting himself against the most challenging equipment. She saw him limping without his cane when surely it would have been easier to continue using it.

He seemed driven, and not just by the need to rebuild his strength.

Part of her ached to help, but there was nothing she could do. His demons were his own.

And as the date for her five-month scan approached part of her was still cringing about having him join her. Why? Because she was scared that he'd see it as a cry for help? As a need for his involvement?

Would that involvement mean more demons for Ben? Part of her knew that it would.

Those first words were still echoing in her mind, as they'd echoed now for months.

'We'll have to get married.'

She was sure that had been his demons speaking.

But she had demons of her own. She could still hear her mother's words echoing down through the years.

'Your father and I had to get married. There was no choice.'

Well, times were different, she told herself, as she'd been telling herself for months. There was no way she was heading into forced matrimony.

But, like it or not, Ben *was* going to be her baby's father and she'd promised.

With the date confirmed, she asked him. They'd been doing a dressing together—one of the researchers had cut himself on coral and had a spreading ulcer that needed careful debridement. As they left the clinic she forced herself to sound nonchalant.

'By the way,' she managed. 'No pressure, but my scan's booked on Friday. So, if you're still interested, you're welcome to…to come with me.'

The last few words came out in a rush, and when she finished the silence seemed loaded.

But he simply nodded, like someone restructuring his diary in his head.

'I can make it.' The words were formal. Cautious?

'Only if you want…'

'Anya, I do want to meet our baby.'

Our baby.

Unconsciously her hands moved to her belly. Was that a whisper of movement? A tiny ripple?

Our baby.

'Martin says it's okay.' Again, she spoke too fast, repeating herself. 'It'll only be for a few hours…'

'You know I want to come.'

His voice was steady, sure. She glanced up at him and his eyes met hers. There was a message in those eyes. *I'm here for you.* And more. *I'm part of this.*

And with that came a stab of something akin to terror. Oh, for heaven's sake… Why was she so afraid of how this man made her feel?

Regardless, two days later she was lying on an examination table in the X-ray department of Cairns Central, her tummy covered with slippery gel, the wand of the ultrasound tracking back and forth over her skin.

And on the screen…

Her baby?

No. *Their* baby. Because when she glanced at Ben's face she saw her awe and wonder reflected back at her.

'It truly is,' he murmured, and she flinched at that.

'Did you think…'

'Oh, Anya, of course I didn't.' His hand covered hers and she was aware of a stab of…warmth? Something more?

Definitely more, but there were ghosts in the way he held her hand, ghosts she didn't want to think about.

Maybe she had to.

'But Rihanna…' Why had she said that? Surely their mutual ghosts had nothing to do with here and now.

'This is nothing to do with Rihanna,' he said, but she heard a catch in his voice that told her there *was* a comparison being made. Those years of lies and manipulation had made their mark. 'Anya, we have a daughter.'

'A daughter?' she said, startled, and the sonographer chuckled.

'That's the problem with doctors' pregnancies. I don't get to spring surprises—boy, girl, twins.' She looked closely at the screen herself. 'Yep, it's a girl.'

'A daughter…' Anya hadn't looked—she simply didn't care—but now, looking closely…

Their little girl wasn't coyly holding her legs together. She was definitely…

Her daughter.

Their daughter?

She was thinking suddenly of her mum, a student, scared, alone, starring at an image on the screen of her, of Anya.

And then she was thinking of her father, Mike, staring at the screen as well.

Ben's words were exploding in her head. *We have a daughter.*

And suddenly she thought…no wonder her mother had travelled half a world from everything she knew and loved, to be with the father of her baby. Ben was still holding her hand and the link felt suddenly unbreakable.

We have a daughter…

Family?

She found she was crying, stupid, helpless tears that tracked down her face before she could stop them. And then Ben was wiping her tears and bending down so his face almost touched hers.

'Hey, it's okay. Please don't cry. It's great. It's wonderful.'

'I… I know. It's just…' She couldn't make herself go on. There seemed no words for what was in her heart.

And then Ben filled the silence for her.

'Anya, please, we need to be married.'

And then he too stopped.

The words hung in the air.

The sonographer was still at work, recording images, making sure measurements fitted with stage of pregnancy, checking, checking, checking to make sure everything was okay.

It *was* okay.

We need to be married.

Her overwhelming instinct right now was to melt into the warmth, the emotion, the…*love?*…that was in this room right now.

She couldn't. Because underneath the emotion were still the stupid, inexplicable seeds of fear.

Fear of what? She was no longer sure, but she knew she had to act on it.

'She looks perfect,' the sonographer said, briskly now. She'd obviously decided to ignore the undercurrents of emotion—or were they over-currents? They were so strong… Maybe sonographers were used to it. 'Your obstetrician will confirm, but I think you two can go out and celebrate that you have a gorgeous little girl in there and she's growing just as she should.' She grinned then. 'You know, a lot of parents take a babymoon at this stage.'

'A babymoon?' Anya asked stupidly. She was struggling to sit up. Ben tried to help but she pushed his hand away. Enough.

'Before your bump gets in the way.' Maybe the sonographer wasn't as astute as Anya had thought—or maybe she'd missed that push as Anya had rejected Ben's helping hand.

'Sort of like a honeymoon where you can enjoy being just you two.' She grimaced. 'You know, I have four kids and I love them to bits but from the time they were born they've been in my life every waking minute. If Warwick and I had our time again and had the chance of a babymoon, we'd be off like a shot. You two should go for it.'

'Maybe we will,' Ben said as he stood back to let Anya rise all by herself. 'I know a great resort. How about it, Anya? How about heading for Dolphin Isles Resort?'

It was an attempt to break the ice and it did—sort of. She gave him a weak smile and struggled to her feet.

'I'll meet you in the cafeteria after I'm dressed,' she managed, then thanked the beaming sonographer and grabbed her basket of clothes and headed for the changing rooms. But when she got there she sat hard on the bench and stared at nothing.

Anya, please, we need to be married.

Think, she told herself. Think!

We need to be married.

That was what her mother had believed, and maybe, given the time and the social mores of the community she'd lived in, that had been the only decision she could have made.

She remembered one of the few times her mother had talked of it. 'I was so frightened, so alone, and my parents were so, so thankful when Mike said he'd marry me. *I* was so thankful.'

And there it was, in a nutshell. Thankful. That gratitude thing.

Was it getting in the way of what she was feeling for Ben?

How could she know? Her emotions were so confused, a kaleidoscope of needs and wants. The way he'd held her hand had felt good, it had even felt right—but surely she was stronger than to let emotion influence her future? She would *not* let herself fall into this man's arms because she needed him.

But…she wanted him?

Yes, she did. She could admit that to herself. Ben was strong, kind, loyal. He was also…sex on legs?

You can cut that out, she told herself fiercely.

So…if you married him…

The need would come first, she told herself, and she knew it was true. Marriage had come up exactly twice now, once when he'd learned of the pregnancy, and today when he'd looked at his daughter on screen.

His daughter.

Unconsciously her hands went to her tummy and held.

'I will not let you be raised thinking your mother needs to be grateful to your father,' she said out loud. 'I will not! And it's his demons making him do the offering. Sweetheart, your relationship with your father is your business, and gratitude to him shouldn't come into that either. So he can take his offer of marriage and stick it.'

She gave a fierce nod and started dressing but dammit, here came the tears again. She swiped them away and hauled on her trousers with a ferocity that startled her. And then she swore because the zip broke.

Of all the…

'Well, that's what he can do while we wait for the return ferry,' she said, and she was still talking to the tiny baby she was carrying. A daughter! 'So the plan is that I'll sit in the cafeteria and hold my trousers together while your father goes out and buys me more. Stretchy ones. And I'll be grateful enough to pay for his coffee—even a doughnut! But that's as far as we should go. We can do this, us girls. We can cope.'

But they might well need his help.

So what, she told herself.

In the days after her mother's death, fighting a fog of depression and despair, she'd picked up a corny self help book. For some reason one of the lines resonated now.

Independence is there for the taking, but a smart women learns the art of accepting help with grace and courage.

Just after that appalling wedding day, a eucalypt had toppled over in her backyard and Anya had tried to clear it. She'd ended up covered with scratches but still with ninety percent of the tree untouched.

The next day she'd rung a neighbour. He'd arrived half an hour later with three mates, a truck, a mulcher and two chainsaws.

She'd hated that he wouldn't take payment, but he'd acted offended when she'd offered.

'Hey, Anya, we're friends, right?'

That night she'd fought an almost irresistible urge to cook him a tuna bake.

The memory made her smile, and the thought grounded her. She and Ben could be friends, and she *would* accept help from him.

But not marriage. That was payment far above the price she was prepared to pay.

Independence was gold.

He'd got it wrong again.

Ben sat in the cafeteria nursing a cooling mug of coffee and expected to feel regret, but this was much worse. This wash of anger, of grief, of helplessness was so strong it threatened to overwhelm him.

Of all the stupid, stupid, *stupid* things to say.

'Anya, please, we need to be married.'

He'd now proposed twice, and the memory of that first proposal was still with him.

'We'll have to get married.'

The look on Anya's face then was still seared in his memory.

And now...

'We need to be married.'

Same thing.

And it was wrong. Anya was a feisty, independent woman, with a career and a planned future. There was no need for a wedding ring.

So why had he blurted it out? Was that what he wanted? For Anya to need him?

He thought of Rihanna, false, manipulative, totally self-centred, and the difference couldn't be greater.

Was that why he wanted her? Because she was so different to Rihanna?

No. Over the last months they'd been a medical team for the island. He'd watched her work and been more than impressed with her skills. More, he'd been pretty much blown away with the relationships she was forming on the island.

She'd come to Dolphin like him, wanting a job where independence was everything, and to a certain extent that had happened. She did hold herself apart, yet there was never a time when she was less than generous with her patients, and less than caring.

And with the islanders themselves? She was getting to know the ins and outs of their lives. Off-duty, she'd be in the shallows happily playing with the island kids, or sitting on someone's porch happily gossiping, or...or just being happy.

She loved her life on the island. Her happiness was infectious too, and as he watched her, more and more he'd been hit by the urge to slough off the remnants of his past and join right in.

Was he falling in love with the island?

Or with Anya?

He was starting to know the answer.

Anya was taking her time—surely it didn't take this long to dress? Maybe she'd stopped to talk to the sonographer, maybe get a copy of the stills of their daughter.

Their daughter.

The idea was messing with his head. The echoes of Rihanna's two announced pregnancies were still with him, and both had left him with a weird sense of loss.

Was that why he wanted this baby so much?

What he wanted, suddenly but quite, quite desperately, was to wind back time. To meet Anya when they'd been med students, when they'd been free of every tie. Free of every ghost.

But Anya would still have had ties, obligations to Mathew and his community, obligations to the mother she'd loved.

He could have helped. He could have found some way of making things work for her.

So she'd be grateful to him rather than Mathew?

Dammit, this was doing his head in.

His leg cramped.

His physio had advised him: 'Whenever you can, choose standing over sitting. These cramps seem to be caused by pressure on your damaged spine, and keeping your spine stretched will help.'

Two hours on the ferry, a taxi ride to the hospital, another half hour's wait for the appointment and then sitting while he watched the ultrasound... What did he expect?

Pain?

He swore and rose and did a slow circuit of the cafeteria,

wishing he still had his cane. It was pride that had made him leave it behind. He wanted to forget...

But he could never forget, and neither could Anya. Her rejection was based on self-protection—he knew that. And his proposal—what was that based on?

Her need? What kind of a basis was that for a proposal? So he'd stuffed it, but he didn't know how to make it right.

He thought of the times he saw her now on the beach, playing in the shallows with the island kids. He thought of her laughter, her empathy and her kindness.

He thought of that night on the river, feeding casseroles to the fish. Of her solitude and her pain.

This was so different to anything he'd felt before. It was a million miles away.

He managed two more circuits of the cafeteria before Anya appeared, looking self-conscious, tugging the hem of her shirt down to hide her hips. Her bump was clearly evident. She looked flustered but she was smiling.

That smile made his heart turn over.

But she wasn't into heart issues, and what should he expect after the stupid things he'd said to her?

'Problem,' she told him. 'Ben, I need your help.'

And that was good. Great even, because it put aside the tangled feelings that were doing his head in.

'Help?'

'My trousers have busted. Unless you want to take me home in my knickers, I need you to buy some more.'

'You're kidding.'

'Nope,' she said, and she grinned. 'I'm a maiden in distress and I need Sir Lancelot. Not for dragon-slaying, though—did Lancelot slay dragons? Regardless, I need a hero for something much more prosaic.'

He chuckled, thankful that the tension had eased. The cramps in his leg had eased as well. They sat while she checked online and located what she needed and then she sent Ben off in a taxi to fetch it.

See, I can help, he told himself ruefully as he left her in the cafeteria and headed off to find maternity trousers.

Just…not enough.

Not in the way he wanted.

CHAPTER TWELVE

WITH ANYA RESPECTABLE AGAIN, they headed back on the ferry. The incoming guests, a high-flying business group, headed for the cabin, quaffing champagne, already in party spirits.

That left Anya and Ben alone, on deckchairs in the bow of the boat.

They sat in near silence. It wasn't a bad silence, though. It was…peaceful.

That had been yet another dumb outburst of Ben's, Anya decided as the mainland disappeared in the distance and the outline of Dolphin Island grew closer. *'We need to be married.'* What a statement! She'd been furious, but time was giving her perspective. It had been the statement of someone who thought he owed her. Of a guy who was offering her the protection of his name.

It had made her feel angry and defensive and small—as if she couldn't cope by herself—but now, lying back in her deckchair, the sun on her face, she decided that it was his history with Rihanna, plus centuries of society norms that were making their marks.

If you made a girl pregnant you married her. Simple as that.

Like her parents.

Let it go, she told herself. She wasn't her mother. She

had a great job, and she wouldn't be ostracised by having her daughter alone. The island was wonderful. She had great support.

And if Ben left?

Okay, that was a heart lurch, but only because he was a friend. There were lots of doctors out there who could fill his place.

Were there?

'Anya?' She was thinking but she was also dozing, letting the sun and the gentle motion of the water lull her to near sleep. But the thought of Ben leaving the island had jolted her and she was still aware of a gut lurch.

'Mmm?'

'What I said this afternoon...it was stupid.'

'So it was,' she said, peacefully enough.

'We don't need to be married.'

'No.' But she answered cautiously. Where was this going?

'I think, though,' he said, sounding as if each word was being considered, syllable by syllable, 'that I may just have fallen in love with you.'

She didn't open her eyes. *Caution!* her brain was screaming.

These words seemed a siren song—a gentle guy, a gorgeous, wounded hero, falling in love with her...

But there were two sets of words preceding this.

'We need to be married.'

'We'll have to get married.'

Was this more of the same? A more considered approach in his attempt to be honourable?

'That's nice.' She tried to make her words light, as if he'd just made a joke and she was responding in kind, but she knew her voice wobbled.

'Anya, I'm serious.'

Uh-oh. She needed to open her eyes. She needed to face this head-on.

'Ben, don't.'

'Don't speak the truth?'

'Don't spoil it,' she said, and the wobble was still there. 'We came here for a reason and that reason holds true. The fact that I'm having a baby shouldn't alter things.'

'The fact that we have a daughter…'

'It's important,' she agreed. 'But it should have nothing to do with the way we feel about each other.'

'So you don't think you could love me?'

She closed her eyes again, a defence, feeling as if a whole lot of balls had suddenly been thrown into the air and she was trying desperately to see where they were. Which ones should she catch? Which ones should she let go?

'Could we,' she said, very cautiously indeed, 'remove that entirely from the concept of marriage? I don't say I don't like you…'

'Wow, that's a start.'

Her eyes flew wide and she met his gaze. He looked almost indignant. Suddenly she found herself close to laughter. Guys, she thought. One declaration that they might just be falling in love and a woman was supposed to fall at his feet? This was being held out to her like a candy bar.

I may just have fallen in love.

It was dumb, it was unfair, but the memory of Mathew was still there.

'We love each other, Anya, and it would make more people than us happy. It makes sense to be married.'

Was this more of the same?

No. This man was a world apart from Mathew. He was strong but gentle, skilled, kind, fun to be with, a pleasure to work alongside.

And he had the loveliest eyes. His gaze held hers and she felt herself begin to melt. What if…?

Get a grip!

'Not…not yet,' she managed. 'Ben, I can't. It's way too soon. I keep seeing Mathew, my mum, my parents' marriage. I need to prove to myself that I don't need anyone. Does…does that make sense?'

'Yes.' His look gentled. 'Yes, it does. Does me being around interfere with that?'

'No. Yes!' She shook her head. 'Ben, I don't know. All I do know is that I'm not ready for…for anything.'

'For being loved?'

'I don't know if I can love back.' She bit her lip, trying to make sense to herself. 'Ben, I like you, a lot, but you… you came along when I was in a mess and you brought me here. It was such an amazing thing to do, and what I feel for you now is all tied up with that.'

'You're saying you feel grateful?' Was there an edge of anger in those words? Regardless, they made her flinch.

'I don't know,' she said miserably. 'But I am thinking you rescued me.'

'You rescued yourself.'

'No.'

'You called off your marriage to Mathew all by yourself,' he said, gentle again. 'That took courage.'

'It did.' She tilted her chin. 'I should have done it years ago though, and here I am, drifting into another relationship.'

'We're not drifting,' he said, the edge back in his voice. 'What happened the night we created our daughter…was that drifting?'

'I guess…it was pretty near a full speed catastrophe.'

'Not a catastrophe,' he said, even more definitely, and he

leaned over and took her hand in his. 'I think...a miracle. A miracle I'd like to share.'

'Well, you can share,' she said a trifle breathlessly. She felt so out of her depth here that she wasn't making sense even to herself. 'But that's our daughter's life we're talking about, not mine.'

'So there's no possibility...'

'Not...no,' she managed. 'This feels like cowardice but I... I can't.'

'But in time?'

'I don't know.' She tugged her hand free and stood up. As she did the ferry changed course into Dolphin Harbour. The direction of the swell changed abruptly and she staggered. Ben was on his feet in an instant, holding her, steadying her.

If felt right. It felt wonderful. She could sink into him, into his strength, into his promise of the future.

No. The boat steadied and so did she.

'Leave it, Ben,' she managed and pulled away. 'We're colleagues with a shared baby between us. Isn't that enough?'

'I guess...' He sighed. 'If that's the way you want it, then I guess it has to be.'

And then they were approaching the wharf. The staff team was there, waiting to take the incoming guests up to the resort, but oddly, Joe wasn't standing with them. He was out on the dock, waving as the ferry approached.

'Docs!'

'Uh-oh,' Ben said. 'What now?'

'We have a problem,' Joe called as the ferry slid into its berth. The gangplank hadn't been put in place yet and the resort guests hadn't emerged from the cabin. 'There's a stranding, a big one. Twenty or so dolphins out of water, around the headland past the research centre. No one goes there much so they could have been out of the water a while. It looks like they're dying.'

'Dying?'

'Yeah,' Joe said, looking gutted. 'Breaks your heart. The research team's there now and any resort staff we can spare as well. But you know what the research team is all about? Coral. If a lump of coral washed up they'd be our experts, but with dolphins they're just as useless as I am. And one of our guests has already been hit by a tail— Dorothy Vanson, would you believe? She and Henry have only just come back from the States, and they found them. They tried to pull one back to sea, somehow it hit her and she thinks she's broken her arm. Meanwhile Martin says he hasn't a clue about dolphins. He's radioed the mainland, but he can't find anyone to help, at least not until tomorrow, and he's already frantic about publicity. Twenty dead dolphins is what we don't need.'

He gestured to the door to the cabins. 'So… With this new lot coming in I can't get away, and even if I could, I dunno what the risks are. I can't imagine you know any more about dolphins than I do, but what's needed is someone with a bit of authority. As medics, you're the best choice. Plus, Dorothy needs attention and she and Henry are refusing to come back to the resort until the dolphins are re-floated. As if that's going to happen fast. Docs, dead dolphins are one thing, but the way things are going…you reckon you can knock some order into things?'

'I'll go at once,' Ben said. 'But Anya…'

'Don't you dare put buts into this equation,' she said before he could finish. 'I'm coming too.'

CHAPTER THIRTEEN

THE SCENE THAT greeted them as Ben steered the beach buggy over the sandhills was a gut lurch, to say the least.

Dolphin Island was the largest land mass of the Isles. Its west side was a sheltered coastline that served to protect the brilliant corals of the Great Barrier Reef, but the cove Joe had directed them to was on the east, open to ocean swells. Large waves rolled in, running up the long stretch of wild beach.

And on the beach…dolphins. Ben pulled the buggy to a halt on top of the rise and they stared in dismay.

Assessment. Here was another edict drilled into them from med school. Don't rush in before you've gained the clearest idea possible of what you're facing.

What they faced seemed chaotic.

The wash of tide had created an almost lagoon type effect, a sandbank far out, with an inner pool of shallower water between sandbank and beach. At high tide the pool would have been deep enough to swim in, the sandbank low enough for dolphins to breach.

But the tide had obviously receded and left the creatures stranded. Their struggles had left them in an even worse situation. They were now lying on almost dry sand.

These were the animals they often saw from the beach near the resort, magnificent bottle-nosed dolphins, constantly leaping from the water in their hunt for the abundant fish around the isles, delighting all who saw them. These were the creatures who'd given the resort its name.

They were in deadly trouble.

But they did have help. A dozen or so people were trying desperately to keep them wet. They all seemed to have buckets and were ferrying them between the sea and the dolphins.

While Ben had been driving, Anya had been scrolling the internet on her phone, searching for information. Now she had a page that told her what they most needed.

'Point form,' she read out loud. 'First, stay clear of the tail, as it's strong and can cause injury. I guess that accounts for Dorothy's broken arm. Then keep them wet, covered with anything you can find, like towels or sheets, and bucket water on them. Apparently sunburn alone can kill them. But be careful not to pour water near their blow hole.'

'That'll be what they're doing,' Ben said, motioning to the helpers. 'But why on earth did they beach themselves?'

'It says here it often happens in a feeding frenzy. Mostly at high tide. Possibly they'll have been chasing a school of fish into the shallows. A big wave makes them think the water's deeper than it is, the wave's sucked out and they're stranded.'

Ben whistled in dismay. 'So what? Grab them by the tail and pull?'

'Definitely not,' she said, reading on. 'They're not used to pressure on their bellies, and it would cause damage. It says here, if possible, dig a trench around them and get water in. Even if it soaks in, the softer sand will help with the pressure. It says to dig holes under the side fins—the pectoral fins—so there's no pressure on them, either. If they're on their sides we need to dig a trench beside them and roll them back to their bellies. If they stay on their side the damage to their pectoral fins can be catastrophic.'

'But re-floating…' He was watching a couple of men already trying to pull a dolphin by the tail.

'We need to get down there,' Anya said urgently. 'The idea is to float them out, using mats or similar to manoeuvre them. But apparently they have to be re-floated all at once. Even when they're in the water, every animal needs to kept under control until we're sure they're stabilised. But if they're not released together there can be some sort of distress signal that'll cause released dolphins to re-strand.'

'Hell,' Ben muttered, staring down at the melee on the beach, then looking at the shallow water and the sand-bank further out. 'So we're talking…next high tide…five or six hours?'

'Yep.'

'And all at once?'

'That's what it says.'

'We'll need an army.'

'I agree,' she said, looking down again at the information she was reading. 'It says here pretty much minimum four people per dolphin. Best bet is a sheet or tarp under them, then someone at each corner. Still protecting the fins, tucking them in, then moving them fast so pressure is kept to a minimum.'

'That means resort guests.'

'They'll come,' Anya said, and suddenly she found herself wincing, thinking of the champagne on the ferry. 'We might need to check for sobriety, but with six hours to go until high tide they have hours to sober up.'

'Will they come?'

'Um,' she said, still smiling. 'Isn't that a lesson that's been drilled into both of our heads? Nothing's more certain, people just love to help.'

* * *

Priority was people—it had to be. They headed down to the beach and found the Vansons, Dorothy and Henry. Since the day she'd helped out at the jet-ski accident, Anya had regarded Dorothy as a friend. The couple seemed to spend almost half the year at the resort, loving its climate, its gorgeous setting, the life away from what sounded a hectic social existence in the States.

But they didn't look social now. The usually flamboyant Dorothy was looking totally subdued, sitting on a rock, cradling her arm and staring out at the scene before her in dismay. Henry was clucking round her, looking worried.

'You can't do anything, dear, I'm sure it's broken.'

A quick glance between Anya and Ben, and Anya accepted her role.

She squatted beside them. As well as helping on that first day on the island, Henry needed constant reassurance that his blood pressure was stable. Dorothy had sliced her foot on a shell just before they'd headed back to the States and had needed treatment for an infected toe. Anya felt as if she knew them well, and she greeted them with a smile.

'Hey,' she said as Ben headed into the melee of dolphins and helpers. 'Dorothy, you've hurt yourself.'

'We found them,' Dorothy told her, obviously fighting back tears. 'You know we just arrived back two days ago? We decided to re-explore the whole island, and when we got here the dolphins were just…here. So Henry took the buggy to the research centre for help and I stayed here. The water was deeper then, and I thought I might just try if I could pull one of the littler ones back into the sea. But I just managed to get a grip and…thwack. Oh, but these poor dolphins.'

'Let's get you back to the resort and fix you up,' Anya said. She was doing a visual assessment as she spoke. Dorothy's multicoloured kaftan had cut-out arms, allowing her a clear view of her lower arm. There was no obvious displacement, but the way she was cradling it, not touching it between wrist and elbow, told its own story.

'No!' She could hear the pain in Dorothy's voice, but also determination. 'If you could bind me up, dear, I'd be very grateful, but I want to stay here. If you tell him what to do then Henry can help, can't he? I know he wants to, and so do I. You can't tell us you have enough helpers.'

'We don't,' Anya agreed. 'But your arm…'

'It doesn't come before these creatures,' Henry said, nodding at Dorothy. 'I won't risk my wife's health, but if it's possible… These dolphins are a big part of the reason we come back here every year. They've given us such pleasure. Please, let us help.'

Hmm. 'Wiggle your fingers,' she told Dorothy, and she grimaced and then tried. She managed to move them though, just a fraction, but enough for reassurance that there was no nerve compression. On the surface, it looked like a simple fracture of the lower radius, not obviously displaced.

And behind her…

'I need your attention.' Ben's deep voice rang out over the beach, startling every helper, and Anya too. Probably even the dolphins. 'Everyone, listen up. If you're willing to keep helping, we thank you, but first priority is to protect yourselves. So absolute imperatives. One, avoid sunstroke. Doc Greer and I have a buggy full of supplies. I need two people—yep, you and you, to cart them down closer. We have plenty of sunscreen—help yourselves and reapply it often. Joe from the resort has loaded hats and a few long-sleeved shirts, so if you're not wearing them already, grab one. Also we have water bottles. Drink lots, often. I'll be checking as I come round and if I don't see empty water bottles I'll send you off the beach.'

'As for the dolphins, keep away from their beaks. They're feeling threatened already and they can bite. Also a swipe from their tail can do damage. These animals need help but if you're ill yourself you'll take resources we can use for them.'

Beside her Dorothy winced, but Anya touched her good arm. 'Hey, don't beat yourself up,' she told her. 'You and Henry got the help these guys need, so well done.'

'Next, care and control of dolphins lesson one,' Ben was booming. 'These guys can't be floated until high tide— that's what the experts tell us. They also need to be released all at once, or we risk them re-stranding. We have a long wait. It'll be dark before they can be released, so if you're willing to help we need to focus on keeping them safe until then. We need to stop them getting sunburned. We need to keep them wet, avoid damage to their fins and we need to take the pressure off their bellies…'

And as she listened Anya could almost feel the surge of communal relief. Someone knew what to do. Someone was in charge.

Meanwhile her priority was Dorothy.

'I'm not going back to the resort,' Dorothy repeated. 'If you can tie me up so I don't do any more damage… What's a broken arm?'

Anya winced but Henry grinned and reached out and patted his wife's cheek. 'That's my girl.' He glanced up at Anya and gave her a firm nod. 'So that's the decision. We're tough.'

'Yeah?' Neither of them looked tough. They were both in their eighties. Henry looked like a retired businessman on vacation—wearing a polo with a golfing club insignia, Bermuda shorts, a shock of white hair and an air of authority. Dorothy was wearing a gorgeous silk kaftan, her silvery-white curls were beautifully bouffant and…were they real pearls around her neck? Regardless, they both looked equally determined.

'Dorothy and I have been through a lot,' Henry was saying. 'We've lost a baby. Our second daughter was born deaf. Dorothy's been through breast cancer. We've been through a business collapse...'

'Oh, and our house burned down when the children were tiny,' Dorothy added, as if it was just a minor inconvenience. 'We're both tough.'

'But I'm not into dolphin care until my Dorothy's fixed,' Henry added. 'We'll take no stupid risks. If you say we have to go back to the resort then we won't fight you, but we both go. No matter what, we do things together.'

'You lost a baby?' Anya said faintly, and Dorothy gave a nod she was starting to realise was characteristic of them both.

'Yes, we did. She lived for just three days. We've had three more since, and now we have five grandchildren. They call us Mops and Pops. Our friends say that's ridiculous, but we think they're the best names in the world. Even so, after all this time, our Miriam's still a hole in our hearts.'

And then she checked. 'Oh, my dear! You're pregnant! I hadn't realised. I'm so sorry—you shouldn't think of such things.'

'My baby's fine,' Anya said, and realised she sounded defensive, but there was no way she could be anything else. 'I...we had a scan this morning. She's perfect.'

'*We* had a scan?' Dorothy's intelligent face brightened with interest.

'Dr Duncan came with me,' she said without thinking. And then, for some reason she didn't understand herself, she found herself adding, 'Ben... Dr Duncan...he's the baby's father.'

Why had she said it? It was the first time she'd admitted

it to anyone but, for some reason, at this moment it felt right. And Dorothy beamed, her broken arm seemingly forgotten.

'Oh, that's lovely! He was so good to us when I had that toe infection. To have someone like that beside you...'

'He'll be great,' she agreed, feeling confused. This wasn't the way most patient/doctor consultations went. 'I... I'm very grateful.'

And Dorothy's beam disappeared, almost as if she'd been slapped.

'Grateful?'

'To have his support, I mean,' she said, too fast. 'Now, let's see to that arm.'

But both Henry and Dorothy were staring at her as if she'd said something obscene. 'Grateful?' Henry said in tones of disbelief.

'I guess... I didn't mean that.'

'But you think it?'

She hesitated and then said honestly, 'He will support us both,' she told them. 'I try not to think it's a cause for gratitude, though. I know he doesn't want me to.'

'I should think not!'

Somehow she recalibrated. Where was this conversation going? 'Enough,' she said, trying to sound brisk, competent—in charge. 'We have twenty or so dolphins needing our help. Let's get you into the buggy. I'll take you over to the research centre, where I can check that arm properly. Personal stuff can come later.'

'Yes, dear,' Dorothy said as Henry helped her up by holding her good arm. 'And I know it's none of our business, but it's not irrelevant. It can't be. Surely gratitude has no place when you love someone.'

'We don't love each other.'

'No?' Dorothy said dubiously, and glanced across the

beach to where Ben was helping lay towels over a dolphin's gleaming back. 'Why not?'

'Because…'

'Because it's none of our business,' Dorothy repeated. 'We get it. But dear, you can't possibly fall in love with someone you're grateful to. It wouldn't work. Why not put that aside?'

'Who said I needed to fall in love?'

'Well, if I were you I would. He's lovely.'

'Hey,' Henry interjected, and Dorothy almost managed a giggle.

'Well, he is. It's just lucky I met you first,' she said demurely as they started walking, a little unsteadily, up the sandhill to their parked buggy. 'And I'm so grateful that I did,' she told her husband. 'But that's the end of gratitude. You and I, love, we've been through the hoops and we're now…well, we're just… Mops and Pops. Us. Gratitude turned into something much, much deeper a very long time ago.'

'And you…' She turned and smiled at Anya, a gentle, considering smile that encompassed not only Anya but also her nicely rounding bump.

'If Dr Duncan is father to your child, if he wants to be a part of your life… Dear, I know I don't have all the details, and Henry'll give me heaps later for putting my nose where it has no business…but…well, he's gorgeous and he *is* part of your life, like it or not. So I surely don't know what you need, but if I were you I'd stop thinking about being grateful and start thinking how to get him into my bed and keeping him there.'

'Dorothy!' Henry said, startled. 'For heaven's sake! She's an incurable matchmaker,' he told Anya. 'Ignore her. For all Dorothy knows, he might have three wives already.'

'I guess,' Dorothy said reluctantly. 'But if he hasn't…'

'Um,' Anya managed. 'Moving on, people. Let's…'

'Move on,' Dorothy repeated. 'Yes, dear, but if he doesn't have three wives…' She sounded almost wistful. 'You know, our second daughter almost missed out on a perfectly lovely relationship because she had qualms. She's deaf, you see, and she thought he was just being kind. It took so long to convince her to go for it, and now she's so happy. And Dr Duncan… He's just…beautiful! But you're right. Enough of matchmaking. Let's fix my arm and go save some dolphins.'

Anya was starting to feeling totally discombobulated. What she needed was to retreat to medicine, and fast.

The research centre was only a few hundred metres around the headland, and she could use their facilities to check Dorothy's arm. She led the couple to one of the buggies, but as she helped Dorothy climb in, she couldn't help glancing back at the beach. Those who hadn't applied sunscreen were busy doing so. Those who had were already starting to dig sand out from under pectoral fins.

Chaos was already starting to look like teamwork.

Ben was… beautiful?

Cut it out, she told herself, but her thoughts refused to be cut.

They had to be cut! What was she doing, thinking that Ben in control mode seemed like sex on legs?

It was not helpful, she told herself. It was not helpful at all, and there was work to do.

Ideally she'd have sent Dorothy straight to the mainland, for X-ray and the immediate care of an orthopaedic surgeon. With their money, transport by chopper was surely possible, as was care by the best of Queensland's medical specialists.

But the couple was adamant they were staying until the dolphins were released, so she settled Dorothy in the director's office and examined the arm with more attention than she'd been able to give on the beach.

She had movement—painful but still possible—in her fingers. There was no numbness, which meant no nerve damage, and the arm was still in alignment. The tail had slapped down hard over her extended arm. She could feel a slight distension and the arm was swelling already. But with movement, with feeling, with the fact that tenderness was at the wrist but not at the elbow, she decided her initial tentative diagnosis of a fractured lower radius was probably right.

'You'll need to go to the mainland to get it X-rayed and set properly,' she told her. 'But I can fix it with a makeshift back slab to hold it firm and bind it tight against your chest. If you promise not to try and move it, I can give you enough painkillers so it can wait until morning.'

'I promise,' Dorothy said. 'But let's do it fast. I want to see what's happening on the beach.'

'You know high tide's not for hours. It'll be a long wait.'

'I can scoop trenches with one hand,' Dorothy said. 'And Henry can use both. There's no way we're leaving now, right, love?'

'No way at all,' Henry agreed.

'Some people—our children included,' Dorothy said darkly, 'think eighty-year-olds should be tucked into bed at nine with a cup of cocoa and a hot-water bottle. Saving dolphins…how cool is this?'

'As long as we can,' Henry said warningly. 'Love, some of them might not make it.'

'Not on our watch,' Dorothy declared. 'Let's get this arm bound and get back to it.'

CHAPTER FOURTEEN

WHAT FOLLOWED WAS five gruelling hours where Ben and Anya's skills as medics were needed almost as much as the skills required to keep the dolphins alive.

Back at the resort, Martin had moved into organisational mode. Within an hour of news of the dolphin stranding, social media had alerted mainstream news outlets. The Dolphin Isles were a source of fascination to the world in general, dolphins were a heart tug, and by dusk a media chopper was hovering over the beach, its lighting flooding the scene. Height had to be maintained in order to stop sand blowing or the noise scaring the dolphins further, but its light was a huge advantage.

As was the influx of guests from the resort. As soon as the news filtered through, guests were volunteering en masse, but Martin was still smarting from the impact on the resort from the drunken jet-ski accident. He thus did a fast and ruthless cull. Volunteers had to be not only fit but able to swim and also able to pass a breath test. Security was sent to block the access track to anyone else.

Martin had also been onto the mainland, requesting veterinary assistance, and both Ben and Anya were updated by phone.

'Check on each animal before release,' the chief veterinarian at a mainland sea mammal rehabilitation centre told them. 'A wounded dolphin can't be released—often its struggles will cause the whole pod to re-strand. Given the urgency of re-floating and the impossibility of getting any wounded animal away from the pod, it's better to euthanise.'

So as the hours wore on, as the tide inched its way back in, Anya and Ben found themselves medically checking each dolphin. It had to be a cursory assessment. Weights, blood tests, internal problems were impossible to assess in this time frame, but the vet gave them enough information to make a best guess.

'They should have included dolphin training in our university course,' Anya complained to Ben. 'They won't cough or stick out their tongues when I tell them to.'

'Inconsiderate critters,' Ben said. They'd been working from one side of the beach to the other and had finally met in the middle, but the work had taken hours.

Each dolphin had been assigned four volunteers, who were continuously wetting the animal's skin or scooping the underlying sand, imperative to stop pressure building. Even more important than assessing the animals, Anya and Ben had also been asking questions of these volunteers, making a best guess of fitness, assigning roles accordingly.

At least four people would be needed to carry each dolphin into the water, and once there, according to the vet's advice, each dolphin would have to be held and gently rocked for at least thirty minutes so they could stabilise. Martin had sent over wetsuits from the resort's water sports supply, the research centre also had heaps, but wetsuits weren't the only need.

As the hours passed, Anya and Ben needed to watch for exhaustion, for any signs that people were working past their limits. Any volunteers who'd managed to get past Martin's fitness assessment had to be gently told they needed to stay ashore.

'And that's not in my skill set either,' Anya complained to Ben. 'I just told Dorothy she'd absolutely need to stay onshore and she almost hit me.'

'She and Henry were the ones to sound the alarm so maybe they should get to give the release signal,' Ben suggested, smiling.

They were both feeling relieved. Even though their dolphin examinations had been necessarily limited, neither of them had found any sign of major injury. The vet had told them that some strandings were caused by an ill and disoriented member of the pod, but these all looked sleek and fit.

'And schools of tuna have been cruising around the headland over the last week,' one of the research team had told them. 'I'd imagine these guys were undone by greed, nothing else.'

So yay, healthy dolphins. They had enough volunteers and enough wetsuits. They'd thought about using sheets to carry the dolphins into the water, but Ben had discarded the idea—too flimsy. Dorothy had come up with a solution. 'Those gorgeous quilts that are on all the beds back at the resort...'

Martin's response to the idea was horror, but...

'That chopper up there's taking pictures,' Henry said, his businessman mode coming to the fore. 'Resort staff carrying dolphins out to sea on magnificent resort-coloured quilts... Tell the man that's publicity gold.'

And a dazed Martin had agreed. The quilts had arrived, had been tested for grip quality, had been approved and were lying ready to slide under the dolphins as the water rose. It was now just a matter of waiting.

'So...you?' Ben asked. He'd been gazing out over the

floodlit beach but now he turned to Anya and his gaze gentled. 'You must be exhausted.'

'I'm tired but I'm okay.'

'I can cope if you need to go home to bed.'

'Are you kidding?' Their position as medics had seen them assume an automatic role of authority, and no one else seemed remotely able to share. Yes, she was tired, but leaving…

'You can't carry,' he told her. 'Or stay in the water.'

'I know that.' She'd accepted it reluctantly. Some concessions had to be made to her pregnancy and a thump from a dolphin's tail could be a disaster. 'Though I reckon I could still get into a wetsuit.'

'Beer belly, pregnancy bump, what's the difference?' he teased, and she chuckled and gave his arm a thump.

'Thanks. But you shouldn't go in either. You know your leg's still weak.'

'I'd imagine I'm one of the strongest swimmers here, though. Try and stop me.'

'Ever the hero. Your role obviously extends past replacing a maiden's busted pants.'

'Too right it does,' he said and grinned, and then silence fell. They stood looking out over the sea of dolphins and helpers, at the floodlit beach, at the sight of so many doing whatever they could—and then Ben looked down into her face and his smile changed. 'Anya, I would so much like that role to extend.'

'Ben…'

'Yeah, not the time,' he said, and fell silent again.

It was a weird time, a hiatus of peace. Checking had been done. Roles had been assigned. Volunteers were now deepening trenches beside each animal. The idea was that as soon as the waves reached them the quilts could be manoeuvred under.

But for the two of them it was now just a matter of waiting. Of being on call if needed. Of standing in the weird light cast by the chopper, or the moonlight when the chopper disappeared—to refuel, to swap machines, who knew? Of watching the waves slowly inching up the beach.

And for Anya…to feel this sensation within grow and grow.

They weren't touching. They were simply standing side by side, and yet it felt as if they were closer. There was some intangible link that seemed to be growing stronger by the minute.

And his words seemed to be echoing.

'Anya, I would so much like that role to extend.'

She knew what he meant.

He'd made two clumsy proposals of marriage. She'd rejected them both and she'd been right to do so. Both had been made at times when emotions were high, the first when they'd discovered she was pregnant, the second when they'd properly seen their daughter. Those proposals had felt like nothing to do with her.

And yet, standing beside him now, the feeling grew stronger that there was far more below the surface of those two awkward declarations.

A hero would have made those first two declarations, she thought. A knight in shining armour, declaring that he would marry his pregnant woman. A hero, looking at the image of his daughter and swearing he would give her a family.

But she stood beside him and she thought, *No. He's no hero. He's just… Ben.*

She was suddenly remembering another night, of Ben wading into the rippling shallows of the river at Merriwood, of his smiles, his understanding. She was thinking of his empathy that first night on the island, disregarding the shallowness of the dumb Mia and guessing the threat of violence beneath the surface. She was thinking of the pain she saw etched on his face when he'd done a hard workout, of the determination he was showing to recover completely.

To recover from the trauma of a disastrous marriage. To recover from betrayal and injury and loss.

She suddenly felt very, very small. This man had asked her to marry him and she'd reacted…with anger.

The chopper swept away into the night—to refuel again? They'd know release wouldn't be until high tide, almost an hour away. She imagined they'd be back then, ready to broadcast dramatic images to the nation.

If this went right, the publicity for the resort would be awesome. Guests helping to save dolphins. It'd be head-line news.

But behind the scenes… She looked across the beach at the huddle of people working by every single dolphin. To the world tomorrow they'd be the resort's wealthy guests, millionaire businessmen and women, actors, politicians, the world's *Who's Who*. But tonight they were just…here. Doing their best.

She glanced along the beach to where Dorothy and Henry were back, sitting on the rock where she'd first seen them. They'd both been scooping sand, but she'd sent them for an enforced break, insisting they drank the coffee Martin had sent over and then rested until the time came for release.

Martin had also sent over blankets—lots of them—so they were now wrapped in cashmere, huddled tight to-gether.

And Dorothy's words were suddenly replaying in her head?

'But, dear, you can't possibly fall in love with some-

one you're grateful to. It wouldn't work. Why not put that aside?'

What if she put gratitude aside? What if she was seeing this man for the first time, meeting him casually, dating with no strings, having a second date, a third? Not getting pregnant. No baggage.

And then…she'd be standing here in the moonlight and she'd be doing…what?

Moving closer. Of course she would.

And she was hearing Dorothy's words again when she'd declared, *'We don't love each other.'*

Dorothy had said, *'Why not?'*

Why not indeed? The question was suddenly almost exploding in her head.

But then it settled, as if panic had somehow been averted. And she was thinking, I haven't blown it. He's still here.

Ben.

And before she could second-guess herself she moved, just a little, so her arm ever so slightly brushed his.

And she lifted his hand into hers and held.

For a moment there was nothing. No reaction at all. It was as if her movement had left them both frozen.

Had she blown it? Panic swept through her. Had she messed with her chances?

The moment stretched on, but still she held. Held his hand. Held her breath.

And then, very slowly, as if caution had to be maintained every inch of the way, his fingers curved around hers, interlinked and held. Strongly, surely, certainly.

He turned and looked down into her face and she looked up at him. Maybe she smiled.

Ben didn't smile. He simply looked into her eyes and what he saw there she didn't know.

Maybe it was a reflection of what her heart was screaming. *Please. Oh, please.*

And then, very gently, his other hand came up and cupped her face. It was a feather touch, so soft, so tender it made her want to weep.

'Anya,' he said, and he needed to say no more. There was such a depth of meaning...

It was okay. No, it was...

She couldn't think. There were no words.

'Hey,' she managed, because she couldn't think of anything else to say, and even the word *hey* was stupid. There was nothing that fitted this moment.

Maybe they needed...nothing.

The moment stretched on. They didn't kiss. They stayed still and silent, the wash of the incoming tide, the moonlight on their faces, the background murmur of the volunteers on the beach, all fading to nothing.

They simply had each other.

And then a wave swept in, bigger than those that had come before. The incoming tide had meant that the pools of water in the trenches beside the dolphins had been filling of their own accord, but this wave swept through the trenches, even managing to slightly lift some of the dolphins closest to the sea.

'It's time to get those quilts under,' Ben said but his voice was unsteady and his eyes hadn't left hers.

'Yes, it is.'

'So it's time for a happy-ever-after for our dolphins,' he said, and then, 'Anya, what about us?'

'We might see,' she said, cautiously, but with slivers of joy suddenly seeming to light her world. 'But...but let's not think of ever after. Let's maybe think about cautious, tentative beginnings.'

* * *

And then the events of the night took over. After that first wave, others followed, surging up the beach, around the dolphins. The tide, however, must have been higher when they'd stranded or maybe—more likely, as these creatures were known for their intelligence—it had been a freak wave that had swept them in. Because as the point of high tide was reached, they were still in a mere six inches of water.

It was enough, though. Each dolphin had had a quilt manoeuvred carefully under its belly, with loops tied at the corner. One of the hotel guests had volunteered that he'd been a Queen's Scout, and he'd personally organised the impressive and, he swore, dependable hand holds.

So as the dolphins felt the water surge around them, as their instinct had them wanting to thrash, the volunteers took up their positions.

They worked under Ben's orders. Each step of the way he was in control.

Anya quietly walked among the groups, silently observing. Watching for any sign of strain among the volunteers, any hint that such a weight might be too much, that no one was disguising or risking injury in their desire to be part of this rescue.

'We're about to move,' Ben told them. 'We'll wait for a decent surge and then we go together. Straight into the water, as fast as you can, over the sandbank and then to chest depth of the smallest person of your party. No deeper. Then we hold. One person, the strongest of the group—work it out now, people—controls the peduncle…'

He was getting his instructions via an earpiece from the mainland vet, and he decided explanation was necessary. 'The peduncle's the base, the stalk if you like, of the tail. If it's loose it'll thrash it and make the dolphin impossible to hold. So one person, the strongest of you, holds that.

The rest of you need to apply weight to the upper body, but still keeping that blowhole as clear as you can. Then you need to rock from side to side, allowing your dolphin to get used to the water. We need to make sure they can self-right if rolled to the side, and that they can surface to breathe unassisted.'

'Why can't we just let them go?' someone called.

'Because we don't want them to re-strand,' Ben called back. 'Our vet says we need to stabilise them for at least thirty minutes, because if one's in trouble they all might be. We keep them as close together as we can, then, on my signal, we release. We make sure the quilt has dropped away—someone from each group can gather it back. Then, on my word, we step behind and form a human chain between them and the beach. We slap the water, kick, yell, make as much commotion as possible, so the clear way for any disoriented dolphin is out to sea. Any questions?'

There were none.

'And the moment any of you are unsure of your footing, feeling unwell, feeling anything other than completely in control, then you get out of there. Dr Greer will be on the beach ready to help. There's no way we'll tell the world tomorrow that we rescued twenty dolphins and lost one investment banker.'

'Now there's a choice,' someone called, and there was general laughter, and then another wave swept in.

Ben called, 'Any time now'. The scene was set.

And it worked.

Anya stayed on the beach with the small group of volunteers who'd self-declared the rescue was beyond their capability. Dorothy and Henry were among them. Dorothy was clutching Henry's hand as if she were drowning and whenever Anya was in range Henry took hers.

This couple were no longer patients. They were friends.

Anya was trying to watch all her little beach tribe. These were people Martin had passed as fit to help but some of them were elderly, they'd been working for hours and they should be showing signs of strain. But without exception they were so entranced by the scene before them that health issues were forgotten.

It was Anya's job to watch their faces and assess, but even Dorothy, pumped full of painkillers, looked far too excited to be worrying about a mere broken arm.

She did have one patient. A woman in her forties, Prue, left her dolphin and stumped to shore in a filthy mood. 'I've cut my foot on a shell,' she glowered. 'Dr Duncan says bleeding can attract sharks or I'd stay. Stupid foot. Can you wrap it up tight, Doc, so I can still watch?'

Anya complied, but with one eye still on the water. It was a rough bandage—she'd have to clean and rewrap later—but there was no way either of them would miss what was about to happen.

Blessedly the moon was full, playing over the disparate group in the water, twenty dolphins and the helpers working to get their dolphins stabilised.

But there were no problems. This might look like a motley band of onlookers, but under Ben's calm directions they became a well drilled army.

Overhead the chopper had returned. It hovered almost motionless, lighting the scene. The waves were washing almost shoulder height, the backs of the dolphins shining in the combined beam of floodlight and moonlight, and the whole world seemed to hold its breath.

And then, finally, on Ben's signal, the order was called by Dorothy in a tone that'd do a sergeant major proud. Ben had planned to repeat it, but there was no need.

'Release!'

There was a moment more of stillness as each dolphin realised they were no longer held. And then…organised chaos. Each volunteer—including those who'd stayed on the beach—now rushed to be part of this final glorious moment. Within seconds they'd formed the most riotous human chain they could manage, banging on the water, yelling, waving their arms, forming a barrier between the dolphins and the beach they'd just left.

And finally, almost as one, the realisation of freedom dawned and the dolphins moved out, into the oncoming waves.

There followed the holding of breath by every person on the beach… *Please…*

And then the pod became a unit, a glorious, leaping surge of gleaming dolphins, glimmering outward through the moonlit waves. They disappeared, plunged down, under again and then up, out, further and further. Not one dolphin faltering. Not one dolphin lost.

And people were laughing, crying, cheering, watching until they were out of sight and then wading through the shallows to hug everyone they could find. Henry and Dorothy—by now everyone knew who'd found them and raised the alarm—were raised on shoulders and whooped in what was almost a tribal dance of celebration. Retirees, businessmen and women, nerdy scientists who spent their lives studying the drift of coral spawn… They were all one.

And then somehow Anya was plucked from the midst of the crowd, scooped up in two very wet arms—clad in wetsuit rubber—and held and twirled and held and held and hugged and held and kissed.

The noise on the beach seemed to die away. Had Ben carried her away from the crowd or was it just that there was no room in her heart for the crowd to exist?

Regardless, she was held against his chest, her weight

apparently nothing. *His leg*, the doctor in her should have screamed. *His back. What are you doing? Are you out of your mind?*

But right now she was no longer a doctor. She was no longer anything but a woman who was deeply intent on returning a kiss she seemed to have been waiting for all her life.

Ben's kiss.

Her kiss.

This was a kiss of love. A kiss of commitment. A kiss with the promise of a future she knew now was inevitably hers.

And when she finally surfaced she found they had an audience. The crowd had come back into focus. The dolphins had finally leapt and glimmered and disappeared, so now, instead of watching the dolphins finally reach their freedom, almost every person on the beach was watching a man kiss a woman. As if it was part of the same promise. The same magic of this night.

She should mind. She should be embarrassed. She should fight to be put down. She should…do nothing.

Nothing else mattered.

Nothing else at all.

'I love you,' Ben whispered when there was finally room for the whisper of words between them.

'Then that's perfect,' she managed before kissing him again. 'Because I believe I love you right back.'

It was past three in the morning before Anya and Ben could make it to bed. Ben had practically ordered Anya to leave him to it, but she'd seen the way he'd limped up the beach to the buggies and she was having none of it.

There was still work to be done. They were risking nothing—every volunteer had to be individually checked.

There were scrapes, bruises, strains. The morning would see this motley crew aching from unaccustomed exertion, and it was Anya and Ben's job to see that there'd be nothing worse.

They cleaned grazes, they stitched the two cuts—one guy hadn't realised he'd cut himself until he stripped off his wetsuit and he still wasn't sure what had happened. They'd fixed Dorothy's arm more securely, had given her painkillers to last the night and had organised a chopper to take her to the mainland in the morning.

They could have organised it now, but Dorothy was having none of it. 'If you think a mere broken arm will stop me sleeping then think again. What a glorious night,' she'd said as the couple had left the makeshift clinic that Martin had organised in Reception. 'Perfect.' One armed, she still managed to hug Ben but she hugged Anya the hardest. 'Oh, my dear, I'm so happy for you.'

And then at last they were done, free to find their own beds. They walked silently along the dimly lit path to Anya's studio—that was the closest. And then they paused.

On the doorstep was a tray. A tiny porcelain casserole and a Thermos.

A note was attached.

Dolphin Isles Resort thanks you for the contribution you've made to tonight's outstanding rescue. Microwave three minutes on high.

'Yay,' Anya said a trifle unsteadily. She was linked to Ben, hand holding hand, and she was starting to feel so tired that she might topple if she let go. 'I hadn't even realised I was hungry.'

'Bless the kitchen staff,' Ben said. 'What's the betting there's one at my place too.' There was a moment's hesitation and then his grip on her hand tightened. 'Anya, what about we pick this up, take it over to my place and put them together?'

And for the first time that night his voice was unsteady. Unsure? She looked up into his face and saw a question.

He still didn't know. She had to say.

And somehow she did. 'Yes,' she said, and then she tilted her face to kiss him. 'Yes, and yes, and yes.'

And he smiled, and all the joy of the night—no, maybe all the joy in the world was in that smile. He scooped up the casserole and took her hand again.

'Don't you need your cane?' she asked suddenly, the thought only just occurring to her. The strain on his injured leg tonight must have been enormous, and she hadn't seen the cane all night.

'I'm done with it,' he said and tugged her closer as they turned to the path to his bungalow. 'You can hold me up when I need it.'

It was enough to make her heart sing. They walked in silence, the emotions of the night almost too much for words.

An identical tray was waiting on Ben's doorstep. They carried it inside and set it on the table.

They were covered in salt and sand. They needed showers. They desperately needed—and desperately wanted—bed. That glorious king-sized bed that was probably still split in two. They could push it together again and...

'But I'm really hungry,' Ben said, sounding apologetic, and as if in reply Anya's stomach gave a low but unmistakable growl. They wanted to make love, right there, right then, but the need for food was suddenly even greater.

'So what do we have?' Ben said, and lifted the casserole lid and sniffed. And then his face broke into silent laughter as he lifted it to let her do the same. 'Anya...'

She sniffed and her eyes widened. 'Tuna bake,' she said

faintly, and they stared at each other, their faces creasing into disbelieving laughter.

'Do we...do we feed this to the fish?' Ben asked at last, as laughter finally eased.

'Don't you dare,' she managed and marched her casserole to the microwave. 'We're going to eat these together—and, what's more, we're going to be very, very grateful.'

CHAPTER FIFTEEN

THE DAY WAS GLORIOUS. The island was sun-drenched, the palms were creating dappled shade over the beach and the soft breeze was creating the merest ripple on the glistening ocean.

There'd been a school of whiting darting through the shallows earlier this morning. A pod of dolphins had eaten their fill and was now cruising lazily out past the waves, occasionally surfacing, seemingly content to drift and maybe even watch the goings-on on the beach.

Who knew what they'd make of what was happening? But dolphins were the most intelligent of mammals. Maybe they could even make sense of it.

They could likely see the cluster of humans, surely different creatures than the wetsuit-clad saviours who'd tugged them to safety six months before. These humans were dressed in the brightest of colours, flowing sarongs, colourful shirts, bare feet, drifts of frangipani tucked into hair or around necks, great garlands of frangipani strung over an arch where a man and a woman stood holding hands.

No. Holding one hand each. The woman—could dolphins differentiate between the sexes?—was using her free hand to cradle...

A young. A bundle of soft white and pink.

Young dolphins were born much larger than this. How

did they survive? a dolphin might have wondered. Put that one in the water and see how it went.

But it didn't seem to be worrying the pair under the arch. They looked as if all was right in their world.

As one, the pod of dolphins rode in on the next wave— maybe to take a decent look? Then they cruised out through the breakers, twisting and leaping and heading back out to sea.

Enough. The humans might be happy, but breakfast was obviously done. Now, what about lunch?

And on the beach…

Vows.

'I, Anya Louise Greer, take you, Benjamin James Duncan…'

'I, Benjamin James Duncan, take you, Anya Louise Greer…'

This wedding was right. It was perfect. It was their day, their glorious affirmation of what was deep inside them both.

It wasn't the grand society wedding Ben's parents would have liked, although they were here too, besotted with their tiny granddaughter and learning to love Anya on her own terms.

Nor was it a formal wedding where everyone who'd ever been good to them had had to be invited. Janet and Beth were here from Merriwood, but they'd mutually decided that Mathew and Jeanie could be left off the guest list.

Because this was simply a gathering of those who they knew wished them joy.

That included all the islanders, the research staff and the resort staff. Martin had warned incoming guests on booking that on this day service would be minimal.

'You're worth it,' he'd told them.

The filming of the dolphin rescue had been broadcast

pretty much internationally. It seemed the corporate guests had been the top echelons of a breathtakingly powerful conglomerate. They'd shared their experience far and wide, and there were consequentially no gaps in the resort's booking for years.

There were, though, places still reserved for 'permanent' guests. Dorothy and Henry had flown back to the States a month after the 'night of the dolphins', but they'd returned before the birth of Aisha Reyna Duncan. And when Anya had gone into labour three weeks before her due date, when the birth had been hard and fast, when there'd been no time to get to the mainland, Dorothy had restated her ex-nurse status. She'd thus acted as midwife as Ben had delivered their precious baby girl.

'Henry and I feel almost like we have another grandbaby,' she'd told Anya the next morning. 'Can we be Mops and Pops again? Oh, my dear, what a wonderful extra reason for spending half our lives here.' She was blinking back tears. 'And do you know, she looks a tiny bit like our Miriam.'

The birth had been perfect, Anya thought mistily as she made her vows. As everything was perfect. This place, this life, this man.

Ben. She loved him with all her heart. He was making his vows now, and the joy in her heart was overwhelming.

They'd stay here, they'd decided. Why not? What had started as an interim step, a place for them both to recover until they could face the world again, had become, quite simply, their world.

The resort was growing—as was the research station. The publicity surrounding the dolphin rescue had prompted voices calling for a marine rescue centre to service the outer islands. Ben had been at the forefront, studying marine veterinary care online, making trips to the mainland to learn more. Anya intended to join right in.

They'd be doctors, vets—and friends.

Best friends, she thought, as Ben slipped a ring onto her finger, and she gazed into his eyes and saw her own deep love reflected straight back at her.

Friends, lovers, partners.

In her arms Aisha gave a tiny squirm and a mew that might have been one of utter contentment. Their little girl surely knew enough not to complain on this day, the beginning of a life that promised so much.

'Our family,' Ben murmured. They looked down into their daughter's perfect little face and then, of one accord, they kissed. It was a sandwich hug, with their baby cradled between them, and there was a collective sigh from the crowd around them.

'You know what?' Ben said when finally they drew apart and there was room again for words between them. 'I'm grateful.'

'Well, how about that?' Anya managed. 'I'm grateful too. But not…not *to* you, Ben Duncan. I'm grateful *for* you.'

'Ditto, my Anya,' he said softly and tugged her close again. 'For you, for our daughter, for this, our happy ever after. And for…life.'

* * * * *

COMING SOON!

We really hope you enjoyed reading this book. If you're looking for more romance, be sure to head to the shops when new books are available on

Thursday 16th February

To see which titles are coming soon, please visit

millsandboon.co.uk/nextmonth

MILLS & BOON®

Coming next month

SECRET SON TO CHANGE HER LIFE
Alison Roberts

'I tried every way I could to contact you,' Brie said
quietly. 'But it was weeks after you'd left. Your phone
was disconnected. You never responded when I tried to
message you on social media. Nobody knew where you
were.'

'So you just gave up?'

'It was during those weeks I found out that the baby
I was carrying had spina bifida.' Brie's tone changed.
She might deserve Jonno's anger but she wasn't the
person he thought she was. She hadn't set out to lie to
him. 'My priorities kind of changed at that point.'

That silenced him. Brie walked ahead and found
another stick to throw for Dennis. Then she turned.

'I never expected to see you again,' she said. 'But
when I'd had a bit of time to get used to you turning
up out of blue, like that, I did try to tell you – the day
I came to your apartment.'

She could hear the echo of what she'd said to him
then, in spite of the background shriek of the seagulls.
She knew Jonno could hear it as well.

I had to come…There's something I really need to
tell you, Jonno…

They both knew why she hadn't ended up telling him
that day.

'You could have told me well before then. Like when I asked you if you had any kids.'

'Oh… yeah… Right after you'd been telling me how thankful you were that you didn't have any dependents? How do you think that made me feel?' Brie's voice hitched. 'I was still trying to get my head around it myself. How was I going to tell my son that his daddy was back in town but might not want to have anything to do with him because he had better things to do with his time? That he wasn't even planning to be around long, anyway. He was going to get rid of the last tie he had here and then he'd be gone again. Forever. Probably on the other side of the world in Australia or New Zealand.'

'I said those things because I didn't know,' Jonno countered. 'Do you really think I'm someone who'd walk away from a responsibility like having a child? That I wouldn't care?'

Brie swallowed hard. Of course she didn't. 'Maybe I was hoping that one day, Felix would be able to find you.'

Continue reading
SECRET SON TO CHANGE HER LIFE
Alison Roberts

Available next month
www.millsandboon.co.uk

MILLS & BOON

THE HEART OF ROMANCE

A ROMANCE FOR EVERY READER

MODERN — Prepare to be swept off your feet by sophisticated, sexy and seductive heroes, in some of the world's most glamourous and romantic locations, where power and passion collide.

HISTORICAL — Escape with historical heroes from time gone by. Whether your passion is for wicked Regency Rakes, muscled Vikings or rugged Highlanders, awaken the romance of the past.

MEDICAL — Set your pulse racing with dedicated, delectable doctors in the high-pressure world of medicine, where emotions run high and passion, comfort and love are the best medicine.

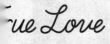 **True Love** — Celebrate true love with tender stories of heartfelt romance, from the rush of falling in love to the joy a new baby can bring, and a focus on the emotional heart of a relationship.

Desire — Indulge in secrets and scandal, intense drama and plenty of sizzling hot action with powerful and passionate heroes who have it all: wealth, status, good looks…everything but the right woman.

HEROES — Experience all the excitement of a gripping thriller, with an intense romance at its heart. Resourceful, true-to-life women and strong, fearless men face danger and desire - a killer combination!

To see which titles are coming soon, please visit

millsandboon.co.uk/nextmonth

JOIN US ON SOCIAL MEDIA!

Stay up to date with our latest releases, author news and gossip, special offers and discounts, and all the behind-the-scenes action from Mills & Boon...

 @millsandboon

 @millsandboonuk

 facebook.com/millsandboon

 @millsandboonuk

It might just be true love...